Thalassa Ali was born in Boston, M daughter of two archaeologists, one British. Her husband was from Lahore, Pakistan, and she lived there for twelve years, spending the last three years of her time there running her husband's business following his sudden death. She became a stockbroker on her return to America and, in 1993, turned to writing. She converted to Islam in 1984, and is a member of a Sufi brotherhood, based in Karachi. *A Beggar at the Gate* is the sequel to her first novel *A Singular Hostage*, which is also available from Review.

Praise for T.

'An exotic historical romance . . . Ali paints a vivid picture of India during the Raj. She also possesses the knack of telling a good story' *Mail On Sunday*

'*A Beggar at the Gate* details in depth and with intelligent sensitivity the increasing desperation felt by an Englishwoman caught between two cultures' *The Big Issue in the North*

'Beautifully written, this novel transports the reader back to the 19th century, British Imperialism and the pull of two cultures in an ever-changing world' *Lancashire Evening Post*

'Does indeed bear comparison with MM Kaye' *The Bookseller*

'One of the best books I have read in a long time . . . beautifully written' *Yorkshire Evening Press*

Also by Thalassa Ali

A Singular Hostage

A BEGGAR AT THE GATE

Thalassa Ali

review

To the memory of my English mother, Thalassa Cruso Hencken

and

my American father, Hugh O'Neill Hencken

Acknowledgements

Arthur Edelstein, who died in the summer of 2003, taught me the craft of fiction. I thank my enthusiastic agents, Jill Kneerim at Kneerim and Williams in Boston and Judy Martin in London. I also thank my extraordinary editors, Jane Morpeth and Flora Rees at Headline Book Publishing, and their assistant, Alice McKenzie.

I would also like to acknowledge the kindness of my writing group, all of whom have been good friends to me and wonderful godmothers to *A Beggar at the Gate*. I had exceptional readers: Gillo Afridi, Deborah Barlow, Diane Franklin, Kamar Habibi, Jon Soroff and Ala Reid, my patient, generous sister.

My website designer was the talented Peter Cepeda, and my assistant was the extraordinary Danielle Charbonneau.

Others have done much to help me: Asad and Farida Ali Khan, Shelale Abbasi, Heidi Fiske, Rifa'at Ghani, Eva Shikhar Ghosh, Mahnaz Fancy, Samia Faruque, Helene Golay, Tariq Jafar, Marjorie Junejo, Tahireh and Zafar Khan, Judy and Bazl Khan, Janet Lowenthal, Kyra Montagu, Cecily Morse, the Pakistan Diplomatic Mission to New York, Susan Paine, Samina Quraeshi, Lucy Ramsey, Sam and Juliet Reid, Zainab

Rizvi, Shakeel and Rehana Saigol, Muneeza Shamsi. The Sind Club in Karachi, and Pinkie and Haroon Yusuf.

I would also particularly like to thank the British Library, whose India Office Collection has been a vital resource to me for many years.

Last of all I thank my remarkable children, Sophie and Toby.

Historical Note

In 1840 the Punjab was still proudly independent. Standing between British India and Afghanistan, irrigated by five rivers and boasting a great treasury of gold and jewels, it was the second richest kingdom in the subcontinent.

But for all the Punjab's success, it had lost its powerful unifying leader. Maharajah Ranjit Singh, who had brought the Punjab under one rule and created a strong disciplined army, had died in 1839, leaving the throne to his only legitimate son, the weak, half-witted Kharrak Singh.

By July 1840, Kharrak Singh was out of power, imprisoned by his son, Prince Nau Nihal Singh. The atmosphere at the Lahore Citadel, the Maharajah's palace and fort, had turned poisonous as opposing factions struggled to gain control of the country.

As these divisions deepened, the British government watched, biding its time. The British, who had recently invaded Afghanistan and installed their own puppet king on the throne in Kabul, were deeply interested in the Punjab, not only for its wealth but also for its geographical position. The shortest line of supply between

British territory and Kabul lay across the Punjab's well-watered plain, and the British government was finding it increasingly difficult to negotiate the use of that route with the fractured government in Lahore.

Most of the British representatives in India, including Lord Auckland, the Governor-General, believed it important to promote a stable government in the Punjab, but there were some who had ideas of their own.

Lady Macnaghten is a real historical figure, as are Maharajah Kharrak Singh, his son Prince Nau Nihal Singh and Faqeer Azizuddin, the Punjab Foreign Minister.

Lady Macnaghten did travel to Afghanistan in 1840 to join her husband, Sir William Macnaghten. The unfortunate events at Lahore in January 1841 took place much as I have described them.

Mariana Givens, her aunt and uncle, Russell Lewis the Political Agent, and Saboor and his family are all products of my imagination.

Glossary

The Urdu language shares much of its vocabulary with Hindi, Arabic, Persian and Punjabi. Only three of the words listed below are not in the Urdu language.

abba	the diminutive of father
a-jao (v.)	come
al Hamdulillah	by the grace of Allah
as-salaam-o-aleikum	may peace be upon you
aloo gosth	a curry of goat meat and potatoes
Baba	a title of respect for a male child, father, or old man
begum	a lady of rank
Bibi	used as second name for a native woman, and also as a title for a Muslim lady
Bhai	brother, also a polite term for an elder male relative
Bhaji	a polite term for an elder female relative

bhang	Indian hemp (*Cannabis sativa*), whose dried leaves, stems or seeds are smoked, chewed or added to a drink for a narcotic effect
burka	an all-enveloping loose garment, worn by Muslim women, that covers the body from head to toe
Burri Memsahib	a title of respect for the most senior English lady
chador	a large sheet of cloth worn by Muslim women to cover the head and body – an alternative to the burka
champa	(*Michelia champaca*) a tropical tree with sweetly scented yellow blooms
Charak Puja (*Bengali*)	a Hindu festival in which men were suspended from a swinging pole by hooks in their flesh
charpai	an Indian string bed with a wooden frame
chora	long
dal	boiled, spiced lentils
darwaza	a door or a gateway
dhobi	a washer of clothes
dhoti	a Hindu loincloth
do	two
dopiaza	a curry of meat and onions
dupatta	a length of material worn by women as a scarf or over the head and shoulders
durwan	a gatekeeper
ek	one
fajr	the pre-dawn, as in the Muslim dawn prayer
faqeer	one who is poor in the sight of God
Granth Sahib (*Punjabi*)	the Sikh holy book

ghat	a path or stairs, leading down to a river
Hai, Allah!	Oh, God!
haveli	a walled city mansion
Huzoor	a title of respect for a man
iddat	the number of days a widowed or divorced woman must wait before she can remarry: four months and ten days for a widow; three months for a divorced woman
Inshallah	God willing
isha	the night-time prayer
jadoo	black magic
jalao (from *v. jalana*)	light
jamawar	a woollen fabric from Kashmir, woven in an intricate, multicoloured design and used for shawls
jezail	a long, heavy Afghan musket, capable of firing a ball a great distance
kachnar	(*Bauhinia variegata*) an attractive Indian tree with delicate mauve blooms
kajal	the black powder used for lining the eyes
Kali	a hideous and terrifying Hindu goddess, wife of Shiva the Destroyer
kameez	a long tunic-like shirt worn over shalwar – loose trousers
keema	a dish of ground, spiced goat's meat
ke saat	with
khanum (*Persian*)	a title of respect for a lady
kismet	destiny
Lalaji	an affectionate, respectful term of address for an elder male
mahout	an elephant driver

Mahraj	the term of address for a Maharajah
maidan	an open space, park or plain
maund	a measure of weight, about 40 kilos, or 88 pounds
mehndi	a plant (*Lawsonia inermis*) whose leaves are ground to a paste and used to dye the hair and the skin
minar	the tall tower attached to a mosque from which the Muslim call to prayer is proclaimed five times daily
mohur	a coin of pure gold, the principal coin of India since the sixteenth century
muezzin	the caller to prayer
mukhtiar	the first assistant to the Maharajah of the Punjab
munshi	a teacher or interpreter of Indian languages
n'hut	the nose ring worn by married women in India
nach	an entertainment by Indian musicians and dancing girls
Nani Ma	grandmother: mother's mother
neem	(*Azadirachi indica*) a tree whose astringent leaves and bark are used as an antiseptic
palanquin	a closed litter carried by bearers. A pole projects fore and aft from the roof of the box and rests on the bearers' shoulders
pan	a folded betel leaf containing chopped areca nut, lime, and other ingredients. Used widely in India after meals
punkah	a swinging fan made of a cloth-covered wooden frame that has been suspended from the ceiling

punkah-wallah	the man who works the punkah by means of a rope that passes through a hole in the wall of the room and leads to the verandah outside
qamar	the moon
Qur'an	the sacred book of Islam. It is the record of the revelations received by the Prophet Muhammad
rezai	a quilt stuffed with fluff from the cottonwood tree
rishta	a relationship, particularly a family one; a marriage proposal
rishtadar	a relative
rumal	a handkerchief or scarf
sahib	a polite title for a man
salaam aleikum	Muslim greeting meaning 'may peace be upon you'
sari	a length of silk or cotton fabric, worn by women, wound about the body
sati	the suicide of a Hindu widow who burns herself on her husband's funeral pyre: considered (at the time of this story) to be an act of great piety
Shaikh	a person of particular spiritual authority, such as the master of a Sufi brotherhood
shalwar	loose trousers narrowing to round the ankles, typically worn with a kameez
Shia	the party of Ali, one of the two principal branches of Islam
Sikh	adherent of Sikhism, a monotheistic religion based on purity and equality, founded in the Punjab by Guru Nanak Shah

sirdar	a chief, leader or general
Shiva	the Destroyer, one of the three deities of the Hindu triad
sowar	a native cavalryman
Sufi	a follower of the Path. A Muslim mystic
tamasha	a show, a spectacle
tandoor	a clay oven for baking bread and meat
taweez	the Merciful Prescriptions: a series of cures and healings practised by Sufis
teen	three
Thug	a member of a religious organization in India whose adherents befriended travellers on the roads, then ritually murdered and robbed them
tulwar	an Oriental sword with a curved blade
ubtan	a paste made of chickpea flour, ground almonds, rose water, turmeric and other ingredients and used to soften the skin
Urdu	a language closely related to Hindi but written in the Persian script, and widely used in India. It contains many Arabic, Persian and Turkic words
valeema	the celebration held by the bridegroom's family after his marriage
zenana	the family quarters of a Muslim household, where the women are secluded from male outsiders

Prologue

No one knew when the city of Lahore, with its tight, airless lanes and thick, defensive walls, had first arisen beside the Ravi River on the flat plain of the Punjab, but everyone agreed that the city's foundations rested upon the ruins of many older, now forgotten versions of itself, and that the Lahore of the seventeenth century had been the finest and most beautiful of them all.

Two hundred years after the Moghul emperors had embellished it with their characteristically elegant architecture, the old city still boasted a grand, marble palace within its red brick fort, and a glorious red sandstone mosque. Beyond the city walls, tiled gateways, irrigated gardens, airy pavilions, and the delicately carved and inlaid tombs of the royal dead were witnesses to the grandeur of a city that had once been the northern capital of a great empire.

In the eastern part of the walled city, near the Delhi Gate, stood another architectural masterpiece of the Moghul era, the mosque of Wazir Khan.

Inside the mosque, the morning air was cool, and faintly scented

1

with roses. Sunlight poured in from the courtyard outside, illuminating the dust that hung in clouds, softening the colours of the high-ceilinged prayer chamber. Near a wall densely decorated with Arabic calligraphy, Shaikh Waliullah Khan Karakoyia knelt, shoeless, on a Persian carpet, an illuminated Qur'an open before him on a carved wooden stand, his tall starched headdress lending him a dignity he did not require.

There was no part of the Muslim holy book that Shaikh Waliullah, spiritual guide of the Karakoyia brotherhood of mystics, had not already committed to memory, but even so, he never failed to perform the ceremony of removing the book's silk wrappings and setting it open on a carved stand, before chanting the familiar Arabic in his quiet singsong.

Today he would recite the beloved verses from the chapter entitled 'Light', Sura Nur.

> Allah is the Light
> Of the heavens and the earth.
> The parable of His light
> Is as if there were a niche,
> And within it, a lamp:
> The lamp enclosed in glass:
> The glass as it were
> A brilliant star,
> Lit from a blessed tree:
> An olive, neither of the East
> Nor of the West,
> Whose oil is well nigh
> Luminous,
> Though fire scarce touched it:
> Light upon Light!

2

After sitting for some minutes, his lips moving, his eyes half-closed, the Shaikh returned the book to its wrappings. He tucked it beneath his arm, rose to his feet and walked barefoot through the vaulted archways of the prayer chamber, then across the mosque's square courtyard, past the ablution tank with its burbling fountain, returning the salutes of other men as he passed them, his forceful expression softened by the passage he had been reciting.

At the entrance, he greeted the hunchbacked Keeper of Shoes, then waited while the little man brought the slippers he had kept carefully aside from those of ordinary men. The Shaikh pushed his feet into his shoes and strode down the mosque's long flight of steps and into its small, cobbled square.

His family's ancestral home stood fronting the square, at a right angle to the mosque. As the Shaikh approached its tall, carved doors, three men who had been squatting outside leapt to attention, and the great doors swung open.

The main courtyard of the comfortable old haveli, with its animal stables along one side, was as warm as the square outside, but it was quieter. The sun caught its frescoed walls, painted with the crescent moons that gave the old house its name, and fell upon the inner courtyard's lone, dusty tree, and onto the platform where, on pleasant afternoons, the Shaikh was accustomed to sit among his followers.

He crossed the small courtyard, turned left into a doorway, and climbed a flight of winding, stone stairs to the ladies' quarters of his house. In a large upstairs room, women and children watched as the Shaikh marched past them along a bright corridor and into a small, whitewashed chamber where his twin sister waited for him.

He returned her half-smile of greeting. 'I was reciting from Sura Nur,' he offered as he lowered himself to the sheet-covered floor. 'For some reason that chapter never fails to remind me of my daughter-in-law.'

3

Safiya Sultana shifted her stout body against one of the bolsters that lined the room's walls. '"An olive, neither of the East nor of the West",' she quoted in her measured Arabic, easily identifying the verse her brother referred to, for she did not often need to be told what he was thinking. 'Yes,' she agreed, 'I think one could say that about the English girl.'

'Inshallah,' the Shaikh said softly, 'she and our little Saboor will soon return safely.'

'Inshallah, God willing,' his sister echoed, nodding gravely.

On that same afternoon, twelve hundred miles southeast of the Shaikh's house, Mariana Givens nudged her mare through a throng of gaily dressed natives, her eyes on the scene before her.

The air around her smelled of frying and spices. Harsh, rhythmic music came from somewhere she could not see. She turned her head, taking in the scene, promising herself she would remember it forever.

This was not the first time Mariana had left the broad avenues of British Calcutta behind her. A dozen times during the previous six months she had escaped her uncle's large house on Chowringhee Road and ventured alone into the native part of town, for she had discovered that when she lost herself in the real India, her misery and boredom lightened for a time.

She had gained this opportunity to see the interesting and macabre Charak Puja only an hour earlier. As she crossed the broad drive in front of Government House on her afternoon ride, several young British officers had ridden past her, talking animatedly among themselves.

'. . . a cross between a Maypole and a whirligig,' one of them had been saying. 'A man is attached to a rope fixed to the top of a mast. A group of men then rotate the mast, causing the attached man to spin about in a great circle. But what distinguishes it from a real whirligig is that the man is suspended by meat hooks that have been forced through his body.'

'We must go there at once!' another had cried. 'We must not miss a moment of it!'

Hoping no one would see her leaving the respectable environs of Government House, Mariana had waited until the young officers were some distance away, then clucked to her mare and set off to follow them, a solitary female figure riding sidesaddle through the native shantytown, where naked babies played in the dust and unrecognizable smells filtered through the air.

The temple grounds at Kali Ghat were filled with a swelling, festive crowd. The cries of sweetmeat sellers competed with the clashing of native music. Groups of dancing girls whirled before prosperous-looking onlookers. Ragged creatures with great gashes through their upper arms danced wildly to the same music while running swords or spits through their wounds. Others held withered arms over their matted heads, their fists clenched, filthy, overgrown fingernails protruding from the backs of their hands.

Two tall poles at the centre of the ground promised even more fearful sights.

The drumbeats began to intensify. The crowd cleared a wide circular space, leaving only a dozen half-naked men standing by two tall masts. Mariana rode forward, craning to see which one of them had hooks through his body, but saw only that several ropes trailed along the ground behind the group, then rose to the top of the pole.

Like bullocks pushing a waterwheel, all but one of the men begin to push the arms of a turnstile attached to the pole. As they ran faster and faster in a tight, shouting circle, the ropes tautened and the last man rose slowly into the air and began to fly.

He swung in a wide circle, his lips moving as he threw flowers onto the crowd below. As he flew past her, Mariana saw plainly that four hooks had been forced through the muscles of his chest, and four through his back. His wounds did not bleed, but remained sickeningly raw and open for all to see.

A male English voice laughed loudly somewhere in the crowd. Mariana gazed upward, unable to look away, a hand shading her eyes. Was it agony or joy that made him draw back his lips into that mad smile? Had he taken bhang to lessen his pain? What had driven him to make this extraordinary sacrifice?

The man swung towards her again, reaching into a cloth bag as he approached. A moment later he sailed over her head, his expression concentrated and ecstatic. A handful of flowers fell around her as he flew away.

A yellow marigold became entangled in her horse's mane. She reached out, but before she could touch it, a male hand appeared suddenly and swept it to the ground where it lay, bright as a jewel, in the dust.

'You should not be here,' the owner of the hand said firmly.

Shocked, Mariana stared down from her saddle. The man who had spoken was clearly Hindu, since his shirt opened on the right side. He stood beside her, clean-shaven and neatly turbaned, his waistcloth flowing to his feet, a white dot between his eyes.

'This is *not* your path,' he continued in a resonant voice, speaking in Urdu, a language Mariana understood, not in the Bengali that rose and fell about them. 'This way,' he gestured at the dreadful figure soaring above them, 'is for others, but it is not for you.'

The crowd had thickened around her, blocking her escape. The discordant music seemed to grow louder. The Englishman laughed again, his voice a distant guffaw.

'Your path lies to the northwest.' The stranger pointed an

authoritative brown hand away from the crowd. 'You must return there to find your destiny. Until then, do not attend festivities such as these. Do not touch the flowers. Do not look again at the man overhead.'

How had he known? Mariana swallowed, searching for a brave, offhand response, but nothing came. When the man did not move, she followed his gaze towards a line of distant green hills.

'Leave this place,' he commanded. 'Go.'

The men at the turnstile shouted. Overhead, the wounded man's ropes and pulleys creaked and sang, telling Mariana that he still whirled above the crowd, dropping his flowers like blessings on their heads. But she did not look up again. Instead, she clucked to her mare and pushed her way without a backward glance past mendicant scarecrows, dancers, and food stalls until she reached the road leading back to her uncle's comfortable English house on Chowringhee Road.

It had not been the Hindu stranger's abrupt appearance beside her or the oddness of his message that had driven her, trembling a little, from the temple grounds. She had seen at once that there was no reason to fear him, that he was no charlatan or trickster. He had been too cleanly dressed, too dignified. He had asked for nothing in return for delivering his message. What had sent her away had been his words.

Your path lies to the northwest, he had said, pointing in the direction of the Punjab, the proud, unconquered kingdom that lay beyond the northwestern frontier of British India. It called to Mariana even now, its faint siren song offering elusive, wondrous things and a world entirely alien to her own, where no word of her language was ever uttered, no morsel of her native food ever prepared. In the venerable walled city house she had left behind in Lahore fifteen months ago, there were no balls, no amateur theatricals, no dinner tables with

7

silver candelabra and lively conversation. Instead, the great Shaikh Waliullah's ladies and a score of their children occupied themselves day after day in an upstairs room that, in Mariana's memory, had seemed to encompass the entire world.

But of her path there had been no sign. How could there be a path when those ladies scarcely ever left the house?

She rode home, lost in thought. Her face felt hot and gritty beneath her top hat. She stared at a brightly caparisoned donkey in front of her, trying to distract herself from her memories of Lahore.

Whatever path the soothsayer had meant, it could surely not lead there. After fifteen long months, Mariana had come to believe that she would never go to the Punjab again.

Chapter One

20 June 1840

Three months later, still in Calcutta, Mariana sat beside her aunt six pews behind the Governor-General and his two spinster sisters, watching a short, red-faced man make his perspiring way towards the pulpit steps of St John's Cathedral.

Around her, the congregation twitched and whispered. A woman nudged her husband. Another woman in black, who had appeared to be sleeping, sat up and began to fan herself vigorously. Two rows away, a newly arrived girl and her sharp-faced companion turned in their seats to look at Mariana, smug satisfaction on their faces. Like her, they knew what was coming. Unlike her, they were enjoying themselves.

Beneath her wilting gown, Mariana's stays felt as if they had been ironed onto her torso. Her hair, difficult at the best of times, had escaped her straw bonnet and now hung in loose brown curls on her neck, causing her skin to prickle in the June heat.

The dean climbed the pulpit steps and mopped his face. He leaned over the carved wooden rail of the pulpit, his eyes drifting towards

Mariana, who yawned deliberately behind a gloved hand, her body tensing against the hard wooden pew.

'I find it delightful to see how much our numbers have grown in the past year,' he began in his high voice. 'It gives me *such* pleasure to see how many eligible young ladies from home have found suitable matches here in India.' His eyes rested briefly on a square-shouldered officer, his moon-faced wife and their overdressed, sqirming baby before returning to Mariana. 'As I look out over this congregation, I am filled with joy at the sight of so many happy little families, and I look forward to seeing many, *many* more.'

'I know someone who will *never* be married in this cathedral,' a voice behind Mariana said clearly.

It would do no good to let the woman know she had heard. Instead, Mariana picked up her aunt's hymnal and began to leaf through its pages.

It came as no surprise that the dean had aimed his remarks at her, for he had done the same in every one of his sermons for the past six months.

The gossip about Mariana's experiences in the northwest had begun to surface on the verandahs and in the drawing rooms of the British capital six months earlier, immediately after she had returned, along with the rest of the Governor-General's vast camp, from his lengthy visit to the Maharajah of the Punjab. After Lord Auckland's state tents had been struck for the last time and the officers who had accompanied him had returned to their families and living quarters, the story of Mariana's shocking behaviour in Lahore had spread rapidly from bungalow to bungalow, defying Lord Auckland's order of strict secrecy and swiftly eclipsing all previous scandals. For, the gossip ran, while in the Punjab, Mariana Givens had done the worst thing an Englishwoman in India could do: she had embarked upon a disgraceful, ruinous liaison with a native man.

Confirmed by the energetic, brown-skinned presence of her two-year-old stepson Saboor and embellished with ever more damning detail, the scandal had clung to her like sticky, invisible clothing, uniting all of Calcutta society against her, and turning her overnight into an outcast among her own people. Worse still, Mariana's ruin had fallen upon her aunt and uncle, neither of whom had been present in Lahore during that tumultuous time.

From the moment of her return, Aunt Claire and Uncle Adrian, the only family Mariana had in India, had been excluded from the cheerful dinners and spirited balls and fetes that made Calcutta the gayest city in India, especially the celebrations that had attended the Governor-General's triumphant return from his visit to the north. A few loyal friends still paid surreptitious visits to the Lambs' comfortable bungalow, but the rest of society had drifted away, fearful of being caught by association in the viscid web of Mariana's disgrace.

'But these people know nothing of what really happened,' Mariana had insisted to her tearful aunt when they had been cut dead for the third time while buying muslin in the bazaar. 'Why should we care what they think, Aunt Claire?'

But Aunt Claire cared very much what people thought. Moments after Mariana had carried little Saboor through the front door of 65 Chowringhee Road and begun a halting, uncomfortable recital of her experiences in the Punjab, Aunt Claire had collapsed, semi-conscious, onto a sofa, eyes shut and mouth open.

Choking tragically from a whiff of smelling salts, she had waved Mariana away and refused to listen to a word of explanation. 'What have I done to be punished so?' she had sobbed later to Uncle Adrian from her pillows, while Mariana eavesdropped in the hallway outside. 'Why has she done this unmentionable thing? And why has she brought a native child into my house?

Make her take it to the servants' quarters, Adrian. Oh, *what* will become of us?'

'You should never have brought that baby into the drawing room,' her uncle told her tightly a little while later, as he stood, his back to her, staring out of his study window. 'Is it not enough that you have ruined yourself? Must you also parade a native child in front of your aunt? Since you insist he has lost his mother, and is of high station among his people,' he added grimly, 'the child may remain with you. But you are *not* to let him into the front of the house, and you are *forbidden* to mention Lahore or the Punjab again in your aunt's presence.'

Shocked at this angry reception by her normally mild uncle, Mariana had been unable to reply.

He turned from the window and glared at her. 'You knew perfectly well,' he said, 'why we accepted Lord Auckland's invitation for you to join his train. You were well aware that it had nothing to do with translating local languages for his sisters. Given such a signal opportunity, why did you not marry one of his officers while you were in the Punjab?'

'I tried to marry one of them, but it all fell to pieces because he was supposed to have—'

'Instead of doing your duty and marrying an Englishman,' her uncle barked, his bald head flushing with emotion, 'you kidnapped the Maharajah's baby hostage and then, with a recklessness I cannot even conceive, you married its father. How could you have done it? How?'

'It was a mistake,' she replied stiffly. 'I did not mean to marry him.'

'You might have thought of the consequences to us,' he went on, his voice rising. 'Before you abandoned your own race and entangled yourself with a native family, you might have considered

12

my brother-in-law, who so generously sent you out here, with *very* different expectations.'

He sighed. 'We must of course extract you from this most unfortunate marriage and return the child, but when and how that is to take place, I have no idea. It will do you no good, of course,' he added, waving an impatient hand at Mariana's sudden tears, 'but in the meantime you must take pains to behave like everyone else. Do *nothing* else to attract comment. *Do you hear me?*'

He had been right. It had been far too late for Mariana to find acceptability. Since then she had been snubbed and ignored, and barred from society's pleasures. She had lived quietly with Saboor and her aunt and uncle at Chowringhee Road, reading Persian poetry with her elderly native language teacher and escaping occasionally to the native part of Calcutta. It was not an unpleasant life, for unlike her Aunt Claire she had never been interested in parties. Only two things caused her real misery: the thought of losing Saboor, and going to church.

'Put on a pretty morning gown and get into the carriage,' Aunt Claire had snapped this morning, after bursting into Mariana's room and finding her still in her dressing gown. 'There is no need for you to feed it,' she had added, averting her eyes from the round-eyed child who sat beside Mariana, eating his breakfast. 'It can have its breakfast with the servants.'

'I loathe church,' Mariana argued, as she deliberately handed Saboor a piece of buttered toast. 'I hate everyone who goes there, and they hate me. St John's Cathedral must be the most *unchristian* place in all of India.'

'It is not,' her aunt had replied sharply, 'and you *shall* go there. If you would only make the slightest show of contrition, I am sure you would be forgiven.'

The dean now raised his voice, interrupting Mariana's thoughts.

'And there is still better news,' he announced grandly. 'Churches are being constructed all over India. The latest, at Allahabad, is nearly complete. What wonders these churches will do!' He spread his arms wide. 'We are all breathless with expectation, for it is now certain that the conversion of the natives is very near at hand. We must keep in mind, however, that until they have seen the Christian light, the natives must be avoided. There is terrible degradation in the native's present character, and vice in his every word and deed. And we must remember,' he dropped his voice and favoured Mariana with a sidelong glance, 'that for those who associate intimately with them, there awaits the same vice, the same degradation, the same perdition.'

Degradation. Perdition. The hymnal Mariana was holding came alive in her hands. As if by itself, it slammed shut, making a noise like a thunderclap that rang satisfactorily through the cathedral's stone interior.

The dean jerked upright. A stringy woman turned in her pew and glared at Mariana.

Aunt Claire's finger jabbed into Mariana's side. 'What are you *doing*?' she whispered, scowling. 'Put down that hymn book and attend to the sermon.'

People stared. The sharp-faced girl nudged her friend.

The dean recovered himself and began to quote the Acts of the Apostles, his florid voice rising and falling. Mariana sat erect, giving no outward sign of discomfort, while her mind wandered to the message she had received in March from the mysterious Hindu man. He had spoken with urgent authority, but Mariana could not fathom what he had meant. What destiny could possibly await her in the direction he had pointed?

She blinked. Could the man's message have had anything to do with the poem her elderly teacher had given her to translate on the day before he began the long journey home to his native Punjab? 'My moon of Canaan, the throne of Egypt is thine,' the poem had read. 'The hour is near. The time has come to bid farewell to the prison.'

As she translated those Persian words, her munshi's feverish old face had brightened with some emotion she could not read, but the old teacher had not told her why he had chosen that particular poem for their last day.

Mariana felt certain he knew more than he revealed; he had long belonged to the Karakoyia brotherhood, and he knew the mysterious Shaikh Waliullah well.

What was the meaning of that verse? Did the prison represent Calcutta for her? If so, where was her promised throne of Egypt? She found her handkerchief and blew into it, trying to imagine herself as wonderful as Joseph, with his coat of many colours.

The dean stopped speaking at last. As he descended from the pulpit, the wooden stairs creaked and groaned in protest, echoing Mariana's sentiments. She longed to jump to her feet, pink-faced and shouting, and teach the old hypocrite a lesson in Christian charity.

Half an hour later, as she followed her aunt towards the cathedral's main entrance, she heard a male voice behind her in the crowd. 'She wouldn't be bad-looking, you know,' it said, 'if she ever smiled.'

When they reached the driveway, Aunt Claire hoisted herself, panting a little, into her new carriage and fought her parasol open against the Calcutta sun. 'What is the matter with you, Mariana?' she demanded, one hand clutching the side of the carriage for balance. 'Why did you bang your hymnal shut in the middle of the sermon? You will never redeem yourself with Calcutta society if you behave like a lunatic.'

Mariana snapped open her own parasol. 'I could not bear to hear one more syllable about my supposed sins, Aunt Claire.'

'Why do you assume he was talking of *your* sins, Mariana?' Aunt Claire sniffed, settling into her seat. 'I am quite certain he was not. In any event, no one can make out what is said in that great, echoing cathedral. I, for one, caught no more than one word in three of that sermon.'

An English family drove past them, wedged into another carriage, the husband stuffed into his frock coat, the children looking wan and ill in the heat. As they passed Mariana and her aunt, all turned their heads away. Mariana winced at the miserable little sound that came from her aunt's corner of the carriage. Aunt Claire might pretend she had not heard the sermon, but there was no avoiding the Broderick family's collective snub.

As they passed the houses along Chowringhee Road, each in its large, walled compound, Mariana studied the brass nameplates on each gate, as she always did. All save two were English.

When they reached number 65, the scarlet-turbaned durwan waved his bamboo pole and four men in loincloths appeared and pushed open the wrought-iron gate. The carriage with its matched horses swung through.

In the echoing entrance hall, Aunt Claire handed her bonnet and parasol to a servant. 'I must look in on your uncle,' she said over her shoulder as she puffed her way up the stairs.

Mariana waited, listening anxiously at the foot of the stairs. Worse than the punishing heat of Calcutta, its mosquitoes, its gossip, even the squalor and starvation of many of the natives, were the illnesses whose sudden descent could wipe out entire families in a matter of hours.

She did not think she could bear her life without Uncle Adrian, who now lay, ill with fever, in an upstairs room. Unlike most of the English, her uncle knew something of the Indian life she craved to understand. An avid student of military strategy since her childhood, she had always cared more for her uncle's stories than for her aunt's silks, lace, and gossip. It had been Uncle Adrian who had introduced her to her munshi, the old man who had taught her both Persian and Urdu, the court language of India.

Unlike his wife, Uncle Adrian had forgiven Mariana's sins.

A sound came from the dining room, followed by a high-pitched hiccupping giggle. Forgetting her worry, Mariana tore off her bonnet and rushed through the archway in time to see a small figure in white erupt from under the table and race through the pantry door, his clothes flying.

'Come here, Saboor, you nuisance, you pest!' Her hair falling from its pins, she burst into the pantry, and found the curly-haired child dancing with excitement, half hidden behind a china cupboard.

Half a dozen men sat on the kitchen floor, eating rice heaped on freshly cut banana leaves. They looked up, chewing.

'Saboor, my little cabbage, my little cauliflower!' she cried as she scooped the child into her arms.

He wriggled and bounced as she kissed him, his broad face alight. 'An-nah, put me down, put me down,' he shrieked. 'I want to run and *run*!'

As she followed the galloping three-year-old figure through the doorway, her aunt's voice rang in the hallway. 'Mariana, come upstairs. There is something we must tell you.'

Chapter Two

Mariana had heard that demanding tone before. She climbed the stairs reluctantly, in no hurry to hear what Aunt Claire had to say, for it almost certainly had to do with Saboor, who now sat on the pantry floor, eating his lunch.

The battle of Saboor at 65 Chowringhee Road, joined by Mariana and her aunt on Saboor's first day in Calcutta, was now in its seventh month, but the child still lived in the house, not in the servants' quarters, and ate his food with her, and she still sang him to sleep in her bedchamber. Confident of victory in the upcoming skirmish, she squared her shoulders and turned towards her uncle's bedroom. She had, after all, protected her little hostage in the past from more dangerous opponents than one poor, snobbish, unhappy aunt.

Out of habit, she paused to listen before entering the room, trying to divine the course of the conversation she was about to join, but heard only the raucous cawing of crows outside her uncle's bedroom window.

'Come in, Mariana, and shut the door.' Still wearing her creased church gown, Aunt Claire fanned herself in an upright chair beside an open window, while Uncle Adrian smiled from his bed, his usually ruddy face now yellowed and drawn.

'We wanted to tell you of this earlier,' Aunt Claire began in her usual ringing tone as Mariana lowered herself into a seat beside the bed, 'but with your uncle's illness there has been no time.'

Mariana nodded. Perhaps this conversation would not concern Saboor, after all.

'Your uncle,' Aunt Claire announced, 'has been posted to Afghanistan.'

'Afghanistan?' Mariana sat straight. 'But I thought he was going home to Sussex.'

'Well, he is not. The British Envoy in Kabul has particularly asked for him.'

'It is quite flattering, really,' Uncle Adrian put in from his pillow. 'We shall be leaving in a month or two.'

'But I thought you hated travel, Aunt Claire. I thought—'

'It does not matter what you thought, and in any case, it is all decided. We are at last to be rid of that native child, and you are to be divorced.' Aunt Claire closed her fan with a snap. 'On our way to Kabul, we shall stop at Lahore, end your marriage, leave the child with his family, and travel on. It's as simple as that.'

Rid of Saboor? Mariana's hand flew to her mouth.

'Think, Mariana,' her aunt was saying. 'The child is small now, but in no time at all he'll be a full-grown native *man*. What on earth would you do with him then? This brings us, of course, to my next point. In his dispatch from Kabul, the Envoy revealed something unexpected about you.'

'Sir William Macnaghten has mentioned *me* in a government dispatch?'

'He has,' Aunt Claire replied, in the grand tone she reserved for government matters. 'Several days ago, immediately after his new appointment to Afghanistan, your uncle was summoned to Government House, but to his surprise it was not to discuss either Afghanistan or the Honourable East India Company. Instead, Lord Auckland's two sisters told your uncle privately – and in strictest confidence – that there was one important fact you omitted to tell us about that horrid native "marriage" of yours.'

Something in her aunt's expression warned Mariana what was coming. 'What have I not revealed, Aunt Claire?'

'That you are still, shall I say, chaste. That you are married in name only.'

Mariana, who had never spoken to anybody about such matters, looked hastily away. 'And the Governor-General and his sisters know this?'

'Of course they do,' Aunt Claire said impatiently. 'Sir William had just told them.'

'But how does he——'

'As you no doubt remember,' Uncle Adrian put in gently, 'every Government of India officer who was present at Lahore that evening was forced to attend your wedding, including Lord Auckland. The next morning, Sir William Macnaghten kindly offered to fetch you from Shaikh Waliullah's house and take you back to the English camp, but when he arrived in the walled city, he found that you had vanished upon some silly native errand.'

'It was not silly,' Mariana protested, stung. 'The Maharajah's armed men came for Saboor, and they had to let him down from a window in the rain, and——'

'Never mind about the child,' snapped Aunt Claire.

'When Sir William inquired as to your whereabouts,' Uncle Adrian went on, his eyes averted from Mariana's, 'the Shaikh indicated that the previous night had not proceeded as expected. Sir

William then asked one or two questions of his own, and divined the truth. He wrote in his dispatch that he had put the whole story from his mind and only thought of it after he requested my appointment to Kabul.'

Aunt Claire glared at Mariana. 'Why did you not tell us this yourself?'

Mariana found her handerchief and mopped her face. Saboor's *grandfather* knew what had happened that night? Who had told *him*? Did they all tell each other *everything*?

'I do not understand,' she said stiffly, 'how Sir William could even *mention* such a delicate—'

'Don't be a goose, Mariana,' interrupted Aunt Claire. 'You had no reason to hide this information. We cannot think how you managed it, but we have all agreed that saving yourself on your marriage night was the first sensible thing you have done since you came to India.'

'If it is true,' added Uncle Adrian, 'then it may be possible to salvage some small part of your reputation. While you behaved foolishly, even provocatively, towards the natives, you may not have been entirely unchaste.'

'*Not entirely unchaste?*' Mariana sprang, hot-faced, from her chair. '*If it is true?*'

'Sit down at once. There is more.' Aunt Claire leaned back in her chair. 'The Eden ladies have told your uncle that they want to apologize to you.' She peered at Mariana over her fan. 'They said that on the way to the Punjab, you wanted to marry a certain Lieutenant Fitzgerald of the Horse Artillery, and that they forced you to sever that friendship. They said that all this occurred just over eighteen months ago. They implied that you took the loss badly, and that the disappointment you felt may have affected your judgement and led to your later entanglement with Saboor's father.'

21

Affected her judgement indeed. Mariana glowered from her chair.

'The ladies said that they forced the parting after hearing that Fitzgerald had jilted a young lady here in Calcutta. They now understand that the story was false, and that Fitzgerald had, in fact, behaved very well.' Aunt Claire paused dramatically. 'Why did you tell us none of this?'

Mariana averted her face. It caused her too much pain even to think of Fitzgerald. What was the use of talking about him?

Fitzgerald's smile had been crooked and knowing. His uniform coat had smelled deliciously musty. At first, the Governor-General's sisters had put no obstacle in the way of her infatuation. Nodding like two bonneted birds, the two spinsters had watched her blossom, watched her follow her young horse gunner with her eyes until the lies that had travelled all the way from Calcutta reached the Punjab. Then, abruptly, they had changed their minds. With no thought of Mariana's feelings or of Fitzgerald's, they had issued instructions that the two were to be separated.

The loss of him had been agony.

Four weeks later, Lord Auckland's much-desired treaty of alliance with the Punjab had been signed and celebrated with Mariana's unexpected native wedding. The next day, Harry Fitzgerald and all the other officers she might have married had marched off with their great army to Afghanistan and victory, leaving her behind them, in disgrace.

'The Eden ladies wish to make amends,' Aunt Claire announced. 'Now that this new information has emerged, they believe they can help you. They have quite generously offered to let it be known in certain circles that your behaviour in Lahore was not as shocking as people suppose. They are willing to suggest that you have been wronged.'

'That is, of course, the great benefit of my appointment to Kabul,'

22

Uncle Adrian added seriously. 'It may be that we, and particularly you, my dear, can make a fresh start there. I understand that Kabul looks set to become a delightful station for our officers, with its superior climate and wonderful fruit.' He nodded with satisfaction. 'Fortunately for all of us, among Muslim natives an unconsummated marriage is easily dissolved.'

Aunt Claire cleared her throat. 'Of course, this brings up the question of your future. Once we are in Kabul, it may be possible to find a husband for you. A widower, perhaps.'

A doddering old man with children older than herself? Mariana opened her mouth to speak, then closed it.

'But one never knows what might transpire,' her aunt went on eagerly. 'After all, Kabul is full of unattached men, including Lieutenant Fitzgerald.'

'No one will marry me, Aunt Claire, and Fitzgerald hates me, after what happened.'

'But my dear girl, your news must be well-known there already. You know how gossip travels. For all we know, the lieutenant may be waiting breathlessly for your arrival. After all, he has had his own experience with unfair gossip and scandal. But if he does not marry you, someone else may. You should have children of your own.' She sighed wistfully. 'You have no idea how happy that will make you. But of course,' she added, 'if nothing takes place in Kabul, we shall take you home to England when we leave here permanently.'

Uncle Adrian nodded. 'Your aunt is right, Mariana. Whatever happens will be better than this. You shall, thank God, be free of your native connections before the end of the cold weather.'

And free of Saboor. Mariana stared numbly at her uncle.

Three days later, at four o'clock in the morning, Mariana woke up with a start to find her manservant Dittoo at her bedroom door, a lamp in his hand, looking rumpled and close to tears.

'There is a courier outside,' he whispered hoarsely. 'He has brought a letter from Lahore. He says he will give it into your hands only.' The lamp jerked in Dittoo's hand, sending moving shadows across the wall.

Wordlessly Mariana reached for her dressing gown.

'He is very ugly, Bibi,' Dittoo went on, his face bunching. 'He is an albino. I told him I could not bring such a strange-looking man into the house in the middle of the night. I said he must wait until the morning, but he is insisting, and his voice is becoming loud. I begged him to give me the letter, but he said he would kill me first.' He straightened his hunched body as far as he was able. 'He says he has not travelled all this distance to give the letter to a servant.'

Mariana crept down the stairs after Dittoo and followed him to the side verandah, where she quickly took in the shadowy form of a burly man in a thick, Punjabi-style turban. The man's beard was as pale as corn silk. She blinked in surprise at the sight of his scabbed and blistered feet on the tiled verandah floor. Although they clearly belonged to him, they were as white as her own.

She returned the man's greeting, but said no more. She did not even ask his name. Instead, she took the sealed letter from his outstretched hand and turned away towards the stairs. Back in her room, she slid the letter into one of her tin storage boxes and went back to bed.

For two days she avoided reading it. For two days the albino sat on the string bed outside the gate, waiting for her reply before starting the twelve-hundred-mile journey home.

She had no need to read the letter. The fact of its arrival told her all she needed to know: that more than one person had plans to take her and Saboor to Lahore. The albino's letter, she was certain, contained the information that Saboor's father, her native husband, would soon be on his way to collect them both and return them to the walled city house where he lived with his mysteriously powerful father and the rest of the Waliullah family.

When it is safe, I will come for you, Hassan had promised on her last evening in the Punjab, before the Governor-General's camp crossed the Sutlej River into British territory. A moment later, he had gone.

In the weeks that followed, she had expected him to come, but he had not. As the distance between them grew, she had put his promise from her mind. Now when she tried to picture him, she found she could remember only a blurred, bearded face and a long embroidered coat.

For eighteen months she had heard nothing from him.

She could not remember when she had stopped believing that she would see Lahore again, but sometime during the difficult months after her return to Calcutta she had begun to imagine a different ending to the story. She dreamed of some chance happening that would allow her to take little Saboor back with her to England when her aunt and uncle left India for good. She imagined Sunday lunch at her father's country vicarage, and Saboor sitting in a high chair at the table, eating roast mutton, beside her little nephew Freddie. She pictured the neighbours patting him on the head, nodding approvingly as he grew up, exotic and lovable, the pride of Weddington village.

Now she must face the loss of the child she had kept safe for so long and loved so passionately, who woke her each day crying, 'An-nah, morning has come!' as he clambered onto her bed.

She must also face her husband, and perhaps his family as well. They would be upset by the divorce. After all, it must be a great honour to have an Englishwoman in the family. But it could not be helped, and when it was over, Hassan would keep Saboor, and she would be left with a broken heart.

The only person who might ease her pain was Harry Fitzgerald, who had once admired her for speaking several native languages, who had not seemed to mind when her clothes were buttoned wrong, who had offered her hot, hasty kisses in the shadow of her tent when no one was looking. But after starting for Afghanistan with his heavy, wheeled guns, the handsome lieutenant had sent her only one bitter letter, from a camp near the Bolan Pass.

Who will dare to be your friend now? he had written.

Since then he had travelled hundreds of miles through deep mountain passes and over barren, waterless land. He had fought battles, real ones, not the imaginary scenes they had conjured up together over breakfast in the dining tent at Lord Auckland's camp. He must have felt terror. He must have seen horrible things.

He might have changed. Perhaps he drank too much now, after all the bloody campaigning. Worse, perhaps he had proved a coward in battle. Even if he were still the same, could he ever love her again?

Your path lies to the northwest. The Hindu from the Charak Puja rose again in Mariana's mind, pointing into the distance. Afghanistan, of course, was to the northwest, but so was the Punjab.

Tangled among thoughts of the fair-haired lieutenant were other memories, vivid, startling ones of a room strewn with roses, of herself in red wedding silks, her skin oiled and perfumed, lying terrified on a bed while her husband bent over her. She tried to put the memory away and recapture the feeling of Fitzgerald's lips on hers, but instead she saw Hassan's bearded face, saw his expression change, saw him pull away from her.

She had not saved herself on her marriage night. Seeing her terror and exhaustion, Hassan had spared her himself.

Sleep, he had said, before padding back to his own bed. *Go to sleep*.

And now, eighteen months later, his courier was waiting outside the compound wall. The letter the albino had brought still lay unopened in her tin box.

Mariana drew a deep breath. She must not keep Hassan's courier waiting any longer.

Chapter Three

23 June 1840

The walled city of Lahore had always smelled of roses. Discernible in the cool winters, the scent became overpowering in the still, baking heat of the Punjabi summer, filling the tiny, stifling shops that lined the city's narrow alleyways, rushing out of its many mosques and temples. Sometimes sweet and mysterious, often corrupted and rotten, the perfume reached into every quarter of the city, staining the air, permeating everything: the food, the water, even the offal swept into heaps in the city's neglected corners.

The only part of the city where the scent did not reach was the red brick fort that took up the northwestern quarter of the city's walled area. There, in a guarded tower room inside the marble palace that occupied the northwest corner of the Moghul Citadel, Maharajah Kharrak Singh of the Punjab had begun raving again. Bent double on the golden throne that had belonged to his legendary father he rocked from side to side, watched by his few remaining loyal courtiers, his hands clutching his midsection, his feet drumming the floor.

'I *want* the magical child, the grandson of Shaikh Waliullah. I *want* him,' the Maharajah repeated, his ugly face creased with pain. 'And I want to leave this place,' he added, peering about his ill-ventilated apartments. 'This is not fit for a king. I must live in the best part of the palace.'

'You will, Mahraj, you will,' crooned a black-bearded gentleman from his place on the marble tiles beside the throne. 'But the child Saboor is not here. He left Lahore more than a year ago, before your father died.'

Kharrak Singh's bejewelled courtiers stood along the walls, their bright silks adding life to the stifling room. They nodded in agreement. One of them held out a hand. 'Come, Mahraj,' he coaxed, smiling encouragingly, 'you must rest.'

'My father would still be alive if that child had not been stolen from him. Everyone knows it was the Shaikh's grandson who protected my father with his magic. No one tells me the truth.' The Maharajah glared at the seated man. 'Not even you, Faqeer Sahib. You know I am being poisoned, and you know that the poisoner is my own son, the usurper of my power. If my father were still alive,' he gasped, 'he would help me. He would never allow this.' He bent over again, his damp face grey.

'We have not lied to you, Mahraj—'

'And what of the child's father?' Kharrak Singh stabbed a quivering finger at a tall, neatly bearded man who stood unobtrusively against a wall. 'What of *him*, with his English wife? He should send me his healing child. I am dying in front of him, and he does nothing.'

'But Hassan Ali Khan's son has gone to Calcutta, Mahraj,' the Faqeer pointed out. 'And how is the Prince poisoning you? The food tasters have yet to show signs of illness.' Beneath his neatly tied turban, the Faqeer's forehead glistened with perspiration. 'Every precaution has been taken to protect you.'

Spittle crawled from the corner of the Maharajah's mouth. He looked up, his eyes unfocused, at his assembled nobles. 'You want me dead, all of you,' he cried. 'Hah! I know what you want, but you will *never have it*.'

Nervous silence fell over the small, crowded apartments. 'Is he cursing us?' whispered a young man whose emerald necklaces covered him from his neck to his waist.

'You want to believe that your future is safe,' Kharrak Singh croaked, 'that you will keep your riches, but I can tell you this, the Kingdom of the Punjab, built by my father, is finished.'

Eyes fixed on their suffering king, his courtiers scarcely breathed.

The Faqeer spoke at last. 'No, Mahraj,' he offered, hunching his shoulders, his voice a conciliatory singsong. 'Surely you do not mean to say these terrible things. Surely you do not mean to curse our beautiful Punjab.'

The Maharajah pushed the Faqeer's hand away. 'It is finished,' he insisted. 'You will see. Ranjit Singh's heirs will kill each other, as my son Nau Nihal is killing me!'

As his shocked guests began to withdraw, he threw his head back, his tightly wrapped beard exposing a knobby throat. 'Opium,' he howled. 'I want my opium!'

That same day, in the eastern part of the city, near the mosque of Wazir Khan, a small shrouded figure had been crouching anonymously for hours outside the tall, double doors of Shaikh Waliullah's house.

The figure sat silently, huddled among the rubbish left by a careless sweeper, a chador the colour of dust leaving only her pointed childlike face visible. Her small, damaged hand clutched the cotton fabric together under her chin.

Moving only her eyes, the girl watched three ragged men cross the cobbled square and approach the carved doors of the haveli, moving slowly, for one of the men appeared to be in considerable pain. She listened silently as the boldest of the three pounded heavily on the door.

'How is it?' he asked, glancing with concern at his suffering companion as the door's heavy bolts slid noisily aside.

The friend did not reply. He just shook his head, his eyes bulging, his breathing shallow and noisy.

With a great creaking sound the great doors swung open. A pair of guards stood back to let the three men pass inside. 'What have we here?' asked one, his voice echoing in the vaulted brick entranceway as he peered at the injured man. 'Is it snakebite, or a scorpion sting?'

'Whichever it is,' put in the second guard, jerking his chin towards the interior of the haveli, 'you should take him to Shaikh Waliullah at once, but you will not find the Shaikh in his courtyard in this heat. On days like this he stays indoors in a sitting room among his companions. After you cross the inner courtyard, you will see a doorway facing you. Call out, and someone will show you the way.'

Distracted by the injured man, the guards did not notice the silent hunched figure rise to her feet and steal past them into the first courtyard.

The girl had felt weak for days. Throughout the morning as she squatted near a festering pile of mango skins and rotting vegetables, her illness had clutched nauseatingly at her middle, threatening to overcome her. Now, as she crept past Shaikh Waliullah's horse and elephant stables and pushed open the gate leading to his quiet family courtyard, faintness gathered in the corners of her brain.

She had taken a great risk in coming this far. Long before the pre-dawn call to prayer had awakened her farrier husband and his harsh-faced mother, Akhtar had raised herself in cautious stages from the floor where she and her husband slept. Avoiding her mother-in-law, who snored on the hovel's only string bed, she had groped along the wall until she found the older woman's chador hanging from its nail, then felt her way out of the crumbling quarter that had been her prison for three long years.

Following her instincts, she had stumbled along the lightless alleyway outside the door, driven only by a chance remark she had overheard the week before from a passerby outside: that in a house near Wazir Khan's Mosque there lived a woman who knew how to cast spells.

What spells they were did not matter to Akhtar as she braced herself, a hand to her head, against the inner courtyard wall. What mattered was the hope she had felt at hearing those careless words, spoken by a stranger whose face she had not even glimpsed.

Spells. The word suggested mysterious happenings and sudden, miraculous cures. It could also mean something darker: wicked spells, wasting away, even death. But from the moment she had overheard the remark, Akhtar had felt certain that this magician lady possessed what she urgently needed: a remedy for the agony she had endured since her marriage – savaged by her husband, reviled by her mother-in-law, worked to exhaustion, trapped in their tiny, airless quarter with no means of escape.

The mosque was not far from her own, miserable home. As the fiery sun rose, and people appeared in the stifling lanes and alleys, she had tried to ask the women among them where the lady she sought lived but had been too ashamed to explain herself properly. Misunderstood, terrified her husband would find her before she reached her goal, she had wandered fruitlessly until a sad-eyed hunchback who guarded visitors' shoes outside the mosque had asked who or what she sought.

'Ah,' he had said when she tried to explain, 'you seek Begum Safiya Sultana, the sister of the great Shaikh Waliullah. She is no magician, my dear child, but her name is well-known. She will help you.' He had pointed across the square to a wide, brick haveli. 'Wait outside the Shaikh's house,' he had told her. 'In time, they will let you in.'

No magician. Unwilling to believe him, Akhtar had crouched down near the carved doorway, telling herself that the hunchback could not know the truth, for he was not a normal man.

She did not know how long she had waited in the heat without food or drink, but for all her discomfort, and as ill as she felt now, her fright was gone, for the doors of this grand house had closed safely and decisively behind her, shutting out her husband, her mother-in-law, and everything else that might harm her.

For now, however, she could walk no further. A carved balcony overhead offered a patch of shade. She sank to the courtyard floor beneath it, rested her forehead on her upraised knees, and closed her eyes.

Moments later, the injured man and his two friends appeared. Nearly invisible in her dust-coloured clothing, Akhtar lifted her head in time to see the three men hurry by, the injured man sobbing aloud as his two friends half dragged him through the courtyard, past closed doors and shuttered windows, past the courtyard's lone, dusty tree, until they halted beside an open doorway.

The heap of discarded shoes outside the entrance told Akhtar that a number of men were inside. The leader of the trio called out a greeting. After an interval, he left his friends and vanished through the doorway, then reappeared followed by two men, one of them an elderly gentleman with a very wrinkled face and a tall starched headdress.

The girl held her breath. This old man must be Shaikh Waliullah himself, for he radiated power. Even in her illness, she recognized the force of his presence, which seemed to reach all the way across the courtyard to the patch of shade where she huddled.

The injured man's friends lowered him to the ground, where he rocked, keening, from side to side, one ankle clutched in both his hands. The old man glanced briefly at the wound. 'Yes, it is a scorpion sting,' he announced in a light, pleasant voice, then turned to his companion and held out a hand. 'A stick, Javed,' he ordered. 'Yes, that one will do.'

The stick in hand, the old man bent over, his headdress tipping dangerously forward, and made several marks in the dust of the courtyard floor. Then, apparently satisfied with what he had written, he threw down the stick and searched through the pile of discarded shoes, poking at them with one foot, while the injured man's wails rose behind him.

At last, the old man picked up a leather slipper. His back to the victim, he began to strike the marks he had made in the dust, gesturing impatiently for silence when the victim's friend tried to speak. The loud cracking of the shoe against the ground attracted other men from inside. They stood in the doorway, craning to see. Shadowy figures of women appeared in an upstairs window behind filigreed shutters.

Within moments it was over. The old man straightened and dropped his slipper among the other shoes. 'Well?' he inquired in his light voice, wiping dust from his hands and turning his attention once again to the victim.

The injured man had ceased keening. 'It was here,' he said in a wondering tone, rubbing a hand over his anklebone, 'but now it's gone.'

Akhtar pushed herself to her feet, trying to see more. What

strange event had she witnessed? This house must be filled with sorcerers and magicians.

The old man nodded several times. 'Well, that's that,' he said in a matter-of-fact tone. 'You should drink something.' He nodded towards the guarded entrance. 'You'll find water and sherbet over there.' The three men backed away, saluting deferentially. 'And now, Javed,' the old man said, turning to his companion, 'let us return to our conversation. It is not every day that I meet someone who is acquainted with Ghalib. My sister finds his poetry quite exceptional. She will be very pleased to hear that he is to visit Lahore . . .'

His voice faded as he stepped over the threshold and disappeared from view.

Akhtar stared after the two men. She wished she could follow the old magician into his sitting room, and pour out all her troubles, but how could she speak in front of all the other men whose shoes lay heaped beside the door? No, she must go to his sister instead, for she must be the lady who cast spells.

Supporting herself with one hand, Akhtar groped her way towards a canvas screen that stretched along the wall ahead of her, supported by thick bamboo poles. Such screens, she knew, were designed to shield ladies from the eyes of men. After negotiating a wide fold in the canvas, she found a doorway, then a brick staircase leading down into darkness, as if to a subterranean room. Women's shoes lay beside this door.

Akhtar scuffed off her own shabby sandals and crept down the staircase.

The courtyard had been bright and fiery hot. As she stepped down into the cool darkness, dizziness bloomed in her head, and her knees buckled. Disorientated, tangled hopelessly in her chador, she plunged forward, twisting an ankle, banging her knees and elbows as she fell, cracking her head, until she landed at last in a pained heap on the brick floor at the bottom of the stairs.

Dizzy and stunned, she heard female voices raised in surprise. Bare feet approached, then stopped beside her. A deep, authoritative voice penetrated the fog in her brain. 'Tell Khadija to bring a sheet,' it commanded. 'This girl is hurt, whoever she is.'

Was it a eunuch who spoke? A woman? 'Please,' Akhtar managed to say, without opening her eyes, 'I don't want anything. I only want to meet the lady who casts spells.'

'Don't move her yet,' the voice continued, as hands laid hold of her. 'I want to see her in the light.'

Too weak to resist, Akhtar let someone remove her chador and push back the dirty sleeves of her kameez. Too ill for shame, her eyes squeezed shut, she did not care what they saw.

Someone gasped. 'As if this ill treatment were not enough,' the voice announced, 'her liver has been affected. Look at the colour of her skin.'

Someone shooed children away. Akhtar forced her eyes open. Women stared down at her, their mouths open. Some of them were young. One was fair, with a high-bridged nose. One or two, including a white-haired serving woman who clucked loudly with dismay, looked very old.

The powerful-sounding voice, Akhtar discovered, belonged to a stout, elderly woman with iron-grey hair, who studied Akhtar with an experienced eye, nodding to herself much as the old man in the courtyard had nodded over his scorpion sting victim. But unlike the old man, this woman gave off no magical power, only the authority of one accustomed to being obeyed.

Disappointed, Akhtar searched among the crowd for the sorceress she had come to find.

'Let her lie there.' The grey-haired woman gestured towards a dark corner of the cool corridor where Akhtar now lay. Through a wide doorway Akhtar could see more ladies of various sizes and ages. Amazed at the kindness of the hands that lifted her, she allowed herself to be led to a sheet-covered mat that someone had spread on the floor.

'Drink this,' the stout lady told her gruffly. 'It will help your nausea.'

Akhtar tried to raise her head. 'But I want to find—'

'Not now, child. Whatever is troubling you, it will, Inshallah, be resolved. But first you must recover your strength.'

Akhtar drank, and as she did, the pure, lovely taste of roses filled her mouth, driving away the rottenness and filth she had breathed in the street. Later, while she slept, she dreamed that she lay in a cool garden, breathing in beautiful scents, while women's voices murmured pleasantly in the distance.

A deep voice penetrated her dream, speaking rhythmically in a singsong tone, drawing some vowels out, shortening others, reciting poetry in a language Akhtar did not understand. A different voice offered an Urdu translation whose words echoed in her half-sleeping imagination:

> With treasure, whose treasurer is the faithful spirit,
> We have come as beggars to the King's door.

As Akhtar drifted into deep sleep, she imagined a pair of ragged beggars crouching by a tall ornate door, their hands extended for alms, while beside them a heap of gold and jewels gleamed and shone.

Several hours later, a dust-covered labourer entered the Shaikh's sitting room and approached his padded platform. He wiped dirty hands nervously on his long, unclean shirt.

'I have never beaten my wife, Shaikh Sahib,' he declared loudly. 'Never, I swear it.'

Behind the platform, water rippled down a carved marble cascade and poured into a trough in the floor, filling the air with a cool, restful sound.

The Shaikh seemed to grow taller as he sat. 'And you never burn her with brands from the fire?' he asked. 'Do not tell lies, Abdul Ghaffar. Your wife's screams have disturbed your neighbours for months. Two of them came to us only yesterday. This morning, unable to bear your ill-treatment any longer, your wife ran away from your house.'

The labourer took a step backward.

'She lies in our family quarters at this very moment,' the Shaikh added, 'covered with the evidence of your beatings and your burnings.'

'She would not obey me, Huzoor. She—'

'Obey *you*?' the Shaikh rasped. 'Her duty is to serve and obey *God*. Your duty is the same. Do you think I beat my wife when she was alive? Do you think these men beat *their* wives?' He gestured towards his assembled followers, who watched silently, strings of prayer beads motionless in their hands. Among them was Yusuf Bhatti, a fighter and a man of action, who had arrived at the haveli looking for his childhood friend Hassan Ali Khan, only to be waved inside to sit among the Shaikh's followers. He hated to sit still, but even he was following the proceedings attentively.

'Her family has land,' said the labourer. 'I need it. They would not—'

'Then it was *greed* that led you to torture the wife whom you are enjoined to protect.'

The man dropped his eyes from the Shaikh's fierce gaze. 'A mistake, Huzoor. Forgive me.'

'It is not the Shaikh who should forgive you,' a pockmarked follower offered from the crowd, 'it is your wife.'

The Shaikh nodded. 'Nasir Sahib is correct. Now then, shall we send for her so you may apologize?'

The labourer stiffened. 'No, Huzoor,' he said roughly. 'She has brought disgrace upon my family by running away. I will starve before I apologize to her.'

'Then she is lost to you.' The Shaikh turned away from the man, flicking his fingers in dismissal. 'Go then, Abdul Ghaffar. And do not attempt to marry a second time. If you try, you will be stopped.'

Yusuf Bhatti nodded his approval with the other men as Abdul Ghaffar backed out of the room. The man was clearly a violent fool. Yusuf thought of his own plain, hard-working wife, who had already given him four sons. When he shouted irritably at her, she ignored him.

He smiled to himself. Sensible woman.

A grey-bearded man spoke up. 'Shaikh Sahib,' he said, 'people in the bazaar are talking about your daughter-in-law.'

The other men dropped their eyes. Yusuf sat up, scowling. How dare this man mention one of the Shaikh's family women in public, especially Hassan's wife? It was bad enough that the woman was noisy, ill-behaved, foreign—

'They say,' the bearded man persisted, 'that she will be the downfall of your family.'

The Shaikh smiled. 'And how has the bazaar arrived at this conclusion, Malik Sahib? What have your fellow diamond merchants to say?'

'They say things have changed since mad Maharajah Kharrak Singh's son imprisoned him and took power. They say the Prince hates the British, that after he has killed his father with poison he will punish you and your family because your son has an English wife.'

39

'Ah, my dear Hassan!' The Shaikh's face lit with pleasure as a tall man with an open face stepped into the room.

'Peace, Father,' replied Hassan, whose light, pleasant voice matched the Shaikh's. He crossed the room with quick steps and greeted each of his father's followers in turn, embracing some and saluting others politely, his right hand to his forehead, before seating himself beside his friend Yusuf.

'The Prince has favourites of his own,' the bearded diamond merchant went on. 'To please them, he may, God forbid, confiscate your lands, even this haveli. This has happened to other families for smaller cause.' He gestured towards the doorway. 'You have a large household, Shaikh Sahib. How will you support them all? Without this haveli, where will they live? Who will help you?'

The Shaikh's embroidered headdress had begun to droop in the heat. He poked a finger under it, and scratched his scalp. 'And what, Malik Sahib,' he inquired mildly, 'do you propose we should do?'

'I suggest that your son distance himself from the British before it is too late. I propose that he divorce his foreign wife.'

The assembled followers drew in a collective breath. Yusuf wiped his hot face with the tail of his turban. He could not help but agree with the man. The faster Hassan escaped from that odd woman, the better. He glanced sideways to gauge Hassan's reaction, but could not guess what his friend was thinking.

'Divorce?' protested a small man with large, watery eyes. 'But that is unthinkable!'

'He need not divorce her, then,' the merchant answered, 'but he should keep her far away. And he should marry again – a nice Punjabi girl. Dozens of families would be honoured to receive a proposal from him. Why, my own brother has a lovely daughter who would be—'

40

'Malik Sahib,' interrupted the Shaikh, 'you think like a diamond merchant. You should spend more time in this house. And now we will ask my son for his response.'

All eyes turned to Hassan, whose warm smile resembled his father's, although his face was not wizened and dark, but fair and broad. 'Malik Sahib,' he replied, spreading his hands, 'in this world, family matters are one thing and politics are another. A man cannot change his wives with each change in the political wind. In any case, the Prince will have greater concerns than my family alliances after he ascends the throne.'

'There,' said the Shaikh. 'You have your answer, Malik Sahib. And now, Hassan, what news of the court?'

'No good news, Lalaji.' Hassan reached for a string of prayer beads from a pile on the sheet-covered floor. 'The Maharajah is still imprisoned. He and his son still quarrel. Meanwhile, the Maharajah continues to decline. His stomach pains increase. I fear the end is approaching.'

'His food is poisoned,' offered someone.

The beads moved through Hassan's fingers. 'The food tasters have not fallen ill yet, but there is one thing the Maharajah eats constantly that is never tasted.'

The Shaikh nodded. 'Opium.'

Hassan sighed. 'This hatred will cease after he dies, but things will not be easy for the Prince. He will face real dangers in the future. He must keep the Punjab united, while appeasing the other contenders for the throne, especially his uncle Sher Singh. And he must deal with the British.'

The men nodded, the clicking of their prayer beads mingling with the whispering of the fountain.

'Now, Hassan,' said the Shaikh, changing the subject, 'I understand that your Afghan trader will be coming from Kabul soon.'

'Yes,' put in another man, 'your poet-trader friend, who brings perfumes—'

'And cats,' added the pockmarked disciple.

'And saffron,' said a shy-looking man who had not spoken all afternoon.

'And occasionally some decent horses,' put in the irrepressible Malik Sahib. 'I want to be the first to see Zulmai's horses. I missed a good Turkoman the last time he came.'

An hour later, the visitors had gone and Shaikh and Hassan were finally alone. The Shaikh's embroidered headdress now lay in a heap beside him on the dais. The skullcap the old man wore made his dark, wrinkled face appear more forceful than ever.

'I have been meaning to speak to you, my boy, about this marriage business,' he began, leaning forward to lay a hand on his son's knee. 'I know you still think of poor little Mumtaz Bano, may Allah Most Gracious rest her soul, and I know well that your new foreign wife is not like her, and perhaps not to your taste. You should know that if you decide to take a third wife, I will not stand in your way. Of course I do not advise keeping more than one wife at a time,' he added, 'but then Mariam is not of our people. You might perhaps make some arrangement by which she remains here, and continues to be a second mother to Saboor.'

'With all the trouble and cruelty at court, who can think of wives and weddings?' Hassan said lightly. Then his expression sobered. 'All I want is my Saboor. I ache to hold him in my arms.'

'I, too, long to see him,' his father agreed. 'It pains me to think my grandson is so far away, with only your English wife to love him.'

'Inshallah, he will return soon,' murmured Hassan.

His father nodded. 'Inshallah.'

Chapter Four

'Take Saboor downstairs, Dittoo,' Mariana called as she sat on her bed, her eyes on the tin box that stood in a corner of her large, bright room. 'Let him watch the dogs having their bath.'

As the sound of Saboor's running footsteps faded, she opened the box. Worn and ragged at the edges, the letter from Shaikh Waliullah's house seemed full of portent, a talisman from another world. Soiled from having been carried across India, it had been folded, then sealed with wax into which had been stamped an imprint in Arabic letters. *The Merciful*, the imprint read.

Knowing the message it contained, she would have preferred to slide it back into its hiding place unread, but it seemed wrong not even to look at a letter that had been carried for twelve hundred miles.

She turned the stained paper over and broke open the wax.

She did not recognize the elegant right-to-left handwriting, but the firm signature at the bottom of the letter read *Hassan Ali Khan*. Holding her hair off her face, she bent over the paper and began to read, a little rustily, as she had not read Urdu since her old munshi's departure for Lahore a month earlier.

I trust that you and Saboor arrived safely in Calcutta, the letter began, *and that your family is well. I am pleased to tell you that all of us at Qamar Haveli are in good condition, and that we send you our salaams.*

Qamar Haveli, the House of the Moon, with its upstairs ladies' quarters, its filigreed balconies, its inner courtyards . . .

Here in Lahore, the letter continued, *the circumstances that caused us to send you and Saboor away have not changed much, but I am happy to say they are good enough to warrant your return. It is believed the Maharajah, who asks constantly for Saboor, will not live more than a month or two. His heir, the Prince, already preoccupied with other matters, is unlikely to concern himself with my son after he ascends the throne.*

I would come for you myself if it were possible, but I cannot leave Lahore at this critical time. However, as your people travel constantly throughout India, it should not be difficult for you and your escort to join one of their caravans.

He was not coming. Mariana let the paper fall to her lap.

Escort. Caravans. Hassan's choice of words made her sound like an Oriental princess travelling in a cushioned litter, surrounded by a retinue of servants and retainers, instead of crammed into a stifling palanquin with only Uncle Adrian, Aunt Claire, hunched Dittoo, and a triple-jointed sweeperess to keep her company.

Moreover, Hassan's words contained no trace of the elusive beauty she admired in Urdu poetry, and no suggestion that he remembered their sole, sandalwood-scented kiss. From its tone, her rescue of Saboor might have been part of a business transaction, although what she was supposed to have gained from it she could not imagine.

She could not help feeling a small stab of disappointment. Shunned by everyone else in India, she had always assumed that Hassan, at least, had wanted her, that he would be hurt when she left him.

Perhaps she had only imagined the powerful feeling that had seemed to emanate from him and surround her as they sat side by side in her tent the evening Lord Auckland's camp had left the Punjab.

Someone rapped at her door. 'Let me in, child,' Aunt Claire hallooed from outside, jolting Mariana's thoughts from the past. 'We have been invited to dine with Lord Auckland's sisters at Government House tomorrow evening. You must get out your grey silk with the lace edging. I want to see if the lace has yellowed.'

Mariana pushed the letter hastily beneath her pillow and opened the door. Her aunt's face was flushed with pleasure at the prospect of dinner at Government House. She held a small leather box in her hand.

'Your uncle is feeling much better,' she announced as she entered. 'I am certain we shall be able to go.' She held out the box. 'I have brought my pearl necklace and eardrops for you to wear. Put them somewhere safe. Now, where are your gowns?'

'How kind of you, Aunt Claire.' Unsure whether she wanted this unexpected generosity, Mariana tugged open the large tin trunk that stood beside her wardrobe, shook out a grey watered-silk gown, and held it up.

'The neck is still all right,' her aunt said, peering at its lace edging, 'but this sleeve is turning. You must conceal it as best you can. I was right to insist on this colour. The grey will make your eyes seem less green.' She shook her head. 'Your eyes must have come from your father's side. *Our* eyes have always been a lovely, clear blue.' She turned to leave. 'I'm going to lie down. I think the mango fool at lunch was too much in this heat. You should rest also. I want you to look pretty tomorrow evening. Sir William Macnaghten's wife is to be present.'

'Lady Macnaghten?' Mariana stared at her aunt. 'You must be

joking. She has cut us dead in the bazaar three times this month. Why should Miss Emily invite us to meet such a conceited—'

'I am not joking, and I do not like your manner of speaking. Lady Macnaghten,' Aunt Claire intoned, adopting her Senior Officer voice, 'is to be escorted by her nephew, a successful young man to whom you are to be civil. He is to be one of our intelligence officers in Kabul.'

'I am *always* civil, Aunt Claire,' Mariana protested to her aunt's retreating back. She would be polite to the nephew, whom she had seen only in the distance, a foppish-looking fellow with oddly long feet, but there was no chance at all that he would return her good manners. How like Aunt Claire to believe that she could ingratiate herself with Calcutta society by being polite to people who were uniformly horrid.

The door closed. Mariana snatched Hassan's letter from beneath her pillow and pushed it back into the tin box.

It was no use telling Aunt Claire about it, for she would be horrified at its very existence. Aunt Claire always stopped short of learning the whole truth of things. She had never even inquired about the albino although she had seen him a dozen times since his arrival. Unlike her uncle, Aunt Claire had only the vaguest idea of what had actually happened to her niece in the Punjab.

Uncle Adrian had waited a week after Mariana's arrival before demanding a complete account of her adventures in the Punjab. He now knew as much of her story as decency would allow. He had also questioned her about Maharajah Ranjit Singh's court and his army, questions that Mariana had been pleased to answer.

'They have a strong, disciplined infantry, Uncle Adrian,' she had told him eagerly, delighted to speak of a subject dear to her heart, 'and their artillery is formidable. At Gobindghar, the Maharajah's arsenal, there are seven hundred heavy guns, from nine to thirty-two pounders. But I do not think much of their cavalry; the horses are uneven in quality and the uniforms looked shabby, but they have a wonderful corps of racing camels, each carrying one man and one swivel gun. Did you know they all wear chain mail?'

Her uncle had smiled. 'And I am sure you have already written about this to your father, the would-be general.'

Yes, she certainly had described the Sikh forces to her gentle, vicar father. Military strategy had long been their private interest, and now it was all she could write about since she had no life outside the house, and she hesitated to describe her forbidden adventures in the native part of the city. She had, of course, told her parents what had happened in the Punjab, knowing as she did so that she was dashing her mother's dream that she would 'marry well' in India, and hurting her father, whose good opinion meant everything to her. But she had told them all of it, without softening the facts.

She glanced up as mynah birds screeched outside her window. Dear Papa was getting old. Would she ever again sit in his book-filled study, pink-faced with pleasure, knowing she had his full attention as she argued the finer points of famous battles – Marathon, the defeat of the Athenians at Syracuse, Alexander's triumph at Arbela . . .

Her parents' letters in reply had been painful to read, but both had said the one thing she had longed to hear – that they loved her still.

Whatever horrors you may have committed, her mother had written, *you are still our daughter.*

The time will come, my brave, foolhardy Mariana, her father had written, *when you must return that poor baby to his family. After you do it, we will be here in Sussex, waiting for you.*

Her married sister had also written. Stiff and censorious at first, Charlotte had later confided that she found the story romantic, *although I should prefer it to have happened to someone else!*

47

Mariana leaned out of the window, her elbows on the sill. Perhaps things would be all right. Perhaps she would one day write home to say that she was, by some miracle, to marry Harry Fitzgerald. Perhaps she would have fair-haired babies who would be hers to keep . . .

Outside, a groom led Uncle Adrian's gentlest horse up the drive to the shade of a tree, then lifted a solemn Saboor onto the horse's back. Mariana sighed. With her teacher and her horse groom gone from Calcutta, only one person remained who knew her story: faithful, rumpled Dittoo. Each day was lonelier without her old munshi; every afternoon when Uncle Adrian's quiet Bengali groom helped her mount into her sidesaddle, she missed Yar Mohammad, the tall, bony-faced dreamer of dreams who had served her since the day she first stole Saboor, eighteen months earlier.

As child, horse and man moved off down the drive, a very different picture intruded on her thoughts – the interior of her tent and Saboor's elegant father beside her on the Persian carpet, leaning on a bolster, his face turned from hers, the shawl on his chest rising and falling as he breathed.

Dreams were like clouds; amorphous and fleeting, they altered even as one watched them. But her memory of the Pubjab, brought back by the arrival of the letter, was sharp-edged and brightly coloured, too real and too fixed to be a dream. It was all true. It had all happened. Saboor, riding up the drive, was proof of that. The small white scars of snakebite on Mariana's wrist were also proof, as was the albino courier who sat on his charpai outside the compound wall, waiting for a reply to the letter he had carried so far.

When the message came that he was to present himself to Hassan Ali Khan's foreign wife, the albino had been sitting in the shade of

48

a champa tree. Deep in thought he scarcely noticed the parakeets that darted in and out of the branches over his head.

With his odd appearance and abrasive manner, Ghulam Ali had never made friends easily, but he did not complain. Since childhood, he had made a point of keeping to himself. He had suffered loneliness throughout his life, but loneliness could mean safety to a man who feared the attentions of others.

Most men feared snakes or scorpions. The albino feared the taunting mob.

Since his earliest years he had suffered at the hands of others. He had been called frightful, possessed by the devil, a man whose very appearance betrayed the sins of his mother. He had been bloodied, stoned, chased from his house, driven out by people who blamed him for ill luck, for sudden floods, for cholera and smallpox.

In his thirty-two years, he had become hard, cynical and afraid. He had also become a perceptive observer of others, anticipating their moods, interpreting their looks and gestures. Always ready to fight or run, he was never without the knife he had stolen when he was ten. But the worst moments of his life had taken place on this last journey from Shaikh Waliullah's house, on the road between Bareilly and Shahjahanpur, when a group of twenty travellers had offered him friendship.

The men had been unremarkable in appearance. None, as far as he had seen, had been armed. All had been cheerful. The only unusual thing about them had been their friendliness.

'We are labourers on our way to dig a canal near Shahjahanpur,' offered one of them, a man whose stomach protruded over his loincloth. 'Where are you going?'

Surprised, Ghulam Ali had stopped walking. 'To Calcutta,' he replied, in his usual gruff tone. 'I am taking a letter there.'

'Ah, a courier. But it is long way to Calcutta. Your letter must be important.'

Unwilling to reveal his affairs to strangers, Ghulam Ali grunted and continued on his way, but the men, walking as fast as he, had kept pace.

'So many people carry weapons on the road,' a young, curly-headed man remarked. 'It seems everyone is afraid of attack. I saw a man yesterday with a chora knife and two swords. These people worry me. I have nothing but this rumal.' Smiling, he flicked his long cotton scarf with his fingers, but his smile faded instantly at a warning glance from the first man.

The group walked on together for some miles, chatting companionably to Ghulam Ali as they went, commenting on the horsemen and donkey drivers and bullock carts that passed them, stopping to inspect fruit for sale by the side of the road. Joking and nudging each other as they walked, they attracted the attention of more travellers along the way.

Some joined them: a Hindu and his son on their way to buy a bull, a trader from Bareilly with some Surati chintz to sell in Lucknow, a lone man with a tall walking stick who was to join a wedding party.

Ghulam Ali had let down his guard in that friendly group. Pushing away his usual unease, he had basked in the unfamiliar feeling of inclusion among men who did not comment on his appearance.

It was only when the group, at its ease and now numbering twenty-five, was finishing dinner in a jungle clearing far from the road that he guessed the danger he was in. At the third unexplained glance between two of the men, he understood to his sudden terror that these friendly folk who picked their teeth and laughed with their heads thrown back were Thugs, fearsome devils he had heard of since his childhood.

Moving only his eyes, he counted the men in the clearing. Several members of the party were missing, but the wavy-haired man who had so casually flicked his scarf was there, talking amicably with the wedding guest. The long scarf was missing from his neck, but lying casually beside him on the ground lay a length of wet, tightly twisted cloth.

A chill drove down Ghulam Ali's spine with such force that he had to fight with himself to remain still. It was true, then. All five newcomers to the group, including himself, were carrying money or saleable goods. All had been lured off the road to be strangled, then robbed.

The missing men, he now saw, had gone to dig graves for them all: the farmer and his son, the trader, the wedding guest, himself.

The signal would be given at any moment, and then one of them would fling a cloth about his neck and jerk it tight . . .

With no time to warn the others, he stood up as casually as he was able, and managed to produce a yawn. 'I will relieve myself,' he muttered, and started towards the road.

'Hurry back,' called out a voice behind him as he strode away from the terrible clearing. 'We're making tea. It will be ready soon.'

The roads of India are unsafe after dark, but nowhere between Bareilly and Shajahanpur was as dangerous as that secluded place where the lonely albino had found companionship. Stumbling and panting, he followed the road for several miles before he felt safe enough to sleep, hidden beneath a thorn tree.

Now, after so many weeks, his terror had faded, but Ghulam Ali had not forgotten that night. He had been thanking God for his escape when the foreign woman's bent-over manservant summoned him into the house.

The courier, who had never seen or spoken to a female member of Shaikh Waliullah's family, was reluctant to follow the servant who shambled in front of him towards the kitchen entrance. How, he wondered, had that great family descended to including foreigners among their women, females who showed themselves openly to men, even to servants like himself?

He had seen English people on his journey to Calcutta. They had sat upright on horses or in carriages with sour expressions on their faces, the men dressed in dusty black, the women in shockingly tight, stiff clothes that revealed the curve of their breasts. Instead of the graceful veils worn by Indian women, these females had worn baskets on their heads, covered with drooping ribbons and bobbing flowers. Unlike his own endlessly inquisitive people who noticed everything around them, these foreigners seemed to ignore even other travellers on the road.

If they cared nothing for what happened around them, why were they here? How were they so powerful?

Hassan Ali Khan's foreign wife was sitting on a cane chair on a bright verandah. Unwilling to look up at her, he made a long business of scuffing off his shoes in the corridor outside.

'*As-salaam-o-aleikum*, peace be upon you.' She addressed him properly in a firm voice, as if she knew exactly what she was saying. 'What is your name?'

'It is Ghulam Ali,' he replied, more harshly than he had intended, his head bent, ashamed of his failure to greet her first.

'Ghulam Ali,' she repeated. Her chair creaked. Unable to stop himself, he raised his eyes.

Her hair was uncovered. Her throat, the same colour as his own, was exposed to his gaze by the cut of her European clothes. Embarrassed, he looked hastily away.

He had, of course, seen the young Englishwoman as she came and went through the gate, alone on a horse or seated in a carriage beside the old woman they called her aunt, but she had always been well covered, and she had never looked him in the face as she did now, her green, catlike gaze full of curiosity, her fingers tense on the arms of her chair.

'How long did it take you to come from Lahore?' she inquired.

'Three months,' he replied, his eyes on the window.

'And what is the condition of the Punjab?'

'The country was in a bad state when I left it, with the Maharajah locked away, and his son poisoning him while he's trying to rule. The people are crying, wishing old Maharajah Ranjit Singh had not died, that his poor, mad son had never come to power, that his grandson were not so cruel. The young Prince has had his father's favourite courtier killed. They dragged him from the Maharajah's bedroom by his hair and cut him to pieces with swords and knives. It will not be long before the Maharajah dies of the poison,' he concluded, still looking away from her, feeling her shocked stare.

'Prince Nau Nihal Singh is poisoning his own father?'

Ghulam Ali shrugged, surprised that a foreign woman cared about such matters. 'Rich, powerful people are like that,' he said, 'but they say in the bazaar that if Saboor Baba were with him, Maharajah Kharrak Singh would never be locked away, eating poison.'

'And as long as Saboor Baba is with *me*,' Hassan's wife said tartly, 'he will never again be the property of *any* maharajah. But do the people still speak of him even though he has been gone for more than a year?'

'Of course they do.' Ghulam Ali could not keep the grandeur from his tone. 'Who could forget the child whose very presence was enough to cure Maharajah Ranjit Singh of all his illnesses? They remember the Maharajah himself saying that Saboor Baba carries a light in his heart that brings health and good fortune. They have not forgotten that the old Maharajah died only months after Saboor Baba went away.'

The child must have heard his name, for he came at once, his embroidered slippers pattering on the verandah tiles. He brushed past Ghulam Ali, trotted to Mariana and threw himself onto her lap, his teeth clenched, his small arms trembling with the strength of his embrace.

'An-nah!' he said fiercely.

Ghulam Ali shifted his feet and glanced up. 'Am I to take your reply now?'

'Not now,' she said sharply.

Their conversation was clearly over. Ghulam Ali motioned with his head, indicating that he wished to leave her. When the English-woman nodded, he backed from the room and pushed his feet into his shoes.

She was a stranger in odd clothing, whose tone of voice he could barely interpret, but Ghulam Ali, the reader of others, would have sworn that she would not have hesitated to die for Hassan Ali's curly-headed child in her lap.

Mariana felt the heat close around her as Saboor slid from her lap and followed Ghulam Ali down the passage. Outside in the garden, a man watered the front lawn from a full goatskin slung across his back.

How different the walled city and Citadel had sounded when described by Ghulam Ali. Lahore sounded crudely violent and dangerous, not at all like the place she remembered or that her old tutor had evoked with his poetry and his hints of escape and redemption.

Even if Lahore were unchanged, it would still seem vastly different to her on this journey. She would be neither a fugitive with a stolen baby nor an unwilling bride fighting for her life but a normal Englishwoman travelling respectably with her uncle and aunt.

And that, she said to herself as she started for the stairs, would surely make all the difference.

Chapter Five

'Before we go to dinner,' Aunt Claire announced the following afternoon as she sat on the verandah drinking a glass of sherry, 'there are things you should know, Mariana.'

'We now have a plan for our journey to Afghanistan,' Uncle Adrian put in. He cleared his throat noisily. Mariana, who knew that sound, studied him warily over the rim of her glass.

'There is a reason why Lady Macnaghten has been invited to dine with us at Government House,' he began. 'She is soon to depart Calcutta in order to join her husband in Kabul. Lord Auckland's sisters have suggested we join her and travel with her party.'

Beautiful, snobbish Lady Macnaghten, of all people! Mariana shook her head vigorously. 'She will never agree. She hates us.'

'Oh, I don't know.' Aunt Claire signalled to a servant to collect the glasses. 'Perhaps she is not as——'

'As the Envoy's wife,' Uncle Adrian continued as if neither of them had spoken, 'she is entitled to a large baggage train and an army escort, which we are not. And we shall be useful to her. Lady Macnaghten had expected to travel alone except for her nephew,

56

which would, of course be a daring, unsuitable arrangement, even for someone as self-assured as Lady Macnaghten. It will be to her advantage to have other European women in her party. Her plan is to send her baggage ahead by land, and then journey as far as Allahabad by steamer. At Allahabad she will rejoin her baggage and travel the rest of the way to Afghanistan under armed escort. As the journey is very long, she expects to stop several times on the way. One of her resting places will be Lahore where, due to her husband's seniority, she has already been invited by the Sikh government to set up her camp in the Shalimar Garden.'

Mariana sat up. 'Shalimar! How lovely. But why talk about it, Uncle Adrian, when we know she will refuse?'

'She *cannot* refuse.' Uncle Adrian smiled. 'Lady Macnaghten will never cross the Governor-General's sisters while her husband is angling for the governorship of Bombay. And there will be other advantages to travelling in her party. The steamer will save us months of travel. The British Resident at Ludhiana is expected to escort her to Lahore, where she will spend several weeks. He will make all her arrangements there, and he can do the same for us. The Eden sisters have already asked him to supervise the dissolution of your native marriage. A few days in Lahore will be sufficient to free you from all your connections there. After we have rested, our party will be joined by a second detachment of troops who will escort us through the Khyber Pass and on to Kabul.'

Mariana sighed. 'I know we must do it, but—'

'We must.' Her uncle reached out and patted her on the knee. 'Miss Emily will broach the subject with Lady Macnaghten this evening. Whatever she may pretend, Lady Macnaghten is well aware that your connection with the Shaikh's family is quite innocent. I only hope,' he added, 'that awful nephew of hers stays out of our way.'

*   *   *

57

'Turn round, Mariana. I must look at you before we leave,' Aunt Claire said breathlessly that evening, after pushing her way into Mariana's room half an hour before the carriage was due.

She stood back and watched through narrowed eyes as Mariana turned a full circle in the middle of her room, already too hot in her grey watered silk. 'Yes, you look all right,' she said, nodding.

Her own gold satin, less fortunately, matched the yellow of her face. Like Uncle Adrian, Aunt Claire had suffered her share of fevers.

'You must remember to reduce your smile, Mariana,' she cautioned as she leaned over to inspect her own teeth in the looking glass. 'A great, beaming smile is pleasant at home, to be sure, but when one is out in society one should make an effort to be fashionable.' She gave a satisfied nod. 'I am pleased to see that your shoulders do not look as square as usual. In fact, your only real difficulty this evening is your hair, although I see you have managed to tidy it up more than usual. Please make sure it does not fall out of its pins while we're having dinner.'

Her yellow face and obvious discomfort from the heat notwithstanding, Aunt Claire looked radiant. Being invited to Government House meant everything to her. Perhaps under Miss Emily's sharp blue eyes, Lady Macnaghten would be civil to foolish, uncomprehending Aunt Claire.

The huge, tasselled velvet fan in the dining room of Government House swung creakily back and forth on its pulleys, sending an intermittent breeze over Mariana and causing the candles in front of her to gutter every time it passed over them.

Only at Government House were things done this well. For all Aunt Claire's scolding of the punkah-wallah who worked the fan by pulling on a rope, the table candles at Uncle Adrian's house were invariably blown out by the fan the very instant they sat down to dinner.

As Lord Auckland was out of Calcutta, this was to be a small, 'family' dinner: just Miss Emily and Miss Fanny Eden, a pair of their favourite bachelor generals, Lady Macnaghten and her nephew, Mariana, and Mariana's aunt and uncle. The assembled diners were seated at one end of a table for twenty; behind each diner a turbaned serving man stood at attention, and behind him, two assistants. Including the head serving man and the cook's assistants, who rushed in and out of the kitchen carrying the dishes, there were thirty-one servants attending eight people.

'I cannot think how I shall manage,' Lady Macnaghten was saying in a fluting voice from her seat beside the older of the generals. 'My husband tells me that the officers in Kabul are expecting balls as soon as I arrive, but as there are still very few ladies, I cannot think how I am to arrange the dancing.'

She seemed to have survived the shock of finding herself at dinner with the most notorious family in Calcutta, although her strategy of pretending that the notorious family was not there at all had begun to wear thin.

'Perhaps the gentlemen will take turns dancing,' Miss Emily offered from the head of the table, while her sister nodded from her seat beside the second general. 'I understand there are some *very* charming officers in Kabul.'

Mariana, who was thinking hopefully of Fitzgerald, arranged her face to show no feeling as Lady Macnaghten's eyes flicked over her for the fourth time in ten minutes.

Lady Macnaghten's nephew, a sour-faced young man in expensive-looking clothes, waved a languid hand. '*I* see no difficulty in finding ladies to join in the dancing,' he drawled. 'Kabul is full of native women. I understand some of them are quite pretty. I am sure they can be taught to dance at a moment's notice.'

'Well, really, Charles,' said Lady Macnaghten indignantly, puffing out the fashionable sleeves of her cream satin gown, 'I scarcely think *that* will be necessary.'

'We understand, Lady Macnaghten,' put in Miss Emily firmly, 'that you expect to travel to Kabul quite soon.'

'Oh, yes. My husband says he cannot bear life without me any longer.' Lady Macnaghten gave a tinkling laugh. She was blushing.

Miss Emily's eyebrows rose.

'And how soon will that be?' the portlier of the two generals asked hastily.

'I expect to leave next month, although one can never tell how long it will take to make the arrangements. I have been waiting nearly a year for a dozen new bonnets and a pair of chandeliers, and I *cannot* leave without them, but I am told they are on the *Vigilant* which is due at any time.'

Why, Mariana wondered, as she helped herself to fricassee of duck, had Lady Macnaghten made that indelicate remark? And how had she contrived not to turn yellow like poor Aunt Claire? How had she maintained all that thick, glossy black hair, now so elegantly folded and pinned above the perfect neckline of her satin gown? Even the Eden sisters, with their fine gowns and their hair attended to by English ladies' maids, were not so well turned out.

Unaware of any awkwardness, Aunt Claire looked eagerly from Miss Emily and Miss Fanny to Lady Macnaghten and back, as if entranced by so much glamour.

'I,' put in Uncle Adrian, 'will also be leaving for Kabul within the next month or two.'

'Ah,' Lady Macnaghten breathed, her response sounding more like a sigh than an answer.

'Since we are to travel at nearly the same time,' he continued, 'perhaps we should combine our forces.'

Lady Macnaghten's knife slid from her fingers and landed on her plate with a clatter. 'Oh, but that would be impossible,' she cried. 'Impossible, am I not correct, Miss Emily? It would be most *improper* for me to travel with—'

'My wife and I,' persisted Uncle Adrian, ignoring the outburst, 'will be travelling with her niece.'

'Her *niece*?' Lady Macnaghten's mouth fell open. Dropping both her good manners and her elaborate pretence that Mariana was not present, she pointed her fork across the table. 'Do you mean *that* girl?'

'Yes, I believe he does,' Miss Emily put in smoothly. She fixed a deceptively innocent blue gaze on Lady Macnaghten. 'And as Mr Lamb and his wife will have their own staff for the journey,' she said, 'there will be no impediment to their joining you, will there?' Miss Emily barely paused. 'No,' she answered herself, beaming with satisfaction. 'There will be no impediment at all.'

Chapter Six

13 July 1840

'Abba! I will see my abba!' Saboor chanted as he bounced on Mariana's bed. 'Abba,' he repeated, smiling into her face as if his prescience were perfectly normal.

No one had told him, not even Dittoo.

Saboor's capacity to read the future did not show itself often, and when it did it came at odd times, as if clairvoyance were not an inherent talent of his but a gift bestowed upon him capriciously according to some incomprehensible plan.

He had not, for example, guessed that Mariana's old language teacher, whom he adored, was leaving them, but he had fretted for days before Uncle Adrian's latest bout of fever.

When she had asked her old munshi about Saboor's strange talent, he had smiled. 'These things,' he had replied vaguely, 'are not for us to know, Bibi. But we should remember that Saboor is the grandson of Shaikh Waliullah.'

Mariana caught the bouncing child and pulled him onto her lap.

'Yes, darling,' she murmured, forcing a smile, 'you will soon see your abba.'

The next day, one hand holding a large black umbrella over her head to fend off the rain, Mariana sat upright on Uncle Adrian's oldest, fattest horse, watching Lady Macnaghten's baggage train being prepared for the long overland journey from Bengal to Afghanistan.

She had risen early, before her aunt and uncle were awake. After waving away Dittoo's offer of coffee and a slice of bread, she had commandeered a horse no one would miss and set off to the muddy open ground where the caravan had assembled.

Her own modest goods had been delivered the previous afternoon to one of the yawning storerooms fronting the rain-soaked ground, but it had not been worry about Saboor's comfort or anxiety about her boxes of food, her trunks, or the elderly settee donated by Miss Emily that had driven Mariana from her bed so early in the morning. It had been curiosity about the journey ahead of her.

How many elephants would the baggage train require? Would the elephants travel all the way to Afghanistan? How large was their armed escort to be? How many coolies would they have? How many servants, blacksmiths, carpenters? Were the tents of Lady Macnaghten and her party to be separated from the rest of the camp by a high canvas wall, as the tents of Lord Auckland's party had been? If so, where would her own tent be? Inside the private compound, or outside?

It would be outside, Mariana concluded as she rode through the rain. The news of her uneventful wedding night, although it had come from Sir William Macnaghten himself, had so far shown no sign of improving his wife's opinion of her and her family.

Mariana shifted her umbrella as she passed a heap of folded canvas tents. Before her, rows of half-loaded donkey and bullock carts and scores of kneeling camels waited, surrounded by bundles and boxes that lay heaped in muddy piles. On one side of the ground, a trio of soporific elephants knelt under a dripping tree.

While the mahouts sprawled lazily on their elephant's necks, scores of half-naked coolies stacked canvas-wrapped furniture and crates into carts and tied boxes and baskets onto the backs of bored-looking camels. The ground rang with the familiar sounds of a travelling camp – the staccato shouting of natives, the groaning of camels, the harsh braying of donkeys.

As well as tents and furnishings for Lady Macnaghten and her party, the caravan was to carry everything she would require for her house in Kabul, save for her best china and wine glasses, a pair of Bohemian crystal chandeliers, and two dozen cases of brandy. These precious items were to go by steamer with the English party, up the Ganges to Allahabad, a means of travel that would spare them three months of hard, cross-country travel. Because Lady Macnaghten's things were not to be used by anyone but herself, additional furnishings had been added to the camp's baggage for the other travellers and for the dining tent, which required a table and chairs for twelve as well as china, linen, and candlesticks. Less elegant but still necessary were the kitchen tents with all their equipment, and the camp food which had to cater for the English palate: coffee, crates of wine, sugar, and hundreds of jars of pickles and chutneys and preserved fruit.

Lady Macnaghten's horses were travelling with the camp, as were many of her one hundred and forty servants, their wives and their children. They, the workmen, the gang of coolies, and the drivers of the animal wagons made up a population of some nine hundred souls, all to be managed by four young and harried-looking English officers, borrowed from the army for the purpose, who now rushed to and fro among the piles of baggage, calling out orders.

Some distance from the baggage train, a company of eighty native sepoys and four officers waited with their own pack animals, tents, fodder, and supplies.

Of course all of this paled before the grandeur of the enormous travelling camp that Lord Auckland had taken to the Punjab; his baggage train with its three complete bazaars, its large army and its countless pack animals had been fully ten miles long.

A skinny boy in a muddy loincloth led a string of camels past Mariana. She yawned, glad that she had sent Dittoo to Uncle Adrian's storerooms to find the carpet, the bolsters, and the little carved table she had acquired in the Punjab. Whatever unpleasantness this journey might offer, her tent, at least, would have a comfortable native floor arrangement.

Besides Dittoo and her palanquin bearers, Mariana would have a sweeperess to brush her tent floor and empty her chamber pot, and, unexpectedly, the albino courier.

'Let him come with us, Mariana,' Uncle Adrian had suggested. 'He seems a resourceful man, and he speaks Punjabi, which may prove useful when we get closer to the northwest.'

She tweaked her damp veil from her face. Within hours all these carts, pack animals, and walking men would set off, taking the old northeast route from Calcutta to the River Ganges. At the river, they would turn west, and follow the Gangetic Plain until they reached the city of Allahabad, at the confluence of the Ganges and Yamuna rivers, both sacred to Hindus. There they would stop and await the English party's arrival by steamer. Then they would turn their faces to the northwest, and set off on the long, final leg of their fifteen-hundred-mile journey to Kabul.

It was nearly seven o'clock. Mariana was hungry for her breakfast,

65

but there was one thing she wanted to do before leaving the ground: examine the elephants.

She clucked to her horse, disappointed to find that only three of the great animals were to accompany Lady Macnaghten's camp. Should the camp find itself forced to ford a swollen river, the elephants would have no difficulty in ferrying the English party across, but they would also be expected to extricate any baggage wagons that became caught in the mud. Having only three animals to do all that work would mean wasted time. Mariana sniffed. If she were in charge of this expedition, there would be more than three elephants in Lady Macnaghten's baggage train.

She stopped a safe distance away from the first elephant and was about to call to its sleeping mahout when an English voice rose behind her.

'There he is, just as I told you,' Lady Macnaghten announced in a high, irritated tone.

She sat stiffly on a bay gelding, impeccable in a grey riding habit, pointing to a beautiful black horse that stood tethered with a dozen others. Despite the dampness and the heat, her hands were encased in butter-yellow gloves.

She turned to her nephew, who slouched in his saddle beside her. 'What a fool you are, Charles,' she said sharply. Her voice carried easily across the space between herself and Mariana. 'That one is Ali Baba, of course it is! I particularly told you that Ali Baba is not to travel with the baggage train. I said that he is to come on the steamer with me. I do wish you would listen when I give you instructions.'

Not wishing to eavesdrop, Mariana searched for way to escape but saw none. What she did see was a camel being loaded with wooden crates that clearly held some of Lady Macnaghten's china or glass. Baggage camels were notorious for their tempers and the

66

coolies in Lord Auckland's camp had been forbidden to load them with breakables. This camel groaned aloud, its neck stretched out as if it were being tortured, while several men, unmoved, went on roping the crates to its back.

Mariana hesitated, then, unable to bear the coming destruction, she rode up to Lady Macnaghten.

Whatever Charles Mott had been saying, it had not satisfied his aunt. 'It *is* your fault,' she snapped as Mariana approached. 'Go and tell them to bring Ali Baba to the house. And tell Sonu to come as well, and he is to bring Ali Baba's tack. I cannot have my horse using an ordinary bridle.'

'Good morning, Lady Macnaghten,' Mariana offered, smiling as warmly as she could manage.

Lady Macnaghten did not return the smile. In fact, she did not even look at Mariana but gave a chill little nod in her direction without taking her eyes from her nephew, who had ridden off towards the horses.

'I see that some of your china is being put on a camel,' Mariana said, now unable to extricate herself. 'That was not allowed at Lord Auckland's camp.'

Lady Macnaghten continued to watch Charles Mott's progress as intently as if he were saving the world instead of delivering a message to a servant. Mariana might have been one of the coolies, for all the attention she was getting.

Fighting fury, she turned her horse and moved away. Let the camel break everything, then.

As she started off, one of the British officers strode up, red-faced and perspiring. 'This is all my fault, Lady Macnaghten,' he barked apologetically, nodding politely to Mariana. 'I had thought Ali Baba was to come with us. I had understood he is rather a fractious animal, and that—'

'He is *not* fractious, Major Alford, not at all.' Lady Macnaghten gave a tinkling laugh. 'Like me, Ali Baba has delicate nerves. That is why I understand him so well. I would not dream of sending him with the *baggage*.' She gave a coy shrug of her shoulders. 'He's an English thoroughbred, after all, not a cheap cob like the horse Miss Givens is riding.'

The major made a blaring sound, as if to exempt himself from that unkindness. Mott, who had returned, cast Mariana a look, not of commiseration, but of bitter triumph.

'Come along, Charles,' Lady Macnaghten ordered. 'You have provoked me enough already. Do not also make me late for my breakfast. And do please sit properly on your horse. I hate to be seen with someone who rides as badly as you.'

She spurred her gelding and trotted with surprising clumsiness towards the main road. As she did so, the baggage camel gave one last bellow of pretended agony and lurched to his feet, sending the coolies sprawling into the mud and several of Lady Macnaghten's wooden crates hurtling to the ground, where they landed with a series of loud, splintering crashes.

Chapter Seven

10 October 1840

'How many times, Mariana,' her uncle admonished her three months later, as they stood watching the bank of the Ganges slide past them after lunch in the dining salon, 'do I have to tell you to leave Lady Macnaghten *alone*? I cannot bear that insufferable female any more than you can, but you must *not* provoke like that.'

'I could not help it, Uncle. If she hadn't said it was a log in that superior tone of hers, I wouldn't have—'

'Oh yes you would. You've been waiting all this time to point out a half-burned corpse in the river. You did not have to do it while she was drinking her sherry. It was only by luck that your aunt did not hear you. Why can you not be more forbearing when her husband has done you such an enormous service? Sir William was not required to reveal the truth of your marriage night to Lord Auckland.' He ran a hand through his fringe of hair. 'And where was the need for you to be so short with her nephew over the soup last evening? He was only asking for the salt.'

'It was the way he asked for it.' Mariana tugged her shawl about her in the afternoon breeze. 'I do not like Charles Mott.'

'You should remember that Lady Macnaghten dotes on that young man, for all that she treats him badly. If I were you,' her uncle cautioned, 'I should be civil to him, and stay out of her way.'

'I'll do my best,' Mariana replied darkly, 'although it won't be easy to avoid either of them in such a confined space.'

The heaviest of the rains were past and the level of the Ganges had begun to drop, but the river still ran rapidly. Murky and brown from its load of upcountry silt, it poured across the breadth of India until it reached the great delta where it emptied into the Bay of Bengal, its silt discolouring the waters across four hundred miles.

Here, sixty-eight miles north of Calcutta, hundreds of white storks stood on the broad expanse of sand that formed the river's shores, while flocks of small birds wheeled and dipped above them. Crocodiles by the dozen lay low in the water there and basked on the riverbanks, while porpoises swam out in the river and jackals howled behind the villages.

Only the tall, isolated hills above Sikri-Gali and the birds and crocodiles saw the steam paddleboat clatter past on its way to Allahabad, its two tall funnels sending a billow of black smoke into the dusty sky. Two square barge-like flats creaked behind it, attached to the steamer by thick chains. The first flat accommodated a load of salt and rice, fifty servants, a dozen horses, and a massive pile of crates. The second, fitted out with six passenger cabins and a spacious dining room, carried Lady Macnaghten, her nephew Charles Mott, Mariana, her aunt and uncle, a young couple on their way to Kanpur, and an Italian painter bound for Delhi.

After the departure of the baggage train, Lady Macnaghten's preparations for her journey upriver to Allahabad had consumed nearly three more months. The Bohemian glass chandeliers and the two

70

dozen cases of brandy had not arrived until the end of September, causing Lady Macnaghten to put off her departure twice.

'It's fortunate I'm not a fashion plate, now that we are allowed only three trunks each,' Mariana had put in crossly as they prepared at last to depart.

'If Lady Macnaghten fears there will be insufficient room for her things, she has the right to curtail our baggage,' Aunt Claire had replied stiffly. 'After all, Sir William is a very important official. And, Mariana, fond of clothes or not, you have plenty of nice things, although you make very poor use of them. Why must you wear great brown boots with that sprigged cotton gown?'

This afternoon they would pass by the Colgani Rocks, something to describe in a letter to her father, Mariana thought. She was, after all, travelling on one of the world's great rivers, whose near-magical waters were said to remain clean, healthy and healing, despite the dead bodies covered with busy, carrion-eating birds that floated on its surface. She smiled to herself at the memory of the corpse that had so gratifyingly appeared before lunch, causing Lady Macnaghten to choke on her sherry.

Ahead of them on the groaning flat reserved for the baggage, Lady Macnaghten's beautiful Ali Baba tossed his glossy head while Saboor stood watching him at a distance, his hand in Dittoo's. In front, hauling them both, the steamboat pulled close to the river's shore, abreast of a loaded barge that was moving slowly upriver, dragged by a team of exhausted-looking coolies with a towline harnessed to their chests.

'There are the rocks.' Uncle Adrian shielded his eyes and pointed to four tall islands in the middle of the river. 'How strangely they are formed, rock on rock, covered with all those trees.'

Her eyes on Saboor, Mariana sighed. 'Uncle Adrian,' she murmured, 'I know we have spoken of this before, but I fear I shall die of sadness after we leave Saboor at—'

Before she could finish, Saboor gave a high-pitched cry, jerked his hand from Dittoo's and began to climb hurriedly over coiled ropes and chains, his little face contorted with anxiety. Dittoo struggled to follow him as he darted across the baggage flat to Ali Baba's side and jumped up and down, too close to the horse's nervous hooves, sobbing, his small hands flapping as if he suddenly needed to fly.

'Ali,' he wept. 'Ali Baba!'

Uncle Adrian stared. 'What is wrong with the child? Mariana, you must do something about these sudden—' but she was already gone, running full tilt towards the shifting gangway between the passenger and baggage flats.

Shouting broke out along the shore. On the bank, the coolies were pointing to the river. Terrified that the high-strung Ali Baba would hurt Saboor, Mariana had lifted her skirts and stepped onto the groaning gangway before she understood what the child had somehow foreseen – that the towline of the barge had snapped, and that the barge, low in the water, heavy with a load of stones, was now loose on the river. Caught in the current, it bore down with increasing speed upon the steamer, while its suddenly freed coolies watched helplessly from the shore.

The steamer captain appeared, red-faced, on the deck, bellowing orders. A moment later, clanking with effort, the steamer turned and pulled towards the middle of the river in time to save itself, but too late for the baggage flat behind it. The steamer had towed the flat straight into the path of the barge.

Most of the dozen horses had been tethered on the side of the flat that now faced away from the oncoming barge. Between them and danger, the orderly pile of Lady Macnaghten's baggage, her good china, her chandeliers, and her brandy had been well secured to the deck of the flat with a web of chains. Only one thing was in real peril, her beautiful, fractious Ali Baba who had been separated from the others because of his temper. The horse now stood alone, save for the frantic child, in the path of the oncoming barge.

Sensing the danger, he began to stamp and toss his head while a score of servants, each one clinging to chains and ropes for safety, shouted at the child to stop his anguished dance, and at the clumsily approaching Dittoo to hurry.

Mariana reached Saboor before Ditto did, snatched him up and pushed him, struggling, into her servant's arms. As Dittoo staggered towards the shifting gangway, she raced back to Ali Baba's side.

'Come back, Mariana, don't stay there!' her uncle cried out from the passenger flat.

Working rapidly, his groom had already begun to unknot the ropes that held the horse captive.

'Leave him tied, Sonu!' Mariana shouted over the noise of the steam engine and the yells of the other servants. 'He'll be safer if you—'

Her voice was drowned out by a shattering crash as the barge struck the flat at its centre, lifting it momentarily out of the water. Flung backwards onto the deck, Mariana scrambled to get away from the horse, who now had only one long halter rope to control him. Half loose, Ali Baba backed, plunging, towards the edge of the flat, while the barge, after one or two more half-hearted bumps, began to slide away down the river.

The stallion lost his footing. One of his hind legs, then the other, went over the side. Halfway into the water, dragged along by his unbroken halter rope, he screamed, his neck stretched to its full length as he fought to regain the flat, his forelegs catching in a tangle of ropes on the deck.

At Ali Baba's head, Sonu struggled fruitlessly to haul him back by his mane. As Mariana got hurriedly to her feet, she saw someone with a shock of white hair race towards her, a long-bladed knife in his hand.

'Yes, Ghulam Ali!' she shouted. 'Cut the ropes!'

The albino pushed past her, and swiftly severed first the entangling ropes on the deck, then the strangling halter. The groom ducked, still holding on to the horse, as the severed ropes snapped into the air. Ali Baba gave one last gurgle of fright, then slid over the side, his forelegs scrabbling on the deck until the last.

'Let go of him, Sonu!' Mariana shouted, but the groom did not hear her. Still clinging to the horse's mane, he, too, dropped into the current.

Side by side, while Saboor wailed behind them from Dittoo's arms, Mariana and Ghulam Ali watched horse and man swirl away together in the brown water.

People began to gather. Servants crowded the edge of the flat, staring after the lost horse and groom. The passengers emerged from their cabins. From the roof of one of the cabins, Charles Mott picked his teeth and gazed down upon the scene.

'What *is* going on?' Lady Macnaghten appeared at the railing of the passenger flat, blinking a little in the sunlight, her hair a tiny bit out of place. 'What were those thundering crashes, and why has Miss Givens been screaming like a banshee?'

'I fear there has been an accident, Lady Macnaghten,' Uncle Adrian announced. 'A barge came loose and struck the baggage—'

'Ali Baba!' she gasped, staring at his empty stall. 'Where is my husband's horse?'

'I am sorry to say that he has gone over the side.'

'Over the *side*? *Into the river?*' For a moment she stood still, a hand pressed to her mouth, then she pointed accusingly at Mariana. 'This is *your* doing, isn't it?' she cried. 'I should have known it was you. I distinctly heard your voice telling someone to cut the rope. *You have drowned Ali Baba!'*

Still breathing hard, Mariana smoothed the front of her crumpled, tar-stained gown. 'The horse would have been killed if the rope had not been cut,' she replied evenly. 'Ghulam Ali's quick action may have saved his life.' She raised her chin. 'Horses *do* swim.'

'But he was *Sir William's* horse!' Lady Macnaghten's own chin wobbled visibly. 'You should have asked *me*, but instead you simply cut his halter rope and pushed him into the river!'

'I did not—'

'It makes no difference now,' Lady Macnaghten cut in mournfully, 'whether Ali Baba lives or dies. All that matters is that he is gone, and I shall have to tell my husband.' She pulled a lace handkerchief from her sleeve. 'I had expected to ride him every day, after we reached Allahabad.' Her handkerchief to her face, she turned abruptly and hurried to her cabin, her fashionable shoes clicking against the planking of the deck.

Mariana took Saboor, still sobbing, into her arms and looked upwards. Charles Mott still watched from the roof, a sour smile on his face.

'Of course she did the right thing,' insisted Dittoo that evening as he and Ghulam Ali sat together on the riverbank where all the servants had cooked and eaten their evening meals. 'Who but a fool would think otherwise?' He raised his hands as he spoke, extending his fingers to emphasize his words.

Over the albino's shoulder, the anchored steamer rocked quietly on the starlit river, its flats creaking. Around him, the fires of the other servants – uniformed footmen, grooms, and grass-cutters – glowed like bright jewels along the river's bank.

Ghulam Ali was no fool, whatever Dittoo might imagine. 'Your memsahib should not have rushed onto the baggage flat,' he pointed out. 'I was already coming with my knife, to cut the horse free. I myself would have caught hold of Saboor Baba and kept him safe. She should have waited on the passenger flat with the rest of the foreigners and let me do the work.'

'But my memsahib is no ordinary foreigner,' Dittoo protested. 'She is very brave. She rescued Saboor Baba twice from Maharajah Ranjit Singh.' He glanced over his shoulder, then motioned the albino to lean closer. 'She did it with magic,' he whispered. 'I saw it with my own eyes.'

Ghulam Ali drew back.

'Didn't they tell you this at Qamar Haveli?' Dittoo asked. 'Did they not say that Memsahib used sorcery to steal Saboor Baba at the Golden Temple?' He nodded gravely. 'She made him disappear into the air in front of the Maharajah's palanquin of coloured glass. Everyone saw it happen. I was there when Baba arrived by magic in her tent. Later,' he concluded grandly, 'she had only to look once upon Maharajah Ranjit Singh himself, and he offered to marry her!'

'*Marry her?*'

When Dittoo nodded his assent, Ghulam Ali shifted his body closer to the fire, his eyes on the passenger flat with its darkened windows. He had heard nothing of sorcery from anyone at Qamar Haveli, but this was not unusual. He was never included in the gossip that flew from mouth to mouth in the haveli's kitchen courtyard.

But a sorceress? This was extraordinary news. It was surprising enough that Hassan Ali's foreign wife had made Saboor Baba disappear into the air, but it was truly astounding that she had, with one glance, persuaded the great Maharajah Ranjit Singh to *propose marriage*.

She must indeed be a great enchantress, this foreign woman, for Kharrak Singh's father, unlike his son, had not been mad. Far from it. The creator of the Kingdom of the Punjab with its armies and its riches must have seen for himself that this female was much too old for marriage, and very plain. Beautiful women, after all, had large, liquid eyes, soft faces, and plump bodies. This one had none of these good features, nor was she attractively shy and placid. She had a high-boned face, pointed shoulders, and tumbling hair, and was much too old to attract a man; she also indulged in unseemly behaviour. This afternoon, for example, she had rushed headlong to where she was not needed, and then had fallen backwards, her skirts flying, revealing an indecent expanse of white leg to anyone who might have been looking. If he, Ghulam Ali, had not already been running, knife in hand, towards the terrified horse, he would have turned and run in the opposite direction.

'She has a good heart,' Dittoo added firmly. 'It was her heart that led her to rescue Saboor Baba two years ago, and to interfere just now with the saving of the horse.'

Ghulam Ali yawned. These people were incomprehensible. First, no lady of Shaikh Waliullah's household would think of having a male servant, and yet here was Dittoo, clearly the established personal servant of Hassan Ali Khan's English wife. Did Shaikh Waliullah and his son know that this man brought coffee to her room each morning, that he counted her sheets and towels for washing, that he served her meals, that he defended her with a loyalty reserved for a master, not a mistress?

Ghulam Ali himself did not care. Dittoo might be seedy-looking and a Hindu who would never eat with a Muslim like himself, but at least he treated him as if he were a normal person. It felt good to have the companionship of someone who bore him no ill will, who could be trusted, even if it was only for this journey. After he returned to Qamar Haveli, he would once again be alone, with only his gruff manner to prop up his pride.

'Ajit, oh, Ajit!' The call came from downriver. The men around the fires stared into the half-darkness as the voice came nearer, following an invisible path along the riverbank, accompanied by the clopping of a horse's hooves.

Fifty servants scrambled to their feet. A moment later, Ali Baba's tired groom appeared from the darkness, leading a beautiful, chastened Arab horse.

'At first I was certain I would drown,' Sonu explained as he tied Ali Baba to a large stone, 'but in the end the water pushed us both towards the bank. We have walked for hours. Is there any food left?'

'So the Burri Memsahib will have her horse back,' said someone a little later, as the weary Sonu stuffed cold bread into his mouth.

'She will,' someone else agreed, 'but it will do nothing to improve her temper.'

That evening, after the servants and the horse had been poled back to the baggage flat by two labourers from the steamer, Ghulam Ali lay awake, rolled in his blanket beside a pile of bagged salt. For all Dittoo's praise of his memsahib, and for all his revelations about her unusual abilities, Ghulam Ali still had reservations about the woman.

She was foreign, and therefore suspect. Her evening dresses bared the skin of her shoulders and chest so scandalously that he made it a point never to look at her or any female member of the British party after sunset.

She seemed to have no sense of propriety. He had seen no shame on her face after she had fallen onto the deck of the baggage flat. She seemed not to care how she looked, appearing on the deck of the passenger flat with her hair loose and her boots untied.

But she had courage. He had seen it in her face the first time they had met. Her actions of the afternoon had shocked but not surprised him. Furthermore, she never ignored the natives. In fact, she looked at them all, including him, with a curious intensity, as if they had something she wanted. She spoke properly to them, unlike most of the other foreigners, who could barely make themselves understood.

Whatever, he wondered, would become of this odd female and her hunched manservant when they arrived with Saboor Baba at Qamar Haveli?

Chapter Eight

14 October 1840

Akhtar squatted in the kitchen courtyard of Qamar Haveli, a brass bucket filled with the ladies' washing at her side. Four months of rose water and proper food had improved her condition, but she was still very thin. Her white Turkish trousers, a gift from the Shaikh's deep-voiced sister, bunched thickly on their waist cord and a plain shirt drooped from her narrow shoulders. Akhtar worked hard, wringing out each delicately embroidered garment energetically before adding it to the growing pile on the sheet she had spread in the sun. Safiya Sultana had offered her a home at Qamar Haveli and her daily food in exchange for simple work, and Akhtar was deeply grateful. Only one need marred her happiness – her longing to discover the identity of the woman who cast spells.

She had begun her search immediately after her precipitous arrival at the haveli. Lying on her makeshift bed in the dark hallway, bruised, aching and nauseated from jaundice, she had tried to divine the truth by listening to the conversations coming from the inside room where the ladies sat, but with no success. The women had spoken of many things, of poetry, of the Qur'an, of various embroidery stitches, of the best ways to cook the buds of the kachnar tree, but they had never once mentioned magic.

The spell-caster could be one of the family ladies or she could be among the women who served them. Since those who practised magic belonged to no single class or religion, she could be anyone, from the Shaikh's sister herself to the ghostly sweeperess who crawled from room to room each morning followed by her stringy-haired daughter, cleaning the floors with her brooms and rags.

Three days after her arrival, too desperate to wait longer, Akhtar had risen unsteadily to her feet and approached a gnarled old servant called Firoz Bibi.

'Is there a woman in this house who practises enchantment?' she had asked the old woman, glancing over her shoulder, afraid to be overheard.

Firoz's old eyes had widened. 'No,' she had declared firmly as she poured out drinking water for the ladies. 'There is no Jadoo practitioner in this house. If anyone were found practising magic here, they would be sent away at once.'

'But I heard a man talking about it,' Akhtar insisted. 'He said there is a lady at Qamar Haveli who knows how to cast spells.'

'People in the bazaars and on the streets know nothing.' The old woman shook her head as she arranged the tumblers on a tray. 'This world is full of ignorance, child. The lady Safiya Sultana is well-known for her wisdom and her healing arts, but she is not known for magic.'

Healing arts — that phrase could mean many things. From that moment, Akhtar watched the Shaikh's sister closely, sidling along the wall to stand close to the lady's customary seat in the underground room. At night, anxious to miss no word of the ladies' conversation, she remained as long as she dared on the sheltered rooftop where the family slept.

Observing Safiya Sultana, Akhtar had seen that she was not an idle person who spent her days taking opium, having her legs kneaded, and sleeping her life away as great ladies were reputed to do. At the first hint of dawn, as the muezzin's call to prayer echoed through the darkness, Akhtar would jump from her string bed on the servants' part of the roof and run to the family quarters to find that Safiya had already performed her own ritual ablutions and was now supervising those of the children. Once satisfied with everyone's cleanliness, Safia stationed herself in front of her household to lead them in the pre-dawn prayer. Akhtar stood behind the rows of children and ladies, following the movements of Safiya's stout body as she stood, bent, then bowed her forehead to her prayer mat, her posture denoting surrender before God. Only after each Muslim household lady, servant, and child had completed that simple observance did Safiya retire to her room to perform her own spiritual exercises, whatever they might be.

Akhtar would have given much to know whether those exercises involved magic.

Every grain of rice, every inch of ginger, pod of cardamom, clove of garlic, every nut, sweetmeat, and piece of fruit served at Qamar Haveli was measured out daily by Safiya Sultana. Each morning, watched carefully by two of the family's unmarried girls, Safiya ordered sufficient food for everyone in the house, and for twelve extra people, in case guests arrived. If the food was not eaten, Safiya herself determined to which needy family the surplus would be sent.

She also oversaw the education of the family girls, not only in the household arts, but in the Qur'an and its meanings, and in the works of Persian and Urdu poets.

In that busy household, there were clothes to be made and embroidered, carpets to be beaten, and weddings to be planned, for the Shaikh's family was large, and many of its members counted upon Safiya Sultana to know the best prices for shawls, silks, and jewels.

There were also the sick and the injured to be treated. Only the day before, as the ladies were finishing their afternoon meal, a breathless male voice outside the curtained doorway had announced that the man who tended the new female buffalo had cut his arm on a piece of jagged metal.

Safiya Sultana had swallowed her last chunk of melon and risen, puffing, to her feet. 'Akhtar,' she had ordered, 'bring one of our torn dupattas and come with me. Firoz, you know where I keep the dried neem leaves. Take two handfuls to the kitchen for boiling. And Rahima,' she had told one of the younger women, 'bring my chador.'

Moments later Safiya Sultana tramped down the stairs, her plain white chador covering her clothes and shielding her face.

Akhtar had not had time to cover herself with her own dirty chador, forgotten on a shelf in another part of the house. Instead, she wrapped her thick cotton veil over her head and face as best she could.

'Never mind all that,' Safiya ordered, reading Akhtar's thoughts as she pushed open the gate leading out of the family court-yard. 'Your clothes are modest enough for the work we are going to do.'

The scene at the stables was disconcertingly bloody. The buffalo driver stared with shock at his dripping arm while a dozen men clustered around him, bloody straw at their feet, offering advice and gazing in fascination at the open wound through which muscle and bone were visible.

'Stand back,' one of them called as Safiya Sultana and her nervous acolyte stepped round a pile of stones and into the stable. 'Begum Sahib has come.'

In the half-hour that followed, while the men watched from a careful distance, Akhtar had learned that Safiya Sultana treated open wounds by packing them with boiled neem leaves before wrapping them in cotton rags torn from old clothes. But Akhtar had learned nothing of magic. Safiya Sultana had been brusquer than ever once the wounded man had been taken away and the sweeper sent to clean the blood from the stable floor.

'You will learn far more from watching me than you will by asking endless questions,' she had rumbled. 'I cannot take the time to teach you when our men keep leaving their work half-finished. Look at those doors to the elephant stables. They are half rotted away, and no one has told me.'

Across the courtyard from where Akhtar was now working, the dhobi and his wife appeared, their arms full of sheets and floor cloths for washing. Akhtar stood up, her bundle of wet clothes in her arms, remembering how important she had felt yesterday, steadying the cooking pot while Safiya poured tepid neem water into the injured man's wound as he hissed in pain, then holding his arm out straight so that Safiya could tie on the strips of bandage. She raised her chin, recalling Safiya's gruff compliment. *You have a nice, gentle touch*, Safiya had told her.

As Akhtar spread the clothes out to dry on the upstairs verandah, a fragile-looking woman appeared at the head of the kitchen stairs and stood uncertainly, one hand on the wall, as if waiting to be addressed.

'*Salaam alaikum*, peace be upon you,' Akhtar offered.

'And upon you,' the woman murmured. She lowered her head so that her veil obscured her face. 'Is the lady Safiya Sultana available?'

Putting down her wet clothes, Akhtar straightened. This woman's manner suggested a need, but was it for something as ordinary as money or clothing? If Akhtar had not been so ill when she had come looking for magic to save her, she would have behaved exactly as this woman did. Here, perhaps, was someone who required magic. Her heart pounding, she ran to the ladies' sitting room.

'Send her in.' Safiya Sultana beckoned from her place on the floor.

While the assembled ladies whispered, the frail woman sat down cross-legged in front of the Shaikh's sister, her head bowed. 'I have been married for two years,' she murmured, her chin on her chest, 'but still I am not with child.'

'And your husband has brought you here?'

When the woman nodded, Safiya Sultana reached out to lay a hand on the woman's knee, then closed her eyes.

Was she reciting a spell? Akhtar crept along the wall, trying to see if Safiya's lips were moving.

After several minutes of silence, Safiya sighed and opened her eyes. 'Come back in three days,' she ordered. 'I will give you something to keep under your pillow at night.'

The woman, who had not moved, now reached out quickly, seized Safiya's fingers, and held them to her lips.

'Do not offer me gratitude.' Safiya rumbled, reclaiming her hand. 'Inshallah, God Himself will help you.'

That night, instead of leading the isha prayers herself, Safiya deputed that duty to a gap-toothed old lady, then retired to her room and closed the door.

Later, Akhtar lay sleepless on her new string bed in the women's servants' quarters, wondering what Safiya Sultana had done behind that door. What would the barren woman receive when she returned? Whatever it was, would it work?

The next morning, engrossed in these questions, she nearly missed Safiya Sultana's words as she spoke to the assembled girls and ladies of the family.

'That is because every beggar has a secret,' Safiya was saying. She was sitting on the white-sheeted floor, one elbow resting on a thick bolster. 'Each beggar, no matter how ill or ragged he may be, always gives something beautiful in return for the charity he receives.'

Beggar. Akhtar remembered her dream of the two ragged men with their pile of gold. Noticing her for the first time, Safiya Sultana frowned and motioned for her to seat herself.

Among the women, several little boys sat watching Safiya's face and her eloquently moving hands, their mouths open in concentration.

'But,' one of them asked, his small face puckering, 'what does a *beggar* have to give?'

'Perhaps he offers thanks, or a blessing,' suggested a young woman.

'Exactly.' Safiya nodded. 'Some beggars do not thank or bless, but even they have a gift to offer.'

'What gift is that, Bhaji?' piped a little girl.

Safiya Sultana smiled, her eyes crinkling. 'Aliya my darling, you must think for yourself what that is. Once you have decided, you must come and tell me.'

Beggars who do not thank or bless. The words cut Akhtar to the heart. Hadn't she herself been a beggar when she tumbled down the stairs ill and friendless, possessing only her torn clothes and her mother-in-law's stolen chador? Although her husband had been a farrier, not a whining beggar of the streets, she, who had run away, could not claim as much. Until this moment, she had not thought even to bless those who had lifted her up and fed her and kept her safe.

What gift had she, the beggar, to give? Unlike the men in Safiya's poem, she, empty-handed, had brought no treasure to the king's door.

Chapter Nine

5 November 1840

'Careful, be careful,' whispered the Prime Minister as court servants lifted the dying Maharajah Kharrak Singh from his bed in the Lahore Citadel. Half a dozen white-bearded priests stood by chanting prayers as the servants lowered their king to the floor of the crowded room, so that he might die in the lap of Mother Earth.

The Maharajah shivered, whimpering beneath the shawls they had laid over him. His long hair unfurled dankly on the tiled floor, lit by the flame of a small, earthenware lamp. A priest knelt beside him, reciting. Other priests joined him. Incense clouded the air, causing the watching nobles to blink and rub their eyes.

'Ram, Ram, Ram,' chanted the priests.

'Say it, Mahraj,' urged the kneeling priest.

The Maharajah attempted to speak but abandoned the effort. His eyes rolled upward. Someone came forward, felt for his pulse, then shook his head.

A high-pitched sound came from one of the nobles. The chanting grew louder. A man wearing several emerald necklaces stepped forward. He set a gold lamp, already lit, beside the shrunken, grey-faced body. An aristocratically dressed youth followed, unbuckling his sword belt as he did so. Dry-eyed, Prince Nau Nihal Singh untied the precious Kashmir shawl he wore round his waist and, with a single swift movement, spread it over his dead father.

Later, in the anteroom, the Prince stood before his father's body, now propped on a wooden stool for the Maharajah's last bath. While servants worked to hold the shirtless corpse upright, the son dipped a brass vessel into a pail of water from the River Ganges and poured it over the dead man's head, reciting as he poured.

After his father's stiffening body had been dressed in saffron-scented clothes and jewels, Prince Nau Nihal Singh strode from the antechamber and past the attending nobles. Alone, the Prince climbed a winding staircase to the sunlit courtyard beyond, while behind him the eunuchs began to wail.

The scent of jasmine and frangipani hung in the air of the queens' garden. The Prince made his way to a fountain in the garden's centre and sat down on its marble edge. There he stayed, so lost in thought that he scarcely looked up when approaching footsteps heralded the arrival of the Foreign Minister.

'May I offer my condolences, Prince?' asked the Faqeer.

The young man nodded an invitation to the neatly dressed man, who sat down beside him and pulled his coarse-looking robe together over his knees. 'I am sorry to be bringing this up so soon,' the Foreign Minister said, 'but there is much to be done. I fear that if you do not act quickly, you may find it difficult to control the other contenders for the throne, especially your uncle Sher Singh.'

The Prince's nineteen-year-old face hardened. 'Most of my family members are as weak as my father was. As for my uncle Sher Singh, he is popular with the army, but no more than I am. I have no fear of him, Faqeer Sahib.'

'And the Prime Minister, with his riches and his private army?'

'I will keep Dhian Singh close to me. His guns and men will be at my command.'

'Ah.' The Faqeer nodded. He got to his feet, embroidered silk peeping from beneath the coarse beggar's robe he had affected for years. 'Your grandfather,' he said smoothly, 'was a great man. He was a brilliant soldier and horseman, and an inspired leader. He loved a good joke, and he passionately loved the Punjab. I pray that you will be able to wield his sword.'

The young man met the Faqeer's eyes with his own level gaze. 'They will be taking my father's body outside now,' he said coldly, then rose to his feet.

The Maharajah's elephants and horses had been given away in charity, as had hundreds of thousands of rupees and gold mohurs. The dead Maharajah's body had been placed on a gold and silver bier and covered with many shawls. The moment had come for the funeral cortège to pass through the city and on to the garden outside its walls, where the square sandal- and aloes-wood pyre stood waiting.

The Foreign Minister and his assistant walked at the end of the procession. Having witnessed the legendary Maharajah Ranjit Singh's funeral only two years earlier, Hassan Ali Khan and Faqeer Azizuddin had no need to see the forced passage of his mad son's golden, shawl-draped bier through the crowded streets, or to hear the praying of male onlookers. They did not need to hear the wailing of the women thronging the latticework balconies above them, or see the people surge towards the four doomed queens who walked barefoot behind their husband's bier, throwing their jewellery into the crowd.

'Sati Ma, Mother Sati, pray for me, pray for my sins!' cried the crowd as it pushed forward, heedless of the guards, to clutch at the clothes of the stony-faced queens.

'Have those poor women been drugged?' Hassan asked the Faqeer as the two men followed at a distance.

'I do not know,' the Faqeer answered, 'but I was told that the four who are to be burned laughed and danced at the Citadel before the procession left. All the rest fainted when the bier was carried out. That should tell us something about those women's condition.' He grimaced and tipped his chin towards the front of the procession. 'But I had not realized that seven serving women were to burn as well.'

After an hour of prayers and ceremony, the crowd sighed gustily as the four queens climbed onto the pyre in order of seniority, followed unsteadily by the seven chosen serving maids, each one helped by two other women. Slowly, as if half asleep, the women lay down, the Maharajah's wives at his head, the servants at his feet.

'The senior queen is not among the satis,' murmured Hassan.

Men climbed onto the pyre and covered the corpse and all the living women with oil-soaked reed mats. Others poured vessels of clarified butter over the logs. The chanting grew louder. The Prime Minister took a flaming torch from a priest and handed it to Prince Nau Nihal, who nodded and began to circle the pyre, his lips moving.

As the fire took hold at all four corners, the Faqeer touched Hassan's elbow. 'Come,' he ordered. 'We can respect this rite of theirs, but we need not watch it.'

The crowd sighed again. Flames shot into the air as the two men, the only Muslim officials at this Sikh funeral, edged their way towards the city gate.

The pyre was still burning two hours later, when Hassan and the Faqeer rode back to join the procession returning the Maharajah's son to the Citadel.

Hassan gestured through the crowd towards the Prime Minister who rode beside the ample, heavily bearded figure of the Prince's uncle Sher Singh. 'Should we ride with them?'

'It does not matter. I believe our posts at court are safe. We should let others push their way to the front.' He sighed. 'I only pray that Nau Nihal Singh will display some of the qualities so lacking in his poor father.'

The afternoon sun threw shadows across the flat ground. An old stone archway stood along the high wall of the great Badshahi Mosque, marking the path to the Citadel gate. Watched by high-circling vultures and ragged villagers, the procession of nobles and courtiers rode towards the archway, while in the distance a black water buffalo lowered its head to charge a passer-by. Preoccupied with the buffalo and its fleeing victim, Hassan and the Faqeer did not turn to look until a heavy rumbling sound came from the direction of the archway, followed by thudding and shouts. The arch, together with the young Prince and his party, had all disappeared inside a billowing cloud of dust.

Men threw themselves from their mounts and ran towards the scene. A horse squealed somewhere, in terror or pain. The dust-covered figure of a man staggered out of the dust cloud, clutching his shoulder.

'The arch has fallen!' someone cried.

'The Prince!' shouted someone else. 'Where is he?'

'Help us! Help!'

Hassan and the Faqeer kicked their horses and galloped towards the scene.

Behind them, a pair of pigeons circled the pyre twice, and then, as if at a signal, dropped into the flames.

The man outside the curtain raised his voice to be heard over the boom of cannon fire. 'They are saluting the accession of Prince Sher Singh to the throne,' he shouted.

'*Sher Singh?*' Rani Chand Kaur, wife of one dead king and mother of another, started forward from her place on the floor of the royal ladies' chamber. 'Which one of you fools has snatched the throne from my family and handed it to the son of a clothes dyer?'

'It was not one man, Maharani-Ji. The decision was made by the full court. Who else but your brother-in-law can be Maharajah now that your son is no more?'

'*Who else?*' Chand Kaur had already screamed herself hoarse. Her face with its bloody, vertical scratches was as wild as her hair. 'Did any of you ask whether my daughter-in-law was with child?' She pointed to a frightened-looking girl who crouched silently in a corner of the incense-filled chamber. 'When my grandson is born,' the queen rasped, '*he*, not an upstart son of shame, will sit on the throne of the Punjab. Pah! You are fools, sons of owls, all of you.'

The cannon fire had ceased. 'We did not know this, Maharani-Ji,' said the male voice.

But Rani Chand Kaur had lost interest in the conversation. Seizing the neck of her long shirt with both hands she tore it wide open.

'They have killed my son!' she shrieked. '*My son!* When I find the man who took my injured son to the Hazuri Bagh instead of to this palace,' she went on raggedly, the tattoo on her chin changing shape with every word she spoke, 'when I find out who locked all the garden and the Citadel gates so that I could not go to him when he was dying, I will put his eyes out with *my own hands*.'

93

Chapter Ten

2 January 1841

Mariana watched from her horse as the first of Lady Macnaghten's three elephants stepped gingerly onto the bridge of boats leading out of British-held India and into the independent state of the Punjab.

Built across the Sutlej River two years earlier for Lord Auckland's state visit to Maharajah Ranjit Singh, the span still held, although it had clearly suffered since that time. Broken timbers now threatened its stability, causing the elephant to tread cautiously on the shifting surface, its mahout watchful on its neck.

As the second elephant joined the first, a chill went down Mariana's spine. If on this journey there were a point of no return, this bridge of boats was it. She glanced behind her, looking for someone who understood, but saw only Charles Mott stopping to blow his nose. It was no use anyhow. No one understood her feelings, not even Uncle Adrian. He had said only yesterday that her divorce would lift a 'terrible burden' from her shoulders.

How could she look forward to her divorce when she was about to lose Saboor?

Needing to think, she guided her mare away from the bridge. The Punjab, now mere yards away, could no longer exist only in her imagination, but what had it become since the death of old Maharajah Ranjit Singh? Lahore must be quite different without the flamboyant, one-eyed Maharajah who had taken the stability of his self-made kingdom with him when he died, leaving lesser men to quarrel over his treasures and his power.

Other things must also have changed in the old city. Shaikh Waliullah still lived, or she would surely have heard otherwise, but was his stout, sensible sister still alive? Mariana could hardly bear to think of arriving too late to see Safiya Sultana again, a woman who had captured her imagination more than anyone else except the Shaikh himself.

Safiya was a poet, Mariana's elderly teacher had told her, and a philosopher, too, one whose fame spread far beyond the walls of Lahore. Mariana had even learned Safiya's best-known poem, composed after the loss of both her daughters to smallpox:

The thief descended swiftly, and as swiftly fled.
Plundered of his load, my hamstrung camel groans outside
    my tent.
Where is his worked leather saddle? Where are my treasures—
My rubies, my saffron, my pure white raisins?
All are lost. What then is the destination of this ruined caravan?

Would she meet Safiya Sultana, or even enter the upstairs ladies' quarters of the Shaikh's aristocratic old house? Her only mission, after all, was to obtain the Shaikh's consent for her divorce. The transaction would properly occur in the men's part of the house, and it was quite possible that she would be excluded from the negotiations.

When it was over, as plundered of her treasure as Safiya Sultana had been, she, too, would be lost.

She tried to imagine Harry Fitzgerald, now aware of her purity and filled with newfound respect for her, sitting down to write an apology for his earlier remarks, hinting that he would like to beg her forgiveness in person, but it did no good.

Hoofbeats approached. 'Come along, Mariana,' her uncle urged, interrupting her thoughts. 'You'll be late to breakfast if you dawdle here.'

Ahead of them, Lady Macnaghten rode towards the bridge, accompanied by the newest member of her party, the British Political Agent and liaison officer to the Sikh court, who had arrived early in the morning to escort her into the Punjab.

Russell Lewis, a thin person whose great, hooked nose and chinless, jutting head gave him the look of a vulture, had arrived that morning with much fanfare and many assistants. Mariana watched without interest as he leaned from his saddle to say something to Lady Macnaghten. He was said to know a great deal about the workings of the Sikh court, but at this moment she cared little for the political intricacies of the Punjab.

An hour later, after leaving her horse with a waiting groom, she stepped distractedly into the camp dining tent, then stopped short at the sight of Russell Lewis at the dining table, hunched over a plate of eggs and lamb kidneys. It was not Lewis's appearance, or even the size of his breakfast, that caused Mariana's sudden halt, but where he was sitting, for he now occupied Charles Mott's place beside Lady Macnaghten, while Mott, newly ejected from Paradise, slouched sullenly in the previously empty seat beside Mariana's chair.

She sat down reluctantly and returned Mott's dismissive nod with an equally dismissive one of her own, which he did not see because he had already looked away. Across the table, Aunt

Claire flapped a hand encouragingly between the silver coffee pots.

'Now that we are on land,' she had confided weeks ago, 'you may converse with Mr Mott out of earshot of the rest of us, whilst still maintaining propriety. You *must* make yourself agreeable to him, Mariana. He is to be an intelligence officer in the government at Kabul. I have several times observed him glancing covertly at you when he believed no one was looking. I am certain he thinks more highly of you than you realize.'

'I do not like him, Aunt Claire,' Mariana had replied flatly. 'He is too pale and damp-looking, and he has—'

'You are not to say again, Mariana, that Mr Mott has *beady eyes.*'

The English party's overland journey had begun some nine weeks earlier, in the last days of October. During the ten days that followed the steamer's arrival at Allahabad, Lady Macnaghten and her nephew had been feted by the station's British society at dinner parties, theatricals, and balls, while Mariana, Saboor, Uncle Adrian, and a very disappointed Aunt Claire had waited in a rented house, ignored by everyone. Only after Lady Macnaghten had grown tired of the festivities had they all joined the baggage train, which had arrived by land from Calcutta some weeks earlier.

Spread out over a large area of flat ground, the train had looked exactly as it had before it left Calcutta, with the same soporific elephants, superior-looking camels, distracted British officers, hordes of natives, and endless mountains of luggage.

Lady Macnaghten had made a great display of nervousness as she watched her more valuable belongings being packed onto the bullock carts, but nothing dire had yet happened to her chandeliers, her porcelain, or her brandy, although the camels had managed to smash more than half her ordinary china before the train reached Allahabad.

The arrangement of the travelling camp had been fixed from the first day. Lady Macnaghten's grand tent and Charles Mott's smaller one were set up together on the right-hand side of a dining tent large enough to seat twelve. Mariana's tent and the one housing her uncle and aunt were on its left. The kitchen tent and the servants' small tents and cooking fires stood some distance behind the dining tent, as did the long lines of horses and pack animals, and the piles of unloaded baggage, both under heavy guard against thieves. The whole area was then enclosed in a wide circle of pickets, sent from the neat army camp that bordered Mariana's tent.

Over the weeks, the camp had fallen into a routine. At five thirty each morning, Mariana and Saboor were awakened by the sound of Dittoo bumbling his way into her tent carrying a tray with coffee for Mariana and an egg for Saboor. Half an hour later, having sent Saboor to travel with Dittoo, Mariana got sleepily onto a horse and rode between ten and fifteen cross-country miles at her uncle's side to the next campsite, while Lady Macnaghten rode clumsily ahead of them, accompanied by her nephew and the Vulture.

The only person who refused to travel on horseback was Aunt Claire, who insisted on riding in a palanquin carried by a team of bearers.

Behind all of them crawled the baggage train with its elephants, creaking carts, and walking servants. If all went well, as it had today, at the end of their ride Mariana and the others could expect a hearty breakfast in the dining tent, which had been sent on ahead the previous evening.

The Vulture swallowed a last bite of buttered toast and looked about the dining tent through half-closed eyes. He nodded to the assembled party, but allowed his gaze to slide over Mariana and her family without acknowledging their presence.

He knew about them already, of course. Who did not, in this gossiping country?

Lady Macnaghten smiled prettily over her fan, revealing a perfectly smooth, rounded arm. 'And now, Mr Lewis,' she cooed, 'we breathlessly await your news of the Punjab.'

'Yes, indeed,' Uncle Adrian put in quickly. 'We have heard nothing but rumours since we learned of the collapse of the archway after Maharajah Kharrak Singh's funeral. Did the young heir die by accident, or by treachery?'

'No one knows,' the Political Agent replied in his high, nasal voice. 'Of course one of my couriers came to me as soon as the accident occurred. In fact,' he added importantly, 'the man killed a horse in his haste to bring me the news. But even I do not know for certain what happened to Prince Nau Nihal Singh. Those most easily blamed had relatives injured or killed in the accident. The stones that fell may have been dislodged by all the cannon fire after Maharajah Kharrak Singh died.' He shrugged, bird-like, inside his black frock coat.

'And will there now be competition for the throne?' asked a baggage officer.

'Oh, yes.' The Vulture leaned back in his seat and made a steeple of his fingers. 'The mad Kharrak Singh's famously difficult widow, who somehow escaped dying on his funeral pyre, has suddenly claimed that her dead son's wife is expecting a child. Insisting that the unborn child will be male, the woman has named herself regent until it comes of age, and has forced the Sikh Council to rescind its decision to enthrone her husband's half-brother, Sher Singh. The Council must now forge a compromise between the two of them. Sher Singh, naturally, is infuriated.'

'And what is he like?' asked another officer.

'I have met Sher Singh twice. He is an entertaining, larger-than-life

99

character, a heavy drinking Punjabi who might be said to resemble Henry the Eighth. He is popular with the army, which apparently supports his claim to the throne.'

'This seems a dangerous business,' observed Uncle Adrian. 'The Sikh army under Sher Singh could be a formidable force.'

'It would. I shouldn't be surprised,' the Vulture added carelessly, 'if there were an explosion of violence between Sher Singh and the Maharani.'

'But we had planned to stay three weeks in Lahore!' cried Lady Macnaghten. 'Surely you do not mean there will be fighting while we're there?'

'Oh, I very much doubt it will come to anything yet,' soothed the Vulture. 'By the time that happens, Lady Macnaghten, you will already be in Kabul, giving your first ball. And, unpleasant though the Rani may be,' he added with a smile, 'she has been most charming to us. She has,' he said grandly, 'offered us the Koh-i-noor diamond, among other things.'

'Which diamond?' Lady Macnaghten leaned forward.

'The Mountain of Light. It weighs a hundred and twenty-nine carats, and is coveted by everyone who has ever seen it. Princes have fought over it for centuries.' The Vulture leaned back in his seat. 'The Koh-i-noor is one of the great treasures of India. I am also happy to say,' he went on, 'that the Rani has co-operated quite well with us in the matter of the Afghan tribesmen who come down through the Khyber Pass to attack and rob Englishmen travelling to Kabul without sufficient escort. Only a month ago, a Major Effington was robbed of his money, goods, and horse, and left for dead. I have persuaded the Rani to take strong action against this sort of behaviour.'

'And all of this is in exchange for what?' inquired Uncle Adrian, taking the words out of Mariana's mouth.

'The Rani has convinced herself that we are going to help her against Sher Singh.'

Uncle Adrian's face had begun to redden. 'And how has that occurred?'

The Vulture shrugged. 'I have no idea.'

Uncle Adrian frowned. 'And what action does the Rani propose to take against the Afghans?'

'Oh, nothing unusual,' the Vulture replied casually. 'All Afghans who come into the Punjab are to register with the Sikh government. Those who do not will be subject to public floggings, being shot from cannon, that sort of thing. Some of them are useful to us, of course,' he added, as he stirred his coffee. 'They bring intelligence and so on, but most Afghans are no more than savages.'

Charles Mott set down his coffee cup with a little groan of boredom. Mariana inched her chair away from him. Why did the fool not listen to this important conversation? Who had appointed him an intelligence officer?

'Whatever happens to the Sikhs and the Afghans,' Lady Macnaghten said, laying down her fan with a decisive little gesture, 'I certainly hope *we* do not meet any savages on our way to Kabul.'

Chapter Eleven

3 Janaury 1841

The forty courtiers had been standing in the delicately mirrored pavilion for nearly an hour, listening to the demands of Kharrak Singh's widow. Water splashed in the sunny courtyard fountains outside as they tried to persuade her to share power with Prince Sher Singh, their eyes on the curtain that blocked off one end of the breezy, shadowed room.

'I will *never* share this kingdom with a low son of shame!' the Rani's throaty voice erupted from behind the curtain. The courtiers shifted and sighed. 'I am the daughter of military heroes. Everyone knows what Sher Singh's mother did behind Maharajah Ranjit Singh's back. Hah! My husband was mad, but at least he had royal blood.'

'The Punjab should have one ruler, not two,' murmured a pearl-laden man in a gorgeous striped turban. 'The Rani should leave the work of ruling to Sher Singh, and wait peacefully for her grandchild to be born. It is up to fate to determine whether the child is male or female, whether the Rani will win or lose.'

A tall Hindu leaned over, his emerald earrings swinging, his lips to the first man's ear. 'Do not speak,' he cautioned in a whisper. 'There is treachery here.'

Hassan Ali Khan leaned against an inlaid pillar, his back to the sun, watching as the most influential men in the kingdom murmured among themselves. Beside him stood Faqeer Azizuddin, his coarse beggar's robe wrapped round him against the chill breeze that entered through the filigreed windows of the pavilion.

'And *you*, little she-camel,' the Rani went on, apparently addressing someone who had joined her behind the curtain, 'remove your face from my sight, you who have killed my son with your ill luck. Black was the day when I married my son to you! Who would want you, but for the child you are carrying?'

The sound of a girl's sobbing reached them.

Hassan brushed a hand over his face. 'How will the Punjab survive such base people?' he murmured to the Faqeer. 'How can the kingdom have come to this?'

'As for you, Dhian Singh,' the harsh female voice continued, 'you who will not let me have the Koh-i-noor diamond, you may be Prime Minister now, but you have come up from nothing. You are a self-made upstart.'

In unspoken agreement the Faqeer and Hassan walked down the pavilion steps and into the courtyard.

'She has gone too far,' the Faqeer said, keeping his voice low.

'Surely after this,' Hassan ventured when they were out of earshot, 'the Prime Minister will abandon her and join Sher Singh.'

'My dear, I believe Dhian Singh already has,' replied the Faqeeer.

'Then she is finished,' Hassan said as they crossed the courtyard. 'Perhaps we are all finished.'

The Shaikh's family courtyard was a pleasant place to sit on winter mornings. Before the sun began its slow descent towards the roof of the upstairs ladies' quarters, its rays fell kindly upon the courtyard, illuminating the haveli's frescoed walls and its single tree.

When Hassan was not at the Citadel with the other courtiers, he and his childhood friend Yusuf Bhatti had the courtyard to themselves. In the hours before the usual crowd of respectful guests began to filter in through the gate to visit the Shaikh, the two men sat together on a string bed beside the tree, the sun on their shoulders, a bubbling hookah on the ground between them.

They made an unlikely pair, Hassan tall and open-faced, whose fastidious style of dress made up in elegance for his broken nose, Yusuf thick-bodied and rough-looking, his heavy curved sword lying close to hand, the handle of a serviceable knife protruding from the sash about his waist.

Today they were not alone. Earlier as they had sat peaceably passing the mouthpiece of the hookah back and forth, a servant had hurried from the outer courtyard.

'The Afghan traders have come,' the man announced. 'They are waiting outside.'

Now, in place of the smouldering hookah, bundles, packets, and caged birds stood before the two men, while opposite them, two traders sat cross-legged, a pair of decorated muskets slung across each of their backs.

The elder of the two traders was a lean man with heavy eyebrows and startlingly pale eyes. Hassan took a teapot from the tray beside him and refilled his guest's glass with cardamom-scented tea.

'So, Zulmai,' Hassan said, 'now that it is winter in Afghanistan, are you not glad to be here in my Lahore, the City of Roses?'

The trader smiled, revealing an even row of white teeth. 'You never tire of asking me that. You have no idea how I miss my country.'

Hassan nodded. 'It is terrible to be parted from what we love most. Your sadness reminds me of my own anxiety for my son. I think often of that poem: "From Canaan, Yusuf shall return, whose face a little time was hidden: grieve no more—"'

'"Oh, grieve no more,"' Zulmai continued, '"In sorrow's dwelling place the roses yet shall spring from the bare floor."'

Hassan sighed, his eyes half-closed. 'You Afghans truly appreciate poetry.'

'Except for him.' Zulmai pointed to his young, fresh-faced assistant, who smiled broadly, his mouth stuffed with fruit. 'Habibullah here knows of nothing but guns and horses.'

Hassan nodded towards the hunched figure of Yusuf Bhatti. 'And Yusuf here is at home only in the jungle, shooting pig. It might kill him to learn a line of poetry.'

'Then why do we not leave those two to each other,' offered the trader, 'while we indulge our appreciation of poetry?'

Yusuf let out a barking laugh. 'Hah! You may be a poet, Zulmai, but you could never spend your days sniffing perfume and reciting verses. Look at you, with your knives and your two jezails strapped to your back. What are your weapons for, if not fighting?'

Zulmai did not reply. Instead, he nodded to his assistant, who strode off through the low gate to fetch something from the kneeling camel that waited by the elephant stables.

'As always, I am happy to see your wares,' Hassan told Zulmai, as they watched the boy reach into one of the camel's panniers. 'One of my cousins is in need of a good shawl, my uncle is desperate for saffron, and I hope you have brought me the amber I asked for.'

Zulmai reached into his clothes and withdrew a small, neatly stitched cloth packet and then a short, wicked-looking knife. He unsheathed the knife and sliced through the cloth wrapping, revealing a small cake of ground amber. He handed it to Hassan, who lifted it to his nose.

105

'Beautiful,' breathed Hassan. 'But Zulmai, you must not take my appreciation for foolishness.'

The trader opened his hands. 'We will discuss the price later. Look at these.' From another pocket he produced a smaller packet and unwrapped the cloth. There on the white cotton lay six beautiful dark red Jagdalak rubies, each the size of his little fingernail. 'Are they not exceptional?' Without waiting for an answer he put them back in his pocket. 'I have forty good Turkoman ponies at the caravanserai, and a dozen fine Arabs. I wanted to show the best of my Arabs to your young Maharajah, but now that he is dead, I will show them to Raja Dhian Singh or one of the other sirdars.' Zulmai rested his elbows on his knees, his pale eyes on Hassan's face. 'Speaking of the Prime Minister, I hear he has deserted the Maharani and offered his allegiance to Prince Sher Singh. That will be bad news for the Rani. Everyone knows that Raja Dhian Singh has great riches and heavy guns.'

Hassan shrugged. 'No one is sure what these sirdars are up to.'

'I also hear that the Rani is trying to buy the aid of the British. I understand she has promised them the Koh-i-noor diamond and all of Kashmir for their help, but that the Prime Minister has said—'

'This looks interesting,' interrupted Hassan as Zulmai's assistant approached with a bundle of dusty woollen fabric in his arms. Hassan stood up as the boy cut open the bundle and spread out its contents. 'These are Moghul shawls. How did you find them, Zulmai?'

The Afghan shrugged. 'Not everyone understands the value of his possessions. The British are everywhere,' he persisted. 'They are building themselves houses near Kabul. They intend to stay in Afghanistan.' He smiled. 'They think they have conquered us,'

'Those British want to take over the world,' said Yusuf harshly, while Hassan inspected the shawls, each finely embroidered in rich, contrasting colours. 'They are waiting for us to stumble so they can come in with their armies.'

Hassan held a yellow shawl with a swirling design in his hands. 'No one likes the British,' he observed, without looking up. 'In any case, their Political Agent will be here in five days. After that we will discover his designs for the Punjab.'

Zulmai nodded. 'Yes, and your wife and son are travelling in his party, is that not so?'

Hassan stared at Zulmai, the shawl hanging from his hands. 'How do you know this?'

'I listen to bazaar gossip.'

Later, as Zulmai's loaded camel rose awkwardly to its feet and followed Zulmai and Habibullah out of the haveli, Yusuf turned to Hassan.

'Do you trust that man?' he asked.

'Not at all,' replied Hassan, staring after them. 'I have known Zulmai for fifteen years, but I have yet to divine what he is thinking. No, I do not trust him at all.'

Chapter Twelve

'An-nah, morning has come!'

Heavy breathing in her ear and tugging on her quilts told Mariana that Saboor was awake. 'Has it, darling?' she murmured as she reached out from the covers, her eyes still shut, to pull him to her, still warm from his own bed.

'Will we ride today, An-nah?' he begged, as he did each morning. 'I want to ride with you all the way to the next camp. I want to gallop so-o-o fast!'

Sitting up beside her, he pumped his elbows to indicate speed.

She yawned. 'We shall see, my little cabbage.'

Perhaps she would let him ride today, astride her lap in the sidesaddle, shrieking with excitement when she gave in and galloped a short distance for his pleasure, one arm wrapped tightly about his middle.

She sat up and surveyed her tent with satisfaction. Fifteen feet square, it was the same size as the one she had occupied on her previous journey to the Punjab, but it was far more comfortable. In addition to the four-poster bed, the bedside table and washstand, it boasted Miss Emily's small, elderly settee, which doubled as Saboor's bed, and an arrangement for sitting, native-fashion, on the floor. The floor arrangement pleased Mariana most; with its thick knotted carpet, its richly coloured bolsters stuffed with cotton wood fluff, and its two tiny carved tables, her tent had a very un-English look.

'Come in,' she called, as a storm of coughing outside her tent heralded the arrival of Dittoo with her coffee tray.

'We are nearly there,' Dittoo announced as he backed into the tent, the tray in his hands. 'Ghulam Ali says we are only two marches from Lahore.'

The evidence grew daily of their closeness to Lahore. Sikhs with their long, bound beards and plain turbans had been evident in every village for a week, along with the usual Hindus and Muslims, but now the villages looked more prosperous, and the flat, dusty fields were full of half-grown wheat.

There had been other changes in the past few days. Charles Mott seemed to have developed a strong attachment to the Vulture, and now hung on the Political Agent's every word. Several times Mariana had seen him pull up a chair and join pre-dinner conversations between the Vulture and two of the army officers.

She often wondered what the four men talked about. *I cannot help thinking*, she had confided in a letter to her father, *that they are plotting something.*

When Mott was not thus engrossed, he watched Mariana. She had caught him several times gazing at her from a distance. At meals, she felt his covert attention on her, distracting her uncomfortably from her food. Aunt Claire, who had noticed this, gave him her small, fashionable smile at every opportunity.

Mariana sighed into her coffee cup. She would not miss Charles Mott at all when this journey came to an end.

At six fifteen Mariana sent a disappointed Saboor to travel on a donkey cart with Dittoo and emerged into the morning to find three saddled horses near her uncle's tent, attended by several dark-skinned grooms.

She watched as her slow-moving aunt emerged from the tent, stuffed into a riding habit and top hat.

'Aunt Claire,' Mariana called happily, after her aunt had hoisted herself onto one of the mares, aided by a groom, 'isn't it lovely to ride so early, while it is so cool and pleasant? I am certain you will enjoy it, and I am sure we shall find interesting villages and ruins on the way.'

'The weather is the least of my concerns, Mariana,' her aunt answered from her sidesaddle, her voice carrying over the shouts of coolies and the groans of camels. 'And you may be sure that I shall not look at a single native ruin or village on the way. I am going straight from here to the dining tent, where I shall eat my breakfast in peace. What an hour to be on a horse!'

By the time Mariana and her aunt and uncle set off, followed by the vanguard of the baggage train, Lady Macnaghten was already too far ahead of them to be seen, having ridden away earlier with the Vulture and one of the army officers. One lone European figure rode in front of Mariana and her family, his horse raising a dust cloud that obscured his identity.

'Is that Mr Mott?' Aunt Claire inquired, shading her eyes with a gloved hand.

'Yes, I believe it is,' replied Uncle Adrian. 'Considering his enthusiasm for Russell Lewis, I wonder why he is riding alone.'

Mariana, who did not care, said nothing.

Half an hour later, after failing to persuade her aunt to stop at the two interesting ruins they had passed, Mariana noticed a mud village ahead of them. Large enough to have a wide lane down its centre, it boasted a busy roadside market, a few tethered goats, lolling dogs, and the usual pack of small, naked children. Across from the market, a crowd of brightly dressed women and girls had gathered at a communal well.

'That is unusual,' Uncle Adrian remarked as half a dozen fierce-looking riders nudged their way through the crowded market. 'One does not often see riding horses in native villages.'

'Look,' Mariana cried, pointing.

Charles Mott was in the village. He stood uncertainly near a mud wall, not far from his tethered horse, his eyes on the women at the well.

The women talked among themselves, ignoring Mott as they filled their earthen vessels with water. As one party of them turned away, hips swaying gracefully, brimming vessels perfectly balanced on their heads, another chattering party arrived.

Mott had not seen Mariana and her family. Still watching the women, he unbuttoned his riding coat and slung it over his arm, displaying a white shirt and a pair of striped suspenders that held up his trousers.

'What an odd thing to do,' exclaimed Uncle Adrian. 'Why has he taken off his coat in front of an entire native village? I call that unnecessarily disrespectful, especially near those women.'

'Why on earth should an Englishman be respectful towards *native* women?' Aunt Claire asked dismissively.

'Because it is silly not to be,' snapped Uncle Adrian. 'I cannot think what the man is up to.'

As they watched, Mott left the mud wall and moved into the shade of a tree not ten feet from the well, his head still turned from Mariana and her family, his pose suggesting inquisitive superiority.

'What is the fool doing now?' demanded Uncle Adrian.

Before Mariana or her aunt could reply, several men on horseback

111

detached themselves from the throng at the bazaar and trotted towards Mott.

Hearing them approach, he turned towards them, frowning loftily. He held his ground at first, but the horsemen spurred their mounts and came on faster, shouting in guttural Punjabi and drawing long, curved swords. Uncle Adrian spurred his horse forward just as Mott abandoned his superior pose and sprinted for his tethered mount.

He was still yards from his goal when the riders reached him. As Uncle Adrian rode towards them and Aunt Claire cried out in horror, one of the horsemen leaned from his saddle, sword in hand, and sliced at Mott's back. Mott's trousers dropped instantly to his ankles, trapping his running feet. Arms flailing hopelessly, coat flying, he pitched forward, full length, into the dirt.

The native women stared. The horsemen grinned and slapped each other. Mott stood up, spitting dirt, his pale legs clad in only linen under-drawers. The men howled with laughter as he struggled to mount his horse while holding his trousers up with one hand.

Aunt Claire had covered her face, but Mariana was unable to take her eyes from the scene. When Mott was safely mounted, Uncle Adrian cantered back to them and herded them off the road, making way for Mott to ride stiffly past, pretending he had not seen them, his ruined suspenders flapping uselessly against his saddle.

Uncle Adrian shook his head. 'Akalis,' he said. 'That's who they were, renegade Sikhs, known for their brutal jokes. Mott was fortunate. They could have killed him. The young fool should have known better than to ogle their women in that insolent manner.'

'They don't seem to have cut him badly, thank goodness,' offered Aunt Claire as they continued on their way. 'I hope someone can give him – oh, *do* stop making that noise Mariana. I am certain Mr Mott has heard you. You really have a shocking sense of humour.'

*   *   *

Four hours later, Aunt Claire glared across the dining table, causing Mariana to duck her head, fighting the broad smile that threatened to engulf her face.

When he entered the tent for lunch Charles Mott failed to offer her even the most cursory nod of greeting. He turned his body away as if he were offended by her presence and fidgeted in his seat, drumming damp-looking fingers on the tablecloth.

At the table's end, Lady Macnaghten interrupted the usual desultory lunchtime conversation with a little cough, laid down her fork and turned to the Vulture. 'This must be the hundredth time we've eaten chicken fricassee,' she announced loudly enough for everyone to hear, gesturing with manicured fingers at the food on her plate, 'but happily I have something other than dull food to occupy me, something that causes my thoughts to flee far away from all *this*.' She gathered her shawls about her shoulders and waved in the general direction of Lahore. 'Now that we are in the Punjab and winter's chill has descended upon the camp, my thoughts have turned to the north, to the ancient mountain passes into Afghanistan. What greatness those passes have seen, what spectacles!'

What, wondered Mariana, had persuaded Lady Macnaghten to discuss the northwestern passes, the ancient mountain routes connecting India with Central Asia? As her aunt let out a reverential sigh, Mariana exchanged a quick, wondering look with Uncle Adrian. Beside her, Mott toyed with the silverware and breathed through his nose, as if he knew what was coming.

'My husband has told me all about the Khyber Pass,' Lady Macnaghten went on in her high, fluting voice. 'He has filled my ears with stories of the conquering horsemen who from time immemorial have entered India by that dangerous defile.' Flushing a little, she cleared her throat, her eyes sweeping the faces at the table. 'For thousands of years, these brave, manly invaders have poured

113

down through the Khyber Pass with but one object in mind: *to ravish the fertile Punjab.*'

Mariana shifted in her chair. Something was wrong with this lecture. Surely she was not referring to—

'Many times,' Lady Macnaghten added brightly, 'my husband has described to me the great conquerors of later centuries, Mahmood of Ghazni, Tamerlane and Genghis Khan, all of whom thrust their way through the pass to *seize and hold the defenceless plains below.*' The red-faced officer cleared his throat noisily, but Lady Macnaghten had already leaned forward conspiratorially. 'Sir William,' she added, 'has often said that had he been present, he would have advised Genghis Khan not to turn back after reaching Multan and Lahore. No indeed,' she finished triumphantly, her cheeks blooming, 'my husband would have urged the Khan to press on without hesitation, and *possess a quivering and helpless Delhi.*'

Mariana glanced at her uncle again, and found him staring scarlet-faced at the chicken on his plate. Like her, he must be remembering Lady Macnaghten's similar behaviour in Calcutta. She clearly thought no one would notice her suggestive choice of words, but why had she chosen this moment to bring up these private conversations with Sir William? And why when they were alone and amorous did they discuss the *passes*, of all things?

'There is, of course, much more,' Lady Macnaghten added, turning to the Vulture who had raised his hands in self-defence, 'but it must wait for another time.'

This conversation needed rescuing. One of the baggage officers took the initiative and cleared his throat. 'Mr Mott,' he put in loudly, 'I saw you arrive at camp this morning after the march. You seemed to have suffered an accident of some sort. Are you all right?'

Beside Mariana, Mott stiffened in his chair. As he mumbled a reply, she squeezed her eyes shut and tried to school her face, but it was no good. A moment later, a hand pressed to her mouth, she rose to her feet and rushed from the dining tent.

Chapter Thirteen

Determined to write some letters, Mariana left the shade of the tree where she had collapsed mirthfully after her escape from lunch. By now Saboor would have gone to have his food with Dittoo, so she would have a peaceful hour to do so.

Absorbed in debating with herself whether Mott's humiliation or Lady Macnaghten's lack of discretion should come first in her letter to her sister Charlotte, she did not hear footsteps behind her. As she reached her doorway a man gripped her powerfully about the waist and forced her past her door blind and into her tent, the length of his body pushing against hers.

Mott must have been holding his breath, for he let it out in a rush as he dropped his arms. Even in the half-light of the tent Mariana could see the perspiration standing on his face.

'How dare you seize me like that? How dare you enter my tent?' she demanded.

'You laughed at me in front of everyone,' he croaked. 'You *laughed*.'

'Go away.' She stepped forward, making shooing gestures. 'You have no right to be here!'

'Who are *you* to poke fun at me?' His voice had thickened. 'Everyone knows what *you* have done. Everyone despises you. But *I* don't mind. I don't mind at *all*.'

Before she could stop him he gripped her by the arm and pulled her towards him. 'Why do you ignore me?' he demanded. 'Why do you pretend I do not exist? I have admired you—'

'*Get out!*' she shouted, twisting her head to avoid the wet, half-open mouth that threatened to close on hers. She leaned away from him, towards her four-poster bed. If she could reach her bedside table, her oil lamp would be weapon enough. But as she threw her weight backwards, he let go of her. Crying out, clutching instinctively at his arm for balance, she toppled onto her bed.

He, too, lost his balance and fell full length on top of her.

As she struggled beneath his weight, he took hold of her face, squeezing her cheeks as he tried to bring her lips to his. She screamed.

'Quiet!' Distracted, he slapped a careless hand over her open mouth, letting one finger slide between her teeth. Heedless that her lip was in the way, that she would hurt herself, she bit down on his finger with all her strength.

For an instant, she thought she had lost, that he felt no pain, but then he jerked backwards with a sharp cry. 'You *bit* me!' he squealed, pulling away from her. 'You savage!'

'Get out!' she snarled into his face, tasting blood, not knowing whether it was his or hers. She struggled to her feet and shoved him, temporarily shocked and unresisting, towards the doorway. She followed this up with a hard kick to his buttocks, sending him sprinting clumsily into the door blind, then out of her tent.

Had someone heard? Had someone come to help her? Her

thoughts whirling, she held the blind aside and looked outside, to see Charles Mott making his escape and Ghulam Ali standing not ten feet from her tent, a long-bladed knife in his hand. The albino stared, his pink eyes wide, taking in the blood on her face, before she let the blind drop into place.

So it had come to this, all the gossip, the disgrace, the lies. She could expect no sympathy. Ghulam Ali had seen and heard. Every servant in the camp would soon know, and they would certainly talk. Pompous and vindictive, Mott could tell whatever lies he chose about her and be believed. He spent so much time with the Vulture and the army officers . . .

Alone against them all, she would have no chance.

Before Mariana had time to move from her doorway, a familiar, ringing voice called from outside. 'I am coming in, child,' said Aunt Claire. 'I have something to tell you about tonight's dinner.'

'Please, Aunt Claire, I am resting,' Mariana protested shakily through the closed blind. *Not Aunt Claire, not now.*

'Why are you resting? You never rest at this time of day.' Her aunt pushed the blind aside. 'It is about Mr Lewis,' she said, holding the blind open, her bonneted head bobbing decisively. 'He will be — but what is this? What is wrong with your face? Blood! Oh my dear child! What has happened to you? How badly are you hurt?'

'Charles Mott did this.' Mariana put trembling fingers to her lip, still feeling his fingers gripping her face. 'He followed me here and tried to—'

'*Mr Mott?*' Aunt Claire started back.

'He came inside and seized me,' Mariana whispered. 'I fell down there.' Tears leaked onto her cheeks as she pointed to the bed. 'I made him leave before he could — but he will talk. He will say bad things about me. He—'

'But Mr Mott is a gentleman,' Aunt Claire interrupted, her eyes glazing with confusion. 'Why should he speak ill of you?'

'Because I *bit* him. Because I would not let him do what he wanted.'

'Do what he *wanted*?' Aunt Claire glanced towards the doorway, as if looking for assistance. 'Mariana,' she said, her face a map of conflicting feelings, 'I do not understand. I am sorry you are hurt, but I cannot believe that poor Mr Mott is capable of the behaviour you describe. What did you do to provoke him into it?'

'What did *I* do?' Fury replaced Mariana's tears. 'I have barely spoken to your "poor Mr Mott" since we left Calcutta!' She dashed at her wet cheeks with the back of her hand. 'Your Mr Mott is a *pig*.'

'You are not to use that language with me,' her aunt said huffily. 'Whatever this is about, the fact is you are to be ready for dinner half an hour early tonight, as we are eating at half past seven.' She twitched her shoulders as if relieving herself of an unwanted burden. 'And tell that bleached ruffian outside to sit somewhere else. I do not like native men sitting so near your tent.'

With that, she swept off without a backward glance.

The bleached ruffian in question had been squatting beneath a thorn tree a short distance from Mariana's tent when she returned from lunch, followed a short while later by the Englishman.

Since the overland journey had begun, Ghulam Ali had made a habit of watching the soldiers of the armed guard lounging outside their tents after their afternoon meal. He liked to imagine that, given the opportunity, he could have become a soldier like them, smart in a red woollen jacket with white cross belts, a flintlock rifle near him at all times. Engrossed in the men's gossip about the other soldiers and their discussion of drilling and marksmanship, he had

119

not looked behind him when the Englishwoman's easily recognizable steps turned towards her tent, but when other, rapid, footsteps had followed hers, taking the same route to her doorway, he had taken notice.

To Ghulam Ali those footsteps had sounded strangely uneven, as if the person approaching were in the grip of some strong emotion. Wondering, he had turned his head in time to see an Englishman's back disappear into Memsahib's tent.

Ghulam Ali had never imagined Hassan Ali Khan's wife to be a loose woman, for all her clumsiness and odd behaviour. Absorbed in caring for her stepson she had never seemed to take the slightest interest in the pallid, black-coated men of the English travelling party. What then was the reason for this mysterious visit? Frowning with curiosity, Ghulam Ali had risen to his feet, approached her tent and leaned forward to listen.

The lady had spoken first. At the sound of her voice, the hair on Ghulam Ali's arms had stood up. Although her words had been unintelligible, there had been no mistaking the sharp fear in her tone.

A man's voice had responded, arguing. Seconds later, Hassan Ali Khan's wife had given a guttural scream.

Bitterly regretting his curiosity, Ghulam Ali had turned to flee those frightening sounds, but then, cursing his own cowardice, he had stopped.

Someone must aid the lady; someone must protect her honour, for surely her honour was at stake. Ghulam Ali had glanced over his shoulder looking for help, but had seen only the soldiers squatting by their tents, too far away to have heard. There was no sign of anyone else. He would have to face this horror alone.

Now the man yelped in pain. Shaikh Walliullah's daughter-in-law, it seemed, was fighting back.

Ghulam Ali drew the long Khyber knife he had carried since his childhood, then hesitated. What could he do to save Hassan Ali's wife? How could he decently intervene? Who knew what fearful shame he might encounter to if he rushed, uninvited, into the lady's tent?

As he hovered irresolutely, knife in hand, the door blind billowed outward and the weak-faced nephew of the senior memsahib burst into the sunlight, clutching his left hand.

A moment later the blind re-opened to reveal Memsahib, panting and scarlet-faced, blood staining her lip. Her eyes met Ghulam Ali's and then she withdrew and the blind thumped dustily shut.

Almost at once her aunt, the fat memsahib, bustled up and pushed her way into the tent, only to reappear soon after and stalk away, her chin held high.

Ghulam Ali squatted beside the tent, his knife across his knees, considering what he had seen and heard. He had guessed from the first that the Englishman was a weakling, but that alone did not explain why the son of a jackal felt entitled to follow Hassan Ali Khan's wife into her tent and to treat her with disrespect, perhaps even violence. And why had her aunt appeared and then gone away without showing sympathy? Surely the fat memsahib was not stupid. Why had she taken the attack so lightly? Why had she not emerged from the lady's tent shouting with rage, bent upon punishing the man?

Ghulam Ali stared down at his knife, remembering what Dittoo had told him: that the English people seemed to abhor the young memsahib's marriage to Hassan Ali Khan, and that as a consequence she had been suffering at their hands.

Believing that anyone would be proud to boast a family connection to the Waliullahs, Ghulam Ali had refused to accept Dittoo's claim, but what if it were true? What if, despised by her own people,

121

Hassan's wife had somehow become subject to indecent attack? If so, that would explain what he had seen in the brief, unguarded moment when she had looked out of her tent: not the shame and rage of an innocent woman but the haunted, hollow stare of the outcast.

Dittoo's theory would also explain the aunt's behaviour. Outcasts were never believed. Defeated before they spoke, such people learned to keep their agonies to themselves. Hassan's wife, it seemed, was having to learn this difficult lesson.

How strange that the woman who had been charged with the guardianship of the Shaikh's grandson should herself be alone and unprotected upon the field of battle.

Ghulam Ali shook his head. By Allah, the woman had courage. How well she had protected herself from a man so much larger than herself!

Shambling steps hurried towards the tent. It was Dittoo, bearing the child Saboor in his arms. The little boy had been weeping. He hiccupped, his fists screwed into his eyes as he rode against Dittoo's chest. At the tent, he rushed into the arms of Hassan Ali's wife who had come outside, the blood still on her face, to comfort him.

Ghulam Ali stood up, the knife still in his hand. 'Wait,' he barked in his crude Urdu, before Dittoo could depart. 'I have a message for your memsahib.'

'There, darling,' Mariana soothed. Her arms about Saboor, she stared over his head, remembering Harry Fitzgerald's final letter, its painful words impossible to forget.

I excuse myself after dinner each night to avoid hearing the shameful things our officers are saying about you. Who will dare to be your friend now?

'An-*nah*,' Saboor mumbled against her breast.

'He would not eat,' Dittoo reported. 'He wept instead, saying something had happened to you, that you needed him. I don't know what is wrong. Nothing happened to make him cry.'

122

He tipped his head towards the albino, who stood awkwardly close by. 'And Ghulam Ali has asked me to give you a message. He says he will sit guard outside your tent. He says he will not let anyone come near you again. What does he mean, Memsahib? Why has he taken out his knife? What is wrong with your face?'

Who will be your friend now?

The child's arms tightened about her. 'Nothing is wrong,' Mariana whispered as she buried her crumpling face in Saboor's hair. 'Nothing.'

Chapter Fourteen

'What are you doing here?' Yusuf shouted that same afternoon, his square face cheering at the sight of Hassan Ali Khan among the showily dressed sirdars crowding Prince Sher Singh's makeshift court fifty miles northeast of Lahore. 'Look at you, in all your finery.' He seized Hassan by an embroidered sleeve and tugged him away from the crowd. 'I thought you were in Lahore, waiting for your son to arrive. Does Rani Chand Kaur know,' he went on, lowering his voice, 'that you have come to Batala to call upon her rival?'

'The Rani knows I have come to suggest a compromise between her and Sher Singh. Other Sirdars are doing what they can at the Citadel, but our work is of no use. In all the time I have been here, I have not been able to speak privately to Sher Singh. His blood is too hot for compromise, and the Rani at Lahore is too proud and stubborn to listen to reason.' Hassan pointed to a graceful, tasselled tent that stood at the centre of a large encampment. 'I see that the Prime Minister has already arrived. The Rani has offered him the Koh-i-noor if he will return to her, not that she has possession of it.'

'But hasn't she already offered it to the British, along with the heads of any Afghans she can find?'

'She has offered it to everyone. She would offer it to me if she thought I could help her. But what of you, Yusuf? Has your irregular cavalry gone over to the Prince? Are all of you in line for the diamond?'

Yusuf leaned over and spat onto the ground.

Silk-clad courtiers continued to ride in through the main gate of the house, weapons clanking at their sides. Black-bearded men stood by the stables, their chain mail and steel helmets gleaming in the sun.

'He is coming. The Prince is coming outside,' the crowd murmured.

A bear of a man wearing a helmet of polished steel appeared. Flanked by heavily armed guards, he thrust his way through the open gateway. 'Do you see these guns?' he bellowed, slapping the nearest cannon with an open palm, sending a crowd of ragged children sprinting to safety. 'If need be, these are the guns that will take back the throne!'

'Yes, Mahraj,' shouted someone in the crowd. 'We will prevail within the first hour!'

'Once we reach Lahore,' the Prince went on, 'more chiefs will come, with many more men. Those who do not come out of loyalty will join us once they see our strength. By the time we march on the city, so many troops will have deserted Rani Chand Kaur that we will not need to fire a single a shot!' He smiled broadly. 'Ah, I see young Hassan Ali Khan, assistant to Faqeer Azizuddin, is here. And you too, Sher Bahadur,' he added, turning to another man in the crowd.

Hassan and Yusuf exchanged glances. 'It is no use my staying,' murmured Hassan. 'I must go to Lahore to meet my son. Are you coming?'

125

'Did you see how many of the Rani's spies are here?' Yusuf said as they mounted their horses.

'I did. They are everywhere, and those who aren't spying for her are spying for the British.'

Yusuf frowned. 'If Sher Singh does attack, I wonder how he will control his men. Troops on both sides have not been paid for months. It would be madness to let them loose inside the walled city.' He sighed. 'I am glad my cavalry has not taken sides. I have no stomach for killing Punjabis. We should be fighting our enemies, not our friends and neighbours.'

'I hope it does not come to violence.' Hassan shook his head. 'My father will never leave Lahore. What a bad time for Saboor to return.'

Yusuf reached over and dropped a thick hand onto his friend's knee. 'Cheer up, man. If there is a battle, it will, Inshallah, be over quickly. In any case, the doors of Qamar Haveli are stout. I doubt your family will suffer. We should be celebrating young Saboor's return. A few days from now, God willing, your whole family will be rejoicing.'

'I wonder,' Hassan said thoughtfully, 'what he looks like after these two years.'

'I shall take you in to dinner myself,' announced Uncle Adrian as he joined Mariana outside his tent in the gathering darkness. 'Your aunt has developed a sudden headache, and will not be joining us tonight. I have already sent her excuses.'

'If Aunt Claire will not be at dinner,' Mariana said sharply, 'I cannot come with you.'

'What?' Her uncle frowned. 'Don't be absurd, Mariana. They're all waiting.'

'No.' Mariana shook her head. Without even her aunt's pallid support, how could she face Lady Macnaghten's party, the officers, the Vulture? How could she sit beside Mott at the table? How could Aunt Claire be such a coward?

Her uncle again offered her his arm. 'Mariana,' he ordered, 'you will come with me. I cannot think what is the matter, but whatever it is, it must wait until after dinner.'

Inside the candlelit tent, Mott stood silently by his chair, his eyes fixed on the silver candelabra in front of him. As Mariana approached the table, she saw Mott's bandaged hand tremble a little on the back of his chair.

What had he told them all? she wondered. Fearing that he had been seen entering her tent, had he invented some ugly tale about himself and her?

Everyone was present: Lady Macnaghten resplendent in blue satin and ruffles, the Vulture draped in a heavy gold watch chain, Uncle Adrian and the four army officers, all chatting comfortably to one another as they took their places.

It was Mott's new friends among the army officers she feared most, but even they seemed absorbed in their conversations. Only Lady Macnaghten stared at Mariana for a moment, then glanced quickly away, a small frown between her eyes.

In the seat to Mariana's right, her uncle leaned forward, his eyes on her face which was now clearly visible in the brightly lit tent. 'Why, Mariana, my dear,' he said loudly, 'you have cut your lip!'

Too mortified to answer, she sat silently, while Charles Mott twitched beside her.

The Vulture cleared his throat. 'I have news from Lahore,' he announced in his nasal voice. 'The thwarted Prince Sher Singh is preparing to advance upon the city.'

'But the Rani is at the Citadel, with her court,' put in a red-faced officer. 'Do you think the Prince intends to kill her?'

127

'I don't know, and to tell the truth, I don't care,' the Vulture replied genially.

Lady Macnaghten put down her sherry glass. 'The Prince will not attack *us*, will he, Mr Lewis?'

'Oh, no. The Prince wants us on his side. We shall be quite safe, even if he attacks the Citadel while we are at Lahore. After all, we shall be encamped three miles from the city.' He eyed his plate of mulligatawny soup with satisfaction. 'In fact, I rather hope he does attack,' he added. 'I wouldn't mind seeing the show.'

Half listening, Mariana flinched as Mott's bandaged hand stirred on the tablecloth beside his untouched soup plate. He had drunk several glasses of wine and she was not surprised to hear his uneven breathing.

'But why should the Prince resort to military force?' asked Uncle Adrian. 'That seems unnecessarily dangerous.'

The Vulture flapped a careless hand. 'The Rani has refused to meet him,' he said, 'but he has possession of Gobindgarh, the fort containing all the Punjab's heavy artillery – some seven hundred guns. The Rani, who is a fool, didn't think to secure it for herself. If she does not capitulate, I expect Sher Singh will smash his way into the Citadel with those guns and terrify her into submission. But of course that would be after he had besieged the walled city.'

'But the city has thirteen gates,' Mariana said too loudly, startling the officer across from her. 'Sher Singh can never besiege it successfully. It will take him too long. He will storm the gates with heavy guns instead. Whatever he does will be disastrous for the population. If he enters by the Delhi Gate, he will endanger Wazir Khan's Mosque and all the houses around it. If he enters from the Bhatti Gate, he will—'

'My dear young lady,' interrupted the Vulture loftily, addressing her for the first time since his arrival, 'I am sure we are all impressed by your knowledge of Lahore, but you are missing the point. The point,' he said, regarding her through half-closed eyelids, 'is that the heirs to the throne of the Punjab will murder each other whether we want them to or not, and that such murders can only advance our interests.'

Mott stirred beside her. 'Quite right,' he agreed.

At the sound of that self-satisfied voice, Mariana's simmering anger turned to fury. What an arrogant fool he was! She looked down at the cutlery on either side of her soup plate. The knives, with their rounded blades, were not dangerous, but the forks had potential . . .

'. . . will fall into our hands, guns, treasure, and all, without a shot fired, and at no expense to ourselves.' The Vulture drew out his words to emphasize, Mariana supposed, his own brilliance. 'Prince Sher Singh's attack on Lahore may cause trouble for the population, but we should remember that it will be their trouble, not ours.'

Ignoring her uncle's warning glare, Mariana fixed the Vulture with a level gaze.

'How,' she inquired, as other conversations died around her, 'can you excuse the slaughter of innocents? How can you justify the plundering of treasures that do not belong to you?' She raised her fork and stabbed it into the tablecloth an inch from Charles Mott's injured hand.

Squealing with fright, he leapt up, turning over his chair and spilling his wine which spread like blood on his white doeskin breeches.

All conversation stopped. Lady Macnaghten stared at Mariana, a hand to her breast, her cheeks suddenly as white as her pearls.

Mariana rose to her feet and nodded towards the head of the table. 'I hope you will excuse me, Lady Macnaghten, gentlemen,' she said evenly, then swept past Charles Mott and out of the dining tent in a rustle of silk.

It was after eleven o'clock when Dittoo scratched on the closed blind. 'Memsahib,' he whispered, 'your uncle is calling you.'

The air in her tent was cold. Mariana reached, shivering, for a shawl. Uncle Adrian must be furious to have summoned her at this late hour, but she did not care. Wild horses could not make her apologize to the Vulture, Lady Macnaghten, or Charles Mott. Politeness had no meaning now. Shunned and friendless at the bottom of some invisible social ladder, she had but one choice – to fight for herself.

She gathered up several shawls, flung them about her shoulders, and marched to her uncle's tent, her chin high, her breath visible in the cold night air.

When she stalked inside, she found him on his feet, still wearing his evening clothes. He acknowledged her arrival with a sharp, red-faced nod, then pointed to a chair near the bed, where Aunt Claire sat against several pillows, her double chin wobbling beneath the strings of a lace cap.

Braced against his anger, Mariana watched him reach for the bedside lamp. 'I want to see your face,' he rasped.

The lamp shook as he held it up. Aunt Claire's plump fingers opened and closed on the coverlet as Mariana stared stony-faced into the light.

He set the lamp down hard on the table, causing his wife to start against her pillows. 'I must know how badly Mott has hurt you,' he said tightly.

Dear, silly Aunt Claire had told him.

Bathed in sudden relief, Mariana answered, 'It is nothing. He has not hurt me otherwise,' she added firmly, comprehending the real meaning of her uncle's question.

He nodded. 'Come, then,' he ordered. 'You can tell me the story while I walk you back to your tent. I shall then pay a visit to Mr Charles Mott.'

The next morning, as she ate a boiled egg, Mariana looked cautiously about the dining tent. Everyone was there but Mott. All seemed occupied with their food, even the officers of the armed escort. Ignoring her, they poured milk into their tea and chewed their toast as they had each morning since Allahabad.

Charles Mott had not, it seemed, boasted in advance of his proposed conquest. He had also, apparently, kept his failed attack to himself.

At the table's head, a pale-faced Lady Macnaghten pretended as usual that Mariana was not there.

Aunt Claire picked disconsolately at a lamb kidney. It had taken her hours to abandon her dream of social advancement and tell her husband of Mott's outrage, but she had done it. Mariana smiled forgivingly in her aunt's direction, and helped herself to a spoonful of sugar. With Uncle Adrian and perhaps even Aunt Claire on her side, she might find the journey bearable after all.

'Mott has admitted to his disgraceful behaviour,' Uncle Adrian had confided on the early morning march as he and Mariana rode together behind Lady Macnaghten and the Vulture, with Aunt Claire's puffing bearers jogging behind them. 'Of course he confessed only after I offered to produce that albino courier of yours as a witness. The thought of being exposed by a servant was too much for him, I suppose. He came clean, but in a most unpleasant manner. I do not like to see a man beg for mercy.' He gave a satisfied grunt. 'I then threatened him with his aunt, Mr Lewis *and* the Governor-General if he so much as looks your way again.'

Feeling as light as air in her sidesaddle, Mariana had glanced back at Charles Mott, who was riding so far behind them that he had almost included himself in the baggage train.

What a difference it made to have allies.

Chapter Fifteen

11 January 1841

When the seventeenth-century Moghul Emperor Shahjahan visited his northern capital at Lahore, he had his tents set up at Shalimar, his pleasure garden, whose name signifies Abode of Love.

Shalimar had suffered in the hundred and forty years since the fall of the Moghul Empire. The lovely old garden had been stripped of its marble, and the dainty pietra dura decorations had been torn from the walls of its airy pavilions, but battered though it was, it was still beautiful. Its three terraced levels were intact, as were nearly all of its pavilions. Water from Hansli Canal filled the three great square pools, one on each level, and the four hundred carved fountains still stood where Mulla Alaumulk Tuni, the garden's designer, had placed them three hundred years before.

Shalimar was at its best in January. Its formal areas boasted cypresses and blossoming fruit trees – mangoes, cherries, apricots, mulberries, and other varieties, although not the hundreds of trees that had once grown there. But for all the loveliness of its trees, the garden's greatest feature had always been its roses. Cultivated by the same tribe of gardeners for many generations, the roses were now on full display, dominating the garden with splashes of colour, sweetening the breeze that ruffled the water in the pools.

On one side of the middle terrace, shaded by old mango trees, the tents of Mariana and her aunt and uncle overlooked both a lacy little building and Lady Macnaghten's grand quarters in the centre of the middle pool, on an island pavilion reached by a marble causeway.

Unlike Charles Mott, whose tent stood across the water, together with the tents of the armed escort, the Vulture had placed his tent far away from everyone else's, near the entrance gate on the lowest terrace.

'I am pleased that Lewis has arranged for us to stay here at Shalimar,' Uncle Adrian told Mariana as they stood surveying the garden, 'although I cannot say I like the man. I find him much too sure of himself. I do not like his making us wait a full week to see the Shaikh. And even if he is responsible for our political information, I don't like him setting up his tent so far from everyone else, and conversing secretly with all those natives out of earshot.'

While Mariana and her uncle watched, a tall native man left an expensive-looking horse near the main gate, then stood briefly outside the Vulture's tent before disappearing inside.

'I hope our government will not allow itself to be dragged into the quarrel between Prince Sher Singh and the Rani,' sighed Uncle Adrian, 'and I certainly hope those two do not come to blows, much though Lewis seems to desire it.' He frowned, his eyes on the birds swooping between the mango trees. 'But none of this is our concern. We shall soon be far away from here. My dear Mariana,' he added, noticing her stricken face, 'you must not grieve over that child. You are doing the right thing.'

He glanced again towards the Vulture's tent. 'Mr Lewis has offered to accompany us to the Shaikh's house tomorrow. In spite of everything, I shall be glad of his assistance. He is experienced with upper-class natives, and will, I am sure, be most useful in explaining our position.'

Mariana stared over the garden wall. A smoky haze in the western sky hinted at the presence of the busy city of Lahore; within its walls stood the comfortable old haveli where the Shaikh and his family waited for her.

This was to be her last night with Saboor.

It was with a heavy heart that Mariana tugged on her boots the next morning. Within an hour she, her uncle, the Vulture, and an armed escort would set off to inform Shaikh Waliullah of the divorce.

The day had not begun well. First, Charles Mott, who had claimed illness and fever for the previous three days due to a severely infected finger, had appeared in the dining room for breakfast. Instead of ignoring her, he had offered her repellent, exaggerated politeness. He complimented her unnecessarily on her blooming health and suggested she borrow his horse grooms when she went for her daily ride. 'I never take servants out with me, and in any case, I shall not be riding today.'

'No, thank you,' she had replied icily, avoiding his eyes.

She sighed as she tightened her bootlaces. As if that were not enough, Dittoo had burst into sudden tears half an hour later, while dusting her bedside table.

'What will become of me after you and Saboor Baba return to your husband in the city?' he wailed. 'Where will I go?'

Saboor ran to comfort him, catching at his callused hands. Mariana glanced away from his damp, tragic face, ashamed at having concealed the truth from both of them for so long. She had not known how to tell them.

'Stop crying, Dittoo,' she said. 'No one is sending you away. You will serve me as you always have.'

'But how can that be?' He stopped dusting the table and stood, his cheeks wet, Saboor's small hand in his. 'How can I serve you after you have gone to live at—'

'Enough, Dittoo,' she snapped, and pushed past him out of the tent.

It was only later, while a shy young groom walked Saboor up and down under the trees on one of the mares, that she told Dittoo the truth.

'I am not going to stay with Saboor at Qamar Haveli,' she blurted out. 'I am going to dissolve my marriage, leave Saboor with his family, and then go on to Afghanistan with my uncle and aunt.'

'But you must not do such a terrible thing.' His face had filled with dismay. 'If you leave your husband and his family, if you leave Saboor, you will be *all alone*!'

After his shocked protest, he had left her alone to watch the groom and the mare with Saboor on her back as they walked carefully along the margin of the central pool, their figures reflected brokenly in the rippling water.

Saboor now waited outside her tent, bathed and ready. Told that he would soon see his father, he had danced with excitement. For all his prescience at other times, he seemed not to have guessed that the price of regaining his home and family was to lose her forever.

She pushed the tiny buttons of her gown rapidly through their loops. It would be best for him to live at Qamar Haveli, of course it would. That venerable house was full of his own people, many of them children who had fussed adoringly over him when he was last there, taking turns carrying him up and down, shrieking with pleasure as they dragged him across the floor, their small hands under his arms.

He would forget her in time . . .

*   *   *

136

An hour later Mariana sat stiffly against the hard pillows in her palanquin, singing one of Saboor's bedtime songs, more to comfort herself than to entertain him.

> Lavender's blue, diddle diddle,
> Lavender's green.
> When I am king, diddle diddle
> You shall be queen . . .

She fell silent. It was no use; he was too excited to listen.

'An-nah, open the side! I want to look out!' he cried, clambering over her in the cramped box, his elbow digging into her middle, his animated face inches from hers.

Outside, the bearers panted rhythmically as they ran, the sound of their breathing joined by the clopping of horses' hooves: Uncle Adrian's, the Vulture's, and those of two officers of the armed guard. They seemed to be covering the three miles to the walled city at an unnatural speed, but it was only Mariana's dread of arrival that made it seem so.

Pushing down her sadness, she fumbled with the side panel and let Saboor put his head out through the opening. The familiar smells of spices, sewage, and bitter charcoal floated into the palanquin.

Uncle Adrian believed the Waliullahs would be loath to part with her. 'Remember, Mariana,' he had told her as they waited for her palanquin, 'that the Shaikh may be very reluctant to give up a European daughter-in-law. As Mr Lewis and I are experienced with natives and know exactly what to say, I advise you to remain silent. Do not interfere in any way with our negotiations.'

As they approached the walled city, she pulled Saboor inside and closed the panel against the stares of the men on the road.

'I'm going to see my abba!' Saboor crowed as they passed

under the Delhi Gate and into the crowded alleyways of the city.

Mariana listened to the cries of hawkers and the voice of her sirdar bearer ordering passers-by out of the way. 'Move out, move out!' he called as the palanquin moved slowly along, its sides scraping against buildings and the bodies of pack animals.

The crowd thinned and the palanquin slowed. Mariana heard the sound of great doors thudding open, and horses' hooves echoing in an entranceway.

They had arrived.

A short while later she heard a gate creaking open. She did not need to look out to know that they were now in the Shaikh's inner courtyard. Was the Shaikh waiting for them in the sunlight on his padded platform, surrounded by his usual silent crowd of followers?

No, of course not. The meeting would be held indoors. Knowing she was coming, the Shaikh would have arranged for her to be shielded from the eyes of men.

'Saboor has come,' said a voice.

'Yes, he has come,' agreed another.

No one mentioned her.

The palanquin stopped. Saboor had started up before it was safely on the ground. 'Hurry, An-nah. I want to get down!'

Mariana looked out. A temporary-looking canvas wall blocked her view of the neat courtyard where, two years ago, the Shaikh had cured a snakebite victim, then interviewed her in the starlight. Above her head, silent filigreed balconies looked down upon the courtyard and the palanquin. Was Safiya Sultana, the Shaikh's poet sister, there, watching from behind the latticework shutters, while other ladies crowded about her, craning to see?

'A-jao, Saboor,' male voices called enticingly from behind the canvas. 'Come to us!'

138

Before she knew it, Saboor had scrambled over her lap and onto the ground. An instant later, he darted round the canvas screen and was gone.

It was too late to embrace him, too late to say goodbye. Before Mariana had time to cry out, her uncle appeared at her side.

'We must hurry,' he urged. 'The Shaikh is inside.' He helped her to her feet, took her firmly by the elbow, and steered her towards the open doorway, tightening his grip when she turned, searching desperately over her shoulder for a last glimpse of Saboor.

Tribal rugs covered the floor of the cool, whitewashed room. Large bolsters in brightly embroidered covers lay along the walls. Three upright chairs stood together. At the room's end, in front of a filigreed marble window, the Shaikh rose to meet his guests.

He was exactly as Mariana remembered him: a wiry man with a wrinkled, animated face, whose tall, starched headdress rose above jutting ears. His gaze held the same magnetic, suppressed power.

His feet were bare. Belatedly, she remembered they should have left their shoes outside the door.

'*As-salaam-o-alaikum*, may peace be upon you.' The Shaikh gestured amicably towards the chairs, then seated himself on his dais, his feet close to his body, his clothes falling into graceful folds. Mariana sat, arranged her skirts and pushed wandering curls into her bonnet. The Shaikh had not asked which of the two men was Mariana's uncle; she had no doubt he already knew.

'Welcome to this house,' he said in polite Urdu. 'I trust your journey was not too difficult?' His words were informal, as if he were addressing family members. Mariana glanced at her uncle and saw he had noticed the same thing.

'Our journey was quite pleasant,' Uncle Adrian replied gravely in his excellent Urdu, 'and little Saboor seems to have enjoyed it.

The child has been looking forward to meeting you and the rest of your family again, after all this time.'

The Shaikh inclined his head.

'But we have not come solely to meet you, Shaikh Sahib, although it gives us great pleasure to do so,' Uncle Adrian continued. 'Other considerations have brought us to Lahore. We have come to ask for your indulgence in the matter of my niece.'

Why did Saboor not come to her? Mariana only half listened to her uncle, her senses tuned to the sounds from the courtyard.

'We have come to request that the marriage between your son Hassan and my niece Mariana be terminated.'

'Terminated?' Mariana could almost hear the Shaikh's eyebrows rise.

Where *was* Saboor? Surely this was not the end. Surely she would see him again, if only to say goodbye . . .

'We understand,' the Vulture interpolated smoothly, 'that *all* the requirements of the marriage have not been met. We therefore ask for the dissolution of the *contract*, not the marriage itself, since, technically, there is no marriage.'

Mariana froze. How mortifying that the Vulture knew her story.

'May I know,' the Shaikh inquired, 'the reason for this request?'

Uncle Adrian cleared his throat. 'My niece is English. Her life and her expectations are those of an Englishwoman. She entered this marriage hastily two years ago, without consulting us, and she now faces the prospect of living as a native lady in a style that is quite foreign to her. I am certain that your family must have had similar feelings.' He paused. 'Surely you would prefer your son to marry a lady from among his own people.' Having accomplished this part of his speech, Uncle Adrian relaxed his grip on the arm of his upright chair.

Qamar Haveli was indeed foreign, Mariana thought, with its

strange food, strange languages, no riding and no picnics, but none of that mattered to her now . . .

A sound came from outside. Silhouetted against the light, a small figure peered into the room. 'An-nah?' he called.

She was halfway out of her chair before her uncle's fingers closed firmly on her wrist.

'My niece is not suited to the life of the zenana,' Uncle Adrian continued, pulling her down again as Saboor pattered away. 'We believe it is in the interest of your family as well as ours to allow her to leave quietly and without hindrance.'

The Shaikh turned his gaze onto Mariana. 'And what,' he inquired, 'does the lady Mariam have to say? Does she, too, wish to dissolve her marriage to my son?'

Mariana blinked, hearing his version of her name. The Shaikh's gaze, deep and knowing, brought back their first encounter two years earlier when she had wanted to stay beside him forever in that dark, shadowed courtyard. He had read her thoughts so easily that night . . .

She would never see him again after her divorce, nor would she see his twin sister, the philosopher-poet whose presence had attracted her so strongly two years earlier, and whom she had longed to embrace during her last moments in this house. Never, she realized, had she been so powerfully drawn to anyone as she had been beckoned to these two. They had fired her imagination and drawn her heart as the flame beckons to the moth. Yet once she was divorced, Qamar Haveli and everyone in it would be as inaccessible to her as Heaven itself. Her beloved Saboor and his stranger father, the Shaikh and his sister would all disappear from her life, and with them the elusive something that had called to her, siren-like, throughout her stay in Calcutta.

Your path lies to the northwest, the man had told her at the

141

Charak Puka nine months months ago. *You must return there to find your destiny*.

Uncle Adrian nodded encouragingly. The Vulture stared impatiently through the doorway.

'Speak, Bibi,' commanded the Shaikh.

Chapter Sixteen

'Go on,' urged Uncle Adrian.

Mariana swallowed. 'I do not know, Shaikh Sahib,' she whispered, unable to stop herself. 'I do not know.'

Uncle Adrian started painfully, as if she had stabbed him in the back. The Vulture snorted, his face bunching in disgust.

What had she done? She leaned towards her uncle. 'I'm sorry, Uncle Adrian,' she murmured, reaching out to touch his arm. 'It's just that I—'

'Little fool!' snapped the Vulture. 'You've played right into his hands!'

Beyond the canvas screen, a man laughed.

'So,' the Shaikh observed, adjusting the shawl on his shoulders, 'Mariam Bibi is uncertain of her opinion.'

The Vulture smiled thinly. 'Of course she is uncertain, Shaikh Sahib. She is a woman. We all know how capricious—'

'Yes, she *is* a woman,' put in the Shaikh. His voice took on an instructive tone. 'Among Muslims, a woman must decide for herself regarding her marriage, and if necessary, her divorce. Since the dissolution of marriage is a very serious matter, if a woman wants to divorce her husband, she must say so herself.'

There was something immovable about the way he sat on his dais, his eyes fixed on his guests. Mariana stiffened beneath the Vulture's hot, angry gaze.

Uncle Adrian stirred uncomfortably. 'We did, of course, consult my niece before we came here. I don't understand how—'

'I should add,' the Shaikh continued, 'that our offer of marriage was made after much consideration. Mariam's bride gift has already been arranged. She now owns a house near Delhi Gate. It has a yellow door. We will show it to you. Her jewellery is with my sister.'

They had given her *property*? Mariana watched Uncle Adrian and the Vulture exchange an astonished glance.

'We have no intention of keeping of your gifts,' returned the Vulture sharply. 'We must not let him think he can buy the girl,' he murmured in English.

The Shaikh turned to Uncle Adrian. 'You suggest that Mariam will suffer among my family ladies. You should know that those ladies love and respect her, and that they have longed for her return since the day she left us.'

'Shaikh Sahib,' Uncle Adrian said carefully, 'we have no doubt that your family is kindly disposed towards my niece. It is just that we feel she should remain with her own people.'

The Shaikh inclined his head, causing his starched headdress to tip towards them. 'Lamb Sahib,' he said, 'you have stated your opinion, as I have stated mine. But the question of divorce is not ours to decide. If Mariam is, in fact, determined to divorce my son, they must decide together what is to be done. It is fortunate that Hassan is in Lahore,' he concluded, waving a hand towards the courtyard. 'He arrived only this morning to celebrate the return of his wife and son. He will meet Mariam in a moment, but first I will tell you a story. It is intended for Mariam, but I believe you gentlemen may find it interesting.'

Out of the Shaikh's sight, Mr Lewis's foot began to vibrate beneath his chair. Uncle Adrian took out a handkerchief and mopped his face.

'In his shop,' the Shaikh began unhurriedly, 'a jeweller sat before two heaps of semi-precious stones, picking stones from one heap and dropping them, one by one, onto the other.

'"What are you doing?" asked a passing friend.

'"I am sorting through my stones," replied the jeweller, "to make certain that there is no priceless gem among them."

'When the friend passed by again, he saw that the jeweller was now picking the same stones from the second heap and dropping them back onto the first.

'"What are you doing now?" asked the friend.

'"I was careless in my sorting," replied the jeweller, "and missed a lovely emerald. I am now trying to find it."

'"Ah, you are looking for an emerald," said the friend. "That explains why you have thrown away a diamond."'

The Shaikh did not look at Mariana, but she felt his attention on her, reading her thoughts, uncovering her secret hopes of Harry Fitzgerald.

'And now,' he said, gesturing towards the doorway, 'if you gentlemen will come with me I will take you to my visitors' room for green tea. Mariam Bibi may remain here to wait for my son. It is best, is it not, for husband and wife to make this decision alone?'

'Now see the damage you've caused,' hissed the Vulture as he passed Mariana on his way to the door.

'You little fool!' Uncle Adrian's voice trembled with anger. 'You should never have shown the strength of your feelings for Saboor. You have given the Shaikh exactly what he wants, and now you must face his son alone.' He gripped her above the elbow. 'Do *not* blunder again, Mariana. Say as little as possible, and *stick to your argument.*'

Left alone, Mariana looked about the chilly, whitewashed room. Now, at last, she understood what she wanted. She must somehow dissolve her marriage to Hassan without losing Saboor or his tantalizing family.

It should not be difficult to persuade Hassan to divorce her, provided that his pride did not complicate matters, for she was, of course, white. But surely he would see the benefit of marriage to one of his own women, someone who understood his habits, who would be satisfied to spend her life in the upstairs ladies' quarters.

But would he allow her to visit Qamar Haveli after it was over? She *must* find a way to embrace Saboor again, to sit once more in the presence of the Shaikh, to lean on a bolster on the floor of the ladies' sitting room and study the calm power that radiated from Safiya Sultana. She sighed. They were all of a piece, this fascinating trio: the prescient Saboor, his magnetic grandfather, Safiya herself . . .

Mariana pictured Safiya in the upstairs room overlooking the courtyard outside, presiding over the score of women of all sizes and ages who sat, shrouded in their soft, loose clothing, waiting for her.

When she had left that upstairs room two years ago, Mariana had failed to say goodbye. Ordered to kiss the silk-wrapped Qur'an, she had felt it pressed against her lips, and then had started down the stone staircase without a backward glance. The ladies had begun their waiting then. The force of their expectation seemed to reach into this room and wrap itself round Mariana's body, drawing her invisibly towards them.

Surely Safiya would see her passion for Saboor and her desire to understand them all. Surely, after the divorce, Safiya would give her the few days she needed, would allow her the time to say a proper goodbye . . .

The sun had moved off and the room became chilly. Mariana drew her shawls closer and pushed her hands into the sleeves of her gown.

A sound at the door made her start. A tall, familiar-looking man stepped into the room on bare feet and stopped short, studying her, his back to the light, a child wriggling in his arms.

'Peace,' he offered.

'An-nah, Abba is here!' Saboor struggled to get down, then rushed to Mariana and threw himself against her knees. Her eyes closed, she gathered him to her breast, but in a moment he had galloped away again and wrapped his arms about his father's leg with a child's fierce, rediscovered love.

'My father says you have something to tell me.' Hassan picked up his son and moved to the dais, his embroidered coat moving gracefully about his ankles. As he sat down and drew the child onto his lap his scent reached her, sweet, mysterious, different from the one she remembered.

He had changed. The broad, neatly bearded face she remembered had thinned. Beneath a crocheted skullcap, his eyes seemed wary and tired. He wore a distracted air, as if he had left important work to meet her. His eyes drifted towards the open doorway as if he were waiting for someone.

It would be best to speak plainly. 'I have come,' she announced, 'to ask for the dissolution of our marriage.'

Hassan stiffened under his elegant clothes. Saboor's animated body went still. An instant later he climbed down from his father's lap and ran out through the doorway, his face averted from Mariana's. She caught her breath, afraid he had understood her words.

'We do not know one another properly.' She forced the words out rapidly, schooling herself not to run after Saboor. 'Our worlds are different. My food, my customs, my language are all unlike yours.

I ride a *horse*. I go out dressed like *this*.' She pointed to her unveiled, bonneted self, her tight bodice, her English stripes, the shoes she should have taken off outside the doorway. 'How could I be happy, living here with your family?'

Hassan shrugged. 'You should have thought of all that before you accepted our proposal in front of the Maharajah's court two years ago. People are still laughing at the way you thrust yourself on us.'

Thrust yourself on us. So much for the supposed honour of having a white wife. 'But your father sent a letter proposing our marriage,' she insisted. 'I saw it myself.'

'That was a private matter, not something to be announced in public by the prospective bride.' He rested his elbows on his knees. Gold gleamed on brown, smoothly tapered fingers. She had forgotten the extraordinary beauty of his hands.

She took her eyes from his hands and drew herself up. 'I'm sorry if I offended you,' she said, 'and I'm sorry to have changed my mind. It's not that I do not like your family. I hope to be able to come back again and visit later on. But for now, please, just agree to divorce me.'

'And Saboor? What of him? Have you forgotten that you were seen in a dream, that you are his guardian for life?'

'*Please*,' she repeated, unable to stop herself from looking towards the door, 'do not speak of Saboor.'

'I married you for his sake,' he went on, pressing his advantage. 'It is your duty to protect him, and my duty to be your husband. How can you not understand this after two years?'

'But that dream came from *your* side,' she argued, 'not from mine. My people do not act upon dreams. How can I be held to a promise I never made?' She shivered, afraid he would refuse her.

He lifted his shoulders. 'But you *did* promise. You agreed to marry me. It is your kismet, your destiny to be here in the Punjab, with us.'

Your path lies to the northwest. You must return there to find your destiny.

Invisible coils seemed to tighten about her. Mariana swallowed, trying to distract herself from the soothsayer's words. Afghanistan, Kabul, were also in the northwest — Harry Fitzgerald was there, with his fine profile, his crooked, knowing smile. He would take her back, wouldn't he? He would give her children, wouldn't he? They would take Saboor's place in her heart, wouldn't they?

'Your clothes don't matter,' Hassan went on, changing the subject. 'My aunt Safiya has made you twenty-one changes of clothing. But please,' he added flatly, frowning at her, 'do something about your hair and attend to your skin. Your hair has fallen out of that thing you're wearing on your head, and I can see that it needs oiling. You were perfectly all right when I married you. I cannot imagine how you could have let yourself go like this. I hardly recognize you.'

'My appearance has nothing to do with this,' she replied as tartly as she could, pushing the offending curls out of sight. 'I am only trying to—'

'Hassan Sahib-Ji,' called a voice from behind the canvas wall. 'Faqeer Azizuddin is here to see you.'

'I must ask your leave to go.' Without waiting for her reply, Hassan gathered his fine coat around him and rose to his feet.

Mariana stared. 'But we haven't decided about—'

'You will stay here, of course.' He waved towards the row of filigreed windows overlooking the courtyard. 'My aunts have been waiting all morning for you,' he said as he stepped over the sitting-room threshold and into a pair of upturned, embroidered slippers. Unexpectedly, he offered her a half-smile. 'We will discuss this nonsense of yours later, when I can find the time.'

As he disappeared behind the canvas barrier, Mariana heard Saboor's excited voice. 'Where are we going now, Abba?' he cried.

A moment later, the call to prayer floated into the room from Wazir Khan's mosque. '*Allahu Akbar! Allahu Akbar!*' cried the muezzin from his minaret. 'God is great! God is great!'

'But how did you fail to make Hassan understand?' demanded Uncle Adrian fifteen minutes later, after he and the Vulture had come to fetch her. 'Did you not speak clearly? Have you forgotten your Urdu?'

'I was perfectly clear, Uncle Adrian,' Mariana replied a little sharply. 'Hassan did understand, but he hardly listened to what I was saying. Then someone called to him from outside, and he went away.'

'Did he show any sign of agreeing to the divorce?'

'He said I must stay here with his family, and that we can talk more about it when we meet again. He seems very busy at the Citadel.'

The realization struck her all at once: here was the perfect solution to her dilemma! If she stayed at the haveli now, she would be able to spend time with the Shaikh and his sister, and with Saboor, before the divorce. Then, having gained all she could from the Waliullah family, she would be better able to bear it if they refused to let her return.

'May I get my things and come back, Uncle Adrian?' Please, please, let me stay! Her eyes on his face, she ignored the Vulture, who twitched impatiently at her uncle's side.

'Don't be ridiculous, Mariana.' Her uncle's tone brooked no argument. 'You have no idea of the perils you would face, left alone with these people.'

'Wait.' His face brightening, the Vulture held up a bony hand.

'The Shaikh's son is assistant to the Foreign Minister, is he not?'

Mariana and her uncle nodded.

'And he was called away in the middle of an important interview with Miss Givens? Hah! I knew it. There must be news of Sher Singh. He must be coming to seize the city. Why else would Hassan have left so suddenly?'

Uncle Adrian stared. 'But what has—'

'The attack may be quite soon,' the Vulture went on. 'Miss Givens's divorce should be accomplished as rapidly as possible. If staying a night or two among the Shaikh's ladies is required for her to gain another interview with her husband, I see no harm in it. Moreover, any information Miss Givens might come upon while she stays with the natives of this house would be of immeasurable value to us. We are, of course, most interested in the fate of the Punjab.'

Of all people to have taken her side! Mariana beamed at him.

'You may see no harm in her staying here,' her uncle said sharply, 'but her aunt will take a *very* different view.'

Chapter Seventeen

13 January 1841

'You must be mad,' Aunt Claire cried the next morning from her folding chair in front of her tent. 'I will not allow Mariana to stay for one moment in a native city full of filth and disgusting diseases!' She glared at her husband from beneath her parasol. 'If you send her there, Adrian, I shall *never* speak to you again.'

'Yes, my dear,' he soothed, while Mariana fidgeted desperately beside him in a basket chair. 'I do not much like the idea myself, but in order to be divorced, Mariana must stay for a day or two with the child's family. We cannot give up now, after coming all this way. She has been there before, you know, and they have never done her any harm. Mr Lewis is very much in favour of the idea.'

'And what of the attack on the city that everyone is talking about? Mariana could be trapped in the fighting. She might be—'

'Sher Singh has not yet reached Lahore.' Uncle Adrian's chair creaked under him as he brushed an ant from his sleeve. 'Even after he comes, it will be some time before he is ready to storm the Citadel. Mariana must escape her marriage now, before the attack, if there is to be one. No one can guess what will happen to Lahore in the future. For all we know, a month from now it may be impossible even to enter the city.'

'If I do not go to Qamar Haveli now,' Mariana snapped, 'I shall never, *ever* be divorced.'

It was unfair to be short with Aunt Claire, but Mariana was too heartbroken and anxious to stop herself. She could think of nothing but Saboor.

Uncle Adrian's 'There, there, my dear, it is for the best' was all the sympathy she had received. Aunt Claire did not even acknowledge her grief.

No one at Shalimar understood her. Dittoo had refused to speak to her since she had told him the truth of her plan. Ghulam Ali had vanished without a word, back to his employment at the Shaikh's house, presumably too disgusted to say goodbye.

'Do not take your temper out on me, Mariana,' returned her aunt. 'If you must sit and scowl, then sit on a horse and scowl at the natives.'

'Yes, go on, Mariana,' agreed her uncle. 'It is a nice, bright day. A ride will do you good.'

When Mariana went to her tent, Dittoo was nowhere to be seen. Saboor's bedding was gone, and so were his small trunk of clothes and the little bullock cart with wheels which Ghulam Ali had carved for him. Her tent, for all its pleasant furnishings, looked comfortless and bare.

What was Saboor doing now? Did he miss her? Had he gone easily to sleep last night without her songs and nonsense rhymes? She *must* see him again. Otherwise, the cruel abruptness of their parting would poison the rest of her life.

Fighting tears, she struggled into her riding habit and top hat.

When Dittoo still did not appear, she shouted, her voice breaking, for the sweeper to go and call for a horse and groom.

How would she bear it if Aunt Claire forbade her to go to Qamar Haveli? What would happen if Sher Singh attacked the city before she was able to get to the Shaikh's house?

She raised her chin. She must not entertain such thoughts. Surely Aunt Claire would give in under pressure from Uncle Adrian and the Vulture, and allow her to return to the walled city. Surely Sher Singh would not appear with his army before then.

She opened her door blind and nodded to the frail young groom who had brought her mare. One thing was certain. If she were allowed to return to Qamar Haveli she would stay there more than one or two days. In fact, she would remain in the walled city as long as she possibly could.

As she rode towards the garden's main entrance, she saw the Vulture sitting outside his tent, deep in conversation with two coarsely turbaned men who squatted on the ground by his chair, long-barrelled jezails slung across their backs. A heavily loaded camel knelt nearby. The men looked like tribesmen of some kind, Afghans perhaps. The Vulture glanced up from his visitors and offered her a conspiratorial nod. She replied with a small nod of her own. Without his support she would never go back to Qamar Haveli. It seemed the least she could do.

God willing, she would leave for Qamar Haveli the next morning. An hour after that, she would again hold Saboor in her arms.

The road west of Shalimar was quiet. A herd of bleating goats, a file of women with baskets on their heads and a group of mounted soldiers wearing chain mail vests over their ordinary clothes were all the traffic Mariana saw as she followed the old road past a deserted walled garden and several small mud villages. A well creaked in the distance, powered by a pair of oxen. The air smelled of dust and dung fires.

An interesting-looking ruin, a house perhaps, or a tomb, lay a quarter of a mile off, between two large stands of thorn trees. Intrigued, Mariana rode towards it, but before she had reached its outer wall the sound of hoofbeats and shouting arose behind her.

A runaway horse galloped towards her across a stretch of open ground, its rider swaying dangerously on its back. Far behind, two men, presumably the horse's grooms, pelted along on foot, losing ground with every step. A large cloud of dust enveloped the runaway animal and it took Mariana a moment to realize that the horse was Ali Baba and his imperilled rider was Lady Macnaghten. An instant later, the horse thundered past, foaming at the mouth, with Lady Macnaghten flopping blindly on his back, her top hat fallen over her eyes, the reins lost, her arms about his neck.

The grooms were too far behind to be of any use. Mariana kicked her mare and gave chase.

The mare would be no match, even for a tiring Ali Baba. In the event he changed direction and careered right, towards a mud village, whose entire population seemed to have emerged from their homes to watch the show. A hundred yards from its walls Ali Baba halted abruptly and stood still, his head hanging, as if he wanted someone to tell him what to do next.

This last was too much for his tottering passenger. As he came to a stop, Lady Macnaghten toppled slowly from the saddle and lay unmoving in a heap of expensive grey worsted, her dented riding hat beside her on the ground.

The villagers and Mariana all arrived simultaneously upon the scene. She glanced behind her, to see Lady Macnaghten's two grooms sloping towards them, in no hurry, it seemed, to learn the outcome of this disaster.

Without being asked, a square, barefoot man took hold of Ali Baba's bridle and led him a little way off, while the others gathered in a silent circle about Lady Macnaghten, their brown faces intent.

Mariana was about to dismount when Lady Macnaghten rose painfully to her feet and took in the villagers standing shoulder to shoulder around her.

'My horse!' She cried out in English. 'Where is my horse?'

When the people crowded closer without answering, she spun about in a circle, her eyes wide beneath dusty, loosening hair. 'Which of you has stolen Ali Baba?'

She did not see Mariana dismount and hand the mare's reins to a bystander. 'Make way,' Mariana ordered quietly.

The crowd parted obligingly, revealing Lady Macnaghten who was now dancing with rage and fright in its centre.

'I'll have you all hanged,' she shouted, still in English. 'Hanged, I say! I'll teach you steal an Englishwoman's horse!'

At the sight of Mariana, she blinked as if she had seen a mirage.

'The villagers mean you no harm,' Mariana offered, as she bent to rescue Lady Macnaghten's sadly dented top hat. 'They are only curious. Ali Baba is here,' she added, taking Lady Macnaghten's arm. 'He seems quiet enough now, but I think you should get onto my mare. I will ride Ali Baba back to Shalimar.'

Lady Macnaghten's grooms arrived and helped her onto Mariana's mare, where she sat shakily, kneading her right arm. Still holding the top hat, Mariana climbed onto the drooping, sweat-covered Ali Baba, then clucked encouragingly. Without another word they set off at a walk for the camp.

The road in front of them was quiet. A bullock cart creaked along, piled high with straw. The armed soldiers rode past again, this time going the other way, guarding a quick-moving donkey cart in which two bareheaded prisoners, their arms tied behind their backs, struggled to keep their balance. A man followed them on foot, leading a loaded camel.

Mariana pointed to a stand of trees. 'Shall we stop there?' she asked politely, not certain how to treat this new, weakened version of Lady Macnaghten. 'We can get off some of the dust.'

'It was a cobra,' Lady Macnaghten offered a little querulously, when they reached the trees. 'I had intended to go for only a short ride, but when we passed some thorn trees, it reared up unexpectedly. Ali Baba saw it first. He bolted before I even took in what it was.'

'Hm-m.' Mariana did not believe her; it was such an obvious untruth. Lady Macnaghten, stiff, awkward rider that she was, had been quite mad to ride Ali Baba, and he had simply taken advantage of her. But one thing was clear, the woman had nerve: first to have ridden the Arab, and second to have defended him, however wrongly, against the villagers. Courage was the last virtue Mariana had expected to find in Lady Macnaghten.

'Mr Lewis advised me this morning not to ride such a difficult horse. My husband, too, begged me never to do it.' Lady Macnaghten pushed her fallen hair from her face and sighed tragically. 'I only wanted to give him a little exercise.'

Mariana nodded silently. She had done more than that. She had worn him out.

'I am afraid of what they will say.' Lady Macnaghten's voice trembled. 'I fear they will all laugh at me.'

'Laugh at you? There's no one at camp but us.'

'Mr Lewis will laugh at me. He's not a nice man, you know. He'll tell the other officers, and they'll tell more people. You do not know how much I dread being talked about.'

Speechless at the irony of this remark, Mariana could only look away.

'What am I to do?' Lady Macnaghten went on, poking dispiritedly at her ruined habit. 'I have hurt my arm, and I cannot even get the dust off my other side. How can I return to camp like this?' She swallowed. 'I have been unkind to you,' she whispered. 'I thought you had – but you hadn't. My husband told me all about it. I do not know what to do about Charles, after he did that awful . . .' She looked away. 'Your face at dinner that evening – I realized what had happened. He has done it before. That is how I knew it was him.'

Mariana did not reply. Instead she nudged Ali Baba closer, and brushed the dust from Lady Macnaghten's riding clothes. She knocked the dents from the top hat and set it on Lady Macnaghten's head.

'Why,' asked Lady Macnaghten, her eyes still averted, 'are you being so good to me after we have all been so cruel?'

She had been cruel, but now she was bruised, frightened, and as dishevelled as Mariana had ever been. And she had the nerve to ride an impossible horse against everyone's advice, and stand up to native villagers in spite of her fears.

Without answering, Mariana took out her pocket handkerchief and carefully wiped the dust and the tears of shame from Lady Macnaghten's face.

Chapter Eighteen

'So,' Yusuf Bhatti asked that same afternoon as he and Hassan returned from Batala for the second time that week, 'now that Sher Singh is preparing to attack Lahore, is there a chance that the Rani will soften her position and allow him to rule?'

'No chance at all. She has been buying every general she can find with cash and treasure. Sher Singh is doing the same, of course. Between them, they have entirely corrupted our magnificent army.' He slapped dust from his clothes. 'The sirdars are choosing sides now, each man desperate to be in the winning camp.' He sighed. 'I suppose one cannot blame people for trying to save themselves when their very lives and fortunes are at stake.'

They edged their way past a file of heavily loaded camels. 'I tell you, Yusuf, more than anything I fear the double-dealing of the British. From what I can tell, their Political Agent is deeply involved in the dispute between the Rani and Sher Singh. He has been making promises and giving encouragement to both sides. Few people see it, Yusuf, but I believe the British are the real enemy of the Punjab.'

'I hate to mention this, but have you considered your wife's position?' Yusuf paused, choosing his words carefully. 'Is it possible that the same Political Agent has ordered her to—'

'No,' Hassan snapped. 'He has not. But then there is . . .' He looked away from his friend, his shoulders sagging.

Yusuf sighed. The woman had been in Lahore for only two days, and he could see that she was already giving Hassan trouble. The poor fellow had no luck with females. It should have been enough that his first wife died.

Yusuf believed Hassan should marry again. Ever since the English-woman's departure two years earlier, Yusuf had done his best to hammer sense into his friend. Prevented by delicacy from inquiring into Hassan's private feelings about the woman, he had nonetheless offered his advice, first suggesting, then encouraging, and finally ordering that Hassan to take another, Punjabi, wife.

'Our women are beautiful,' he had insisted. 'They are the envy of India. A good Punjabi wife will give you six, seven more sons.'

But Hassan had remained immovable. 'Yusuf,' he had said finally, 'our family men do not keep two wives.'

Yusuf had dropped the subject after that. There was no sense in arguing with the Waliullahs. Like all mystics, they were an impractical lot who relied upon dreams and visions when they ought to be using reason. It had been exactly like Shaikh Waliullah, God bless him, to force his son to wed a foreign woman because of a horse groom's dream, and it was just like the son to stubbornly refuse to see the hopelessness of his marriage. What did Hassan see in that noisy, unmanageable woman, beyond her fondness for his son? Surely he had not come to love her . . .

As they waited for her return, Yusuf had tried to forget what he had witnessed two years before: that same female writhing on the floor of her tent in agony from snakebite, her clothing bunching about her legs. It had covered him with shame to have seen the face of his friend's second wife. That he had seen more than her face was too horrible to dwell upon.

To be sure, she had proved herself courageous by rescuing Saboor twice from serious danger, but in Yusuf's view nothing she had done warranted Hassan's chaining himself to her for ever. If only there were some way to get him out of that mistaken alliance.

'The British are trying to dissolve my marriage,' Hassan said abruptly.

'What? How do you know?' Yusuf slapped at a fly on his horse's neck, concealing his satisfaction at this news.

'Their Political Agent and her uncle brought my wife to Qamar Haveli yesterday. They tried to make my father agree to a divorce. The reasons they offered were complete nonsense. When my father asked her straight out whether she wished to divorce me, she could not reply. When I spoke to her myself later on, she became confused.' He smiled bitterly. 'I don't think she could remember what they told her to say.'

'But why would the British interfere with your family matters? Surely they have more serious work to do.'

'Perhaps they wish to sever my wife's connection with Lahore before Sher Singh attacks. If so, then at least they are honourable enough to protect one of their women.'

Yusuf nodded. 'When will Sher Singh march on Lahore?'

Hassan shrugged. 'Soon, if things continue as they are. By the time this contest is finished, nothing will be left of the kingdom.'

A hollow booming came from the direction of the city. Yusuf raised his head. 'Artillery fire! What are those fools doing now?'

They urged their horses into a gallop, the two men leaning forward, their loose clothing flapping behind them.

A messenger rode out through the Delhi Gate and waved to

them. 'Come quickly,' he shouted above the bustle of the crowded roadway. 'They are blowing men from cannon!'

On the plain below the Citadel's walls, a large body of infantry, some in flowing native dress, others in European coats and cross belts, had been marshalled to form three sides of a square. Inside the square, a trio of twelve-pound cannon had been set up to face the open side. Trussed and tied over the mouths of the guns were three men, one of them only a boy, scarcely old enough to have a beard.

'Sons of foulness.' Yusuf cursed loudly as he and Hassan guided their mounts through a thick press of shouting onlookers, all striving for a better view. 'Which sons of shame have done this?'

'Lower your voice, Yusuf,' Hassan cautioned. 'This is what the Rani does to please the British. She cannot give them the Koh-i-noor diamond, so she executes Afghans to please them.'

The condemned men did not flinch. None of the three faces showed fear, not even the boy's, but their bodies had already betrayed them. Yusuf could see that their hands and feet had gone rigid, and that the boy's shalwar was soaked from his groin to his ankles.

'Look there.' Yusuf gestured. 'They have caught your trader and his fat-faced assistant.'

Hassan followed his friend's gaze. Across the firing ground, guarded by soldiers, a dozen more Afghans squatted in a line, their heads bared, their arms tied behind their backs. Some had narrow, hawk-like faces and some did not, but all had the same emotionless demeanour as the men on the guns. All save two were dressed in coarse, ragged clothing.

'You said you did not trust Zulmai and his friend,' Yusuf commented. 'Perhaps you were right.'

Hassan stared at him. 'Those men are human beings, Yusuf.'

Someone shouted an order. The three cannon fired, almost in unison.

A cloud of black smoke obscured the scene in front of the gun barrels, then drifted towards the two horsemen as they calmed their startled mounts.

When the smoke lifted, Yusuf grunted in disgust.

The ground in front of the cannon was sprayed with blood. Body parts littered the dirt. Prodded by their officers, a few reluctant soldiers tied their turban ends over their faces and moved to cut down the shredded remains that still hung from the gun barrels.

Hassan rode his horse towards the line of Afghan prisoners. Following behind him, Yusuf noticed a tall European in dusty black clothes standing at the front of the pushing crowd, observing the carnage with undisguised satisfaction. While Yusuf watched, the man glanced towards the waiting prisoners, caught the Afghan trader's eye, and started abruptly.

'What is this?' Hassan had reined in his horse. He glared down at the Punjabi officer guarding the trussed prisoners. 'What have these men done? Who has ordered these executions?'

From the corner of his eye, Yusuf watched the foreigner move closer, then hesitate, listening.

The officer shrugged. 'The Rani's orders,' he replied. 'These men are unregistered criminals.'

Beside Zulmai, young Habibullah looked up, hope lighting his face. The other prisoners knelt impassively on the ground.

Hassan pointed to the two traders. 'These men are no criminals. I know them personally. Let them go at once.'

'They are spies for the Rani's enemies,' offered a soldier, pointing his gun barrel into Habibullah's face for emphasis.

'No, they are spies for the British,' put in another.

'Let them go,' Hassan repeated.

The officer spat. 'Pathans are vermin. They rob and beat people for nothing. They kill the English who travel through the passes.' He gestured vaguely. 'Even if these men have not yet committed such crimes, they will. They always do. Why should we wait? We may as well kill them now.'

'Let them go, son of a pig!' Yusuf bellowed. 'These men are not even Pathans. Can you not tell a Tajik when you see one?'

'Wait, Yusuf,' Hassan murmured. He dismounted and approached the officer. 'Come this way if you will,' he said politely, gesturing away from the soldiers and their prisoners. 'We can speak over there.'

As Hassan and the officer moved away, Yusuf looked for the black-coated Englishman, but he was gone.

A moment later, Hassan and the officer returned. While Yusuf watched, the officer jerked his head towards Zulmai and Habibullah. 'You may leave now,' he grunted, then glowered his startled men into silence. He pointed towards the back of the crowd. 'Your camel is over there. As for the rest of you,' he jerked his head, 'go.'

'But why are you setting them free? You have only killed six of them!' shouted someone in the crowd.

'Do not let them go! Kill them, kill them!' shouted the others.

The officer waved his musket menacingly. 'Disperse!' he thundered. 'Disperse, before we kill you instead.'

'Do not cut it,' said Zulmai sharply a little while later, his upper arms still tied behind his back. 'That's my turban.'

'So it is.' Yusuf sheathed his knife, then smiled crookedly at the sight of Hassan carefully untying the yards of coarse cotton fabric holding Zulmai's arms together.

Habibullah had already kissed their hands in gratitude. Zulmai had merely nodded his thanks. The twelve other men now filed past, each one with his right hand pressed over his heart in grateful acknowledgement.

When his arms were free, Zulmai rubbed them and flexed his fingers to restore circulation. '"Oh heart, when a time of sorrow overtakes thee,"' he quoted, '"It will vanish if thou hast a kind friend. Friends are commonplace in times of comfort, but in a time of trouble, one friend is enough."'

Hassan smiled. 'You flatter me, Zulmai, to be reciting Jami over such a small matter.'

Later, as they rode towards the city, Yusuf glanced at Hassan's unadorned hands and let out his barking laugh. 'I hope,' he said, 'that you weren't too attached to those gold rings of yours.'

Chapter Nineteen

14 January 1841

When Hassan Ali Khan's foreign wife had arrived at Qamar Haveli two days earlier after a two-year absence, all the Waliullah women, even Safiya Sultana herself, had hurried to the verandah windows to look down through the filigreed shutters to the scene in the courtyard below.

Little Akhtar had stood with the other servants at a window with a lesser view, sharing the ladies' pleasure as they watched a small child who resembled Hassan Ali climb out of the palanquin, then run round the canvas screen and into the arms of his waiting father. But it was Hassan's foreign wife who had interested the girl more. Revealed in a horse groom's dream as a lioness, she had apparently rescued Saboor twice from Maharajah Ranjit Singh, thus meriting the honour of becoming Shaikh Waliullah's daughter-in-law.

While the ladies exclaimed over Saboor's beauty, his healthy energy, and his father's obvious joy at his return, Akhtar had wondered about the woman who had performed those feats of bravery and won the family's heart. Surely she must be tall and queenly, as elegant as her husband, someone whose superior character was written in her every gesture . . .

Akhtar had been stunned at the dishevelled figure that emerged from the palanquin next, a figure so odd that Akhtar had thought she must be dreaming. The woman's boldly striped garment, shockingly tight at the bodice, had been so wide from the waist down that her legs might have been terribly deformed for all anyone could tell. A basket headdress obscured her face. Escaped hair tumbled carelessly onto her shoulders. She was the strangest creature Akhtar had ever seen, but when a foreign man in black dismounted and disappeared with her into the Shaikh's sitting room, it was plain that she was indeed Saboor Baba's legendary guardian.

The ladies and the other servants had drifted away after that, to await the woman's arrival upstairs, but Akhtar had not left her post at the window. Anxious to see the extraordinary creature again, she had watched Shaikh Waliullah and two foreigners emerge from the sitting room, to be replaced shortly afterwards by Hassan Ali Khan himself, who swept out of sight over the threshold in his long embroidered coat, the child Saboor in his arms.

It had been Akhtar who had witnessed Hassan's foreign wife come out again. It had been she who had reported that, instead of climbing the stone stairs to the family quarters, the woman had re-entered her palanquin and left the haveli with the foreign men.

That unexpected and disappointing departure had been explained later, when Hassan Ali Khan brought his son upstairs and lowered himself to the sheet-covered floor beside his aunt while the other children, boys and girls, clustered, crooning, about Saboor.

'The British are asking for our marriage to be dissolved,' Hassan told his aunt quietly, overheard only by Akhtar, who should have removed herself from the room when he entered but who had remained, wrapped to her eyes, for decency's sake, in a large veil.

'They say Mariam agrees, but I believe they are forcing her.' He gestured tiredly as Saboor rushed away with two older children. 'Those people like to meddle in all our affairs . . .'

Safiya Sultana had laid a plump hand on his knee. 'Do not worry, my dear,' she said in her husky voice. 'Allah is kind. Let her come here. Let us see what can be done.'

When the same palanquin had returned this morning, the ladies crowded the windows once again. This time Hassan Ali Khan's wife did not depart. Instead, she disappeared into the doorway that led upstairs.

Moments later, a rustling in the verandah announced her arrival.

Akhtar stared open-mouthed at the creature who now stood uncertainly in the doorway on none-too-clean stockinged feet, her skirts billowing about her, her bodice revealing the swell of her breasts, a headdress decorated with dusty ribbons dangling from her hand.

Close up, she was startlingly unattractive. Her features appeared sharp and intense. The front of her hair was dry, and her skin looked chapped. Akhtar, who had been studying the beautification of ladies for months, found herself longing to do something about the woman's hands. But for all the foreigner's plainness, when Saboor Baba ran to her and she knelt in the doorway to embrace him, her face softened and took on a curious beauty.

'Peace,' rumbled Safiya Sultana, approaching them, the silk-wrapped Qur'an in her hand, 'and welcome to your home.'

Hassan's wife jumped to her feet and saluted Safiya respectfully, the closed fingers of her right hand to her forehead, while Saboor darted ahead of her into the room. 'Peace upon you, Bhaji,' she replied in slow, perfect Urdu. 'Forgive me, I—'

'There is nothing to forgive.' Holding the book high, Safiya Sultana motioned for her to walk under it. Then she tucked the book into a high cupboard and moved to her usual place against one of the walls. 'Come. Sit with me.'

Akhtar poured a tumbler of water for the new arrival, who sat stiffly upright beside Safiya Sultana, as if her clothing would not allow her to relax.

Why, Akhtar wondered, did the lady's people want to dissolve her marriage? It was possible that Hassan Ali might be an unsatisfactory husband, a wife-beater, or an impotent man, but there had been no time for these difficulties to make themselves known. Everyone knew the lady had left Qamar Haveli the morning after her wedding and had not returned until this moment. If she divorced Hassan, she would leave him wifeless for the second time in two years. Yet if she remained, her frayed intensity would certainly jar the calm atmosphere of the Shaikh's household.

Apparently untroubled by the oddness of the woman beside her, Safiya Sultana gave a satisfied sigh and reached over to pinch Saboor Baba's cheek.

What special information did Safiya have about Saboor's guardian? Akhtar wondered. Was it really Safiya, after all, and not some lesser person who was the caster of spells?

For all her close observation, Akhtar had not yet learned anything of Safiya Sultana's healing methods, although she had seen their effect. She had recently witnessed the return of the barren woman who had come a few months earlier – now pregnant and offering tears of gratitude and a gift of honey from her village. Akhtar had seen the calming of a little boy who had suffered frightening dreams after his father's death, and a number of other lesser cures, but she was still no closer to the truth of how these healings occurred. Nothing had yet explained the sense of peace that she had felt from the moment she fell down the stairs and into Safiya Sultana's care, her need to offer her prayers when Safiya did, or her desire to emulate Safiya's every move.

'Akhtar,' Safiya ordered, 'take Mariam Bibi's things from the trunk in my room and help her choose something to wear.'

While the foreigner stood in the doorway, Akhtar tugged the trunk from its corner and raised its lid. Inside were twenty-one sets of clothes, each one basted into a neat, individual packet. They were all alike: a pair of shalwar – loose, baggy trousers – a camisole, a long kameez to go over it, and a dupatta to be worn as a veil over the head and upper body, but they varied in the weight of their fabric and the elaborateness of their decoration. Some were of made starched, embroidered muslin for summer, and others were of thicker cotton for the colder months. Eight sets were of silk, of varying degrees of formality, each with a delicately embroidered design on kameez and dupatta. There were shawls of many colours. Everything was of the finest quality, Akhtar noticed without surprise as she laid them out on Sasfiya's spartan string bed.

'I shall wear this one.' Hassan's wife pointed to a set of yellow clothes, and a fine pale yellow shawl, richly embroidered in green and violet. When Akhtar looked closely, she saw she had been mistaken about the shawls. This one was old, with a tiny brown stain at its edge. She tried to conceal her shock at this discovery. How terrible, to give old things to a family bride . . .

She tore open the threads holding the suit of clothes together, shook out the camisole, kameez, and dupatta and laid them on the bed. Then she threaded a waist-cord into the shalwar.

It would not take much to smooth the frizz from the lady's hair or relieve her chapped lips and roughened hands, but Hassan Ali's wife refused Akhtar's offer to oil her hair and rough skin.

'I have no need of your help,' the lady said, politely enough, pushing dry curls behind her ears, 'I will not be—' She stopped abruptly with a little intake of breath.

So it was true, thought Akhtar. The lady did not intend to stay.

Akhtar nodded to Mariana and left the room, closing the double doors behind her. Hassan's wife obviously preferred to struggle alone with the many fastenings of her foreign clothing.

Her refusal to be oiled disappointed Akhtar; she had seen an opportunity to display her skills, for in the past months it had become her duty to maintain the family women. Although there was little idleness in the Waliullah household, all the ladies needed the basic attentions — their body hair removed, their eyebrows shaped, their hair and skin oiled. For years this work had been done by Safiya's ancient servant Firoz, but it had now fallen to Akhtar and her light-fingered touch. She performed each task with her usual energy, perfecting her skills as she worked.

There was plenty to do. With no rain for the past month, the winter air of Lahore had become so dry that even Safiya Sultana, who never wasted time on such activities, had asked Akhtar to massage oil into her thinning, iron-grey hair.

The ladies, who had been talking eagerly among themselves, fell silent again as the doors opened and the foreign woman stepped smiling into the room, then stopped short, her eyes on the place where she had been sitting. It was now occupied by two small girls who knelt beside Safiya Sultana, their shoulders touching, nodding as the older woman spoke to them.

The lioness looked better in normal clothes, Akhtar decided. Her movements were more graceful than she had thought they would be, but the lady clearly did not know how to wear the shawl, and her hair, which should have hung down her back in a single plait, was still pinned loosely to her head, much of it escaping onto her neck. She paused, her mouth turning down, her eyes sweeping the room, then went to sit alone beneath a window, while around her the ladies made space.

'An-nah!' Saboor Baba threw himself into her lap. 'Where did you go? Why have you put on new clothes?'

She said nothing, only embraced him, her gaze on the open window. When he leaned against her breast, she began to croon some rhyming nonsense to him in a foreign tongue.

As she sang, Hassan Ali Khan's green-eyed wife emanated such sadness that the other women looked away, as if they were unwilling to intrude upon such pain. If anyone had asked Akhtar, she would have said that of all the women in Lahore who required the mysterious services of Safiya Sultana, the one who needed them most was the wife of Safiya's own nephew.

Chapter Twenty

'Diddle diddle dumpling, my son John, went to bed with his trousers on . . .'

Mariana bent over Saboor, ignoring the glances of the shrouded, whispering figures around her. It was silly to feel hurt because those two little girls had usurped her place beside Safiya Sultana. It was perverse to want Safiya to stop talking to the girls, to look up, to smile, to notice her in her native clothes.

But silly or not, as she sat beneath the latticed window, she ached with an all too familiar loneliness and humiliation.

It had not occurred to her that this might happen. Early in the morning, having at last received permission to stay at Qamar Haveli, she had thought only of Saboor, and of her soon-to-be-satisfied fascination with the Shaikh and his twin sister. Imagining Saboor sitting on her lap while great vistas of mysterious knowledge opened before her, she had flung her hairbrushes and a change of clothes into her smallest trunk and waved a cheerful goodbye to her bewildered aunt and uncle. It must be a rare household that boasted both a respected Sufi Shaikh and a person like Safiya Sultana. How many

Englishwomen, she had wondered as her bearers huffed along the dusty road from Shalimar, had spent even a morning with such a family?

Her head full of dreams, she had been halfway up the stairs to the ladies' quarters before it occurred to her that there would be more to this reunion than she had imagined. They knew of her request for a divorce. Safiya and all the family must already be aware that she had returned from Calcutta only to reject Hassan as her husband, and to abandon Saboor.

As she had bent to untie her boots outside the sitting-room doorway, her thoughts had been racing. How would the family treat her? Would they refuse to acknowledge her presence, then speak loudly and disparagingly of her within her hearing, as the English did? She had managed to survive those cruelties – she despised Calcutta society, after all – but this haveli, with its mysteries and magnetism, was no Calcutta bungalow. Rejection by the Waliullah ladies, she feared, would hurt her more than she could bear.

But Saboor had come running, and Safiya Sultana had followed, marching towards her on flat, purposeful feet, the wrapped Qur'an in her hand. *There is nothing to forgive*, she had said.

Now the women murmured to each other, too softly for her to hear. No one spoke to her, only Saboor, who soon wriggled off her lap when a curly-haired child approached and beckoned to him.

Across the room, Safiya Sultana cleared her throat. 'It is time,' she declared, her gaze sweeping the room like that of an experienced governess, 'for us to speak of beggars.'

Mariana bit her lip. Perhaps she should not have come.

'I am certain,' Safiya began in her deep voice, 'that all of you remember that we agreed some time ago that all beggars, however filthy or ill, offer something beautiful to those who give them charity. While we recognized that some offer thanks or blessings, we also

174

asked what the beggar offers who neither thanks nor blesses. Aliya here has found the answer.' She looked at one of the two girls sitting beside her. 'Speak,' she ordered. 'Tell us what you have learned.'

Hand in hand, the two children turned solemnly to face the room. 'Even the most dirty beggar,' piped the smaller of the two, 'offers an opportunity to please God.'

Safiya nodded. 'That is correct. No one offers that opportunity as plainly and simply as the beggar does. It is his purpose in being a beggar, whether he has asked for that duty or not. And of course God's pleasure is hidden in our good deeds, and his blessings are far better than any human bounty, thanks, or praise.'

Mariana bit her lip. How many good deeds had she done recently? She had certainly offered no charity to any of the ghostly, unnerving beggars she had seen outside the gate at Shalimar. *Do not give them anything,* the Vulture had instructed her. *If you do, hundreds more will come.*

'But what if a beggar only pretends to be poor?' asked a boy who looked like Aliya's elder brother.

Safiya smiled. 'In that case, Munawar, we remember our Prophet, who said, "Give to those who deserve, and to those who do not. It may be that God will give you something you do not deserve." We must be kind to all God's creatures,' she added, glancing at Mariana, 'for those who are in need do not always ask for help. We must also remember that each one of us is a beggar before God.'

Mariana shrank into her yellow shawl, aching for this wise woman to include her, to meet her eyes.

'And now,' Safiya continued, 'I will tell you a story, or rather the first part of it, for it is too long to tell all at once.'

Around Mariana, women murmured with anticipation. Across the room, a fat, serious-looking girl dragged Saboor onto her lap.

Safiya looked about her, signalled for Akhtar to sit and listen, and then for a brief moment looked straight into Mariana's eyes.

'Far away in the north,' she began in a singsong tone, shifting her gaze from Mariana, 'lived a king whose rich palace overlooked a teeming city. When his three sons were grown, feeling the need to choose his successor, the king called his eldest son to his side.

'The king gave the prince, who was a fastidious fellow, two silver coins and the garb of a merchant. "Go into the city, my son," he said, "and observe the comings and goings of the people. If Allah wills, you will gain knowledge that will one day help you rule this kingdom. You may return to the palace when you have found a worthwhile use for your two silver coins."

'The prince put on his disguise and set off, but before the sun had set he returned to the palace. "Father," he said sadly, "I wanted to do as you told me, but in all the city I could find no clean, sweet-smelling place to sit while I watched the comings and goings of the people. All I found were dirty upturned stones or the worn steps of houses to sit upon. As I could not follow your first instruction, I never came to the second."'

An elderly, round-backed lady near Mariana sniffed. 'Silly fellow,' she murmured, 'what did he expect to find in a city?'

Mariana glanced at her, surprised. Surely this lady had never looked out of her closed palanquin, even when travelling through Lahore's cobbled alleys . . .

'Disappointed in the eldest prince,' Safiya continued, 'the king sent for his second son, a person of exemplary behaviour. He gave the young man the same merchant's clothing, the same two silver coins, and the same advice that he had given his first son.

'The younger man set off as his brother had done but he, too, returned before the evening. "Father," he wept, "I wanted to observe the comings and goings of the people, but wherever I

176

went I saw thieves and cutpurses, gamblers and dishonest merchants. Distressed by the vices of the city, I found nothing to buy with my two silver coins."

'The old king sighed and sent for his third and last son, a playful, inquisitive young man. "My boy," he said sorrowfully, "I have failed to teach my sons enough of the world beyond this comfortable palace. Had I foreseen how much the city would disappoint them, I would have warned your brothers before sending them there. But having given them no advice, I cannot favour you. Go, wear this merchant's garb and observe the comings and goings of the people. When you return, you must tell me what you learned there, and what you found to do with your two silver coins."'

The women nodded and exchanged glances. Mariana fidgeted, uncomfortably aware that she, the children, and the bird-like servant girl who was listening open-mouthed were the only people in the room who had not heard this story before. Had there been a veiled message in Safiya's expression when she looked into her face before beginning the story?

Safiya shifted her bulk against her satin bolster. 'As his brothers had done,' she told them, 'the youngest prince set out for the city. There he found cobbled streets lined with houses whose latticed balconies nearly touched each other, so narrow was the way. He met musicians, jugglers, tinsmiths, thieves, and rich men. He saw baskets heaped with bright-coloured spices, and shopkeepers weighing mouth-watering fruit on iron scales. Customers lounged on carpets while barefoot merchants unrolled jewel-coloured silks for their inspection. Gold and diamond merchants displayed their wares in tiny stalls near fragrant shops selling attar and incense.'

So this was how the round-backed lady had received her know-ledge of the walled city she had never seen . . .

'At nightfall,' Safiya continued, 'tired and hungry, the prince sought rest in a teashop. As he sat enjoying his tea, a beggar shuffled towards him. The man was bent nearly double, and smelled so foul that the people moved out of his way, grimacing with disgust.

'"Alms," the beggar whined, crouching beside the prince, "alms to help me pass the night."

'Moved to pity, the prince smiled. "My friend," he replied, "I have only two silver coins. The first will pay for this bread and tea, but you are welcome to the second. As for passing the night, I, too, have nowhere to sleep."'

'But why did he have nowhere to sleep, Bhaji?' inquired a small boy, his voice full of concern.

Safiya smiled. 'He had stayed too long in the city, Rehman. But you must wait for the rest of the story.

'The prince gave the beggar his second coin,' she continued. 'At once the beggar reached into a sack he carried and drew out a lovely silk carpet, woven in many colours, more fine and supple than any in the king's palace. "Offer your prayers on this carpet and give regular charity," he said, handing it to the astonished prince, "and you will always have enough to eat and a fine resting place." And with that, he was gone.'

'Bhaji, Bhaji,' little Aliya burst in, 'the youngest prince pleased God and then received a blessing, did he not?'

'Indeed he did, my darling,' rumbled Safiya Sultana. 'But you must let me finish.

'That night the prince spread his new carpet in a doorway, offered his evening prayers to Allah, the Sender of Blessings, and lay down. At once the rank, gutter smells of the city vanished, and the air was filled with the scent of jasmine and roses, amber and musk. The shuttered silence of the street was gone, and in its place was the sweet sound of playing water and the cry of the nightingale. Beneath the carpet the prince felt soft grass. Too tired to wonder

178

about such mysteries, he closed his eyes, and in an instant fell deeply asleep.

'The next morning, as he stood to offer his dawn prayer to Allah, the Satisfier of Needs, he found two silver coins lying on the edge of his beautiful carpet.'

Safiya dropped her hands, indicating that she was finished.

A satisfied murmuring filled the room. Mariana glanced about her, startled to realize that in her imagination the prince, soberly disguised in coarse wool and a plain, starched turban, had been Hassan Ali Khan.

'When I get married,' announced little Aliya, 'my husband will be exactly like that prince.'

Chapter Twenty-One

Sent to the kitchen to help old Firoz with the afternoon meal, Akhtar squatted on the stone floor across from the two great wood-burning stoves, a stack of worked copper trays at her feet. Beside her, piled high on banana leaves, ninety-four large rounds of bread waited to be added to the trays. Akhtar knew there were ninety-four because Safiya Sultana had counted them five minutes earlier, during her customary pre-meal kitchen visit.

'Never try to steal food,' a burly cook had cautioned Akhtar on her first day of kitchen duty. 'Safiya Bhaji has the eyes of a vulture and the memory of an elephant.'

As an apprentice ladled boiled lentils, curried goat with turnips, and spiced chicken into the serving dishes, Akhtar thought about her dreams.

The first had come unexpectedly seven nights earlier, as she lay waiting for sleep in the servants' quarters. Fully formed, unclear as to its meaning, the vision had intruded upon memories of her village childhood, confronting her with the unfamiliar picture of a woman sitting beside an open gate, her figure nearly obscured by a multitude of rose petals that blew out though the opening and enveloped her.

The woman and her cloud of roses had remained with Akhtar all week as she washed veils, served food, and plucked eyebrows. Telling no one, she had hugged the dream to herself, enjoying its frequent reappearance in her mind's eye: the woman, anonymous in her wrappings, the heaps of dawn-coloured petals, the scent of roses. Such a dream, Akhtar was certain, could never have entered the foul hovel where she had lived with her husband. No, these visions were meant only for places like this haveli, where cleanliness and common sense combined with power and mystery.

The second vision had come yesterday morning just after she had been awakened by the call of the muezzin. It had revealed the same woman and the same gate, but this time the woman crouched, head bent, engulfed by a raging dust storm that had scattered all her rose petals save for a small handful that she clutched to her breast.

What did they mean, these two visions and the story they seemed to tell of blessing followed by disaster?

Akhtar lifted her first tray and started for the stairs, but then, struck by a thought, she stopped so suddenly that old Firoz, behind her with the next tray, gave a grunt of irritation.

In Safiya's story, the prince had dreamed. Although his vision had been different from hers, it had been just as vivid. If the prince's dream was an important part of his story, then her two visions might have some importance too.

It occurred to Akhtar that having no gift to lay at Safiya Sultana's door, perhaps she could offer her dreams.

Now was not the time, for she had ladies and children to feed, and Safiya, who thoroughly enjoyed her food, must never be interrupted while she was eating. But Akhtar determined that she would find the right moment, later on perhaps, when most

181

of the ladies had gone to rest, and Safiya sat alone, composing her poetry.

This might prove more interesting than any search for a caster of spells. Why had she not thought of it before?

Mariana sat against the wall, her arms about her knees, watching the trays arrive, with their thick rounds of bread and covered copper serving dishes. Ladies and children settled on the floor with their food or carried it to other rooms. The fat girl took Saboor's arm and led him off, a sheaf of banana leaves in her free hand. Mariana looked away from him, schooling herself to let him go.

The last person to be given a tray was Safiya Sultana. 'Come, Mariam,' she called, pointing to the empty place beside her. 'Join me. I will show you how to eat with your hands.'

Mariana watched carefully as Safiya ladled a helping of chicken from a zinc-lined serving dish onto the banana leaf in front of her, then tore off a small piece of bread and used it to detach a bit of meat from its bone.

'You must learn to eat properly, with the right hand only,' she instructed before putting the bread with its cargo of chicken and sauce into her mouth. As she chewed she looked Mariana up and down. 'And do not try to eat while you are wearing that shawl. You might spoil it. Hassan bought it for you a week ago, from an Afghan trader.'

Hassan. Mariana stiffened but Safiya had already turned back to her meal.

A group of women close by nudged closer.

'She does not know how to wear her shawl,' said one. 'Here, Tehmina, show Mariam how to drape it.'

A young woman with a high-bridged nose took the edge of Mariana's yellow shawl between her thumb and finger while Safiya continued to chew and swallow beside them. 'This is a beautiful old jamawar – such delicate work,' she said. 'The purple colour is unusual. See how the green embroidery matches her eyes.'

'You must wear it like this,' offered another woman, who wore a braid down her back as thick as Mariana's wrist. She reached forward and arranged the fabric loosely about Mariana's shoulders. As she did so, her sleeve fell back, revealing a smooth, hairless forearm.

Mariana stared. Where had she seen such a well-kept arm before? Unable to remember, she pulled her sleeves lower, suddenly aware that her own arms were covered with fine, blonde down, that her flyaway hair was too dry in spite of all her brushing, that for all her use of Aunt Claire's precious store of rose water, her lips and face were sore and chapped.

No Englishwoman of quality used artificial means to improve her appearance, but there was no avoiding the fact that while she had seemed perfectly presentable at Shalimar, she looked dreadful beside the well-tended ladies of this household.

Why were these women so nice to her now, after ignoring her all morning? Did they know she had come to divorce Hassan and abandon Saboor? How was she to behave?

'Look at her condition,' put in a gap-toothed aunt. 'Someone must attend to her appearance.'

'No.' Mariana shook her head vigorously. She had been plucked and dyed once before, and that experience had been sufficient for a lifetime. Besides, any native beautification of her would be noticed at Shalimar, if not by myopic Aunt Claire, then certainly by Lady Macnaghten. She could not possibly risk their fledgling friendship by appearing at camp looking like someone's native mistress.

'Oiling her hair will do little to help.' The first woman peered into her face, then took up one of her hands and examined it.

'Look at her hands,' she exclaimed. 'They are a pretty shape, but they might belong to a coolie's wife.'

Mariana jerked her hand away. 'I am English,' she snapped. 'Englishwomen do not—'

Wait. The creamy forearm she had remembered a moment ago belonged to Lady Macnaghten.

But that was not all. Even in this cold, dry weather, Lady Macnaghten's skin remained moist. No stray hairs marred the delicately shaped brows framing her face. Her smooth coiffure showed a hint of the auburn colour Mariana had seen in her own curls after they had been treated with henna paste.

'Have you no woman servant to do these things for you?' inquired the gap-toothed aunt.

Mariana shook her head, remembering with growing comprehension the two quiet, sari-clad women who rarely left Lady Macnaghten's tent. She herself had no female servant to polish and pluck her, but it seemed she knew someone who did.

She reached up and touched her hair, imagining Lady Macnaghten stretched on a chaise longue in her grand tent, her dark hair falling heavily, thick with paste, over the chair's back while one of the women pressed a wad of sticky substance against her white skin, then jerked it away, tearing the hair from her arms, then her underarms, then her legs, then her—

No. Not even brave, irritating, snobbish, deliciously wicked Lady Macnaghten, who had fooled everyone but her, would do that.

Mariana studied her red hands. A little judicious dyeing and oiling might not do any harm. Lady Macnaghten would, of course, notice immediately, but she would never tell. They already had one secret, after all. At breakfast this morning, she had offered Mariana a small, private nod of greeting . . .

For the first time since Mariana had entered the haveli, she gave her wide, beautiful smile.

'And now,' Safiiya announced a little while later, 'we will finish the story of the beggar prince.'

She cleared her throat and settled herself against her bolster. 'The youngest prince,' she began, 'spent the second day as he had spent the first one. After hiding his beautiful carpet behind a stone, he again wandered the streets of his father's city, observing rich and poor, idle and hard-working, good and evil.

'At the day's end he returned to the teashop, anxious to discover the secret of his magical carpet, but the beggar did not come. Remembering the beggar's advice to give regular charity, the prince gave his second coin to a blind woman who sat silently outside the teashop door.

'It must be admitted that the prince felt lonely. He watched sadly as men embraced each other in greeting, for he dearly missed his brothers. When chattering maidservants let down baskets over the balconies of the houses to be filled with sweetmeats for the ladies hidden upstairs, he sighed, thinking of his mother and his sisters.'

'We let a basket down from our windows,' a small boy with a shaven head put in loudly.

Safiya smiled at him, but did not reply. 'That night,' she continued, 'the prince spread his carpet once more, offered his evening prayer to Allah, the Lover of His Good Servants, and lay down to sleep. Again, as soon as he closed his eyes he was transported to the invisible garden, but this time, as he drifted off to sleep, he heard a sweet voice singing an exquisite, mysterious song.

'The beauty of that voice pierced the prince's heart, giving him a joy so profound that when he awoke on the third morning, he felt that his soul had become as new as the two little coins that shone on the edge of his silk carpet.

'Thinking only of the music he had heard the night before, the prince walked aimlessly about his father's city, waiting for the sun to set. Doubly anxious to meet the beggar, he again ate his simple meal at the teashop, but again the beggar did not come. With a sigh, the prince gave his second coin to a crippled man.

'As he lay on his magical carpet, he scarcely noticed the garden's perfumed breezes, its splashing fountains, or even the sound of its nightingale. All he cared for was that lovely, mysterious voice, for he had come to believe that it was the voice of his beloved.'

Mariana shifted on the floor. It was as evident as ever that the grown-ups in the room already knew the story of the prince and his dream. Had Safiya chosen it for her benefit, to teach her some allegorical lesson? If so, what was she supposed to learn? Could it have to do with Saboor, whom she could see playing with clay animals in the verandah? Or with Hassan?

'One evening,' Safiya went on, 'a curtained litter was carried past the teashop. As it passed, the prince thought he heard a voice more beautiful than a playing fountain, whose song was more lovely and haunting than a nightingale's. His heart filled nearly to bursting. His beloved of the garden was near – his own beloved, whose song had filled his dreams with joy and longing . . .

'Flinging down one of his two coins in payment for his food, he leapt into the crowded street, thinking only of seeing her face. Pushing aside cripples and beggars, he strove to reach the litter, but found his way blocked by the crowd thronging the narrow street. Mad with longing, he watched helplessly as the litter glided further and further away, then turned as if to leave the city.

'By the time the prince reached the great city gate that opened onto the countryside, there was no sign of a litter anywhere.

186

'"Come inside, sir," called a gatekeeper, beckoning to the prince. "It is sunset, and we must lock up for the night."

'"O gatekeeper," said the prince, "have you seen a litter with silken curtains pass this way?"

'"No, sir, I have not," the gatekeeper replied gently, for he could see that the young man's heart was breaking.'

A small green lizard crept cautiously across the wall near a window. Mariana followed it with her eyes, but in her imagination Hassan stumbled to a halt outside an unfamiliar city gate, searching desperately for someone, but not for her.

Safiya sighed dramatically. 'Desolate, the prince returned to the city and found his doorway. Blinded by tears, he reached behind the stone for his magical carpet, but it was no longer there.' She lifted her thick hands expressively. 'With nowhere to go, surrounded by the shuttered silence of the city and the rank smell of its gutters, the prince offered his prayers to Allah, the Transformer of Hearts. Then, exiled from the garden of his beloved, he lay down on the stones of the doorway and wept himself to sleep.'

Little Nadir tugged at his mother's clothes. 'But the prince was a grown up,' he said in a stage whisper.

'*Chup*, hush,' his mother whispered back.

'When the prince awoke, there were no silver coins to greet him, but after he set off to wander the city streets, he remembered the solitary coin from the day before that was lying forgotten in his purse.

'"I will find the beggar who gave me my magical carpet," he said to himself. "I will give him my last coin, and then I will ask him the way to the fragrant garden of my beloved. For if I cannot return there, I will die of grief."

'For days, the prince searched fruitlessly. As time went on, he began to look like a beggar himself. He grew weak and thin, but he would not use his coin to buy food, for he could think only of finding his way back to the lost garden of his beloved.

'One evening, as he sat, ragged and starving, near the door of the little teashop, he saw a child covered with sores, her hair matted and unclean, trying to beg for food. After some time in which no one but the prince seemed to notice her, she dropped the filthy little hand she had been holding out and crept to the corner of a stairway, where she lay down, a small bundle of misery, and closed her eyes.'

A wispy little girl in front began to snuffle. As Safiya went on with her story, a woman draped an arm about the girl's thin shoulders and murmured into her ear. Mariana dropped her eyes, imagining Hassan sitting tired and distracted on the teashop step, exiled from Paradise. Surely Safiya did not mean the divorce . . .

'The prince took the silver coin in his hand, the same coin he had hoarded even to starvation, believing that nothing could be more important than finding his way back to the garden of his beloved. But now he saw that he could never reach that fragrant paradise at the cost of a child's life.

'Stooping from weakness, he entered the shop, bought bread and tea, and carried it carefully outside.

'As the wretched little girl sat up and took the first swallow of tea and the first bite of bread, the beggar he had sought for so long appeared beside the prince.

'"O prince," he rasped, "Allah Most Gracious forgives all who repent."

'"O beggar," sighed the prince, "I had hoped to give you my last coin, but now it is spent, and I have nothing to offer you."

'"There is no need," replied the beggar. "You have used your last coin wisely. When you first came to this city, you spent one of your two coins each day, without greed, for your own sustenance. The other you gave in charity, and with kind words, to the least of your father's subjects. In return for this good use of your coins, you were shown a little of the Garden of Bliss.

'"To travel upon the Straight Path is to seek the Face of the Beloved, the Sender of Blessings, the Satisfier of Needs, the Lover of His Good Servants, the Transformer of Hearts. You were travelling on the Path until, following your own desires, you forgot charity and lost your way. Now you have returned, humbling yourself and feeding a starving child with your own hands.

'"Therefore," said the beggar, removing various items from the basket on his back, "wear this princely robe, and eat these savoury dishes, for you alone are wise enough to rule your father's kingdom.

'"And Prince," he added, drawing one last gift from his sack, "you have earned the return of your magical carpet. Offer your prayers upon it, and every night without fail you will visit the Garden of Bliss. In time, when you have journeyed far, far along the Straight Path, you will indeed, if Allah Most Gracious is willing, see the face of the Beloved."' As she said these words, Safiya turned and looked into Mariana's eyes.

Mariana breathed in, her head full of nightingales and musk, jasmine and splashing fountains. Had the story been told for her benefit? And if so, why? Surely Safiya did not think her ignorant of the values of charity and courage.

Perhaps the story was an Oriental parable of some kind, containing a mystical secret that she must unravel for herself.

'An-nah!' Saboor appeared from nowhere and leaned against her shoulder. 'What are we going to do now?' he inquired loudly, his face against hers.

Chapter Twenty-Two

Late that afternoon, from his vantage point beneath an ancient mango tree, Dittoo jerked his chin towards a tall, black-clad Englishman who paced alone near a bed of rose bushes, his hands clasped behind his back. 'That man is to blame,' he declared. 'It is he who is responsible for the mad English plan to leave Saboor here in Lahore, and then take poor Memsahib back to Calcutta. It is he who wants to ruin her life.'

He turned to Ghulam Ali, a hand extended, palm up. 'Should the Political Agent decide what family Memsahib belongs to? Is it his affair that she is guardian of Saboor Baba? I have known her for more than two years. She would never leave Baba, and she would never harm another human being. It is they who are forcing her into this shameful separation.' He hunched his shoulders. 'There is something cruel about that man. I know for a fact that two Afghans were arrested on the road after spending hours in his presence, and that he then went to the city to watch them executed. One of our cooks saw it all. But they got away, those two Afghans. Apparently two men on horseback saved them. And there is more. Ever since you left for the walled city, bad-looking men have been coming daily to see Lewis Sahib. Our people think they are spies.'

'Spies?' Ghulam Ali raised bushy white eyebrows.

'Yes,' Dittoo replied firmly. 'The other servants are saying that Lewis Sahib is plotting some treachery against the Sikh court behind the backs of the other English. His scheming may cause terrible damage. But one thing is certain. We should leave Shalimar now, and remove ourselves from danger. If these kings and queens want to kill each other, it is no concern of ours. If there is serious peril, we should bring Memsahib and Saboor Baba away with us for a short time, and when it is safe, she must return to the Waliullah family.'

Ghulam Ali shrugged. 'Whatever happens, there will be no need for her to leave Qamar Haveli. It is very strongly built.' He picked up a small stone and turned it over in his hand. 'And if she refuses to separate from Hassan Sahib?' he said carefully, afraid to let his eagerness show, 'will you, too, come and live with us? Of course you will serve only the men, but there will be Saboor Baba to care for, and Hassan Sahib is a good—'

'No.' Dittoo shook his head as they watched the Political Agent stride away towards his tent. 'Memsahib is the only person I want to serve. If I cannot serve her,' he added, his voice roughening, 'I will return to my village.' He turned away to wipe his eyes.

The small stone fell from Ghulam Ali's fingers and dropped to the ground between his feet.

A moment later, he stood and banged dust from his clothes. 'I must go back to the city,' he declared with his customary abruptness, pointing to a pair of donkey carts that waited inside the main gate, one loaded with oranges, the other with pomegranates. 'They are expecting me. It does not ordinarily take this long to fetch the fruit.'

'Be careful on your way back,' cautioned Dittoo. 'The villages along here are full of cholera. Two of our soldiers are ill with it already.'

'Wait, Ghulam Ali!' A starched-looking servant hurried up, waving a folded paper. 'Memsahib's uncle wants you to take this message to her.'

As soon as the servant was out of earshot, another man appeared. 'You, courier,' he ordered, planting himself in front of Ghulam Ali. 'Go at once to the Political Agent Sahib's tent. You are to deliver an urgent letter to Memsahib in Lahore. You are then to wait for her reply, and return with it.'

'Memsahib is no spy,' Dittoo insisted as Ghulam Ali pushed aside a basket of pomegranates and climbed onto one of the donkey carts. 'She will never aid Lewis Sahib in his treachery, whatever it may be. You will see for yourself how bravely she refuses.'

An hour later, wedged between two baskets, his pink, blistered feet dangling from the back of the cart, Ghulam Ali watched the dusty walls of Shalimar recede into the distance. He, who had seen Hassan Ali's wife looking out of her tent after the Englishman attacked her, did not share Dittoo's point of view. Brave she may be, but Ghulam Ali knew too well that, being an outcast, she had little protection against the evil of others. As a child with only a poor mother to protect him, he himself had been a thief in the walled city, apprenticed to a man with a fierce grip and a wicked leather strap, until he made the fortuitous mistake of snatching a bunch of grapes from a barrow in the Kashmiri Bazaar just as Shaikh Waliullah emerged from a nearby shop.

He had been fortunate, for after the Shaikh had made him return the grapes and apologize, he had brought Ghulam Ali and his mother to live at Qamar Haveli, but who would intervene on behalf of Hassan Ali's wife? Bound by pride and shame, she would never take her troubles to the only people who could help her – the Waliullah family.

He reached for the railing as his cart jolted over some loose stones. That trusting uncle of hers knew nothing about the second letter. The Political Agent, a powerful, devious man, had seen to that. How, then, could she stand up to such a man? How could she refuse to spy? She could not, and Lewis Sahib knew it.

Ghulam Ali sighed. When the Waliullah family discovered what she was, they would hasten the divorce and send her away as swiftly as possible.

That morning, eating alone as usual in the kitchen courtyard, he had allowed himself to imagine that she would stay, and that his first real friend would soon be there, to sit companionably beside him after the meal, talking of her as he always did, his hands moving in grand arcs as he spoke, as if she were the stuff of legend.

Ghulam Ali snatched a pomegranate from one of the baskets and flung it, hard, into the road.

But he had no reason to complain. His return to Lahore after a six-month absence had produced no hero's welcome, but he had been treated with more respect than he had expected. The guards had wished him peace after he pounded in his usual impatient fashion upon the carved haveli doors. The Hindu carpenters at work in the elephant stable had looked up and nodded as he passed.

Later, summoned to the small courtyard, he had been flattered by the length of time the Shaikh had given him to describe his adventures and offer an account of his expenses. His back to the sun to ease his eyes, Ghulam Ali had stood at attention beside the padded platform, softening his harsh voice as best he could while he told the story of his escape from the gang of Thugs, and described Calcutta, a city the Shaikh had never seen.

He had, of course, made no reference to the lady, or to her people's shocking determination to see her divorced.

After Ghulam Ali finished speaking, the Shaikh had nodded. 'You have done well,' he observed, causing Ghulam Ali to flush with pride. 'There are few couriers in this city who can be trusted to undertake such a long journey. You are among the best of them.'

Now, after delivering the cartload of fruit to the haveli's kitchen entrance, Ghulam Ali made some inquiries and then wove his way through the busy streets until he reached a small teashop near the Golden Mosque.

Inside the shop, on a carpet-covered platform with teapots and glass tumblers in front of them, sat Hassan Ali Khan, his friend Yusuf, and two Afghan traders whom Ghulam Ali had seen before. Unlike Hassan and Yusuf, the Afghans appeared perfectly relaxed.

'I only give him the same bazaar gossip he hears from everyone else,' the pale-eyed trader was saying. 'Why should I tell him anything more? Do you think I did not see the son of shame in the crowd, gloating over my countrymen who were to be blown from cannon? Do you think I did not see him recognize us, then run away when you came to our rescue?'

'Then why call on him at Shalimar?' Hassan's face had hardened. 'What sweetness, what trade, does the Englishman offer, Zulmai, that would cause you to swallow your hatred of him and go there?'

The Afghan smiled broadly, revealing even, white teeth. He glanced at a quartet of elaborately decorated jezails that stood, barrels pointing upward, against the teashop wall. 'My hatred of him is unchanged, brother. But if I do not visit him, how can I discover his plans? How can I help you?'

'What, then, are his plans? What help are you offering us?'

'I cannot tell you just yet, but as soon as I know, I will come to you. Do not worry, my friend,' the Afghan added softly, signalling to his young companion. 'I will not fail you.'

With one swift movement he stood and picked up his guns.

Ghulam Ali waited until the two men had disappeared into the crowd before he stepped forward and offered his salaams. 'I have come from Shalimar,' he told Hassan and Yusuf as he reached into the pocket hidden in his clothes. 'As I was leaving, I was given two letters. Both are for your wife, Hassan Sahib.'

'Who wrote these?' Hassan asked sharply. He stared at the folded papers, each one addressed in foreign writing.

Ghulam Ali pointed. 'This one is from the tall Englishman who wears black all the time. The other is from Memsahib's uncle.'

Unable to bear the expression on Hassan Ali's face, he left the shop as hastily as he could.

Yusuf watched Hassan push the folded letters into his coat pocket. 'Why do you care if these British are spying?' he asked. 'It is Sher Singh, after all, who is marching towards us, bent on seizing the throne. What threat does that foreigner offer, with his puny, cannonless escort?'

'He offers no threat now, but I tell you, Yusuf, the British are ambitious and arrogant,' Hassan replied. 'They want to possess all of India. When we have exhausted our energy fighting each other, the British will take the Punjab for themselves. I see the Political Agent's hand in everything around me – in the slaughter of Afghans, even in my wife's attempt to dissolve our marriage. Why has he written to her, Yusuf? What could he want from her?'

Knowing how fiercely the Waliullahs clung to their dreams, Yusuf hesitated before answering. 'What he wants is information,' he said, stating the obvious as gently as he could. 'The Political Agent wants your wife to repeat what she is hearing in the ladies' quarters, and what she learns from her conversations with you.'

Hassan shook his head. 'With me? Why would I discuss these matters with my wife? I never speak of private court business with anyone but my father.'

'Of course you don't.' Yusuf shrugged. 'But in any case, you should let her receive the letters without knowing you have seen them. When you meet her again, listen to her. See if she questions you. You will learn easily enough if she is a spy. If she is, then by her questions alone she will reveal much of the Political Agent's plans. And if she is not,' he added gently, pained by Hassan's stricken face, 'you will have no further need to worry.'

Hassan dropped his head into his hands. 'All I know now,' he murmured, 'is that we must, from this moment, regard the British as our bitter enemies.'

Chapter Twenty-Three

Akhtar did not find an opportunity to speak to Safiya Sultana alone until after the ladies had finished their meal and dispersed to doze in their bedrooms or against bolsters in the sitting room. After carrying in a number of the cotton-filled quilts that would cover the ladies as they slept, she crept to the private room where, each afternoon, Safiya wrote poetry and prepared cures for various illnesses. Afraid to interrupt such important work, the serving girl hung back in the shadow of the doorway, listening to Safiya's voice rise and fall as she composed aloud.

You live with fear, who move with outrider and scout,
Compassed round with bristling steel.
Unlike you I travel weaponless;
Desiring only the Beloved, I step unarmed onto the path
    of fire.

'No,' Safiya rumbled to herself, 'each line should end with *ke saat.*'

Pen in hand, she looked up from her string bed to see Akhtar standing nervously by the doorway.

'Bhaji,' the girl whispered, 'I have had two dreams. The first was of a woman and an open gate and roses, and the second was of dust and—'

'Come in, child,' Safiya said quickly, laying her pen on a square of cloth beside her, 'and close the curtain behind you.'

In the end, one description of her dreams was not enough. Safiya did not let Akhtar stop until she had recounted each dream three times, omitting no detail. When Akhtar had finished, Safiya closed her eyes briefly and recited something under her breath.

'You were right to tell me about your dreams,' she said, opening her eyes. 'If you see anything else, you are to come to me at once. And Akhtar,' she added, frowning, 'come again tomorrow at this time. I will give you something to recite. And from now on, make certain you do not miss any of your prayers.'

Why, Mariana asked herself, had Safiya's beggar prince seemed so much like Hassan?

This was no time to be thinking of a stranger with a crooked nose and a tired brown gaze, who spent all his time at the Sikh court and treated her as if she was no more than an unpaid guardian of his child. She had serious work to do, and she must begin it soon. After all, she did not have much time to learn the secrets of this household. This first afternoon was already slipping away, and she had not even uncovered the mystery of Shaikh Waliullah's cure for snakebite. It was maddening to see him through the latticework shutters, surrounded by his silent followers, while the afternoon shadows lengthened in the courtyard behind him.

Someone coughed on the verandah outside. More people had

come: two women, a new distraction for Safiya. Mariana felt a twinge of resentment as Safiya motioned them to enter.

The older one had already taken off her burka, revealing the lively round-cheeked face of a countrywoman. She carried a child in one arm, an infant only a few months old. The other woman stood, unmoving and still shrouded in her burka, until the first woman lifted away the fabric, revealing a lanky-haired girl whose shoulders drooped so badly that she seemed ready to collapse onto the floor.

Horrified at the girl's despair, Mariana looked away.

Saboor burst from a knot of children and rushed headlong towards the two visitors, determination on his face. At the doorway, he gripped the hem of the girl's kameez. 'An-nah,' he cried as he tugged the girl into the room. 'Come and help!'

While the women and other children made way silently for the new arrivals, Safiya caught hold of a fat little girl with a thick braid. 'Rifhat,' she ordered, 'go and fetch another bolster and a rezai.'

The young visitor moved to a corner of the room. Without removing her burka, she lay down on the floor and drew her knees to her chin.

Saboor sat down beside her. 'An-nah,' he repeated, flapping his hands, as the fat girl arrived, puffing, with the bolster and quilt in her arms. 'Come!'

Mariana hesitated. What did Saboor want her to do? Why was he stroking the girl's shoulder with a small, kindly hand? How could she be of use when she had no idea what was wrong? The girl's sadness repelled her as if it had an evil life of its own.

In the corner, the older woman put the infant down, lifted the girl's head and pushed the bolster under it, then covered her legs with the rezai. She leaned over, fussed with the girl's clothing, then picked up the baby and arranged it beside her.

A moment later the quiet room was filled with the sound of a baby's noisy sucking.

'Go to my room, Akhtar,' Safiya said, 'and bring jasmine oil and cotton wool.'

When the servant returned, Safiya signalled to Mariana. 'Come here,' she said.

It was an order, not an invitation. When Mariana approached, Safiya handed her a little tuft of cotton fluff and a tiny glass vial. 'Roll the cotton into a ball like this, put a little oil on it, and then tuck it into the fold of that girl's left ear. Like this.' She uncovered her own ear and pointed. 'That is the first thing to do in such cases.'

From the corner, a beaming Saboor patted the floor beside him. Aware that Safiya was watching, Mariana went reluctantly over and sat down, careful to avoid contact with the supine girl.

An ugly, sweetish smell came from her, as if she had not bathed for weeks. The hand holding the baby to her breast looked grubby.

Was this, Mariana wondered, a test of some kind? If so, whatever her revulsion, she must somehow pass muster. She held her breath, leaned experimentally forward, and saw that the girl's eyes were tightly closed. Hoping she was asleep, Mariana took a strand of unwashed hair and held it gingerly aside.

'No!' At once the girl flung up an arm and struck Mariana's hand away, then curled her body into a tight ball round her child.

Mortified, Mariana glanced over at Safiya, but she was deep in conversation with the gap-toothed aunt.

'Speak,' advised the countrywoman as Mariana searched for the fallen cotton ball. 'Say something to her.'

At a loss, Mariana could think only of a Persian poem she had learned a year earlier:

And heart bowed down beneath a secret pain,
Oh stricken heart, joy shall return again,
Peace to the love-tossed brain — oh weep no more.

She stopped. These women spoke Punjabi. Why had she chosen a Persian poem that they would not understand? And why had she chosen one that reminded her so powerfully of her own sadnesses, of her father growing old so far away, of her coming loss of Saboor, of her hopeless dream of marrying Harry Fitzgerald and having fair-haired babies of her own?

Tears stung her eyes. When would her losses end? When would she have her own people to love?

No one was paying attention to them. Safiya was still talking to the aunt while the ladies formed into groups for some activity involving tiny yellow limes.

Saboor stopped patting the girl and came to lean his small, comforting weight against Mariana. She went on reciting, her head bowed, while tears dripped from her chin.

Mine enemies have persecuted me.
My love has turned and flown from out my door.
God counts our tears and knows our misery.
Ah, weep not. He has heard thy weeping sore—

The older woman nudged her. 'Look,' she said, pointing.

The girl, too, was crying. Her thin shoulders shook. The hand that had been clenched against the baby's small body was now open. Mariana dashed away her own tears, lifted the girl's hair out of the way, and pushed the cotton ball into place before she had time to protest.

The older woman lifted the baby and handed it, a brown parcel

201

with a tiny, crumpled face, to Mariana. 'Safiya Sultana Begum knows everything about cures,' she confided as she grasped the girl's arm and turned her over, 'it is said that she can even cure cholera.'

'Well done, Mariam,' said Safiya Sultana as the woman took the infant back and put it without ceremony to the girl's other breast. 'You have done the first part of the work. The next part is for me to do.'

She frowned as she caught sight of a figure in the verandah doorway.

A female servant stood there, papers in her hand. 'There are two letters here for Mariam Bibi,' she announced.

Chapter Twenty-Four

'Eat,' Safiya ordered, holding out a spoonful of something brown and aromatic that looked like minced meat. 'You have not even tried the keema.'

Mariana pushed away her banana leaf. 'I am sorry, Safiya Bhaji,' she said, hiding her shaking hands in her sleeves, 'but I can't manage any more.'

She had done her best with the evening meal. Under Safiya's tutelage she had used small pieces of bread to scoop up curried vegetables and a yellow mush that tasted of earth and unfamiliar spices, but her thoughts had not been on the savoury native food in front of her, so different from the insipid fare at Shalimar. All she had been able to think of were the two letters that crinkled in the waistband of her shalwar. She had read Uncle Adrian's letter first.

My dear child,

    You must return to Shalimar at once. Sher Singh's men are expected to attack the city any day, and I fear they will run riot.

    As if that weren't enough, Russell Lewis has been intriguing with both the Rani and Sher Singh, a very foolish thing to do, and absolutely forbidden by the authorities. By meddling in their affairs, Lewis may have put us all in danger.

Please leave the walled city as soon as you can. Bring Saboor if you like. If you fail to complete your divorce now, we may be able to arrange it later.

I would come for you myself, but I have been quite unwell since yesterday.

Frowning with worry, Mariana had laid that letter aside, and opened the second. She did not recognize the handwriting.

Dear Miss Givens,

I trust that the formalities of your separation will soon be completed.

As we agreed, while you are with the Shaikh's family, you are to discover all you can about the present situation at court. I am particularly interested in the exact date and time of Sher Singh's coming attack upon the city. I have my own informants, of course, but your confirmation of these facts will prove invaluable to me, and, naturally, to the Government.

Your husband, who is expected to return to Qamar Haveli tomorrow evening, will know the full details of Sher Singh's plan.

As the natives are not to be trusted at this perilous time, I suggest that you return to Shalimar as soon as you have obtained the necessary information. You may then convey what you have learned to me in person.

I would advise you not to mention this letter, or anything I have said in it.

I am certain, Miss Givens, that you will be scrupulous in carrying out your promise to me.

I remain etc.

Russell Lewis

What had she done? What had she committed herself to when she had let him argue for her at Shalimar? Why had she given him that small, conspiratorial nod?

An hour after the evening meal, she lay under a heavy quilt, staring at the lamplit ceiling of a quiet room off the corridor's end, Saboor asleep beside her. Her arm tightened about his body. She had been here only one day and already she was being told she must return to Shalimar.

Nothing on earth would persuade her to spy on the Waliullah family or help the Vulture with his pernicious intrigues. But when she refused him, how would he punish her? *He is not a nice man,* Lady Macnaghten had said. Mariana had not needed to be told that, but what was he capable of? Would he tell cruel lies to Lady Macnaghten and spoil their budding friendship? Could he ruin the little time remaining in Uncle Adrian's career?

Fear closed over her. She had no sense of what was happening outside Qamar Haveli. Should she tell the Waliullahs about the Vulture and his faintly menacing letter? But what would she tell them? Would they despise her for involving herself in his scheming, whatever it was? If she did not warn the family, would she put them in danger? And what was wrong with Uncle Adrian?

She tried to imagine her next move, but it was late, and her eyes were closing. Still wearing her yellow clothes from the morning, too weary to think, she reached over and turned off the oil lamp.

'I have been waiting for you,' Safiya said the next morning, when Mariana and Saboor emerged, hand in hand, from their room. 'Now, Saboor, you must find Khadija and ask her to get your breakfast.'

Motioning for Mariana to follow, Safiya marched into her room and wrenched the curtain shut.

'I watched you and Saboor working with that melancholic young mother yesterday,' she began, with a satisfied nod. 'You both did well. You are not a healer as he is, of course, but the girl needed you, all the same. I prepared something for her to drink every morning, and sent them off after the dawn prayer. But that is not why I have called you here.'

She took a small leather bag from a shelf. 'One of the maids has had a dream, two dreams in fact. In the first, a woman is greatly blessed; in the second, some emergency arises, and she is thrown into grave danger that threatens her soul as well as her life. I believe you are the woman of the maid's dream.'

What had they uncovered in that dream? Was it the Vulture's letter? Mariana glanced about her, wishing she was somewhere else.

'As these are the girl's first visions since she came to this house,' Safiya went on, 'I am uncertain of their seriousness. But I have nonetheless taken a precaution.'

Reaching into the bag, she drew out a small silver box with a ring welded to its top, through which had been strung a thick black cord. 'We awakened our silversmith in the night to prepare this. You must not take it off,' she warned as she lowered it over Mariana's head. 'Inside it are verses from the Qur'an. Inshallah, it will keep you safe.'

The shiny little box was covered with carved arabesques. Mariana turned it in her hand, and saw that its sides had been carefully welded, so that it could not be opened.

'You are a brave girl,' Safiya said gruffly. 'Who knows what Allah Most Gracious has in store for you, but whatever it is, you will, Inshallah, survive it.' Her face was sombre. 'It is called a taweez,' she added. 'Keep it inside your clothes. It is not for people to see. And now,' she added, her face softening as she reached to open the curtain, 'you should have yourself oiled and prepared for Hassan's return.'

206

'But Safiya Bhaji——' was all Mariana had time to say before Safiya moved rapidly away, leaving her standing, open-mouthed, in the doorway.

What was Safiya up to? Surely Hassan or the Shaikh had told her about the divorce. Was she trying to interfere? As Mariana reached down and touched the papers in her waistband, she felt the family's coils tighten about her.

She must not let any of this disturb her. Hassan would come in the evening. It would make no difference whether or not she had been oiled and plucked. She would show him her immovability on the subject of their divorce, he would be forced to agree, and that would be that. Then, tomorrow morning, having spent too little time in the haveli, she would take her painful leave of darling Saboor and bid Safiya and her ladies goodbye. When she returned to Shalimar, she would refuse, flatly, to speak to the Vulture alone.

'Memsahib,' whispered the bird-like servant at Mariana's shoulder, 'if you will come with me.'

An hour later, Mariana sat on the sitting-room floor, her eyes closing, while Akhtar massaged oil into her scalp with gentle, scarred fingers.

Mariana imagined her family in Sussex, her mother cutting flowers in the vicarage garden, her father in his study, poring over his battle maps with their rows of neatly drawn artillery and dotted lines. If she married in Afghanistan, she might never see them again.

Where was Fitzgerald now? Was he skating with his fellow officers on the frozen Kabul River? Was he training his men, having them fire practise shots at distant targets outside the city? Whatever else the blond lieutenant was doing, he might also be waiting for her. After all, there were very few Englishwomen in Kabul, and all were married. Tainted by her history or not, she was all he could have.

'And now, Bibi, we must move to the window, so I can see to

thread your eyebrows.' The servant girl nodded towards a string bed under one of the verandah windows.

Trying not to wince with pain as the girl pulled hair from one of her eyebrows with a twisted string, Mariana imagined Lady Macnaghten's face when she reappeared, newly beautified, at Shalimar. Of course there would be the difficulty of maintaining her carefully cultivated looks after they began to wear off, but who knew, perhaps Lady Macnaghten might lend her one of the quiet women from time to time.

The elderly maidservant who had brought the lunch trays puffed her way up the stairs. 'Hassan Sahib has arrived,' she panted, gesturing for Mariana to get up. 'He is coming upstairs any moment to see Mariam Bibi. He is only here for a short time.'

Mariana sat up, dislodging the girl's hands. '*Now?* But I cannot see Hassan now!' Where was Safiya Sultana? Where was everyone else? Mariana looked about her for aid, but apart from the girl and the elderly maidservant, there was no one on the verandah but a very old lady who sat dozing against the wall. No sounds of conversation came from the sitting room.

'But my hair is covered in oil, and you have done only one of my eyebrows, and—'

'It is too late to worry about such things,' wheezed the old servant. 'You must change your clothes and conceal your hair. Go, Akhtar,' she ordered the girl. 'Find fresh clothes for Mariam Bibi to wear. And another shawl. She cannot wear that yellow jamawar. She may get oil on it.' She turned back to Mariana. 'I will tie your hair into a knot at your neck. You can cover it with your dupatta.'

When the old servant had finished with her hair, Mariana hurried to her room where Akhtar had laid out fresh clothes. She pulled a brown kameez over her head, careful not to disturb the oily bun at the back of her neck, and tied on a brown shalwar. After draping her dupatta over her head and shoulders as she had seen the ladies do, she emerged from her room.

Uncertain what to do next, she looked about her. Akhtar held out a plain shawl which Mariana wrapped about her shoulders. Then both servants pointed to a small room near the stairway. Through its open doorway she could see a man's knee, and a hand resting on it.

Chapter Twenty-Five

15 January 1841

Aware that the two women were watching her, Mariana walked as confidently as she could across the verandah, past a pair of male slippers at the door, and into the little room.

There were two string beds in the small space, and little else. Hassan sat on one of them, looking even more elegant than usual. Saboor, his hands and face dirty from some adventure, lay sprawled across his father's knees.

'Abba,' he cried, starting up. 'An-nah has come!'

'Peace,' Hassan offered, as Mariana lowered herself uncertainly to the second bed, as drab as a peahen in her brown clothes, her letters crackling at her waist.

The beds were so close together that her knees were less than a foot from his. She reached across the space between them and patted Saboor's beaming face, then jerked her hand away, realizing how close she had come to touching Hassan's heavily embroidered sleeve.

'Are those your court clothes?' she asked, not knowing what else to say.

'They are.' He frowned; a gold earring glinted as he cocked his head. 'Why are you covered in oil? What is wrong with your eyebrows? Did they not tell you I was coming?'

'They did, but too late.'

'Abba has come!' Saboor slid from his father's knee, his face alight. 'He is taking me on his horse tomorrow,' he cried, dancing beside Mariana. 'You must come and see!'

'I cannot stay long.' Hassan caught Saboor's grubby little hands from behind, raised them above his head and bounced him up and down. 'Are you comfortable here?' he asked Mariana. 'Do you need anything?'

'No, thank you. If you remember, I shall soon be returning to Shalimar. I very much like your family,' she added over Saboor's squeals of pleasure, preserving her bridges. 'I hope to call on them again, after our separation. I would like to learn more about your father and your aunt Safiya Sultana. I would also like to visit Saboor.'

'Then why leave us at all?'

'Our marriage was a mistake,' she said primly. 'What more is there to say?'

Unable to tell whether Saboor had understood their conversation, she looked away from the child's sudden scowl.

Hassan did not reply. Instead, he drew Saboor onto the bed beside him. His eyes on Mariana, he began to run tender fingers over Saboor's curls.

She must convince him to let her go before she smelled his sharp, woody perfume again, before she found herself staring at the graceful hands that caught Saboor and held him as he tried to wriggle away . . .

Harry Fitzgerald, with his straight back and his Roman profile, was nothing like the man who sat before her. She tried once more to imagine herself at Fitzgerald's side, a fair-haired baby in her arms, but this time the picture would not form clearly in her mind. How could it, when Hassan sat only feet away, with his broken nose, his silk garments and princely jewels?

Why had she chosen this moment to look so awful? It weakened her position to be half-plucked and oily. She looked down, mortified, at her ill-kept hands.

'There's no need to turn away; I have already seen how you look.'

She glanced up sharply and met Hassan's gaze. A wave of intensity seemed to come from him and cross the space between them.

'I must leave soon,' he said softly. 'I am needed at court.'

She looked away, knowing he still watched her, aware that he was now stroking his son's back. She must not allow herself to fall into the dark, inviting chasm that he was opening before her. If she gave in, she would have no future, no fair-haired babies, no friends . . .

Hassan had mentioned the court. Here was the opportunity to do as the Vulture had asked. If the Vulture were here, he would be signalling her to ask the date and time of Sher Singh's assault.

He could signal all he wanted. She would never ask.

But wait. She herself needed that information. If she knew when the attack was to take place, she would know how long to remain in the city. If there were another two or three days of safety, she could have more time with the family, with Saboor . . .

'When is Sher Singh's attack to be?' she asked, as carelessly as she could, avoiding Hassan's gaze, surprised at the thickness of her voice.

He stiffened. 'Why do you want to know?'

'I do not know how long I can stay here. If I could have even one more day, I—'

'You have no wish to leave Qamar Haveli.' His voice had a knife's edge. 'You do not want a separation. You have been forced to ask this question by the British Political Agent. Admit it.'

'That is not true.' Mariana watched tensely as Saboor ran from the room. How much did Hassan know? Had he seen the letters? Schooling herself not to touch the papers at her waist, she cast about for a way to change the subject.

'I do not have to admit anything,' she told him flatly. 'I am British.'

Had she really said those words aloud?

'You will not distract me with your rudeness.' His expression hardened. 'The Political Agent has written to you. I have seen his letter. What does he want?'

'I cannot tell you.'

'You *will* tell me. It is he, and not you, who desires to know the date and time of Sher's attack. He wants your aid in some treachery against us. Speak. What is his plan?'

'I do not know.' Unable to stop herself, she reached down and felt the letters at her waist. 'My uncle has also written. He says Mr Lewis has been intriguing with the Rani and Sher Singh without the knowledge of our government. Our political officers are forbidden to do such things. I would never give information to a man like that.'

'And what power has he over you that he can force you to spy in your own husband's house?' Hassan's face had grown icy and still. He might have been a complete stranger to her.

'He has *not* forced me to spy,' she cried, the words tumbling from her. 'Mr Lewis is not a nice man,' she added desperately, 'but it was he who persuaded my uncle to let me come here to stay. All I could think of was seeing Saboor again. I had no idea why the Political Agent wanted——' She felt her face crumple.

Hassan leaned forward, his hands on his knees, his face level with hers. 'You are to remain in this house,' he ordered, heedless of her filling eyes. 'You are to take no part in the Political Agent's schemes, whatever they are. You are to tell him nothing. You may not send any message to Shalimar, and you may not go there. I cannot guarantee your safety if you try to visit the English camp. Do you understand me?'

Sniffing, she drew herself up on her string bed. 'You have no right to tell me what to do. If I wish to write to my uncle, I will do so. If I wish to leave this house and go to Shalimar, I will do that, too.'

'You will not.' His voice held a heavy finality. 'You will remain here until everything has been resolved.'

There was clearly no point in arguing with him now. Later on, she would ask Ghulam Ali to take a letter to her uncle, requesting him to send a palanquin and bearers to fetch her. She gathered herself, thinking the interview was over, but to her surprise Hassan made no move to stand. Instead, he peered at her neck. 'What is that black cord you are wearing?' he asked coldly.

'It is for a taweez. Your Aunt Safiya made it for me.' Mariana fingered the silver box through her clothes. 'One of the maids had a dream about a woman who seemed to be in danger. Your aunt believes I am the woman of the dream. I am sure it is nothing,' she added lamely, hoping he would look at her again as he had a little while before.

'If my aunt made a taweez for you, it is far from nothing. You are likely to face real danger. Hai!' Hassan ran a hand over his face. 'I only pray that Allah will keep this family safe.'

'I will always protect Saboor,' Mariana said quickly, and then pressed her lips hastily together.

He did not look at her, or reply.

She shrank into her drab clothes, her unplucked eyebrow weighing down her lid like a hairy caterpillar. 'Will Sher Singh besiege the city, or will he storm it?' she asked in a small voice.

'Neither one. I am sure he has already paid the Rani's troops to open the gates.' Hassan sighed. 'Were you supposed to ask me that, also?'

'No.' She lifted her shoulders. 'I am interested in military history.'

'You study military history.' He nodded, watching her. 'I used to think you were like other English people, but you are not. You are not like anyone, are you?'

He got to his feet, unsmiling, his embroidered coat swinging at his ankles. 'We will speak again when I return later this evening. Inshallah, I will be coming upstairs for dinner.'

As he stepped into his slippers outside the door, she realized she had stretched out a hand to him as he passed her.

'Yes, this is how the wife of Hassan Ali should look!' An elderly aunt slapped both her knees and smiled broadly as Mariana made her self-conscious way across the crowded floor that evening, her delicately worked gold bangles jingling on her arms.

Safiya Sultana gave a satisfied nod and pointed to an empty place near her.

It had taken the whole afternoon for Akhtar to finish her work, and even then she had complained at the lack of time.

'To prepare a bride takes days and days,' she had mourned as she rubbed Safiya's special mixture of almond oil, rose water, chickpea flour and spices into Mariana's dry skin. 'There is so much that I must do to make you beautiful.'

'I am not a bride,' Mariana had pointed out as she lay on the string bed. 'I am only letting you do this because you want to,' she added, more forcefully than she intended.

Now, as she sat down near Safiya, she was glad of Akhtar's work. Some of that meticulous plucking had been painful, but at least she would look less of a fright for tonight's meeting with Hassan. Her hair, oiled and hennaed, fell down her back in a silky, auburn-tinted braid. Her hands and face had been smoothed, her eyes carefully outlined with antimony. Her skin, scented with rose water and saffron, felt sensuous and velvety under her finely embroidered silks.

She fingered the pretty necklace of rubies and pearls that Safiya had sent into her room while she was dressing. Presumably, after Hassan came, he would eat his dinner with all of them, and then he and Mariana would meet alone in some private corner, or perhaps in the small room where they had spoken earlier. After their previous conversation he would, naturally, agree the divorce was inevitable. She would thank him, and that would be that.

They had been married for twenty-four months. She had loved and protected his son all that time but she had never come to know Hassan. Now it was too late. She pictured him leaving her for the last time, his bare feet silent on the covered floor.

She must stop imagining her losses and concentrate on her future. She would certainly be well prepared for her next meeting with Lady Macnaghten. That meeting, with all its implications for her future, would be very soon – tomorrow perhaps. After all, once Hassan had agreed to end their marriage, his insistence that she remain in the city would no longer apply.

She would leave in the morning. She needed to know the state of her uncle's health, and she needed to confront the Vulture. He must be told in plain language that she refused to spy for him. From the tone of his letter, poor Uncle Adrian was clearly deeply disturbed by Lewis's dangerous intriguing. She had never known him to sound so upset.

Around her, the ladies discussed the intricacies of a coming family wedding. The bride-to-be, a pretty, plump-faced child, sat

216

near Mariana, smiling in the evening lamplight. A silver of wood protruded from one side of her nose where it had been pierced, ready for the n'hut, the nose ring all married women wore.

The sun had set hours before. The lamps flickered, throwing shadows against the wall, softening the features of the ladies who shifted in their places, murmuring among themselves, their hands moving expressively. From time to time, they would look over at Mariana and smile approvingly. None of them seemed to know that her marriage to Hassan was about to end and that she would soon be leaving. Safiya had spoken little all evening. Now she yawned.

Mariana's finery weighed on her shoulders; her earlobes ached, pulled down by her long ruby earrings. She glanced past the shutters at the neighbouring houses. Their windows had gone dark. What time was it? Surely last night's dinner had not been served as late as this.

'Akhtar,' called Safiya Sultana, 'bring the food.' She raised her voice. 'Hassan must have been delayed, wherever he is,' she announced to the room. 'Do not worry, my child,' she added, reaching out to pat Mariana's knee. 'He will, Inshallah, come to see you tomorrow morning. And then, tomorrow evening, Akhtar will put kajal on your eyes again, and dress you in something else equally good. As I remember, we gave you five sets of wedding clothes.'

Her disappointment must have been transparent. Annoyed with herself, Mariana smoothed her gold-coloured silks with an impatient hand. 'But Bhaji,' she began, 'I do not think—'

'Hush, child.' Safiya raised a warning finger. 'There is no need to speak.'

Later, after everyone but Mariana had enjoyed a lavish dinner and the food had been taken away, Safiya turned to her.

'Now, Mariam,' she said quietly, 'there is something we must discuss. I do not wish to frighten our family ladies, but we must decide what preparations will be needed to protect this house in case of violence in the city. I am confiding in you because, of all of us, you are Saboor's protector. It occurs to me that you might have some ideas on the subject.'

Flattered, Mariana sat straight, her energy returning as she imagined the haveli surrounded by a yelling mob, and herself in charge of its defence. 'The kitchen entrance should be blocked off,' she offered quickly, remembering the open passageway connecting the kitchen to the family courtyard. 'The main doors are thick enough to hold, but the back door from the kitchen courtyard might be battered down. And we should protect the upper windows. If anyone were to scale the outer walls, they could easily climb in from there.' She pointed to the shuttered windows overlooking the narrow street outside.

Safiya nodded seriously. 'The old elephant doors might prove useful to close off the passageway to the kitchen entrance.' She opened a carved silver box, lifted out a tray with wells filled with intriguing pastes and nuts, and removed a thick piece of betel leaf. 'I had not even considered the windows,' she said as she scooped out a little white paste and spread it on her leaf. 'We will have to talk more about it in the morning.' She sighed. 'I am going to bed after I have this *pan*.'

Mariana looked about her at the quiet room, now emptying of its occupants. Hassan had not come, but still the evening had offered her some small pleasure. There had been restfulness in the company of these undemanding ladies, who smiled at her as they sat comfortably on the floor. She closed her eyes as Safiya chewed beside her, imagining the reception a bride from this family would receive from the ladies of Weddington village, with their stays and bonnets and stiff chairs. After her own experiences in Calcutta, she did not wish to imagine how they would treat the poor girl . . .

She wrenched her thoughts to the present. Hassan would come in the morning. After she met him, she would ask for a palanquin to deliver her to Shalimar. Before leaving, she would kiss Saboor, and pray that it was not for the last time. First, Hassan must agree that she should be allowed to come back and visit Saboor. Then she must gain Uncle Adrian and Aunt Claire's permission to return. The Vulture would, of course, withdraw his support once she refused to spy for him. Aunt Claire was bound to make a scene, and not without reason. One of the points of their long journey had, after all, been for Mariana to rescue her reputation, not to shred it further by paying unexplained visits to native families.

If she was not allowed to see Saboor again, she must somehow turn her attention away from Qamar Haveli and its occupants. Even with her heart breaking, she must think of her future in Afghanistan. She must, above all, be charming to Lady Macnaghten, the Envoy's wife.

When Safiya lurched, groaning, to her feet, and started towards the corridor, Mariana gathered up her yards of embroidered silk and trailed disconsolately behind her.

Her visit to the walled city had been a failure, far too brief, and full of misunderstandings. She had not spoken to the mysterious Shaikh Waliullah even once. For all her desperate desire to learn from Safiya Sultana, she had not asked her a single question. Even tonight, with Safiya sitting right beside her, she had been so absorbed in waiting for Hassan that she had squandered a whole evening's opportunity to gain knowledge. Unable for some unfathomable reason to make a clean break from Hassan, she had bungled their parting, and left herself open to hopeless longing. She had tried to disengage her heart from Saboor, but had found herself watching him every moment, wishing he would come to her and breathe into her ear, as he had done for half of his short life.

She sighed as she reached the end of the corridor and pushed her door curtain aside. Saboor did not seem to understand that she was leaving him. Perhaps it was just as well. One parting, after all, would be enough for both of them.

Chapter Twenty-Six

As she lay in a shadowed corner of Mariana's bedchamber, Akhtar tried to push away her disappointment at the evening's failure.

It was Hassan Sahib, and not she, who should have been here.

She pulled her quilt over her shoulders as silently as she could, knowing how little she was wanted. Of course Mariam Bibi's objections to sharing her bedroom with a servant had fallen on deaf ears. 'No one sleeps alone in this house,' Safiya had decreed after the evening meal. 'Since Saboor has gone to his cousins' room tonight, Akhtar will stay with you.'

The whole household had waited breathlessly for this evening. Akhtar had received her own instructions immediately after Mariam's arrival at Qamar Haveli.

'Each of us must do her part by encouraging Mariam Bibi to remain with us,' Safiya Sultana had told Akhtar in the passageway, after calling her out of the sitting room. 'It is you who will relax her. You will oil her and paint her with henna. It is you who will make her feel beautiful for my nephew. That is your duty. And stop pretending you do not understand what I mean.' She gave Akhtar a

221

pointed look. 'I saw you listening when Hassan Ali told me of the British plan to dissolve his marriage.'

This morning, after watching Mariam emerge shakily from her interview with Hassan, old Firoz had insisted that the moment had come, that the foreign lady was ripe for passion.

'Do you see that faraway look on her face?' she had whispered to Akhtar, pointing a gnarled finger at Mariam's back as she moved away. 'She cannot help loving my Hassan, so tall, so handsome, the light of my eyes since his birth!'

Akhtar closed her eyes. Her task this afternoon had been simple. She had needed only to take Mariam Bibi's best feature and make the very best of it. That feature was her smile. Mariam had smiled only once during her stay, but in that moment Akhtar, who had previously thought Hassan Ali's wife awkwardly plain, had suddenly understood her beauty. Wide, feminine and full of mischief, the smile had lent her face a joyful translucence, as if it were lit unexpectedly from within.

It had been Akhtar's responsibility to make Mariam Bibi happy enough to smile for her husband.

As she mixed rose water with powdered almonds and spices, she had felt that the tiring arts she had learned from Firoz had brought her to this one great moment. Certain of her coming success, she had imagined Hassan Ali Khan arriving at the top of the stairs, and Mariam waiting for him in the sitting room, a queen among the other ladies. She had pictured him sitting down beside his aunt, his eyes lowered to conceal his joy at the loveliness of his wife.

The dreams she had reported to Safiya Sultana would be nothing compared to the honour of delivering Mariam Bibi to her husband, beautiful, smiling, and ready for his embraces.

Akhtar yawned, exhausted from the efforts of the day. As old Firoz had instructed her, she had not only done her work, she had also talked, persuading Mariam of the advantages of remaining at Qamar Haveli. While washing Mariam's hair, she had told her of Safiya Sultana's greatness. She had related the stories she had heard of Safiya's wisdom, her far-reaching knowledge, her ability to help those in distress who were brought into her presence, and even some who were not. While scrubbing and painting Mariam's feet, she had described her own arrival at the haveli and the many kindnesses she had received. While removing the hair from Mariam's legs, she had recited one of Safiya's poems.

But there had been other information to convey. Nudged by Firoz, Akhtar had hinted at the pleasures this marriage offered Mariam, the passion Hassan Ali would surely ignite in her when they were alone, so different, Firoz had assured Akhtar, from the torments of her own experience.

Perhaps Mariam had not understood her suggestions, for the lady had closed her eyes and turned her head away. But Firoz, who had taken the sheets from Mariam's marriage bed two years earlier, had whispered that Akhtar must go on with her counselling, for Bibi was still a virgin and needed her advice.

'It was not my Hassan Ali's doing that there was no blood on those sheets,' the old woman had declared later, glancing over her shoulder to make sure they were not overheard. 'He would never leave his bride unsatisfied. But, the foreigner was alone then, with no family members to encourage her, as our brides are encouraged. Perhaps she panicked. Perhaps he was kind. Inshallah,' she had added fiercely, 'such a disaster will not happen again.'

But nothing had taken place as it should have. First Mariam Bibi had allowed the removal of only part of her body hair, and not even the most important part. What, Akhtar had fretted as she put away her threads and her pastes, would Firoz say if she knew? What would Hassan Ali think when he discovered his wife's unremoved pubic hair?

Second, and worse, it seemed that the lady was still bent on divorce. When Akhtar had taken one of Mariam's slim hands, ready to decorate it with fine, henna arabesques, Mariam had jerked it away. 'Not my hands,' she said sharply, as if Akhtar's beautiful work were somehow distasteful or wrong. 'My countrymen do not understand these things. You may decorate my feet as much as you like, since you have already mixed the paste. They will not show when I return to Shalimar.'

Mariam's tone had been firm when she said those words, but Akhtar had noted with relief that her eyes had wavered.

'Do not worry, child,' old Firoz had assured Akhtar over the afternoon meal. 'My Hassan Ali will change Mariam's mind for her. All will be well when he arrives this evening and they see each other by lamplight. Yes indeed,' she added, nodding emphatically. 'The evening will tell.'

But Hassan had not come, and the awakening desire Akhtar had carefully nurtured all day would have to be revived before he came again.

She shifted miserably under her quilt. Near to weeping with disappointment, she had put away Mariam's lovely gold clothes and taken from the small trunk the garment that Mariam insisted upon wearing to bed: a voluminous embroidered dress that fell from her shoulders to her feet.

Mariam now sat, her back against the wall, reading a letter by the light of a small oil lamp, the paper smoothed out on her upraised knees. Like her clothes, the letter in Mariam's hands looked foreign. How, Akhtar wondered, could Bibi be looking at those strange markings with such perfect, worried understanding?

Curtain rings clicked quietly.

On the bed, Mariam looked up, startled, the paper fluttering in her hands.

Hassan closed the curtain behind him and entered her room, bringing with him the heady scent of pure amber.

Akhtar held her breath. Intent upon his wife, Hassan had not seen her or sensed her presence. She raised herself silently on one elbow.

'I am late,' he said simply, then sat on the edge of the bed, the lamp's flame casting a warm light on his clothes. Her letter on her knees, Mariam Bibi watched him warily, her legs still drawn up close to her body, her loosened hair falling over her shoulders in auburn waves.

'You missed dinner,' she said, a little tremulously.

Had Hassan known Akhtar was present, he would not then have reached forward, gold gleaming dully on one wrist, and laid his hands on his wife's feet.

Mariam Bibi resisted him at first. She pressed herself against the wall behind her as he ran his fingers over the contours of her carefully painted toes, her high arches and her narrow ankles, bereft now of their fine hair. His eyes on hers, he murmured:

> Oh, sacred bird,
> Be my guide in the way of my desires,
> For the journey I propose is a long one,
> And I am new to travelling.

'New?' Bibi breathed. 'But you have already—'

'For all that you behave like one,' he interrupted softly, 'you are no spy.'

Ashamed to have seen Hassan Ali Khan lean forward and cover his wife's mouth with his own, Akhtar rose silently, her back turned to protect the lady's self-respect. As she padded barefoot towards the doorway, she heard a sigh. Unable to stop herself, she glanced over her shoulder.

Mariam Bibi's eyes had lost their focus. Her mouth began to open as Hassan put his hands on her knees, and pushed them a little way apart.

It was a small gesture a suggestion, not a command, but it was enough. As Akhtar moved the curtain carefully aside and slipped from the room, she knew that Mariam Bibi had abandoned the world and entered the dwelling place of the senses.

Akhtar spent the rest of the night in the passageway. It was cold there, and she caught a chill without the quilt she had abandoned in the corner of the bedchamber, but the sounds she had hoped for came from behind the curtain, whispers, rustling, then a small sob. There had also, as she had feared, been a gasp of surprise from Hassan, but to her relief it had been followed by muffled laughter.

She smiled to herself as she shivered on the tiled floor. She would forget neither this moment of triumph nor the verse Hassan had murmured to his wife.

Tomorrow morning when the dawn prayer was finished and she took Safiya aside, she would finally lay her treasure at the king's door.

Chapter Twenty-Seven

16 January 1841

Mariana awoke to the sound of the call to prayer. Her eyes half open, she watched the door curtain sway briefly, then hang unmoving on its rings.

He was gone.

Akhtar's corner was empty. The second bed had not been slept in. Its padded quilt was still covered, as it had been last night, with carefully arranged packets of clothing from Mariana's native trousseau.

The events of last night really had happened. Smears of dried blood marked the bed sheet. Mariana's nightdress, too, was stained. Her unused bolster had fallen to the floor. She closed her eyes, remembering the pillow she had slept on: warm, human, a man's chest. Beneath the amber he wore, Hassan's skin had smelled hot, as if it had been scorched. The scent had both terrified and exhilarated her.

The intensity on his face had made her draw back at first; it reminded her of the look in Charles Mott's eyes and the painful grip of his fingers. But Hassan had been different. He had murmured poetry, his hands on her feet, his eyes on her face.

'Forgive me,' he had breathed into her ear when, at last, he had hurt her.

Later, speechless at what she had done, Mariana fingered the oblong medallion Hassan wore on a gold chain, trying to read its tiny letters by the lamp's flame.

'It is Arabic, from the Qur'an,' he said, stroking her cheek, his eyes glowing in the lamplight. 'A jeweller made it for my grandfather, who gave it to me when I was born. The verses on it are from from Sura Nur. They say that Allah is like a beautiful light enclosed in glass as brilliant as a star.'

'And did your grandfather believe you would be the next leader of the Brotherhood?'

Hassan smiled. 'Oh, no. He always said I was sent into this world as a peacemaker, not as a Shaikh.'

Unexpected as they had been, the events of last night now felt inevitable.

She drew her shawl closer over her shoulders. She had no choice but to stay at Qamar Haveli now. She would help to secure the house against invasion, and then she would live out her life here, never needing to part with Saboor again, learning from Safiya Sultana by day, and from Hassan by night, just as Akhtar had told her in that irritatingly suggestive tone.

But first, although Hassan had forbidden her to do it, she must go to Shalimar and tell Aunt Claire and Uncle Adrian of her decision. She shivered, picturing her aunt's desperate tears, Lady Macnaghten's arch, horrified stare, the Vulture's dismissal, Charles Mott's sneer.

They would never forgive her, but she was different now, with her body tired and sore, and the imprint of Hassan's kisses on her mouth. Across the room, her beautiful yellow jamawar lay folded on her trunk. He had bought it for her himself . . .

She no longer cared what they said at Shalimar.

An hour later, when Mariana entered the sitting room freshly dressed and blushing, the younger women stared and the older ones cooed, while Safiya offered her a satisfied smile. Someone had obviously reported the stains on her sheets while she was bathing.

She took her usual place beneath the window, but this time, instead of sitting stiff-backed on the floor, she rested an elbow on one of the bolsters. She sighed with pleasure when Saboor came to lie across her lap. Why should she not give in to it all? Why should she try to remain an Englishwoman in this atmosphere where women spent their days in perfect intimacy? Why pretend she did not eagerly await Hassan's return tonight?

She had thought there would be work to do in the house, and she was correct. After threading a mountain of small turnips onto strings for drying and filling a row of earthen pickling jars alternately with salt and tiny yellow limes, she and the other women watched Safiya resolve a dispute between a neighbourhood woman and her very angry sister-in-law over a copper cooking pot.

Then it had been time for Safiya to teach her how to eat rice properly with the fingers.

After the dishes had been removed and Mariana was sitting contentedly with a nursing mother and a gaggle of chattering girls, a familiar voice floated in through the window above her head.

'But Yusuf,' the voice said, 'I do not see how they can succeed.'

Anxious to hear and see Hassan again, she got quickly to her feet and pressed herself against the filigree shutters. He was out of sight below the window, speaking to a heavyset man whom she could see, and whom she vaguely recognized.

'First,' Hassan continued, so close by that she could hear the intake of his breath, 'they must get into the garden, which will, of course, be under armed guard. Second, each of them must get a clear shot, in spite of the confusion and the intervening trees.'

A garden? Clear shots? Mariana tried to unlock the shutters, but they creaked too loudly. The girls across the room looked up.

'But they are Afghans, my dear fellow.' The other man sounded impatient. 'They will enter by stealth. Their marksmanship is second to none; even at night they will have no problem. All they will need is time to make themselves ready. What I want to know is where they are to be positioned.'

'Zulmai says they are to conceal themselves near the centre pavilion. Their orders will be to shoot on sight.'

'All five?'

'Yes, all five.'

'I do not see any difficulty with the plan, Hassan. Unless the man is warned, he will never expect assassins. His attention, and everyone else's, will be diverted by the assault on the Citadel. If you ask me, the assassination will be accomplished in ten minutes.'

The man? Did they mean the Vulture? Mariana wondered. There were five English people at the Shalimar Garden: Uncle Adrian and Aunt Claire, the Vulture, Mott, and Lady Macnaghten, whose tent was at the centre pavilion.

'And what of your wife?' Yusuf asked Hassan. 'After all, she may have been—'

'I am keeping her here.' Hassan dropped his voice. 'She is to know nothing about this. Hai Allah, Yusuf,' he added bitterly, 'I cannot tell you how much I hate these British.'

Trembling, Mariana crept away from the window, trembling, and started for her room.

The natives are not to be trusted at this dangerous time, the Vulture's letter had said. She flung herself onto the bed, her thoughts racing. Was that why Hassan had come to her last night: to seduce her into trusting him, to persuade her to stay voluntarily at Qamar Haveli so she would not be at Shalimar when the assassins came?

How long would he keep her a prisoner after he had murdered Uncle Adrian and the others? Surely, after he had tired of her, he would have her killed, like the others. He would never risk her escaping and telling the British authorities what he had done. Surely the murder of senior British officials by a member of the Sikh court would spark terrible reprisals.

Now she understood the Vulture's need for information. How could she have doubted the man, when he was only trying to save all their lives?

She raked back her hair. What had she revealed when she had spoken to Hassan of his intrigues?

She must warn the Vulture. She must write to him and persuade Ghulam Ali to deliver her letter to Shalimar. But Hassan had forbidden her to communicate with anyone there. Her request for paper and pen would certainly be denied.

Very well then, she would tear off a scrap of her nightgown, then cut herself and write the message in her own blood. Perhaps that would make up for the other message that was already written on the sheets, on her gown . . .

She froze. Hassan stood in the room. He smiled. 'You look nice in those clothes. Red suits you well.'

She should have returned his smile and pretended nothing was wrong, but she could not. Instead, she shrank from him, her arms raised, as he approached her.

His smile vanished. 'What is it?' he asked, moving closer. 'Has someone hurt you?'

'*You* have hurt me,' she whispered savagely, anger and fright blotting out her self-control. 'How could you have done that to me last night, when all along you were planning to kill the English people at Shalimar? How can you talk of my clothes while you are sending marksmen to kill my poor old aunt and my uncle who is ill? I was so wrong about you.' Her voice broke. 'Why did I not see the danger in your father's insistence that I come to stay here, in your Aunt Safiya's refusal to speak of the divorce, in the servant woman's sly suggestions? Why did I let myself believe that you loved—'

'Quiet!' He stood over her, his eyes flat and expressionless. He was much taller than she was, and she had no weapon . . .

'Trust,' he said in the level tone that he had used yesterday, 'was the one gift I wanted from you. I looked for no dowry from your family, no jewels, no lands. I entrusted my son to you. You kept him for two years. In all that time, did I demand to know where he was or how you treated him? Did I imagine, for one moment, that you meant him harm?'

'But I was worthy of your trust.' Distraught as she was, Mariana refused to drop her eyes from his. 'I love Saboor, but you hate my people. You said so, just now, outside the window. Not only do you hate them, you are going to have them murdered. And what of me, your English wife? Am I to be your prisoner now, or will you kill me as well?'

'I am Punjabi,' he snapped. 'I do what is best for the Punjab. You should have thought of that before you agreed to marry me.' He shook his head. 'You have no idea what all this is about. You do not know what evil is being planned at Shalimar, and I will not tell you. I have had enough of you. You do not behave decently, you shout, you fight, you interfere, you have been sent to spy on me.

You may have your divorce,' he added coldly, waving a dismissive hand. 'I will tell my aunt. Your iddat begins tomorrow.'

Without looking at her again, he turned, crossed the room, jerked the door curtain aside, and left her.

Chapter Twenty-Eight

Divorce? Her heart racing, Mariana stared after Hassan. Had he really expected to keep her as his wife after he had massacred her people? If so, then for all his calm elegance, he must be mad.

She got up shakily and pushed her feet into her new leather slippers. She must escape to Shalimar and warn her uncle and the Vulture, but how? No one in this house would lend her a horse, and even if they did, how could she ride safely, alone and uncovered, through the crowded streets of the city? A palanquin would be better, but where would she find one? Who would be her bearers?

Someone spoke quietly in the passageway outside. Mariana stiffened. Who was there? Was it Safiya Sultana, whose calm presence and compelling storytelling had masked her cruelty, or was it the sly Akhtar, whose paints and unguents had prepared her for Hassan's treacherous, stroking hands?

She crept to the doorway and peeped round the curtain. The corridor outside was empty, save for Akhtar, who hurried towards her.

'Peace, Bibi,' she offered, smiling. 'Safiya Sultana is calling you. She wants to show you—'

'I need a burka.' Mariana gripped Akhtar's arm and dragged her into the bedchamber. 'I must cover myself,' she whispered fiercely, remembering a rainy morning two years earlier, and herself shrouded in yards of dusty white cotton. 'I must leave this house immediately. My uncle is ill,' she added, searching for a plausible excuse. 'I must go to him at once.'

Akhtar stared. 'But you must not leave now,' she protested. 'You must stay here with the ladies. Hassan Sahib will be coming again tonight. Everyone is so happy now that you and he have—'

'Bring it *at once*.' Mariana dug her fingers into Akhtar's thin arm.

'I have no burka,' Akhtar whispered tremulously, wincing with pain. 'I have only an old chador. It belongs to—'

'*Bring it.*'

Akhtar fled. The family ladies could not have been told the truth. Mariana imagined them watching her now, shaking their heads at her fear and her fury, imagining she had gone mad. 'What a pity,' they would cluck to each other. 'Poor Hassan. He was so patient, so good to her.'

Safiya Sultana and Hassan knew quite well that she was not insane. And they must have known all along how and when the English were to be murdered. After all, they had sought no information from her. Instead, they had drawn her in slowly, firing her imagination with their stories, their kindness to strangers, their poetry and perfumes . . .

Why leave us when we want you here? Hassan had asked her.

Mariana turned back into the bedroom, remembering the poem Akhtar had recited to her yesterday, one that Safiya had written when she was eleven years old:

Like the muezzin who leans from his minaret
The nightingale gives voice from high in a cypress tree.
Perhaps the bird bewails his thwarted passion for the rose;
Perhaps he celebrates her beauty.
In either case, like Safiya, the nightingale can be heard,
Although he is not seen.

Yesterday, that poem had been seemed lovely and compelling. Today, with its reference to hidden women, it had a sinister tone. Mariana shivered. Safiya knew how to cure many illnesses with her potions and her amulets, if Akhtar was to be believed. But could she also destroy? If she chose to, could Safiya actually drive her mad?

The natives are not to be trusted in this dangerous time. Why had she not seen that Safiya, good as she was to her own people, had no compassion or understanding of outsiders? How had she missed the hardness beneath Safiya's calm exterior? Why had she trusted her?

Trust had been Hassan's word.

Enough. She must stop thinking of herself and go to Shalimar. She might never recover from last night's terrible mistake, but for now she had vital work to do.

She crossed the room and opened her small trunk. There, neatly arranged, were her hairbrushes, her best set of stays, and her second-best gown. She must leave them all behind. They were no great loss; after all, her appearance would not matter any more.

Akhtar burst into the room, a length of stained cotton fabric the colour of earth balled up in her hand. Mariana snatched it from her and put it over her head. It smelled evil.

'There is no time to talk,' she said, fanning away the smell, 'but before I leave, what does "iddat" mean?'

Akhtar's sharp little chin had begun to wobble. 'It is a woman's waiting time after her divorce. After she has been with her husband, she must let three monthly periods go by before she is allowed to marry again. But Bibi, please,' she pleaded, 'do not think of—'

'And where would she spend those months?'

'Here, Bibi.' Akhtar wiped her cheeks with her fingers. 'You would spend it here, at Qamar Haveli.'

'Never,' Mariana snapped and started for the door.

Outside, two women sweepers moved crabwise across the floor, patiently gathering little heaps of dust, their long, grass brooms flicking along the wall and into corners. Mariana drew the chador over her nose and mouth, lowered her head and hurried past them and down the back stairway. Once safely through the kitchens and across the servants' courtyard, she would open the back gate and gain the narrow street that ran beside the house. She would be anonymous there . . .

She had almost reached the kitchen when a deep, familiar voice issued from inside. 'We are not so poor, Khadija,' the voice decreed, 'that we must give our guests watery aloo gosht.'

Her heart thundering, Mariana flattened herself against the wall, praying that Safiya had not finished giving instructions, that she would not emerge from the kitchen on her way upstairs.

'And I want you to add more chilies and salt to the lentils,' the voice continued, growing closer. 'They were too bland yesterday.'

With no time for fear, Mariana sprinted back upstairs, the chador flying. Looking neither right nor left, she scurried past the room where she had spoken to Hassan, then hurtled down the spiral staircase and into the Shaikh's empty courtyard.

'Who are you?' One of the guards peered suspiciously at her a moment later, after she had made her breathless way past the busy stables. 'Why do you want us to open the gate?'

'My name is Akhtar,' she lied. 'I serve Safiya Bhaji and the other ladies. Please let me out. My uncle is ill.'

Her head lowered, her face covered, Mariana tried to conceal her pale hands. She bent her knees to lengthen her chador, aware that the bright designs on her feet were barely concealed by her dainty leather slippers. Terrified that Akhtar had already told Safiya, that people had already begun to search for her, she forced herself not to look back over her shoulder. 'Please,' she begged.

'You say you are Akhtar, who works upstairs with old Firoz? The one whose husband burned her with—'

The first guard put up a hand for silence. 'The next time you want to leave,' he said gruffly as he tugged the bolt open on the great double doors, 'go out through the kitchen.'

A quarter of a mile from Shalimar, Mariana leaned against a dusty tree and pulled off one of her shoes. She had not dared to look at her feet during her three-mile walk in her inadequate slippers, but now she wanted to see the damage.

It was worse than she had imagined. Blood from her blisters had seeped into the slipper's thin leather sole. Grimacing, she forced it back onto her foot and continued her painful progress towards the English camp.

Her journey had been difficult, if uneventful. Once free of the haveli, she had hurried as rapidly as she could along a narrow lane between tall, ramshackle brick houses and boarded shops. She had passed the Delhi Gate Bazaar with its shouting merchants and heaps of grains and spices, then joined the mass of people with bundles on their heads making their way out through the heavy, pointed archway of the gate and into the heaving crowd of men and animals emerging from the great open caravanserai outside.

Afraid of being trampled, coughing in the clouds of dust, Mariana had tried to hug the worn brick wall opposite the great caravanserai gate, but it was lined with squatting men and no safe place for her.

Instead she had struggled along in the crowd, buffeted by donkey carts and pushed aside by groups of hurrying, barefoot men, until she had emerged at last onto the road to Shalimar.

No one had tried to stop her on the way, although she had certainly been noticed. A merchant here, an old woman, a group of children there, had watched her pass, taking in the good cotton clothes that peeped from beneath her chador, studying her hands, her feet. Word of the route she had taken would, she was sure, reach the Waliullahs within hours of her escape, perhaps sooner.

A mile from the city, the road had been less crowded, but still there had been donkeys, files of silent camels, creaking bullock carts as tall as ships, and gangs of turbaned horsemen, all, curiously enough, heading away from the city instead of towards it, but in all that crowd, there had been no lone woman. The only women visible on the road had been stuffed into the back of carts with groups of children, or walking single file with huge bundles of straw on their heads, safe in each other's company. Hot under her chador, her feet blistering, aware of the stares of her fellow travellers, Mariana had longed to ask for a place in one of the carts, but with nothing to offer the driver and no man to protect her, she had kept to herself.

The sun had been overhead by the time the dusty walls of the garden had appeared in the distance.

At the gate, ignoring the row of beggars who pleaded for her attention, she lowered the chador from her face and breathed deeply. Once she was inside the garden, sounding the alarm would be easy. She had only to repeat what she had overheard beneath the verandah window, and the Vulture and Uncle Adrian would understand at once and do everything necessary to thwart Hassan's plan. But what of her? How was she to forgive herself? How would she ever recover from her remorse at letting herself be fooled by the Waliullahs, deflowered by Hassan, ruined for life?

Throughout her year of gossip and ostracism in Calcutta, she had taken refuge in the knowledge that she was pure. Now even that small comfort was gone.

She must tell no one, not her mother in England, not her sister Charlotte. She could never marry. Even if she met Harry Fitzgerald again, even if he fell to his knees and begged for her hand, she must refuse. She would never have a fair-haired baby of her own. She would never see Saboor again.

She had not even kissed him goodbye . . .

Minutes later, red-eyed and bone-weary, she entered the gate and presented herself at the Vulture's tent.

'Political Agent Sahib is not here,' declared his head servant, a liveried fellow with a superior air. 'He is sitting over there, with visitors.'

He pointed to a distant tree where the Vulture sat in an upright chair, waving his arms at four armed men in coarse, Afghan clothing who stood in front of him, listening.

'Call him at once,' Mariana ordered. 'Tell him Miss Givens is here to see him.'

'Miss Givens! Good heavens, I hardly recognize you.' The Vulture looked her up and down a moment later, astonishment on his face. 'How have you come? Is your divorce arranged? Why are you wearing native dress? Why are you so dirty?'

'I have walked from the city, Mr Lewis. I have something important—'

'Have you discovered the time and place of Sher Singh's assault on the city? Have you learned anything else I should know? Will the Rani accept his offer of safe passage, or will he launch an attack upon the Citadel?'

She hesitated, aware of the need for care in telling her story. If the Vulture thought she was hysterical, he might not believe her.

'I overheard a conversation between my husband and one of his friends,' she began, measuring her words. 'They were speaking of an assassination in a garden.'

'Yes?' He leaned forward eagerly.

'My husband said there were to be shooters and victims. They mentioned a centre pavilion. They hate us all. I was shocked at the bitter, murderous way they spoke of us.' Mariana shivered. 'As soon as I heard those words, I escaped the haveli in disguise and came to tell you.'

He flapped an impatient hand. 'I am sorry to hear all that, but what I want to know is the day and time of Sher's attack.'

Why was the man so fixed upon Sher Singh? Mariana raised her voice. 'Mr Lewis, I am trying to tell you that Hassan Ali Khan is sending Afghan marksmen to Shalimar with orders to enter the garden, station themselves near the centre pavilion, and shoot all of you on sight — everyone: you, Lady Macnaghten, Mr Mott, and my aunt and uncle.'

The Vulture drew himself up, his adam's apple bobbing. 'My dear young lady,' he said, his eyebrows raised in astonishment, 'whatever has given you that idea?'

He was mad. They were all mad. Without another word, Mariana turned on her heel and limped away, leaving the Vulture gazing after her, his mouth agape.

She had nearly reached her tent when someone called out to her. 'Miss Givens,' he shouted. 'I thought it was you!'

Mariana looked in the direction of the voice and saw Charles Mott running awkwardly towards her, his expensive frock coat flapping about him. 'We must speak,' he panted, stopping short. 'I have something—'

'Get out of my way,' she snapped. 'I have nothing to say to you.'

Of all the people she did *not* wish to see . . .

'But Miss Givens, I—'

'Memsahib?' Before Mott could say anything more, Dittoo appeared in the doorway of Mariana's tent, his eyes wide. 'But how have you come here? Where is Saboor Baba? Why are you wearing those clothes?'

'I will explain later,' she replied, then hobbled into her tent and sank wearily onto her bed. 'Bring me a bucket of hot water and a cup of salt,' she ordered as she peeled away her ruined slippers.

Before he shuffled off, Dittoo turned to her, his ugly face creased with worry. 'You should know, Memsahib,' he said, 'that your uncle is very ill.'

As the door blind fell into place behind Dittoo, Mariana, bit back hot tears. With Uncle Adrian ill and the Vulture refusing to listen, there was no one to turn to for help. How could any of them be saved?

After soaking her feet and bandaging them as best she could with several handkerchiefs, she changed her clothes, forced on a pair of boots, and hurried to her uncle's tent, only to be shooed outside by an exhausted-looking Aunt Claire.

'He has finally fallen asleep,' she whispered, waving Mariana away from the entrance. 'It is cholera, just as we thought. For several days he was unable to eat, and then he developed a pustule on his hand. The real illness set in yesterday afternoon. His purgings went on all night. They have ceased this morning, but that only makes me fear the worst.' She stared briefly at Mariana. 'Why do you look different?' she asked, then shook her head and pushed bedraggled hair from her face. 'I cannot think of these things now. I am quite at my rope's end. Will you sit with your uncle until dinner, while I lie down in your tent?'

Mariana nodded.

'Thank you, my dear. If his thirst should return, there is a jug of sweetened vinegar water beside the bed.' Aunt Claire gestured towards a grizzled old servant who stood anxiously by the doorway. 'Adil will help you if you need anything.'

Uncle Adrian had curled his body so tightly under the sheets that Mariana could see only the bald top of his head and a fringe of grey hair. Perched stiffly on a chair beside him, she willed him to awaken, to hear her story, to tell her what to do.

It seemed like hours before he spoke. When he did, his voice sounded slurred and indistinct beneath the covers.

'It's Mariana,' she told him quietly, leaning over the bed. 'What did you say, Uncle Adrian?'

'Lewis,' he said with difficulty, 'is up to no good.'

'Yes, you told me that in your letter.' He was clearly too ill to be told of the coming attack. Mariana pressed a hand to her forehead, forcing herself to put aside her own desperation, to be patient with her uncle's irrelevant concerns.

'Mott will give you the details of Lewis's plan. I know you do not like Mott, but you must speak to him about this. You must try to stop them before—' He groaned.

'Of course I will, Uncle,' she lied. He began to thrash about, throwing himself from side to side on the bed. She reached out, then pulled back her hand, unsure whether to touch him.

'What are you doing?' Aunt Claire burst through the doorway, a dripping cloth in one hand. 'You are not to let him exhaust himself talking.' She applied the wet cloth to her husband's forehead. 'Go and have your dinner. Tell them to send me a tray. And for goodness sake, wash your face before you go.'

Dinner had already begun when Mariana entered the dining tent; she found everyone already sitting down. In his seat beside Lady Macaghten, the Vulture was buttering a piece of bread. 'It a pleasure

243

to be dining with you, Miss Givens,' he observed, nodding as Mariana took her seat, splaying his fingers on the butter knife, 'although you certainly surprise me with your *extraordinary* appearance.'

His tone was especially unpleasant. Mariana glanced up to see Lady Macnaghten staring covertly at her face.

'Your face is dirty,' Lady Macnaghten hissed. 'It is smudged with dust.' She leaned across Uncle Adrian's empty place. 'But your eyebrows are nicely done,' she added, offering Mariana a conspiratorial half-smile before straightening in her seat, 'and I quite like your hair.'

'Miss Givens,' the Vulture interjected, 'arrived precipitously this afternoon from the walled city. I am quite mystified as to why she has come. She has brought us no information of value, nor has she achieved her divorce.'

'You know exactly why I have come, Mr Lewis.' Mariana did not bother to keep the anger from her voice. 'I am here to inform you that sharpshooters are being sent from the walled city to kill us all.'

Lady Macnaghten gasped. Around the table, the various officers exchanged glances.

'You are quite wrong, Miss Givens,' snapped the Vulture. 'Nothing of the sort is going to happen. You must pay no attention to her.' He inclined his head towards Lady Macnaghten. 'We are perfectly safe here at Shalimar.'

'But how can you—'

'You, Miss Givens,' he said coldly, dropping one of his hands onto the table with a thump, 'would have done well to have remained at Qamar Haveli. You should have made it your business to confirm information instead of rushing here with false intelligence and trying to frighten everyone.' He sniffed. 'I certainly do not need advice from a young woman with a grimy face and a dirty black cord round her neck.'

At the end of the table, the senior baggage officer cleared his throat noisily, as if to drown out the Vulture's appalling rudeness. The three other officers began to speak at once.

Charles Mott put down his napkin and leaned towards her. 'I have been trying to tell you, Miss Givens,' he murmured, 'that the sharpshooters you fear belong to Mr Lewis, not the Punjabis. They are to assassinate not us but Prince Sher Singh in the Hazuri Bagh while his troops are storming the Citadel.'

Mariana's face paled. Before she had time to pull herself together and begin asking the many questions crowding into her mind, Charles Mott shook his head warningly.

'I will tell you more after dinner,' he said quietly.

Later, after ushering Mariana from the dinner tent, Mott told her what he had discovered.

'The Hazuri Bagh, the Garden of Nobles,' he said, 'lies between the Badshahi Mosque and the main Citadel gate. It is from there that Sher Singh will blow open the gate and launch his attack on the Rani. Lewis's plan is to send sharpshooters into the Hazuri Bagh. They are to lie in wait near the centre pavilion and shoot Sher Singh during the battle.'

Mariana's mouth went dry. 'But why?'

'Lewis is ambitious, Miss Givens. He wants the Punjab annexed to British India while he is Political Agent. The simplest way is to make sure this country has no decent ruler, then to step in during the inevitable chaos. Sher Singh is too popular and too competent for Lewis's taste. Of course, in time the Sikhs may kill each other off without any interference from us, but Russell Lewis is not a patient—'

'Are you certain of this?' Mariana interrupted.

Mott wiped his forehead with a damp-looking handkerchief. 'I know you think me a fool, Miss Givens,' he said bluntly, 'and I have been one. But I also have a great deal of respect for your uncle since he . . .' Mott fidgeted awkwardly. 'Perhaps now is not the time to go into that. In any event, your uncle suspected that Lewis was up to something and he asked me to discover what it was. As Lewis had taken me into his confidence, I was able to learn the details of his plan. I am an intelligence officer, after all,' he added with a sour smile.

'But now Mr Lamb is ill,' he went on, 'and I do not know what to do. We are, of course, forbidden to engage in any sort of intrigue with the natives, but Lewis is our most senior officer here. There is no one for hundreds of miles with the authority to stop him.'

What she had done?

'Men in the city already know of the assassination plot,' Mariana said shakily. 'They will prevent it.' Then she turned and walked painfully to her tent.

Lady Macnaghten had been quite correct about her face. As Mariana held up her looking glass and stared into it, she saw that her cheeks were smeared with the dust and tears of her journey. Pointlessly elegant brows now framed her face. Her skin, where it was clean, looked uselessly fresh and dewy.

On another day, Lady Macnaghten's friendly words would have given her joy. Now that she had thrown away her chance at happiness, they only added to her misery.

Why had she not asked Hassan whose assassination he had been discussing as he stood with his friend under that open window? Why had she rushed so hastily to judgement against people who had offered her nothing but acceptance and love, who had only wanted to protect her from the Vulture's treachery?

I am keeping her here, Hassan had said. *She is to know nothing about this.*

She gulped back tears. From the very beginning when she had accepted his proposal in front of the court, she had done everything wrong. Blinded by ignorance and her own stupid, headlong nature, she had behaved again and again like an ogre in a fairy story.

You shout, you fight, you interfere, Hassan had told her, in that cold, level voice.

He was right. She had done all those things. Worst of all, she had not trusted him.

She must return at once to Qamar Haveli and throw herself on his mercy, and the mercy of his family. Safiya had forgiven her before, perhaps she would again; but what of tender, elegant Hassan? His last words to her had carried such heavy finality. What if he refused to take her back, to let her be his wife, to let her be Saboor's mother? She would surely die of unhappiness.

But she could not leave for the city now, with her uncle so desperately ill. And even if he survived, she and Aunt Claire would face days and nights, perhaps weeks of difficult nursing before he was fully recovered.

Whatever decision she made now, whether she returned to the haveli or stayed at Shalimar, the consequences would haunt her for the rest of her life.

Suddenly she straightened.

Who had told her that Safiya Sultana knew a cure for cholera?

It had been the woman who had brought the young, despairing mother to be cured. *It is said that she can even cure cholera*, the woman had confided.

'No, Mariana, this is madness.' Aunt Claire drooped in the upright chair, her eyes large in her yellow face. 'You must stop asking me.

It is much too dangerous. I could not bear to lose both of you.'

'But it is his only chance.' Her uncle moaned on the bed beside them. Mariana summoned the last of her persuasive power and knelt beside her aunt's chair. 'I shall ask Safiya Sultana to return here with me,' she insisted, gazing into her aunt's face. 'She is a native, but she is renowned for her ability to heal. They would never have told me she had a cure for cholera if it were untrue.'

Her aunt closed her eyes. 'Very well,' she sighed. 'You may go, but not until the morning. And after you do, you must return as quickly as you can.'

Chapter Twenty-Nine

The Citadel and the Badshahi Mosque occupied the northwestern quarter of the walled city of Lahore. On its western edge, the Citadel's ninety-foot-high Alamgiri Gate and the mosque's equally tall, carved entrance faced each other across the rectangular expanse of the Hazuri Bagh, or Garden of Nobles.

While Mariana had been making her painful way to Shalimar, four men, three of them heavily armed, stood deep in conversation on the upper floor of the two-storeyed marble pavilion that adorned the garden's centre. As the men talked, the unarmed member of their group pointed towards the Citadel Gate whose pair of massive towers stood less than fifty yards away.

'If your information is correct, Zulmai,' said Hassan Ali Khan, 'then Prince Sher Singh will watch his men storm the Citadel from this vantage point. Nowhere else in the garden has a better view of the gate. And if the assassins succeed, it is here on this parapet that he will die.'

'Hah!' Yusuf Bhatti clapped him on the back. 'Stick to negotiating, my fine friend,' he advised, 'and leave fighting strategy to others.'

249

He waved dismissively about him at the pretty upper floor of the pavilion, with its scalloped arches and marble inlay. 'This upper story is wide open and unprotected. Look there.' He pointed through the trees to the thick, crenellated wall that stretched away on either side of the heavy gate, separating the Citadel from the garden. 'The Rani's own marksmen will be shoulder to shoulder up there, each one praying for an opportunity to shoot Sher Singh.'

'He cannot conduct the battle from the ground floor, either,' Zulmai said, in his accented Punjabi. 'It is as open as the upper storey, with all those archways. You can see straight through it.'

Habibullah grinned. 'I could see well enough from the far end of the garden to put a bullet into the Prince's heart wherever he was standing.'

'There is an underground room,' offered Hassan, 'where the old Maharajah used to spend hot summer days.'

Yusuf and Zulmai nodded.

'Then that will be Sher Singh's command post,' Yusuf stated. 'The assassins may not know of that underground room yet, but they will learn of it when they see men going up and down the stairs.'

'And where will the snipers hide themselves?' Hassan leaned his arms on the parapet and stared down at the garden.

'One may hide there.' Habibullah joined him and pointed towards an ancient tree whose gnarled roots offered enough cover for a prone man.

'And another there.' Yusuf tipped his head towards a low, ruined wall.

Zulmai shrugged. 'There are a hundred places where a man might conceal himself and wait while the garden fills with soldiers and artillery. What matters is this: at some point during the heat and noise of battle, Prince Sher Singh is bound to show himself and look towards the gate, and the assassins will take their shots. At

250

least the Prince has managed to keep the day and time of his attack vague. The uncertainty has been driving the British Political Agent to distraction.'

The sky behind the four men had turned pink, but no muezzin summoned the faithful to their sunset prayers at the Badshahi Mosque. Now converted to a Sikh powder magazine, the mosque was silent.

Hassan sighed. 'We can only pray that the assassins learn the time of the attack too late, or that Sher's men catch them in time. In any case, Yusuf, we must be off to warn him.'

'Tell me, Zulmai,' Yusuf inquired, as he descended the marble staircase, his weapons clanking at his side, 'who besides us knows of this plot?'

Zulmai lifted his shoulders. 'People know of it,' he replied casually, 'but none of them care. They are all Afghans. The Political Agent has paid them well to hold their tongues.'

'So you learned all this from one of your countrymen, not from a higher source.' Yusuf's tone had roughened. 'How can you be certain that it is true?'

'I was not told of these plans by an Afghan. I learned what I have told you from the Political Agent himself.' Zulmai smiled as he stepped out into the sunlight. 'He thinks I am one of the five assassins.'

'I am told that Sher Singh has bought and paid for twenty-six thousand infantrymen from Mianmir and Begampura,' Hassan remarked to Yusuf as they sat in the courtyard of Qamar Haveli half an hour later. 'They are to march sometime in the next two days, under cover of night.'

'And what is his plan?'

Hassan drew a circle with the toe of his shoe in the dust of the courtyard. 'When they arrive,' he said, pointing towards the right side of the circle, 'half of them will enter the city from the east, by the Delhi and Yakki Gates.'

'So near this house.' Yusuf blew out a long breath. 'Are you worried?'

'My father has refused to leave the haveli. I must therefore put my trust in Allah. The rest of Sher's army will come around to the Citadel side. Of those, half will enter the city through the Taxali Gate, and the remainder will enter the Hazuri Bagh and prepare to blow in the Alamgiri Gate and take the Citadel by force. I understand that Sher Singh's representative has been handing gold mohurs to the troops guarding all three city gates. Each one is to be opened at a signal, without a shot fired.' He shook his head. 'Our army seems to have sold its blood to the highest bidder.'

'And Sher Singh will order the Rani to surrender after he has subdued the city.'

'Yes, and of course she will refuse.'

'Of course. It will be good riddance when she leaves,' barked Yusuf. 'I never could stand what I heard about the woman. At least Sher Singh is a fighting man.'

Hassan nodded as a man approached them from across the courtyard.

'Peace,' Ghulam Ali offered, his white beard jutting aggressively. 'I have news for Hassan Sahib. I have come from the direction of Shalimar,' he continued, without waiting to be asked. 'There were soldiers and artillery on the road. I asked where they were going, and they said they were on their way to Buddhu da Awa to join Prince Sher Singh's forces.'

'And?' Hassan raised his eyebrows.

'They told me they were marching on Lahore tonight.'

Hassan nodded his thanks to the courier. 'Wait for me, Yusuf,' he said, before striding towards his father's sitting room.

Ten minutes later Hassan reappeared and he and Yusuf mounted their horses and rode towards the Delhi Gate.

'Let us hope Sher Singh has not left already,' Yusuf commented. 'I do not want to chase him over the countryside in the dark. But then,' he shrugged, 'if he is not at his camp, we can always send him a warning message.'

'No, Yusuf.' Hassan shook his head. 'It would be too risky to entrust such an important message to anyone. There is treachery everywhere these days.'

Yusuf thrust a meaty hand towards the crowd trying to get through the gate. 'Look at these wretches, running away from the city. I hear that half of them have buried their valuables, not that it will help them.' He shook his head dolefully. 'Whatever happens, Punjabis will soon be killing each other.'

White-uniformed infantry soldiers in black cross belts and silk turbans were in evidence everywhere, lounging in groups near shuttered bazaars, standing tensely in front of tall city houses. At the gate, their hungry eyes studied the crowd and the animals and the heavy bundles men and beasts were carrying.

Hassan sighed. 'And look at our soldiers. Who knows which side any of them have taken. Once they were our pride. Now they behave like common criminals.'

On horseback and elephant-back, in carts and on foot with their possessions on their heads, the crowd streamed out through the gate, the men wearing dhotis or shalwar kameezes, their women bare-faced or shrouded in burkas according to their faith, the children silent and staring.

'Have you noticed,' Hassan asked as they rode under the gate's thick, pointed arch, 'that nobody in this crowd has looked back?'

The two men followed the road to Shalimar. Clouds overhead obscured a half-moon, leaving only nearby villages to offer frail, glowing landmarks until their inhabitants fell asleep, and they, too, disappeared into the darkness.

'The turn-off must be somewhere here,' Hassan muttered. 'I have seen it a thousand times by daylight.'

'Wait.' Yusuf held up a hand in the darkness. 'Do you hear that sound? Something has disturbed the dogs in that village over there.' Without waiting for Hassan, he wheeled his mount and left the road.

New sounds joined the barking of the dogs: the clopping of hooves, the murmur of men's voices, the tramp of marching feet. As the clouds parted overhead, allowing a thin light to fall upon the scene, a ghostly column of white-clad figures appeared, muskets on their shoulders. They marched rapidly along a track at right angles to the main road, accompanied by two dozen men on horseback. As the file approached, more dogs added their voices to the first ones, signalling the presence of more soldiers.

While Hassan and Yusuf watched silently, the column gained the main road. They turned, four abreast, towards Lahore.

'At the rate they're travelling,' Yusuf murmured, 'they will be outside the city in less than an hour.'

It took some minutes for the column to pass. After it had disappeared into the darkness, a file of camels strode into view, each carrying a soldier and a swivel gun. Behind them rolled fourteen horse-drawn artillery pieces. The column numbered over five thousand men.

'Sher Singh's force for the Hazuri Bagh,' Yusuf muttered.

'Then we must hurry.'

But in that uncertain light they could not hurry. They let their horses pick their way over the path taken by the army until they came to the forbidding mound of brick and earth where Sher Singh had set up his court. After passing hundreds more milling soldiers and mounted officers, they urged their horses up the broad stone steps leading to the summit and its ruined pavilion. Tents had been set up to accommodate the members of Sher Singh's temporary court. 'No one is here,' a guard told them, looking up from his meal, his elderly face lit by a cooking fire. 'They left hours ago. No, I cannot say where they have gone, or when they will return.'

'If Sher Singh is not with that column, we may not be able to find him,' Yusuf said thoughtfully as he and Hassan returned the way they had come. 'In that case, preventing the assassination will be up to us. I will collect Zulmai and his fat-faced friend from the caravanserai, and then you can go home to Qamar Haveli and leave us to deal with the assassins ourselves.'

'I am not going home. I am coming with you.'

'But you are not needed,' Yusuf countered flatly. 'There will be only four assassins, and Zulmai is worth two men. He comes from a family of crack shots. His father killed a hundred ibex in his youth. He told us so himself. And we will have the advantage of surprise, at least at the beginning. Both Habibullah and I are used to these things,' he went on, softening his tone. 'You, Hassan, are a courtier.'

'I cannot ask the three of you to risk your lives while I sit safely in my house.'

Why did the fellow sound so bitter? By the moon's frail light, Yusuf thought he saw fury on his old friend's face.

'Something has happened,' he said sharply. 'What is it?'

'My wife has run away to Shalimar. She left this afternoon.'

'But you said she wanted to divorce you. Why did she not follow the proper procedure?'

'She has it in her head that you and I intend to kill her relatives and the other British at Shalimar.'

Yusuf groaned aloud.

'She must have run away to warn them.' Hassan shook his head wearily. 'You were right, Yusuf. I should have divorced her long ago.' He turned in his saddle, his face unreadable in the dimness. 'I can shoot, you know. I would hate to kill, but I would do it for the Punjab. I have a musket at home. I even have a Khyber knife. Nothing,' he said fiercely, 'will stop me from coming with you to the Hazuri Bagh.'

'If that is truly your wish, my friend,' Yusuf replied, shaking his head, 'then I can only pray that Allah Most Gracious sends us luck.'

Chapter Thirty

17 January 1841

Mariana banged on the roof of the palanquin, urging her bearers to hurry, then sat back on her cushions and looked at her timepiece. It was a quarter to six.

All night, she and her aunt had watched helplessly as her uncle thrashed under his quilts, his face damp and taut with agony. Once he had grasped Mariana's hand and tried, frantically, to tell her something, but Aunt Claire had leapt from her chair and forbidden him to speak. Once or twice he had gulped down the sweetened vinegar water. Otherwise, he had shown no improvement.

It had been nearly daylight before Mariana had been allowed to leave. She had rushed to her tent, shaken the dust from her native clothes, and put them on. Unable to wedge her bandaged feet into the ruined native slippers, she had laced them into her English boots, snatched up a few shawls and Akhtar's filthy chador, and sent for her palanquin.

The morning air felt misty and cold. The palanquin jogged along, its bearers breathing loudly in unison as they ran, while the lead bearer murmured the condition of the road to those running blindly behind him. Inside, Mariana shifted beneath the quilt and abandoned herself to the exciting memory of Hassan's weight upon her body.

Once she reached Qamar Haveli, she would beg his forgiveness and promise never to leave again. She would admit her mistake. She would swear that she trusted him absolutely, and that she would do whatever he asked if he would let her inhabit even a small corner of his life.

He would not deny her that much. Surely, in time, he would stroke her face again while she turned his beautiful gold medallion over in her fingers. Surely, she would once again breathe in the burnt perfume of his skin . . .

The smell of frying, filth, and corrupted roses replaced the tang of dung fires that had scented the air since Shalimar. The shouting of agitated men and the braying of animals reached her in the palanquin. She must be nearing the old caravanserai, and the Delhi Gate.

Shortly afterwards, jolts and tremors told her that her bearers were having trouble with the crowd. The crush must be even greater than it had been the previous afternoon. Staccato voices shouted angrily nearby. Animal bodies scraped against her palanquin. Inside the tightly closed box, she reached for a handhold, hating her sudden fear and her inability to see out.

'Hurry,' she ordered, banging on the roof with an anxious hand, willing them to get her out of this tumult and into the normal, busy lanes of the city, where she would be safe.

'Move out,' her head bearer shouted. Scuffling erupted close by. An animal let out a mournful groan. Metal clashed against metal beside her.

At last the palanquin moved forward with fewer jolts, as if the way had finally been cleared. Mariana's heart slowed its jumping.

The echo of her bearers' harsh breathing told her that she was under the heavy stone archway of the Delhi Gate.

She leaned back against her cushions, relieved to be away from the mob, but why were the streets around her now so strangely silent? Where were the carts that should be rumbling past her? Where were the footfalls and voices of the busy inhabitants of the walled city?

Without warning, her palanquin dropped to the ground.

She opened the panel and saw she was only a hundred yards inside the Delhi Gate. There was no sign of its bazaar, with its colourful piles of spices and sacks of grains. All that remained were dull, faceless boards and padlocked doors. The street, as far as she could see in either direction, was deathly still.

'What are you doing, Munnoo?' she called, leaning out of the palanquin. 'Why have you stopped? This is not Qamar Haveli.'

Her sirdar bearer turned to her, his proud, wizened face puckered with unfamiliar emotion. 'We must go back,' he said.

'But you must take me to the haveli, Munnoo. We cannot simply turn—'

'No, Memsahib.' He pointed to something Mariana could not see. 'If you will not let us take you back to Shalimar,' he said, his voice suddenly wobbling with fright, 'we will leave you here alone.'

Leave her there? Only the most dishonourable palanquin bearers did such things. 'Munnoo, you cannot possibly—'

Munnoo and the other bearers abruptly let go of the palanquin's carrying poles and sprinted like a flock of long-legged birds towards the Delhi Gate.

A harsh voice from above her head said, 'Do not stay in that palanquin, Bibi.'

'What?' She put her head out of the box and craned upwards,

looking for the owner of the voice, but saw only silent, shuttered balconies.

'I am up here,' the invisible speaker continued. 'Take my advice and walk away. If the soldiers see you in it, they will think you are rich. If they believe you are hiding jewels, they will kill you.'

'Soldiers?'

'Sher Singh's men entered the city half an hour ago, let in by the Rani's traitorous soldiers. For now all have gone to loot the Kashmir Bazaar, but they will return. Go home while you still can.'

'Home? But—'

'Listen.'

Distant shouting and the popping of gunfire broke the eerie silence of the street.

'Hurry!' commanded the invisible speaker.

Numb with fright, Mariana gathered up her shawls and Akhtar's chador, put a booted foot out of the palanquin and stepped gingerly onto the cobblestones. She unfolded the chador with shaking fingers and covered herself with its smelly folds.

It was not far to the small square where the austere façade of Qamar Haveli stood at right angles to Wazir Khan's mosque. If she walked quickly, she would be safely inside in no time.

She had taken only a few steps when she started, gasping.

The dead body of a middle-aged man lay in a broken heap near a flight of stairs, as if he had fallen from an upper window. If her palanquin had advanced only a few more paces, her bearers would have had to step round it. No wonder they had rushed headlong out of the city.

But where was the dead man's family? Where were his mourners?

Mariana already knew. They were inside, too terrified to show themselves on the cobbled street where she now stood out in the open, with nowhere to hide.

Unseen eyes bored into her, as if the whole city were watching her through loopholes and latticework shutters. Truly frightened now, she hurried past the dead man, lifted the awkward folds of her chador, and ran towards the haveli.

Qamar Haveli stood silent, its double, iron-studded doors tightly shut. No guard lounged outside to signal her arrival.

Her heart thudding, she crept along the front of the haveli, then turned into the dark alley that ran along its side. Avoiding the open sewer that ran along its margin, she hurried past shuttered doorways, looking for the entrance to the haveli's kitchen courtyard.

The low wooden door, set into a high, brick wall was tightly locked.

She called out and knocked on the heavy planks. Raising her voice, she knocked harder. Finally she shouted until her throat ached and beat on the door until her hands were bruised.

No one came.

The gunfire seemed to be coming closer. Someone had turned into the alley.

Heavy footfalls approached. Mariana pressed herself into a doorway.

'This is the short cut,' said a male voice.

'Good,' replied another. 'If we hurry, something will be left.'

Two soldiers in dusty white uniforms rounded the corner of the haveli and strode towards her, muskets on their shoulders, curved tulwars clanking at their sides, taking up the width of the alley.

The tall one saw her first. 'What,' he asked his companion casually, 'are women doing out of doors?'

'Pah, what a filthy chador!' The smaller man made a face as he passed her. 'She must smell as bad as that sewer.'

The tall one stopped and turned back to her. 'You should go home, Bibi,' he said.

'I am home.' Breathless from fright, Mariana struggled to marshal her thoughts. 'I need to get into this house,' she said quickly. 'Would you please beat on the door for me? They cannot hear me from the inside.'

'We do not serve women,' sneered the small soldier. He made a swaggering gesture with his shoulders. 'Knock on the door yourself.'

'My uncle is very ill.' She addressed herself to the taller, politer man.

'It is too late for your uncle.' The tall soldier shook his head. 'Prince Sher Singh has taken over this city. We are shooting his enemies like dogs. Can't you hear the firing in the Kashmiri Bazaar? This is no place for a woman. The fight will move into the square at any moment.'

'They should have told us they were going to the Kashmiri Bazaar first,' the second soldier complained, as the pair continued down the alley, no longer interested in her. 'Why should we miss all the fun?'

'There will be plenty more looting to do,' the first soldier assured him. 'You will see. In a few hours, only the beggars will be safe.'

The second soldier giggled and hitched up the belt of his tulwar. 'They'll be safe as long as we are killing only Sher Singh's enemies. Beggars will make perfect targets when we kill for sport.'

When they were out of sight, Mariana rushed to the front of the haveli and hammered hopelessly on its tall doors until she could beat on them no longer. She stood beneath the shuttered balconies and called until her voice was gone.

Exhausted, she pressed her forehead against the brick wall. She must think of a way to save herself. The Prince's troops were loose in the city without order or discipline, now joined, most likely, by the Rani's soldiers. All those too poor to barricade themselves behind stout haveli doors were in as much danger as she was. Even the people inside Qamar Haveli itself might suffer, if Sher Singh's men thought of putting it and other large houses to the torch.

The soldiers would arrive in the square at any moment, armed and bent on looting and death. She could not hide in the narrow alley, for she would surely be trapped there. She must find somewhere in the square to wait out the coming horror.

Looking as inconsequential as she did, she might live through the first hours of Sher Singh's invasion, at least until the soldiers began to kill for enjoyment . . .

She crept along the front of the haveli and looked for a place to hide. All the wooden doors and shutters that would ordinarily have been propped open to let in the air were now closed and locked. But she found a narrow recess in the wall where Qamar Haveli joined the wall of another house. With luck, if she squeezed herself into that poor bit of cover and stood still, no one would notice her.

The distant boom of howitzers came from the direction of the Citadel.

Prince Sher Singh had begun his attack from the Hazuri Bagh.

A gang of heavily armed soldiers erupted from a side street, brandishing unsheathed tulwars and bayonets. Ten abreast, sweating, their faces contorted with excitement, they charged past her, their weapons stained with blood.

What had happened to Maharajah Ranjit Singh's disciplined army, with its intricate drills, its almost European uniforms, and its foreign mercenary advisers? Were its officers so corrupted by politics and gold that they stood idly by and watched their men run wild? As Mariana stood paralysed at her post, she imagined herself lying dead outside her husband's house, unknown, unrecognized, her chador soaked in blood . . .

Yelling soldiers rushed into the mosque and a score of others splintered the frail shutters of the shops at its base – shops that sold items no looter would want: Illuminated copies of the Qur'an, books, and perfume. Disappointed, they hurled the books into the square and smashed vials of precious oil. The scents of musk, sandalwood and attar of jasmine filled the square.

A man leaned from a rooftop opposite Mariana's hiding place, a musket in his hand. He aimed carefully, then fired into the crowd of soldiers below. Mariana flinched as the ball struck home and a burly Sikh fell to his knees. *Run, run,* she begged silently, but the man on the roof lingered to see the effect of his shot.

Half a dozen soldiers raced to their wounded companion, who pointed weakly at the rooftop. The soldiers smashed their way into the sniper's house, reached the roof and dragged him and three other men from the house and flung them onto the street. Mariana sank to the ground and tried fruitlessly to stop her ears.

When she looked up, sickened at what she had heard, four decapitated bodies lay in front of the mosque.

Yelling and screaming, a dozen soldiers ran towards her along the front of the haveli, their steel bayonets and curved swords at the ready. Unable to breathe, she pushed herself against the wall, her arms raised in a hopeless effort to protect her face.

Ten feet from her, they swerved as one man and charged towards the centre of the square.

How had she escaped death? Mariana looked after the soldiers, her pulse racing. Was it her taweez? She reached up and felt for the silver box with Safiya's Qur'anic verses folded inside. Perhaps it was working. Perhaps, after all, she would survive this horror . . .

Only the beggars will be safe. There was wisdom in that cruel statement. Mariana did not stand up again. Instead, she began to transform herself. She rubbed against the dust-stained wall, adding stripes of grit to her already filthy chador. Gagging at the smell, she pushed her hands into the foul, urine-smelling dirt at the bottom of the wall, forcing it under her fingernails and into the skin on the backs of her hands, and rubbing it onto her face. She unlaced her English boots, hid them, then rubbed more dirt onto her feet and their bandages, wincing at the icy cold of the cobblestones under her bare toes. At last, filthy and terrified, she crawled to the haveli's front door. Making herself as small as she possibly could inside the folds of her chador, she reached out a dirty hand, palm up.

'Alms,' she croaked, 'alms, for the love of Allah.'

Chapter Thirty-One

By the time Mariana's bearers abandoned her in the city, Hassan, Yusuf Bhatti, and the two Afghan traders had already spent long, cold hours inside the Hazuri Bagh.

They had arrived after midnight to find the ground outside the torch-lit garden swarming with soldiers and pack animals and the side gate heavily guarded, but Yusuf and his companions had had no difficulty in entering. It had taken only a few rupees from Hassan to persuade the pickets to look the other way, allowing the four men to slip inside, pistols, jezails, muskets, and all.

Hassan had gone straight to the centre pavilion, identified himself, and asked to speak to Prince Sher Singh, but to no avail.

'He is not here,' a bearded officer said abruptly, turning him away at the marble steps.

'It is our fate, then,' Zulmai observed, 'to deal with these assassins alone.'

As they crouched, waiting for morning, against the garden's boundary wall, Yusuf pointed towards the side gate where they had entered. 'That's the last of the Prince's guns,' he said, as a team of horses dragged a nine-pound cannon inside by the light of a dozen torches. 'Fourteen artillery pieces. Sher Singh is taking no chances.'

Habibullah grinned as the horses hauled the piece into position before the massive Alamgiri Gate leading to the Citadel, encouraged by shouts and blows from a swarm of gunners. 'It will be a fine thing to see those huge doors blown off their hinges.'

'Let us see how much resistance the Rani offers,' cautioned Zulmai, glancing over his shoulder at the garden. Behind him, Sher Singh's infantry waited in groups while their officers rode to and fro, pointing and shouting orders.

'And who wins in the end,' Yusuf agreed.

Now, by the morning light, shivering beneath his heavy shawl, Yusuf glanced at Hassan who sat, his own shawl over his head, his breath visible in the raw air. Since midnight, he had spoken little.

'There is the Prince,' Hassan now said sharply, pointing towards the pavilion. 'On the verandah – the heavyset one in the shawl turban.'

The other three men followed his gaze in time to see a group of men disappear from sight down an interior flight of stairs.

Habibullah laughed. 'Your prince is a confident man, to be showing himself so early. Habibullah and I will search for them on this side of the pavilion. You, Hassan, go with Yusuf and watch the other side.'

Zulmai rose to his feet in one swift motion and adjusted his jezails. 'We have seen the target,' he said quietly. 'Now we must find his assassins.'

Zulmai proposed that he and Habibullah should search for Sher Singh's attackers on one side of the marble pavilion while Yusuf and Hassan covered the other.

A wall similar to the Citadel's surrounded the garden. The wide, flagstone walk along its top and its defensive stone battlements provided perfect hiding places for snipers and a good line of fire

267

at anyone in the garden, but the wall was heavily guarded by the Rani's troops. The assassins would have to execute their deadly work from ground level in the busy garden.

'Stay here,' Yusuf told Hassan. He rose stiffly, brushed dust and leaves from his clothing, then marched purposefully across the garden, leaving his musket in Hassan's care.

Yusuf picked his way clumsily along the edge of a ruined walkway, his eyes travelling from the ground to the branches of the mango trees near the path and down again. Ahead of him, a mangy donkey loaded with ammunition let out a squealing bray. Dust blew in all directions.

Seventy-five yards from the pavilion, hard by the boundary wall, he found what he sought: a man crouched behind a pile of broken stones, his eyes on the pavilion, his back to Sher Singh's cannon, nearly invisible in his ragged, dust-covered clothing, a long-barrelled jezail across his knees.

Yusuf did not stop walking. Instead, careful not to attract the man's attention, he continued to follow the wall, searching for the other assassin. For all he knew, these men, like themselves, had chosen to work in pairs. If they had, the other was watching him . . .

But he found no second sniper.

'I have seen one of them,' he told Hassan a little while later. 'Stay here. I am going back to kill him.'

'What can I do? How can I help?' Hassan was on his feet in an instant, his musket in his hand.

Yusuf smiled grimly. 'You can stay under this tree and protect the weapons. Shoot anyone who tries to take them. I will cut the man's throat, for the garden is quiet where he is sitting, and I do not want another assassin to hear my shots, but after this, without a gun, I'll be as useless as if I had stayed at home in bed.'

A short while later, his tulwar at his side, and his heavy, triangular-bladed dagger tucked into his sash, he stood hidden behind a simbal tree, studying the sniper.

The man had not moved. He still squatted close to the boundary wall, his back to Yusuf, his pile of stones protecting him against retaliatory fire from the pavilion. From beneath his coarsely tied turban, greasy hair hung to his shoulders.

Broken stones littered the ground between the two men, complicating a running charge. Careful not to create unease in the assassin, Yusuf kept his eyes averted as he moved quietly toward a thorn bush, thirty feet from the Afghan.

The man's thick turban drooped down over his neck. Yusuf fingered the curved tulwar at his side, gauging the blow that would sever the head from those hunched shoulders, then loosened his grip on the sword and reached for his dagger instead. With so much obstruction at the man's neck the sword might fail to do its work. It would be safer to seize the sniper by his beard and slit his throat.

Like his enemy, Yusuf waited. His head ached and his eyes burned from lack of sleep, but he made no move until a great, thudding roar came from the direction of the Citadel gate, blotting out all the other sounds around him. Without waiting to confirm the cause of the din, he launched himself at the crouching man.

But he had not counted upon the assassin's curiosity. Too late to stop, he saw the man turn towards the sound of the guns, then start with surprise as he caught sight of Yusuf running at him full tilt, his dagger in his fist.

The assassin reached rapidly into his clothes and withdrew his own wicked blade, but the jezail across his knees stopped him from turning his body to meet Yusuf straight on.

Yusuf struck the assassin on the shoulder, and they both went

269

sprawling on the stony ground. Before the assassin could scramble away, Yusuf caught his arm, and plunged his dagger deep into the man's side.

The assassin's body jerked. A high, whistling sound came from him as he tried to breathe, but he did not drop his long Khyber knife. He made a fearful effort to rise, his fingers tightening on the knife's haft.

Yusuf was no butcher, but he did what he had to do. Setting his knee on the arm holding the man's knife, he pulled back the turbaned head and drew his dagger blade across the man's throat.

As he did so, a second shattering roar came from the entrance to the Citadel. This time he looked up, and saw that the gate had been blown open. Unaware that the Rani's own guns had been set up inside the gate, Sher Singh's men had stormed through the opening, to be caught in a barrage of cannon fire at point-blank range. When the smoke cleared, more than a hundred of Sher Singh's soldiers lay dead and dying in the gateway, among broken carts and shattered pieces of the great wooden doors.

'We may lose this battle,' Hassan announced when Yusuf reappeared and flung down the sniper's weapons. 'Is the assassin dead? Where is your turban?'

'He is dead. Have you seen Zulmai?'

'No.'

Yusuf ran tense fingers over his face. 'There must be another sniper on this side of the garden.' He glanced towards the Citadel. 'Look,' he added, 'they're going make a second—'

Another cannonade arose from inside the gate. Again, once the smoke lifted, a hundred more dead and dying bodies clogged the entrance.

Yusuf made up his mind. 'Come, bring your musket,' he barked, dragging Hassan to his feet. 'With the battle going so poorly, the

Prince will want to see the damage for himself. Any moment now he will come out onto the verandah and make a target of himself. There is no time to lose. We must find our second sniper.'

As they started off, a crackling sound came from the high walls on either side of the Alamgiri Gate. The Rani's troops were now pouring deadly musket fire down upon the Prince's infantry who were massed along the wall, seeking cover from the cannons inside the gate. In a panic, the Prince's men broke ranks and sprinted away from the danger. Bloody, shouting, tripping over their dead and wounded, they surged past their own silent guns, and made for the side gate through which they had entered the garden.

'Look there.' Hassan caught Yusuf by the sleeve as half a dozen soldiers flew past them.

Between the trees, oblivious to the panic surrounding him, a beardless man crept towards the centre pavilion. Like the first assassin, he wore a coarsely tied turban and carried several weapons.

He came to a stop no more than twenty yards from Yusuf and Hassan, and squatted on the far side of an old mango tree, a corner of his shawl just visible to the two men.

'He looks even younger than Habibullah,' Yusuf muttered.

Soldiers hurried by, obstructing Yusuf's line of sight.

'Come,' he ordered. With Hassan following, he made his way through the mob of escaping soldiers until he reached another tree.

'We cannot shoot him yet, in all this commotion,' he said into Hassan's ear. 'When we are near enough, you take the first shot. Aim carefully, and do not shoot until I say so. We must not alarm him, and we must not miss.'

When Hassan nodded, Yusuf patted him on the shoulder. 'You can do it, my friend,' he murmured.

They were yards away from the sniper when Prince Sher Singh

appeared with his armed guard, framed in a scalloped archway on the pavilion's verandah, his bearded face puckered with worry.

The sniper raised his jezail.

'Now,' Yusuf said quietly. 'Shoot him now.' He closed one eye, controlled his breathing and raised his own musket, taking aim at the boy assassin's head.

Hassan did not fire.

'Now,' Yusuf ordered again, knowing even as he did so that Hassan would not fire, that he could never shoot a child, even to save the future of the Punjab.

Fighter that he was, Yusuf pulled the trigger.

The boy's jezail leapt in his hands an instant before Yusuf's shot struck home, but he must have sensed some impending danger, for his shot went wild. He missed his mark, but as he rolled, bleeding, into the dust under the mango tree, confusion erupted in the pavilion.

Someone had been wounded.

'Get down, Hassan,' Yusuf shouted, reaching for his friend, but he was too late. Before he could to get them to safety, a dozen musket barrels lifted, aimed at them, and fired.

Chapter Thirty-Two

It was well past noon. The sun had dropped behind the high, decorated gate of Wazir Khan's Mosque an hour before, robbing the little square of its warmth.

Throughout the day, as the sun moved and the shadows in the square changed, Mariana had crouched, waiting for death, outside Shaikh Waliullah's door.

Only once had she moved from her post. Late in the morning, during a lull in the violence, she had crept round the corner of the house, past the small, boarded shop built into the corner, and into the lightless alley leading to the haveli's back door. There, panting with fright, she had relieved herself into the fetid channel running along one side of the alley, then crawled back and folded herself down once again, becoming as small and invisible as she could against the wall.

The day had been a nightmare of slaughter and misery, with gangs of soldiers smashing their way into the dwellings beside the mosque, all of them easy to plunder, for the city had not seen this kind of violence for forty years. Time and again the soldiers dragged men out of their houses and beat them until they agreed to turn over their small treasures. Her face pressed against her upraised knees, Mariana had tried not to hear as the poor souls pleaded that they had no riches and no gold and were executed on the spot, and their bodies left on the bloody cobblestones where they had fallen.

The soldiers would swarm away, carrying their pillaged goods and bloodstained tulwars, but no sooner had one mob gone than another charged in from a different direction, waving weapons and shouting curses, and the little square erupted into violence once more.

With each new orgy of looting and killing, Mariana had expected to die, but the soldiers carried out their ugly work without taking any notice of her.

During all those hours, the tall haveli doors had remained tightly locked against her; they might have been the gates of Paradise and she the worst of sinners.

The afternoon air, filled with the smell of blood, rotted roses, and rare, spoiled perfumes, had turned cold. She shivered. Like the prince in Safiya's story, she had surely earned her banishment. Like him, she had forgotten charity, for what could be more uncharitable than suspicion?

She had not appreciated the Waliullah family's generosity or the love Hassan had offered her. Instead, proud and mistrusting, she had lost them both. As debased and filthy as the beggar prince, she too was exiled from the perfumed garden of her beloved.

How arrogant she had been when she had arrived at Qamar Haveli.

She had misjudged Hassan and underestimated his family. How could she have imagined that the Shaikh would teach her his magical snakebite cure, or explain his ability to read minds, all in a day or two? What had made her think she could master Safiya's healing arts and the source of her stout, inner calm in the same time?

Instead of seeing her folly, she had felt slighted when the busy Waliullah household had offered her no long hours alone with either Safiya or the Shaikh. Blind to Hassan's feelings, she had not even bothered to ask why he had refused to divorce her.

She hugged herself under her thin wrappings and wiped her running nose on her foul chador. It would do her no good to think of these things now. She badly needed food and water, but most of all she must find a way to warm herself. Her half-bare, bandaged feet ached miserably against the cobblestones. If she were forced to pass the night in the square, she would surely die of cold.

A corpse lay half hidden by a small dome near the centre of the square. From where she sat, Mariana could see that its shoulders were wrapped in a woollen shawl. Clenching her chattering teeth, she looked cautiously about her. No live person was visible in the square. She took a deep breath, rose, sidled over to the dome, and bent over the dead man.

He had been so badly beaten about the head and face that no one could have recognized him. Averting her eyes from the ants crawling on his blood-encrusted features, she loosened a corner of the shawl and gave it a sharp tug, but it did not come free. Much of the fabric seemed to have bunched beneath his body. Growing bolder, she nudged his corpse with a filthy foot and tugged again.

She was no nearer to having the shawl but she had gone too far to turn back. She sat down on the stones and braced both her feet against the dead man's stiffening shoulder. Grimacing with distaste, she wrested the fabric from under him.

Back again in her place against the wall, she examined her prize. It was not a rich shawl, but it was thick enough, and it had only two bloodstains. She spread it gratefully over her chador and wrapped its end about her toes, then leaned back against the brick wall of the house, her eyes closing.

'Peace, sister!'

She started. Whoever this was, he must have witnessed her thieving. She looked nervously about her, but could see no one.

'Sister, I am here.' The cracked voice came from close by.

A tiny, misshapen person stood half hidden by the corner of the building. He raised a hand and beckoned to her.

He was no soldier. Such a small person could scarcely do her harm, crippled as he was. Glad to see a live, human being among all the carnage, Mariana gathered herself and stood, careful not to drop her stolen shawl.

Standing, he came only to her shoulder. His spine was so severely curved that his head, covered with a length of cotton, seemed to have been put on sideways, but his clothes were neat and clean. 'I am the keeper of shoes for Wazir Khan's mosque,' he told her, gesturing towards the tall gateway with its Arabic inscriptions that fronted the square. 'I have spent the day hidden behind a door in an empty student quarter. I have only ventured out now because the soldiers are hungry and have gone to raid the food bazaars.'

'Will they come back?'

'Yes, I fear they will.' The little man looked sideways into her face. 'If Prince Sher Singh had prevailed in the Hazuri Bagh, he would have entered the city by now and the pillage would have finished, but he has not.'

The hunchback gave no sign of disgust at her condition. Instead, his long face held only concern. He pointed to the square with its fallen bodies and broken glass. 'You should not be out here with all this evil-doing, sister. You must take shelter as I have, in one of the empty quarters in the courtyard of the mosque. Allah Most Gracious would not forbid you, a woman, to seek safety in his house. There is water in the courtyard tank,' he added gently, glancing at her filthy hands. 'I will take you there.'

Water. Weak with relief, she could only nod. She allowed him to lead her towards the high, tiled entrance to the mosque.

'I do not want to stay away from Qamar Haveli too long,' she told him as they began to mount the gateway stairs. 'I am waiting for someone to open the doors.'

'Ah, Qamar Haveli, the home of Shaikh Waliullah . . . I entered that house once, when I was a child.' His sigh echoed in the decorated archway behind Mariana. She did not answer him, for she had seen the brimming water tank in the centre of the mosque's broad, open courtyard.

She licked her lips. 'Is there a cup to drink from?' she asked, hiding her unclean hands behind her.

The hunchback shrugged. 'I am a poor man,' he replied.

She would have to wash before she drank from her hands. After laying her shawls carefully beside her, she removed the dirty chador and knelt and dipped her fingers into the tank.

The water was very cold, but she did not mind. She dug the filth from under her fingernails, scrubbed the dirt from her arms, and splashed water onto her face. Then she moved to the far side of the tank, knelt again, cupped her palms, and drank.

Satisfied, she sat back, and found the little hunchback staring at her across the water, his mouth ajar.

'You are not what you pretend to be,' he declared as she turned hastily away to cover herself. 'I knew this from the first time you spoke to me in court Urdu instead of the coarse Punjabi of a beggar. Who are you, then, and how have you come to ask for alms at the gate of Shaikh Waliullah?'

'I am no one,' she faltered.

'You are very fair, if you do not mind my saying so,' he went on. 'Your white skin puts me in mind of Shaikh Waliullah's foreign daughter-in-law. They call her the Lioness, for it was she who rescued Saboor, the Shaikh's baby grandson, from Maharajah Ranjit Singh when the child was dying of grief and neglect. The Maharajah was still alive then, of course, and—'

'I must return to the haveli now.' Her face averted from the hunchback's gaze, Mariana bent and snatched up her shawls. 'Thank you for the water,' she said over her shoulder as she hurried across the mosque's courtyard.

But the little man would not be dismissed. 'I will wait with you at the Shaikh's door,' he announced and trotted beside her towards the entrance. 'You must hear this most interesting story.'

He talked as they descended the staircase, recounting Mariana's own past adventures to her as if they were now a part of the city's history. From time to time she tried to interrupt, to change the subject, to ask if he, too, were cold, where he lived, if he had a family, but to no avail.

'And then,' he went on as they skirted the horrors in the square, 'having seen her bravery and her love of the child, the Shaikh determined that the foreign Lioness should become his son's wife. The wedding took place at the Citadel. Muhammad Ahmad, the diamond merchant, prepared beautiful jewellery for the bride, clothes were stitched, and a bride gift was arranged. You may have seen the gift,' he said, lifting his chin towards one of the streets leading from the square. 'It is a house with a yellow door, only one lane away from the Delhi Gate.' He shook his head. 'But these stories do not always end happily.'

They had reached the haveli. Mariana prayed that the little man would cease talking and return to his hiding place in the mosque, but he did not stop.

'The bridegroom's family had no time to celebrate his marriage. Before the valeema festivities could take place,' he said, lowering himself painfully to the ground and signalling her to join him, 'the

Maharajah's armed men came and tried to take Saboor Baba away again. It was only because of the quick thinking of a Hindu sweetmeat seller that Saboor Baba and the foreign lady were saved.

'The Waliullahs sent them to Bengal for two full years, but they have now returned.' He nodded significantly as Mariana arranged herself on the stones a few feet away. 'The family rejoiced at first, but now it seems that all is not well. The English people who brought Hassan's wife and Saboor Baba from Calcutta are seeking a divorce. They want the Lioness to go away with them when they leave.' He bent forward and rested his weight on his elbows, his great shrouded hump giving him the look of an oddly shaped ghost. 'Imagine the shame of it! But of course she is a foreigner. Who can understand these people?'

In spite of her cold and hunger, Mariana winced.

'It is said that she loves Saboor more than life, and that she wants to stay. Let us hope she does. It would give the family happiness.' He sighed gustily. 'No family deserves happiness more than the Waliullahs.'

Mariana closed her eyes. Everyone in the city must know her story. The hunchback himself would learn soon enough that she had run away from Qamar Haveli.

She had never suffered in that house for wanting to divorce Hassan. Instead of trying to punish her, or even arguing their case, the household had offered acceptance, and the hope that she would change her mind.

'I tell you,' the little man went on grandly, 'there are great men in this city but the greatest is Shaikh Waliullah. He is known far and wide for his wisdom and his generosity. I have kept watch over the shoes outside Wazir Khan's mosque since I was a child. In all that time, the Shaikh has never failed to treat me with consideration. He sees to my health, and his sister sends food to my house, but there is more to his generosity than that. When Shaikh Waliullah greets me, he speaks to my soul, not to my station as a keeper of shoes.' He raised a finger and waggled it in the air. 'In this world, it is a rare man who respects the humanity of a hunchback.'

He fell silent beside her. Mariana reached forward and wrapped her feet more closely in her stolen shawl. What a fool she had been. During her short stay at Qamar Haveli she had been carefully tutored by Safiya's regular teaching sessions. Thinking back, Mariana remembered each one, and the significant glances Safiya had sent her way, indicating that the lesson was intended for her.

She had broken each one of those carefully imparted rules.

First, she had ignored the importance of charity, forgetting that every beggar, indeed every creature on earth, represented an opportunity for the generous to gain God's blessings. On her return to Shalimar, she had failed to offer the beggars there so much as a greeting. She had been rude to Charles Mott. She had abandoned her uncle in his desperate need.

And she had taken her own blessings for granted, disregarding Safiya's second lesson. Like the beggar prince who had forgotten to give away his second silver coin while he ran after the unknown lady's palanquin, she had forgotten what she owed Hassan and his family, and allowed herself to be seduced by suspicion instead.

The third lesson was contained in Safiya's care for the desperate young mother who came to the haveli, and this, too, Mariana had failed to learn: that doing the right thing often required self-discipline. Ignoring this truth, she had abandoned her uncle and aunt at Shalimar, pretending that the cure for his cholera was her only reason for returning to Qamar Haveli.

She must improve herself, before it was too late. She glanced across at her small, silent companion. Now that she was a beggar, she suddenly wanted to offer charity to as many people as possible. What a pity that her audience consisted of only one lonely hunchback . . .

She sat straight. But the hunchback had given *her* charity. He had shown her the water in the mosque. He had told her a story. What else did a keeper of shoes have to give?

She regarded him with a softer eye as he leaned on his elbows, his long face puckered with discomfort. Although she must smell far worse than that young mother in the upstairs room, he had shown no sign of disgust when he approached her with his offer of safety and water.

Here was a man of charity and discipline. With only a cotton sheet to keep out the cold, he had made no move to steal the clothes of the dead. Although he had certainly seen her thieving, he had made no reference to it.

She dropped her head onto her upraised knees. *Please let the haveli doors open soon. Let Safiya possess the cure for cholera, as the woman told me. Let the cure arrive at Shalimar in time. If I have failed once in my duty to Uncle Adrian, let me find a way to save him in the end . . .*

'Look!' The hunchback raised his head and pointed towards the edge of the square.

A group of men had started across the square, carrying something in a sling between them. Whatever it was, it appeared to be heavy.

As she watched, the men put their burden down and began to argue among themselves and point towards the haveli. When she craned forward, trying to hear what they were saying, they saw her and dropped their voices.

Although she could not hear their words, she was certain they were speaking Persian. Their earth-coloured clothing and their coarsely tied turbans told her they were Afghans, like the ones she

281

had seen speaking to the Vulture outside his tent when she arrived at Shalimar. Each man had one or two elaborately decorated guns strapped to his back.

Their argument resolved, they bent to pick up the object they had been carrying, and strode away. As they did so, Mariana saw that it was the blood-soaked body of a man.

Just after they disappeared from the square with their grisly cargo, the sound of muffled footfalls followed by a heavy scraping came at last from behind the haveli door.

Before one side had creaked open enough to allow a man to look cautiously out, Mariana had jumped to her feet and hurled herself against the door.

'Let me in,' she ordered. Behind her, the hunchback rose, grimacing, to his feet.

The guard leapt aside as if he thought she might be a ghost. Taking advantage of his hesitation, she pushed her way inside.

The high, brick entranceway of the haveli with its single, carved window looked exactly as it always had. Amazed at such extraordinary normality, Mariana stopped short, then realized that her little companion had not followed her.

'Wait!' she cried to the guard, then turned and flung herself past him and out into the square.

The hunchback must have saluted her before he left, but she had missed that politeness, for in her haste to reach the haveli, she had turned her back to him. By the time she was outside again, he was on his way towards Wazir Khan's mosque.

'O Keeper of Shoes,' she called after him, 'please come into our house!'

He looked over one bent shoulder, then shook his head. 'No, Bibi,' he replied in his high voice. 'Qamar Haveli is no place for me.'

Coarse shouting erupted in a nearby street. The soldiers were returning. Heedless of the pools of blood or the broken glass that glittered on the cobblestones, Mariana ran after the little man.

Bibi. He had used a title reserved for the high-born. He must have known who she was all along.

'The soldiers are coming back,' she panted as she reached him. 'Listen.'

He shook his head again and moved to pass her. She opened her arms and barred his way. 'Please. We must hurry,' she pleaded, walking towards him, her arms still spread, forcing him to retreat, knowing he would not allow her to touch him.

The shouting grew louder. She stepped forward again. His long face puckered with grief or shame, he backed away from her, towards the haveli door, where a crowd of staring guards had now collected. Knowing they were all watching but too desperate to care about the little man's feelings, she flapped her hands in his face.

'Hurry,' she repeated, shooing him inside.

'Look after him,' she commanded the guards, then raced out again, tearing off her stolen shawl as she flew towards the small domed structure in the square.

She stopped only long enough to fling the length of stained fabric down beside its dead owner, then darted back again, just as a mob of yelling soldiers appeared alongside the mosque and boiled into the square.

By the time she gained the haveli, the great double doors were closing. An instant after she had rushed inside and the sweating guards had forced the iron bolts home, something thudded heavily against the doors from outside.

'We were ready to lock you out,' grumbled one of the guards, glowering at Mariana who stood trembling inside the arched entranceway. 'Do not think we would risk the lives of the Waliullah family for the convenience of a beggar woman.'

The little Keeper of Shoes opened his mouth, then closed it again.

A guard jerked his chin towards the hunchback. 'I know this man,' he said, over the din of hammering fists. 'Take him over there and give him food.'

'May Allah protect you, Bibi.' The little man saluted Mariana before he was led away.

Another guard pointed to Mariana. 'What shall we do with her?' he asked carelessly.

'She can wait here,' the first guard replied. He turned to Mariana and raised his voice. 'When we opened the door,' he shouted as if she were deaf as well as dirty, 'we were expecting to find a lady of our house. Have you seen anyone who—'

'I *am* a lady of this house,' she snapped. 'I have been waiting outside this gate for hours.' Chilled to the bone, she tugged her chador more firmly over her head and strode on her filthy, bandaged feet towards the inner courtyard.

As the guards stared after her, a small figure arrived at the bottom of the stairs leading to the ladies' sitting room.

'An-nah, An-nah!' Saboor shouted as he hurtled toward her. 'You have come!'

Chapter Thirty-Three

The upstairs corridor with its filigreed shutters was nearly as cold as the square outside, but a brazier of hot coals stood in the centre of the sitting room. Saboor dragged Mariana to the door, and a score of ladies and several older girls looked up from their conversations.

The gap-toothed aunt stared. 'How has a beggar woman gained entry to the house on this day of violence?'

'It is An-nah!' The only person who had recognized Mariana danced up and down, still grasping a handful of her chador.

She had no shoes to remove before entering. Instead, drooping with exhaustion in the doorway, she lowered Akhtar's chador from her face.

'Forgive me,' she murmured, not for the first time, swallowing nervously as Safiya Sultana pushed herself to her feet.

'She has come back!' Saboor panted, tugging her into the room with all his strength.

Beyond him, the room with its innocent, seated women appeared so peaceful that it might have been a dream. Mariana reached dizzily for the doorframe, wondering how to explain herself.

As Safiya Sultana approached, a deep frown between her eyes, all the ladies began talking at once.

'Why did Mariam leave the house?' they cried. 'Where did she go? Why is she wearing such dirty clothes? Look at her feet!'

'Akhtar, Firoz,' Safiya called over her shoulder, 'bring food for Mariam Bibi, and heat water for her bath.' She nodded to Mariana. 'Peace,' she offered in her man's voice. 'How long have you waited outside?'

'Since early this morning,' Mariana whispered.

'Hai Allah, how she has suffered!' chorused the ladies. 'But why did she leave us? Why?'

So they knew at least part of her story. But what did it matter? She must offer her confession here. She must tell these ladies that she had unjustly accused Hassan of plotting murder. She must beg them all to forgive her . . .

'It was wrong of me to run away,' she murmured faintly. 'I have made many terrible—'

'Not now.' Before she could say more, Safiya lifted a silencing hand. 'Mariam has endured much,' she intoned. 'We will hear her story later. Saboor is right to be happy.' She nodded at the delighted child and laid an arm about Mariana's shoulders, drawing her towards the brazier. 'You might easily have been killed. Several times we sent men to look out through the front windows, but they could see only the corpses of the dead. Then something seemed to move on the ground below, so the men opened the door, thinking an injured man might be seeking shelter with us. Come.'

Fighting tears, Mariana stepped onto the covered floor.

'Akhtar tells me that your uncle is unwell.' Safiya pointed to a place in front of the brazier.

'He is ill with cholera.' Mariana sniffled as she sat down. 'Someone told me that you had a cure.' She glanced up anxiously

286

at Safiya. *Oh please, let it be true. Let her at least be able to save Uncle Adrian* . . .

'Sit with your back to the brazier,' Safiya ordered. 'What is his condition?'

'Early this morning the heaving and purging had ceased, but he still had a raging thirst and horrible cramps. I left him just after sunrise.' Afraid to hear the truth, Mariana lowered her eyes.

Safiya nodded. 'Then there is hope, provided that he did not relapse badly during the course of the day. I have a store of crystals that were sent to me by a European doctor. They are quite effective, but they may only be given by someone with proper training. I will gladly send our man to Shalimar, but we must wait until it is safe for him to travel.' She sighed. 'Even though your uncle is now a member of our family, I cannot risk our man's life.'

A member of our family. What was Safiya thinking beneath that powerful serenity of hers? Surely she knew of that terrible scene with Hassan . . .

'Is Hassan at home?' Mariana whispered, unable to bear the suspense any longer.

'No. He left suddenly yesterday afternoon. His friend Yusuf came, then his two Afghan traders arrived and the four of them went off together. Hassan told his father he was going to see Sher Singh.' Safiya signalled Akhtar to approach. 'Bring the ewer for Bibi to wash her hands,' she ordered, 'and then take that disgusting chador away.' She turned to Mariana. 'I do not know where Hassan and the others have gone,' she added, seeing the unhappiness on Mariana's face, 'but you must eat now. While you are eating, you will tell us your story.'

Mariana swallowed nervously as she sat in front of the tray of rice and curried goat, one arm round Saboor, her unspeakable feet tucked out of sight beneath her. 'I left the house yesterday for two reasons,' she said, so softly that the ladies around her nudged closer in order to

287

hear. 'First, my uncle was unwell, and second, I mistakenly believed there was to be an attack upon the English camp at Shalimar.'

'An attack on Shalimar?' Safiya frowned. 'Who told you such a thing?'

'No one told me,' Mariana replied lamely. 'I overheard someone talking outside the windows and thought they were discussing a plot to kill the English people. I was wrong to believe it,' she added, dropping her eyes. She took a mouthful of rice and dopiaza. Why did Safiya not ask about her angry scene with Hassan, and his decision to divorce her? Had she not been told?

'Bhaji!' A young girl with a braid that reached to her knees turned breathlessly from an open window. 'The alley outside is full of soldiers!' she cried. 'They are crowding about the back door. They are shouting something about the enemies of Prince Sher Sigh!'

'Come away from there, Khadija!' implored one of the ladies.

Her mouth full of rice and curried goat, Mariana sat straight.

'Girls, leave the room,' Safiya ordered over the clamour of voices. 'Nadir,' she added, deftly collaring a small boy, 'you must go quickly and call Yahya from downstairs.

'I made the guards practise yesterday,' she added, turning to Mariana and gesturing for her to continue eating. 'First they are to call every man, woman, and child in from the kitchen courtyard, and then they are to bring the old elephant doors and close off the kitchen from the rest of the house. My grandson, Yahya, is to give the signal. But why,' she asked, 'are those soldiers calling us Sher Singh's enemies?'

As the little boy dashed off, several adolescent girls hurried into another room and closed the curtain. A moment later, a leggy youth with a small moustache appeared in the sitting-room doorway. Safiya motioned for him to enter.

'Soldiers are outside the back door, Yahya,' she told him. 'You must go to the stables and tell the men to put the elephant doors in place.'

'Wait,' Mariana said urgently as the boy prepared to leave them. 'What of those windows?' She pointed past the sitting-room door to the verandah whose balconies overlooked the narrow alley below. 'If the soldiers bring ladders, they can easily get inside.' She turned to Yahya. 'There were some long wooden planks downstairs, near the stables. Are they still there?'

He nodded, his eyes travelling to the verandah and back again.

'We will need one for each window,' Mariana told him.

'And how will we use these planks of yours?' Safiya inquired, after a single nod of her head had sent the boy clattering down the stairs.

'If the soldiers try to climb inside, we can use the planks to push them out again, even without the help of men,' Mariana replied, as confidently as she could, aware that the ladies had stopped talking and were now listening intently.

Safiya nodded thoughtfully. A moment later something landed heavily outside the sitting-room door.

'They are throwing bricks through the verandah windows!' a woman cried out.

Where was Saboor? Mariana pushed away her tray, leapt to her feet, and raced out through the curtained doorway.

The brick lay on the tiled floor. Near the pile of women's discarded shoes, a pair of girls huddled, round-shouldered with fright. Saboor crouched between them.

Guttural shouts came through the open window. As Mariana launched herself towards the children, she caught a glimpse of a soldier perched on a ladder across the alley.

He raised his arm. Mariana hurried the children into the sitting room, protecting them with her body as one brick, then another and another crashed to the floor around them.

Moments later, Yahya appeared, bent double with the effort of dragging three heavy boards up the stairs.

'Please,' he panted, 'Allahyar is with me.'

Understanding, Mariana jerked the door curtains shut behind her, shielding the ladies from the eyes of Shaikh Waliullah's personal servant. The planks clattered to the floor outside, accompanied by more crashes and a muffled curse.

'Nani Ma!' Yahya called through the curtain, his voice thin with excitement. 'Do not come out! I am bringing more men to protect you!'

Mariana crossed the sitting room and peered out through the shutters. Below, in the family courtyard, male servants hurried to and fro carrying bedding and food, while a crowd of female servants and their children squatted beneath the courtyard's lone tree, as if waiting for instructions.

Safiya Sultana sat calmly in her usual place against the wall, while missiles continued to land beyond the closed curtain, provoking gasps from the ladies, who crouched together in anxious groups, clutching their children.

One daring old aunt had stationed herself with her eye to the gap in the door curtain. 'Look!' she cried suddenly. 'They are coming inside!'

Mariana hurried to her and peered out.

The verandah was littered with thrown bricks. Dust motes danced in the light from the middle window, where, framed by filigreed shutters, the top of a bamboo ladder wavered back and forth, then came to a stop.

A pair of brown hands grasped the top rung, followed a moment later by the sweating, bearded face of a Sikh infantryman.

'Quickly!' Scaracely thinking, Mariana tore open the curtain, caught hold of the three nearest women, and shooed them through the doorway to where Yahya had dropped the wooden planks. 'We must use these to push him out,' she ordered, then reached down and began to tug at one of the boards.

The women nodded. Panting with effort and haste, they lifted the long, heavy board and turned together to face the window.

The whole man had now appeared in the opening. At the sight of four uncovered women, the solider reached, grinning, for the window frame.

'These enemies of Sher Singh are women,' he shouted to his companions below. 'This will be easy!'

'When I count three!' Mariana shouted. '*Ek, do, theen!*'

All four women rushed forward. Gripped between them like a battering ram, the plank caught the soldier squarely in the chest. He toppled backwards, his eyes bulging, and disappeared.

A new sound came from one end of the verandah. Mariana and her companions turned towards it and there, framed in the opening of the far window, a second soldier stood poised to enter, a tulwar swinging at his side, one foot on the windowsill, the other on a bamboo ladder.

Below him, Mariana saw the turbaned head of another man.

'Be quick!' the second man shouted.

Safiya Sultana stood alone in front of the window, the end of one plank wedged firmly into her midsection, the other end balanced on the windowsill.

Before Mariana had time to go to her aid, Safiya threw her considerable weight against her end of the plank.

The infantryman had taken a firm grip on the window frame, but Safiya, who stood squarely, feet apart, on the verandah tiles, had the advantage. Again and again, while he scrabbled, grunting, to keep his balance, she drove her plank into his body. At last, his fingers slipped from the window. The soldier below him let out a cry and the two men dropped, their arms flailing, from sight.

Safiya Sultana laid down her plank and wiped her scarlet face. 'Well, that's that,' she said.

'Cowards! Owls!' Little, bird-like Akhtar appeared from nowhere, rushed to the window and spat through the opening. 'Attack women, will you?' she shrieked, and snatched up a brick. 'You will see how we fight!'

'No, Akhtar!' Mariana hobbled forward and caught hold of the girl's arm as the women and girls ran excitedly to surround Safiya Sultana. 'Do not throw the bricks yet. We will need them if the soldiers return.'

Male voices echoed up the stairs. The girls stopped dancing and hurried away when Yahya bounded up once more, followed by several men, all of whom halted and spun on their heels, their backs to Mariana, who stood alone, dirty and dishevelled, in the centre of the verandah, Akhtar's brick still in her hand.

Yahya stared at her, then put his head round the door curtain. 'What has happened, Nani Ma?'

'The soldiers have been repelled,' Safiya Sultana replied from inside the sitting room. 'That is all. Go and tell Lalaji that there is no need to worry about us.'

Later, as she washed her feet, Mariana imagined what it would be like to have lived in this house for ever.

How would it have felt, never to meet another man face to face? How would it have been to know that if she appeared uncovered, men would turn their backs in order not to see her? How much would she have missed her daily rides, the dinner parties, fetes, and balls?

She sighed. All that would have been difficult to part with, but oh, what she would have gained – the indomitable Safiya Sultana, the brave ladies who had risen to the occasion and knocked the first soldier from the window, dear little Saboor who had somehow known that she was waiting outside like a beggar at the gate, and who even now leaned against her, his broad sticky face turned up to hers, and Hassan, her gentle husband, the only person who had ever called her beautiful.

Oh Rose, what art thou, he had murmured, *in the presence of her lovely face?*

Surely, when he came home he would see that she belonged here. Surely, once she asked his forgiveness, he would relent and allow her to stay. Surely, someday, he would care for her again.

'Lavender's blue, diddle diddle,' she crooned to Saboor, 'lavender's green. When you are king, diddle diddle, I shall be queen.'

If only it could be so . . .

The old elephant doors still blocked off the kitchen, and so dinner was only rice and boiled dal, cooked in copper vessels over a wood fire in the courtyard.

The ladies did not mind. Still repeating the story of their triumph, remembering its smallest details, they crowded happily together in the upper room, Mariana in their midst. She sighed with pleasure as many hands patted her and voices elevated her to the station of heroine, second only to the redoubtable Safiya Sultana. What would her dear, faraway father think of her first battle, the Battle of Qamar Haveli?

The door curtains parted abruptly. Surprised, the chattering women fell silent.

Young Yahya stood in the doorway, bent over as if in pain. 'Lala is in your room, Nani Ma,' he blurted, already backing towards the stairs. 'He wants to see you.'

Safiya nodded. 'Come, Mariam,' she ordered and rose to her feet.

293

'We must not keep my brother waiting. Leave Saboor here.'

As she left the room, Mariana glanced over her shoulder and saw the gap-toothed aunt watching her silently.

A single voice rose behind the two women as they made their way down the verandah. It began on a low note, then climbed, gaining volume, until it was as high and sorrowful as a muezzin's cry.

God is great. It was Saboor.

Shaikh Waliullah sat on the bed, his knees drawn to his chest. Without speaking, he made room for his sister and daughter-in-law. When he met his sister's eyes, the dread already clawing at Mariana's middle rose to her throat.

'Hassan and his friend Yusuf have been killed at the Hazuri Bagh,' he said, his voice creaking like an old man's, while Mariana held her breath and Saboor's wails echoed on the verandah outside.

'When?' Safiya asked hollowly.

'This morning.'

'Where is his body?'

'I have sent two men to bring it here, but they have not returned. It could be that the streets are too dangerous.'

Mariana reached out numbly and steadied herself against the wall. Safiya lowered herself, grey-faced, to the bed beside her twin brother. Together, while Mariana watched, stricken, unable to join in, Safiya and the Shaikh raised their cupped hands before them and offered a series of half-whispered prayers.

'Go, Mariam, and bring Saboor,' Safiya ordered when they had finished. 'From his cries, it seems he has already guessed the sad news.'

The Shaikh ran a hand over his face in a gesture so like Hassan's that Mariana nearly cried out.

Her legs barely carried her to the sitting room. As she stood in the doorway, the women and girls stopped whispering.

'It is Hassan, is it not?' asked someone, her words piercing the ringing in Mariana's ears.

Nodding mutely, Mariana looked for Saboor, and found him hiccupping miserably in the fat girl's lap.

He saw her. 'Abba is hurt!' he sobbed, running to her and catching at her clothes. 'We must help him! No, no!' he insisted, struggling when Mariana scooped him wordlessly into her arms. 'We must go and find Abba!'

'Two men have already gone to look for him,' Mariana replied carefully. Her arms tightened round his squirming body. 'We must wait for them to return.'

God help her, she must find the courage to tell him the truth.

At Safiya's door she put him down, took his hand, and forced herself through the doorway.

Saboor pulled away from her and ran to his grandfather. 'Lalaji,' he cried urgently, 'my abba is hurt. We must hurry and find him!'

'Ah, my darling, the men will bring him. Yes, they will bring him.'

While Mariana stood, mute, in the doorway, Shaikh Waliullah raised his head and looked bleakly into her eyes.

Chapter Thirty-Four

The gap-toothed aunt had begun to beat herself again, her closed fist thudding rhythmically above her breasts. Waves of grief rose and fell around Mariana as the ladies rocked in their places on the floor.

Word of Hassan's death must already have spread through the city. Even on this perilous night, the Shaikh's torch-lit courtyard was filling with male mourners. Looking down, Mariana could see the Shaikh, swathed in shawls against the cold, sitting upright on his platform, surrounded by a sea of silent men.

Unnerved by the vocal agony of the ladies, Mariana slumped against the sitting-room wall, wrapped in the shawl Hassan had given her, unable to make a sound, wishing senselessly that Hassan's funeral were being held in church. There, at least, all these people would be forced to restrain themselves.

Mariana was no stranger to funerals. By the time she had sailed for India three years earlier, her family had already buried two of their babies and a five-year-old boy, one of her uncles, and her two favourite grandparents.

Unlike Safiya Sultana, who now groaned rhythmically at Mariana's side, Mariana's mother had not used her lace handkerchief once on those occasions, not even at the funeral of little Ambrose, who had died when Mariana was twelve. Mama had even sung all the hymns, including the saddest ones, in her usual clear soprano.

Mariana's father had been equally brave, his wobbling chin the only indication of his pain as his child's coffin was lowered into its grave.

But here, pained voices filled the haveli, leaving little room for Mariana to think or to express her own despair. Helpless to offer solace to any of them, even to Saboor, who lay open-eyed across her lap, she sat, tearless and paralysed, waiting for the nightmare to end.

'Abba is hurt,' Saboor repeated mournfully.

'Oh, darling, I am so sorry,' was all she could think of to say.

She looked out at the sky. She did not know what time it was. The night must be wearing on, but what if it did not? What if it stood still instead? Perhaps for all time Qamar Haveli would be perpetually dark, with no bright days to end the blackness, nothing but the flickering of dim lamplight against these sad sitting-room walls.

Saboor stirred on her lap. All night he had lain heavily against her, his energetic little body turned sodden and hot, but now he sat up and looked into her face, his eyes clear and wide.

'Dilly,' he said emphatically. 'There was a dilly. There was a—'

'Hush, my love,' she whispered. 'Diddle. You remember our poems – "Hey diddle diddle, the cat and the fiddle – The cow jumped over—"'

'No, An-nah.' He shook his head firmly. 'Dilly. There was a—'

'Sleep, my darling,' she murmured as she shifted him to a more comfortable position. 'Sleep. Everything will be better in the morning.'

But he would not sleep. Instead, he turned his face from hers and

297

crooned sorrowfully to himself, as if his small heart was breaking. 'Dilly,' he wept. 'There was a dilly, there was a—'

That high, despairing little sound cut into Mariana like a knife. 'Please sleep, Saboor, sleep,' she whispered.

'Let him grieve.' Beside Mariana, Safiya Sultana turned, red-eyed, and laid a hand on her knee. 'It's better.'

Worn down by exhaustion and by the agony around her, Mariana began at last to weep aloud.

She must have cried herself to sleep, but she had not dozed for long, for when she awoke, remembering what had happened with a sickening lurch, the scene around her was unchanged except that Saboor now slept beside her, his brow furrowed as if by terrible worry.

As she shifted against him, a scene appeared in her mind's eye. As still as a painting but strong and vivid, it offered her a single, unchanging scene of a walled city street. Empty of people or animals, the street curved so that only three small havelis were visible to her. They stood in a row, each one with an elaborately carved balcony and a pair of heavy double doors. The doors of the middle one were painted yellow. As she watched the scene before her, she felt an urgent need to knock on the yellow door. At the end of the curved street, past the third haveli, rose the arched bulk of—

The Delhi Gate, the Delhi Darwaza. *Dilly. There was a—*

Hassan was there, at the Delhi Gate. Saboor had known. What vision or dream had he seen and tried to tell her? How wrong she had been . . .

Abba is hurt. She bent over the child's sleeping form. 'Do not worry, my darling,' she whispered, as she lifted him from her lap and wrapped him in her quilt. 'I will go now to the Delhi Gate and find your abba at the house with the yellow door. I only pray,' she added softly before she rose to her feet, 'that he is still alive.'

Mariana touched the carved silver box that still hung about her neck on its black cord. In her dream, she had stood alone outside the house with the yellow door. Her taweez had kept her safe before . . .

The weeping ladies still showed no sign of sleep, but even so no one asked where she was going as she slipped out of the sitting room and searched among the row of discarded shoes for a comfortable-looking pair of slippers.

She found Akhtar's chador on the floor of her room, where the little servant must have dropped it earlier in the day. She picked it up gratefully and returned to the verandah, then crossed to one of the windows and leaned out of it, listening intently.

The city outside the haveli was silent. No sounds of firing or shouting echoed in the streets below. Holding her breath, allowing herself no time for fear, Mariana flitted past the sitting-room door and down the stairs, leaving the sounds of exhausted grieving behind her.

It would take some time for the ladies to realize that she was gone. By that time, if she was fortunate, she would have found Hassan still alive and returned with the good news. If, God forbid, he had already died, at least she would have found him . . .

At the bottom of the stairs, she once again put on Akhtar's foul chador and then crept along the courtyard wall, away from the light of the torches, past the silent, hunched figures surrounding the Shaikh's platform.

Why had she not listened to Saboor? The poor baby had tried for hours to make them understand. No wonder he had wept so forlornly.

Taking care not to be seen, Mariana passed through the low gate and began to negotiate the stable courtyard, with its groups of shrouded, sleeping figures, all refugees from the servants' quarters by the kitchen.

She would need a guide.

Guards had been posted at the gate. They squatted together around a small brazier on one side of the high brick entranceway, their hands held out over the coals. They looked up, frowning, as she approached.

'I need to find Ghulam Ali, the courier,' she announced in a whisper.

'Why? Who has sent for him?'

'It does not matter. Call him,' she replied, raising her voice a little, hoping an imperious tone would make an impression.

'Ghulam Ali, oh, Ghulam,' one of them called out, without bothering to stand.

One of the bodies in the courtyard stirred, then sat up. A woollen shawl was pulled closely over his head but his pale, jutting beard identified him. When he came near, Mariana signalled him to move out of earshot of the guards.

'It is Memsahib,' she whispered, lowering the chador from her face. 'Peace be upon you.'

'Peace.' Ghulam Ali returned her greeting doubtfully, peering at her through the darkness, his voice thick with sleep.

She cleared her throat. 'Do you know a haveli with a yellow door in a curving alley near the Delhi Gate?'

'Of course I do. It belongs to this family.' He shifted his shoulders as if he was about to leave her and return to his place on the ground.

'Take me there,' she said.

'It is dangerous,' he replied gruffly.

'I know.' She glanced towards the guards before bending towards him. 'I believe Hassan Ali Khan Sahib lies wounded in that house.'

Ghulam Ali did not reply. Instead, he gazed over her shoulder as if she had not spoken.

'Will you take me there or not?' she whispered fiercely.

'We will knock twice when we return,' Ghulam Ali told the guards, 'so you will know to let us in.'

He stopped short as the heavy doors banged shut behind him and their iron bolts slid home, leaving him and the foreign woman to their fates. At his back, Hassan Ali Khan's wife drew in her breath.

Illuminated by a cloud-covered half moon, the bodies of the dead lay on the cobblestones, much as they had earlier when he had peered out through the haveli's front window.

They were not alone, for the square was alive with scavengers. Emaciated, half-naked, as stealthy as rats, they crawled in and out among the bodies of the dead, tugging at them, stripping them of every shred of clothing, while dogs skulked in the shadows, waiting their turn.

But what caused Ghulam Ali to hurry away from the door with Shaikh Waliullah's foreign daughter-in-law following behind him was not the scavengers or even the dogs, but the sight of the broad flight of steps that rose towards the entrance of Wazir Khan's mosque, fifty feet away. For on those steps, like a flock of murderous, resting birds, lay a hundred sleeping soldiers wrapped in stolen shawls and quilts, their muskets and swords ready at their sides.

Not all were sleeping. Awakened, perhaps, by the creaking of the haveli doors, three of them had sat up. They reached for their weapons.

Ghulam Ali glanced anxiously over his shoulder as he fled the square, but Hassan Ali's wife showed no sign of flagging. She hurried

301

behind him, anonymous in her chador, her slippered feet nearly silent on the cobblestones.

More scavengers appeared, flitting like shadows among the carnage in the alleyways near the Delhi Gate, searching for anything they could use.

'Sons of shame,' the albino muttered as one of them limped past him on a homemade crutch, a dead man's shawl about his shoulders. 'Vermin.'

In the brief time since the haveli doors had closed behind them, Ghulam Ali had seen enough horror for a lifetime of nightmares. Compared to the violence of the Prince's soldiers, even the Thugs he had met on the road to Calcutta had been decent. Thugs, at least, showed their deadly intentions only at the last moment. They buried their victims, instead of leaving their bodies in the open, to be stripped naked, then eaten by dogs and crows.

Ghulam Ali spat onto the wall beside him. Hassan's foreign wife must be made of iron to venture into this unholy atmosphere, even on a mission to find her wounded husband. For all his boastful exaggeration, Dittoo had been right about her courage.

But brave or no, the woman did not belong in this rescue party. The work of finding Shaikh Waliullah's son should have been left to men. If Hassan Ali Khan were dangerously wounded when they found him, he would be a dead weight to carry, Depending upon his injuries, it might not be possible for Ghulam Ali to lift him onto his back. For all her courage, Hassan's wife would not have the physical strength to help her husband when he needed it most.

They found the house in a curving, dimly lit alley, between two other similar houses, not a hundred feet from the Delhi Gate.

Ghulam Ali pointed. 'This is it,' he whispered.

'I cannot see the colour of the door,' Hassan's wife whispered back. 'You are certain this is the one?'

Ghulam Ali nodded, and then, before he could stop her, she climbed onto the haveli's high, stone front step and rapped smartly on the door.

She was making too much noise. Ghulam Ali started towards her, but before he reached her the yellow doors opened inwards with a jerk. A pair of hands, one holding a long knife, reached through the opening and snatched her inside. An instant later, the door opened again, and a shadowy, turbaned figure appeared. In two strides the man was beside Ghulam Ali.

'Stop, he is our friend!' cried Hassan Ali's wife. 'He is our *friend!*'

The figure halted. Ghulam Ali made out a familiar-looking face beneath the turban. 'You're the Afghan trader,' he said, his eyes on the knife, now lowered to the man's side.

The turban inclined. 'Wait out here,' the man said. 'We may need you later.'

Ghulam Ali nodded, then turned away, before the Afghan saw his tears.

He had never cried when he was abused or beaten, not even when he was young. Proud of his toughness, hardened against fear and sorrow, he had not even wept at the announcement of Hassan Ali's death. But he cried now, standing in the alley by the Delhi Gate, his shoulders shaking under his shawl, his tears dripping down his sunburned face and losing themselves in his white beard.

Friend, the foreign lady had said. At last, someone had called him friend.

Chapter Thirty-Five

'Who are you?' demanded the man in accented Urdu.

'Before I tell you,' Mariana replied, breathing hard through the folds of Akhtar's chador, 'I must know if you have hurt that man outside.'

'I have not. Now, who are you?'

She drew herself up and raised her chin beneath the filthy chador. 'I am the wife of Hassan Ali Khan Karakoyia.'

He took a step back, a hand to his heart. 'My name is Zulmai,' he offered. 'Please forgive us. We were not expecting—'

'Where is my husband?'

'This way.' He pointed towards a faintly lit doorway fronting the courtyard.

A rapid clicking sound filled the square, low-ceilinged room. In the centre of the floor, a single earthen lamp threw shadows onto the ceiling, its exposed cotton wick burning like a candle flame. The air was heavy with the smell of unwashed bodies. Along the walls of the room squatted a dozen heavily armed men. Suddenly exhausted, her head whirling, Mariana looked for somewhere to sit, but there was no furniture in the room other than an occupied string bed in a corner.

Beside her, Zulmai shifted his weight, as if he expected her to say something.

'How badly has Hassan been . . .' Her voice seemed to come from very far away. She tried to focus her gaze upon the long figure that lay, shivering, on the bed. She must act, but first—

An unexpected force suddenly pressed her hard against the wall. Her body felt heavy and immovable. Her eyelids were like lead. The murmuring male voices around her became silent.

One of her wrists began to ache. She opened her eyes and saw to her shock that she lay not against the wall but upon the floor, her cheek resting on bare, gritty tiles, one arm bent beneath her. Mercifully, she had not knocked over the oil lamp as she fell. It stood, still lit, beside her elbow.

She raised her head. Zulmai and the other Afghans must have rushed away in embarrassment when she fainted, for she was alone, save for the man on the string bed.

Too weak to stand, she crawled to the corner, grasped the bed's wooden edge with her good hand, dragged herself to a sitting position, and studied the trembling figure in front of her.

It was Hassan. His eyes were open, but he did not seem to see her. One leg of his shalwar had been cut off above the knee, revealing a tangle of bandages on his left thigh, from which blood seeped onto the floor. The clicking sound she had heard came from the convulsive chattering of his teeth.

She laid a cautious hand on his forehead. He was not hot yet, but with a wound as severe as this, the fever would soon be upon him. His shaking was due to loss of blood, and the icy temperature of the room.

She wanted to speak to him, to beg his forgiveness, but suddenly she could think of nothing to say. She removed the chador and pulled the beautiful Moghul shawl from her shoulders and spread it over

Hassan's body. It was all she had to offer, and he needed much more: a brazier of hot coals at his feet, heavy cotton-stuffed rezais to cover him, someone to clean his wound and stop the bleeding.

With luck, he might be saved. She was no doctor, but she knew that Hassan's only hope of survival lay a few hundred yards away, at Qamar Haveli.

She turned towards the door. 'Water,' she called.

A moment later, a fresh-looking boy stood in the doorway, a brass vessel in his hand, while behind him, several hawk-faced men craned to see inside.

Mariana raised herself to her knees, took the vessel, and poured a few drops of water between Hassan's shaking lips. 'Where are the people of this house?' she asked, her own teeth beginning to chatter. 'Surely they can help us.'

'All three families that were living here have run away,' replied Zulmai, who had reappeared inside the room. 'There is no rezai, no cooking pot to be found in the house. One old watchman remains. He let us in. Your husband is lying on his charpai.'

She set the water vessel on the floor and pushed herself unsteadily to her feet. Behind Zulmai, the other men stood waiting, their eyes on Hassan's trembling form. Some of them were old, some were young. Most were dressed in half-torn clothing and turbans with long tails. Each one had a thin shawl draped over his shoulders. Like Zulmai, each one carried knives, and at least one jezail.

An unarmed man, the old watchman perhaps, stood apart from the others. When she looked at him, he offered a respectful salute.

'There is no time to lose,' she said, reaching out to steady herself against the wall. 'We must take Hassan to Qamar Haveli at once.'

'Impossible.' Zulmai shook his head. 'People are looking for him, with orders to shoot him on sight. We were in the Hazuri Bagh this morning,' he went on, before she could ask, 'to stop an attempt upon

Prince Sher Singh's life. One of the assassins nearly got off a shot at the Prince. Hassan's friend Yusuf killed him in time, but the guards saw the musket flash and opened fire. They wounded Hassan, and killed his friend. I could do nothing,' Zulmai concluded, 'but carry Hassan away before he was finished off by the guards.' He shook his head. 'The Prince now believes Hassan is a traitor. He will pay a fortune to the man who brings him his severed head.'

Sickened, Mariana squeezed her eyes shut. 'Soldiers tried to storm the haveli this afternoon. They were shouting something about "enemies of the Prince".'

'Then?' Zulmai shrugged. 'How can we take him there?'

'He will certainly die if he remains here.'

'We passed by the house this afternoon,' Zulmai told her. 'The doors were closed, while soldiers rampaged in the square. We could not risk Hassan's being seen, so we came here. By now, his enemies will be watching the house. They will kill him at his own door.'

So these were the Afghans who had passed by her in the square, carrying their bleeding burden. If only she had known . . .

Hassan's enemies certainly were watching the house – at least a hundred of them – but she would not tell Zulmai this disturbing fact.

'News has arrived at the haveli,' she said firmly, 'that Hassan is dead. Guards are at the door, waiting for his body to arrive.'

A grey-bearded Afghan stepped forward. 'If soldiers have attacked Qamar Haveli once, they will attack it again. We should be inside, waiting for them, when they come.'

'Yes,' agreed a younger man, whose greased hair fell to his shoulders beneath his turban. 'We will see how they attack the house of Hassan Ali Khan.'

Zulmai nodded. 'Well then, we should leave now, before it becomes light.' He turned to Mariana. 'Your husband's bed will not fit through the doorway without being turned on its side. He must be carried out by two men. Will you excuse us?'

'Give me a moment with him first.'

When the men had gone, Mariana reached inside her clothes to where Safiya Sultana's silver taweez lay against her skin. She tugged the black cord over her head, then bent towards the string bed.

Hassan did not seem to notice as she lifted his head and slipped on the amulet. She opened his dusty shirt and tucked the silver box carefully out of sight beside his gold medallion with its delicately executed Qur'anic verses. Crude it might be, compared to the work of a master goldsmith, but Safiya's taweez had artistry and power of its own.

'Oh Allah Most Gracious,' Mariana whispered, a hand on Hassan's chest, 'please protect him.'

As she waited outside near the yellow doors, a series of heavy groans broke the silence behind her, followed by staccato whispers and the shuffling of feet. A moment later several men appeared, carrying the string bed, with Hassan twitching upon it, followed by Zulmai, the fresh-faced youth, and the old watchman.

'Be careful. The doorstep is high,' someone whispered.

Mariam's bride gift, Shaikh Waliullah had said, *has already been arranged. She now owns a house near the Delhi Gate. It has a yellow door . . .*

Unable to help and too exhausted to weep, Mariana followed the men out of the little haveli that might have been hers.

The streets were quiet as the small procession made its way to the square in front of Qamar Haveli. Mariana looked away from the unclothed dead they passed, who lay huddled against the doors of houses and the steps of small shops. Trying not to notice how cold she was, or how weary, she avoided broken doors and shutters, and

308

the splintered wood and shards of pottery that carpeted the street, passing her own deserted palanquin that now stood stripped of its cushions by the wall of a house.

At last they reached the square. The soldiers were still encamped on the high, broad steps of Wazir Khan's mosque but this time all of them seemed to be asleep.

Zulmai gave Mariana a glance she could not read in the half-moon's light. Without a word to her, he turned to the other men.

'The signal is to knock twice,' he said.

The grey-bearded Afghan hitched his two jezails higher on his shoulders. 'I will go,' he said. 'Cover me with your fire.'

'No! The soldiers may not shoot a woman.' Mariana did not need to add that once the soldiers on the steps began to shoot, it would be impossible to get Hassan into the house. Before the grey-bearded volunteer could start for the doors, she gathered her remaining strength and stumbled into the square ahead of him.

The soldiers on the steps did not move as she approached the house. Praying that the guards inside had not fallen asleep or forgotten the signal, she struck the great doors once, then again, the sound of her fists thudding hollowly around her.

She willed herself not to look towards the steps of the mosque.

They will make perfect targets when we kill for sport.

She heard footsteps behind the door, the bolts rasped, and one of the tall doors creaked open.

'Quickly,' she whispered as she limped hurriedly inside, nearly bowling over the surprised guard, 'open both doors fully. Hassan Ali Khan Sahib is coming!'

'Get inside, inside!' shouted someone behind her. She stepped out of the way and the men bearing Hassan's string bed rushed past her into the stable courtyard, followed by the rest of Zulmai's men,

Ghulam Ali and the old chowkidar from the haveli with the yellow doors, all of them running.

As the great doors swung shut again, musket fire erupted behind them.

Mariana looked about her. The guards were staring at the Afghans who carried their wounded companion through the low gate and into the inner courtyard. The family servants, who had been sleeping, swathed in quilts, near the stable doors, sat up and rubbed their eyes. Someone spoke sharply by the Shaikh's platform, where scores of sleepless men had been telling their prayer beads by torchlight, while they waited for Hassan's dead body to arrive.

Moving like a sleepwalker, Mariana began to follow the Afghans into the inner courtyard, then stopped to watch as Ghulam Ali stepped forward, his pale beard gleaming proudly in the torchlight, to announce the arrival of Hassan Ali Khan, gravely wounded but still breathing after being found by his foreign wife. She turned away only when the Afghans and the Shaikh's guests turned as one man to look at her.

Leaving the assembled men staring after her, Mariana toiled her way up the spiral stairway towards Safiya Sultana, warmth, and comfort.

'Hassan Ali Khan has come,' she croaked, swaying in the sitting-room doorway. 'He has been badly wounded, but perhaps he can be saved. He is very cold. Please tell Saboor—'

Her knees gave way and she sank to the tiled floor.

Chapter Thirty-Six

The air in the dimly lit room smelled of burning charcoal and incense. Sleeping, quilt-wrapped children lay about the floor, deserted by the excited women who now crowded about Mariana's collapsed form.

'Hassan is alive?' they cried, bending over her. *'Alive?'*

'Saboor told me.' Mariana blinked tiredly into their faces. 'He said that his father had been hurt, and then he kept saying "the Delhi Gate, the Delhi Gate." I thought he meant something else until I saw the house with the yellow door in a dream, and understood that I must go there and find Hassan . . .' Her voice trailed away. Where was Safiya Sultana, the one person she wanted to see?

The women gazed down at her, their astonished faces puffy from recent weeping.

'You went *out*?' they cried.

'In the *night*?'

'To the *Delhi Gate*?'

The gap-toothed aunt peered sceptically into Mariana's face. 'Where is Hassan now?' she inquired.

'He is downstairs, with Shaikh Waliuillah.'

Old and young, the women turned and ran to the windows.

'I see him!' An old lady pressed herself against the filigreed shutters. 'He is alive! Allah is great!'

'May Hassan live a hundred years!' cried another woman.

'I do not understand,' the gap-toothed aunt said as she helped Mariana to a satin-covered bolster. 'How is it possible for Hassan's wife to have gone out alone at night, into the streets? How is it possible that Hassan is now covered with the very same yellow jamawar shawl that Mariam was wearing this afternoon?'

A decisive voice came from the crowd at the window. 'Mariam's activities of tonight will be explained soon enough,' intoned Safiya, who, alone of the women, had not rushed to Mariana's side when she fainted. 'In the meantime, she is to warm herself, and rest. As for Hassan, there is much to be done. Bina, have grooms clear the way to the kitchen, and tell the cooks to light the stove and put water on to boil. Akhtar, bring me all the neem leaves we have in the house, and two dozen yards of clean muslin.'

A bright-coloured quilt lay in a heap near Mariana. As she pulled it to her chin, pounding feet on the verandah heralded the appearance of young Yahya at the doorway.

'Hassan Bhai should be kept downstairs,' he panted, 'in case there is another attack on the house. Lalaji has said we should stay in the underground room tonight.'

'But we haven't used that room since the hot weather ended,' protested the girl with knee-length hair. 'It will be full of—'

'Yahya, you must awaken the sweepers.' Safiya looked about her, frowning. 'Tell them to clean the underground room at once, and then send four menservants up here to carry down the carpets, the floor sheets, and enough charpais for all of us. We will bring the linens and the rezais ourselves. And Yahya, take the brazier downstairs but do not try to carry it as it is. Make sure you

312

empty the burning coals into a bucket first.' Then she approached Mariana.

'*Salaam-o-alaikum*,' Mariana offered weakly from her bolster.

'And peace be upon you, daughter.' Safiya Sultana bent to study her in the lamplight. 'You are not well,' she said. 'Rest now. We will hear your story later. You have much to tell us,' she added, looking hard into Mariana's eyes. 'You have not yet explained to us your previous absence, when you vanished the day before yesterday.'

As Safiya turned away, Mariana reached out a dirty hand and caught at her sleeve. 'Is there a chance that Hassan will live?' She must be allowed to beg his forgiveness, to atone for her stupidity, her accusations . . .

'I have not seen him yet,' Safiya replied gently, 'but in any case, Mariam, only Allah Most Gracious can save Hassan. If it is His will that Hassan should live, he will live. If it is not, he will die. We must remember that without Allah's permission, even you and I cannot take our next breath.'

Mariana lay on a charpai against a wall of the windowless underground room, her eyes too heavy to open, as the Waliullah family worked to save Hassan's life.

Murmured Arabic prayers surrounded her, filling the air, half covering the sounds of tearing cloth and splashing water, of Safiya's whispers of encouragement and Hassan's groans of distress.

'You must drink this, my boy,' Safiya said in a firm undertone. 'I will give you opium for the pain in a moment, but first you must drink this.'

Throughout the remainder of the night, Yahya and the women servants came and went, following orders, bringing news. When a man's voice, light but full of authority, returned the ladies' greeting, Mariana knew the Shaikh was in the room.

He must have sat down, then, for Hassan's bed creaked beneath someone's weight.

'Abba,' Hassan sighed.

'Here I am, my darling,' replied that pleasant voice, so much like Hassan's own.

'Akhtar, go and bring tea for Shaikh Sahib,' Safiya Sultana ordered. 'Wali,' she added in a businesslike tone, 'lift Hassan's shoulders while we turn him over.'

Later, when Hassan grew quiet, the Shaikh and his family spoke softly of his bravery in trying to halt the assassination. They mourned the ill fortune that had caused his wound, and the death of his oldest friend, Yusuf. They lauded the courage and tenacity of the Afghans who had rescued him from the Hazuri Bagh. Lowering their voices, they discussed Hassan's grave symptoms, the muscles now torn from his outer thigh, his clammy, pallid skin, his terrible weakness and, later, his rising fever. From time to time they mentioned Mariana's name, but too softly for her to make out what they were saying.

Desperate to help Hassan, longing to touch him, she tried several times to rise, but found she could not lift her head from the pillow. Even when Saboor was brought to her and laid, sleeping, beside her on the bed, she did not have the strength to stroke his curls. She lay, unable to move, her thoughts racing, while the conversations and the prayers rose and fell around her.

What was the use of hoping for Hassan's forgiveness when she had done everything wrong? Why had she accused him of treachery? Why had she ignored Saboor when he tried so desperately to save his father? Why had she waited so long to go the haveli with the yellow doors?

Now, with his life hanging by a slender thread, there was every chance Hassan would die before she could even speak to him.

Only Allah Most Gracious can save him, Safiya had told her.

If only there were one more thing she could do before it was too late – one more service she could perform that would finally atone for her sins, tip the scale and allow Hassan to live . . .

In her waking dream, a pair of grey ears bobbed in front of her as her donkey trotted up the steep, gritty path that ran between folded, brown hills. Aching from the difficulty of riding a donkey without a sidesaddle, she shifted on the animal's back, her foot nearly sweeping the ground.

She was not alone. Other people walked or rode along the same path, under the bright blue sky, keeping her company, a few in front of her, but many more behind. Because she dreamed, she was unsurprised to find her old language teacher, Shaikh Waliullah's elderly friend, behind her on another donkey. She had sent her munshi home to the Punjab from Calcutta many months ago, but now he gripped his animal's saddle with knotted hands, while her tall, trusted groom, whom she had also believed was lost to her, strode at the donkey's head, its reins held loosely in his hand.

Behind them all plodded a long file of camels, some burdened with huge panniers of food, some carrying tents and other equipment.

In her dream, Mariana wept as she rode, making small, miserable sounds to herself, her tears leaving prickly pathways down her cheeks.

Behind her, as thunder began to rumble in the sunny hills, she heard the sound of running feet. Whoever the runner was, he was both strong and determined, for he had already passed the rest of the caravan.

He was running alongside her now. 'Wait, Bibi!' he gasped, holding something out to her. 'I have been sent to give you this . . .'

Chapter Thirty-Seven

18 January 1841

Mariana woke to find Saboor gone from her side. She had indeed been weeping, for wisps of her hair clung wetly to her temples. A deep, rhythmic snoring came from the back of the room and mingled with the ladies' continuing murmured prayers.

She opened her eyes. A sliver of sunlight had found its way down the stairs and onto the floor of the passage outside the doorway of the underground room, but whether it was morning or afternoon, she could not tell.

She peered through the gloom of the chamber and found that the source of the snoring was Safiya Sultana, who lay on a string bed in one of the back corners, her generous chest rising and falling with the noisy rhythm of her breathing.

Safiya's snores explained the mysterious thunder in Mariana's dream, but what had the rest of it signified? Why the donkeys and the bare, unfamiliar landscape? Why had her munshi reappeared to join her on that unexplained journey?

Uncle Adrian had been nowhere in sight along the stony path.

316

Oh please, let him still be alive. Let him survive until the fighting stops, until I am able to bring him Safiya Sultana's crystals . . .

Hassan must still be alive, for there were no wails of mourning, but where was he? Without raising her head, Mariana peered about her and found that his bed had been moved forward into the light. Two seated women talked together beside his still, sleeping profile, their elbows resting on the wooden edge of his bed, a plate of pistachio nuts between them on the floor.

'. . . no need for more jewellery than she already has,' the younger of the two was saying primly between Safiya's snores. 'Listen – Mariana has stopped crying in her sleep,' the girl added, lowering her voice. 'I wonder why she was weeping,'

It was the girl with the high-bridged nose, who had admired Mariana's yellow shawl on a morning that seemed to have receded far away in time. Although she spoke in an undertone, her voice carried easily across the low-ceilinged chamber.

'Perhaps she weeps for shame,' the old gap-toothed aunt suggested.

Shame? What were these women talking about? Feigning sleep, Mariana arranged her head so that she could watch them through half-closed eyes.

The girl leaned forward. 'So you think, Bhaji, that she knew there was to be an assassination in the Hazuri Bagh?'

'Of course, Rukhi.' The gap-toothed aunt spoke in a soft, emphatic singsong. 'Of course she knew.'

'She received a letter from the English at Shalimar before it happened,' agreed the girl.

'Two letters, Rukhi, *two*. And the very next day, only hours before it was to take place, she left this house secretly, wearing Akhtar's chador.' The aunt opened a pistachio shell with a snap. 'No woman,' she added decisively as she pried the nut from its shell, 'not even a European, would leave her house disguised as a servant unless she was up to no good.'

Rukhi nodded her agreement.

'And as to her dreaming of the house where Hassan was to be found,' the aunt continued, chewing as she spoke, 'I do not believe a word of that story. She went out in the middle of the night to meet someone who led her to it, just as she ran away the day before to meet someone who would take her to Shalimar. Mark my words, Rukhi, there is more to our Mariam Bibi than we have guessed. I believe,' she finished grimly, 'that she has been spying for the English.'

'No!'

'I believe she has been aiding the British Political Agent. Everyone is saying he is the author of the assassination plot, the very man who is to blame for Yusuf Bhatti's death and poor Hassan's dangerous wound.'

The girl's hands flew to her mouth. 'Hai!' she breathed. 'How terrible!'

Mariana twitched angrily beneath her quilt. These accusations were not only wrong and unfair, they were also dangerous. If the old aunt believed she was the Vulture's spy, then others must think the same. If they all did, down to the little keeper of shoes with his penchant for gossip, then the story would soon spread into the city, and to the Citadel beyond.

Someone might already have told Prince Sher Singh.

At the back of the chamber, Safiya gave one last, echoing snort, followed by a series of coughs. 'Firoz,' she called an instant later, wide awake, 'bring the food.'

Footsteps approached Mariana's bed. Uneasily aware of someone's eyes on her, she looked up to find Safiya Sultana standing over her, wrapped in a voluminous brown shawl. 'Are you feeling better?' she inquired, peering into Mariana's face.

When Mariana nodded, Safiya gave a satisfied little grunt. 'Good,' she said decisively, 'for the time has now come for you to explain yourself.'

'Explain myself?' Lying down put Mariana at a disadvantage. She glanced sideways towards Hassan's bed and saw the gap-toothed aunt and her companion watching her, their faces alive with curiosity.

'We must be told,' Safiya replied, 'what need or impulse drove you to leave this house twice in the past three days, disguised as a servant. We must hear what happened to you while you were gone. You will also tell us your real reasons for returning with Saboor to Qamar Haveli.'

'Us?' Mariana whispered nervously. Surely she was not to recite all her sins in front of a score of suspicious Waliullah women?

'My brother and I. He will be having his food with me today. When he comes, you will tell us your story.'

Telling Safiya and the Shaikh together would not be much easier than telling a roomful of women, but she had no choice. Mariana cleared her throat.

'Yes, Bhaji,' she croaked.

Safiya turned away. 'Akhtar,' she called, 'bring warm water and a basin, and help Mariam Bibi to wash.'

The meal was as simple as dinner had been. No milkman had come, so there was no yoghurt, nor had the bread dough been sent to the local tandoor for baking. And for two days the only animals that had been slaughtered in the city had been killed by Sher Singh's marauding soldiers.

The room where Mariana ate boiled dal, rice, and a few spiced vegetables with her two interrogators was small and dark, a dry storeroom almost, that opened into the large underground chamber, but it offered privacy as long as they did not raise their voices.

Through the room's curtainless doorway, Mariana could see the ladies bending over trays of food. Across from the doorway, the fat girl laughed as she pushed wads of rice into Saboor's open mouth.

Instead of his usual tall, starched headdress, the Shaikh wore a knitted skullcap on his narrow head. He sat opposite Mariana eating neatly with his right hand, kneading his rice and dal with long, precise fingers before putting them into his mouth, getting no food under his fingernails, unlike Mariana, who already wanted desperately to wash her hands.

She had spent half an hour giving him and his sister an account of her time in Lahore. Unable to lie in their presence, she had told them the full story of the previous four days, omitting no sorry detail: not the furious accusations she had made against Hassan, not his angry agreement to the divorce, not even her temporary theft of the dead man's shawl. The only part she left out was the night Hassan had spent in her bed.

When she was finished, the Shaikh nodded. 'You have told us of your actions since your arrival in Lahore,' he said in the same deceptively light tone he had used since the beginning of the meal, 'but you have not told us why you changed your mind about the divorce.'

'When I first returned here,' Mariana admitted, 'I expected to end my marriage, and leave Lahore behind me forever. Although I knew that losing Saboor would cause me terrible pain, I could not imagine spending the rest of my life cut off from my own people. I expected to go on to Afghanistan with my uncle and aunt after the divorce, and find an English husband there, but instead I stayed here, and Hassan was so, so . . .'

Unable to meet their eyes, she looked down at her newly bathed feet. Surely they did not expect her to give them details about *that*?

'Do not be shy, Mariam,' Safiya rumbled as she helped herself to rice. 'This is not a house of secrets. We know more of your sentiments for my nephew than you realize.'

'Although I did not want to stay,' Mariana hurried on, 'I desperately wanted two things: to keep Saboor for ever, and to learn everything I could about Lalaji.'

Safiya and the Shaikh looked at one another.

'Ah,' said Safiya Sultana.

'I know that Saboor is to be the next leader of the Karakoyia brotherhood,' Mariana went on, her half-formed thoughts tumbling from her. 'I have seen him predict events. It was Saboor who knew that Hassan lay wounded at the house near the Delhi Gate when everyone else, even you, Lalaji, and Safiya Bhaji, thought he was dead. If Saboor can do these things at his age, then what greater mysteries has the Shaikh grasped? What marvels can he produce? Does he influence events? How can I be certain that he did not cause me to fall in – to like Hassan so much?'

The Shaikh and his sister smiled.

Mariana looked at Safiya. 'And you, Bhaji,' she added. 'You are always so calm. Even now, with all this danger and Hassan so gravely wounded, you seem at peace.'

Saboor crept into the room and sat silently down, one small hand on his grandfather's bony knee. 'An-nah,' he said, his bright eyes on Mariana.

She pushed the last grains of rice together on her banana leaf and kneaded them anxiously with her fingers. 'In the beginning, I believed I could learn everything about Lalaji within a few days. Later, I saw that it would take years to approach his power and knowledge. Now I realize that I can never be like him, no matter how hard I try. After all, I am a woman . . .'

She fell silent, realizing what she had said. Where had these mad ideas and ambitions come from? Did she really want to be like Shaikh Waliullah?

The Shaikh pushed a long finger inside his skullcap and scratched his head. 'Daughter,' he said, 'you have misunderstood something: there is no barrier to a qualified woman who wishes to follow the Path to Peace. You have not recognized it, but my sister here is a member of the Karakoyia brotherhood. In fact, should I die while Saboor is still a child, the regent who will guide the Karakoyia until he is grown will not be a man from among my followers but my sister Safiya, for she is as qualified as I am to be Shaikh of this brotherhood.'

Mariana sat up, too shocked to say anything.

'Safiya,' he went on, 'has travelled further along the path than all but one of the men who come to sit beside my platform in the courtyard. That exception, of course, is my old friend Shafiuddin, whom you call Munshi Sahib, and who sends his salaams from Firozpur where he has arrived safely.'

Too upset to be pleased that she had foreseen her old teacher's arrival in her waking dream, Mariana shifted beneath the Shaikh's gaze, her heart aching. There were not one but two Shaikhs in this house. What losses she had brought on herself . . .

'Safiya's abilities and skills, to be sure, are different from mine,' the Shaikh said, ignoring Mariana's pain, 'but they are no less important. Unlike me, she is well versed in the difficult science of taweez, the Merciful Prescriptions. It was she who knew which verses to include in the amulet which I can see you are no longer wearing.'

Hardly listening, Mariana stared at her hands. For a few short days the Shaikh, Safiya, and Hassan had been hers. During that brief time, she might have become a real member of this extraordinary family. She might have been happy. She might have learned

322

much more than a few simple facts about Shaikh Waliullah and his sister.

Had she qualified, she might have begun to follow the Path herself . . .

Why had she not held her tongue with Hassan, and kept her evil suspicions to herself? Why, struck with terror at the unexpected strength of her feelings, had she lashed out, and lost him?

Holding her greasy right hand away from her clothes, she gulped back tears of fury at herself, at the Vulture, at the whole, awful turn of events. She could never gain Hassan's forgiveness while he lay, wholly inaccessible to her, in an opium-induced sleep, surrounded by gossiping women. For all she knew, he would die before he awoke.

Seeing the heartbreak on her face, Saboor left his grandfather and crawled to Mariana, past trays, serving dishes and banana leaves. 'No, An-nah, don't cry,' he said as he crawled onto her lap and patted her wet face. 'Do not cry.'

Chapter Thirty-Eight

Akhtar tried to hide her astonishment at what she had just heard. *Safiya Sultana was as powerful as Shaik Waliullah.* More powerful, perhaps, since she had also learned the Merciful Prescriptions, whatever they were.

She took the food away and carefully carried in a brass ewer and basin, but her hand shook a little as she poured clean water over the great lady's fingers. How could she have been such a fool, searching for a cheap caster of spells in this house of mystery and power? How had she failed to see the greatness in front of her eyes?

'Enough, Akhtar,' Safiya said sharply. 'There's no need to pour all the water over my hand. Keep some for my poor brother.'

Her tasks completed, Akhtar folded herself into a corner to hear the rest of the conversation. But then shouting erupted outside. Hurried footsteps crossed a room overhead. The Shaikh's old, gap-toothed relative put her head round the door.

'Sher Singh's soldiers are attacking us again,' she announced. 'They are trying to get inside through the back entrance.' She pointed towards the stairs as intermittent thudding came from the courtyard. 'Hassan's Afghans are firing down at them from the roof,' she added, fastening her eyes on Mariana, still swollen-eyed after her tearful confession. 'We are not certain whether—'

'Thank you, Rehmana.' The Shaikh spoke respectfully but with such finality that the old lady recoiled in the doorway.

After she had gone, Safiya Sultana turned to Mariana. 'Are you afraid? Is that why you are weeping?'

'I weep because I have lost Hassan, and in losing him, I have lost both of you as well,' she said sadly. 'Hassan hates me now. That lady who came in hates me also. She thinks I am a spy.'

'Rehmana is Lalaji's sister-in-law,' Safiya informed her a little severely. 'She is a silly woman and a gossip, but she hates no one.'

'As to your complaint that you have lost all of us,' the Shaikh put in. 'I must speak the truth, although it is bitter. You have indeed behaved badly, especially to my son. Two years ago, although he barely knew you, Hassan did not hesitate to entrust you with his child. He did not take another wife during your long absence, in spite of many suggestions that he do so. Yet, you failed to treat him with trust and respect. I am not at all surprised that he abandoned hope for this marriage after listening to your unjust and unconsidered accusations,' he went on, ignoring Mariana's renewed tears. 'How could you have thought him capable of killing the Maharajah's guests, some of whom are your own relations?'

'I heard him saying he hated the British, and that he—'

The Shaikh held up a silencing hand. 'The matter of Hassan's hating or not hating your countrymen can be taken up another time,' he said sharply. 'Since your arrival at this house you have acted wildly, and with indiscretion. You ran away alone to Shalimar, risking your life and your modesty, and bringing shame upon this house, for of course you were recognized upon the road. As if that were not enough, you went out again last night without a word to us, and exposed yourself to every kind of assault. Again you shamed us, this time in front of Hassan's Afghan friends, and also in front of my followers, after you returned.'

Mariana wiped her cheeks with the back of her hand. 'I am so sorry,' she whispered.

'But as foolish as your actions have been,' he said, his tone softening, 'it is clear that they were prompted by a warm heart. You ran to Shalimar to protect your relatives and the other English people. You went out again last night to rescue Hassan and bring him home to us. What is more, during this time of trial, you proved yourself in ways that you may not have guessed.'

Safiya Sultana nodded solemn agreement. Akhtar leaned forward, unwilling to miss a word.

'Yesterday,' the Shaikh continued, 'you reached our gate and found it closed against you. Seeing this, you humbled yourself and took on the guise of a beggar. While waiting for our doors to open, you treated the little keeper of shoes with decency and respect. Later, at risk to yourself, you brought him into the safety of this house. Although the doors had already begun to close, you undid your theft by returning the dead man's shawl.'

Mariana brightened. 'If I have proved myself,' she said eagerly, 'will Hassan change his mind about the divorce?'

The Shaikh spread his hands. 'My son is a patient man, daughter, but when he turns his back on a thing, that thing is finished for him. There are people in this house with whom he is no longer intimate who can attest to this fact. Inshallah, he will survive his wound and tell you himself whether he still wants to divorce you. Until then, you will remain here and begin your iddat.'

Mariana shook her head urgently. 'But I must go to Shalimar. My uncle has cholera, and—'

'You will do no such thing,' Safiya Sultana interrupted impatiently. 'You will wait here while *we* attend to your uncle. We must know whether you are with child. And should you leave this house during your iddat, you will bring even more disgrace upon us than you have already. Do you understand me?'

Mariana stared. 'With child?'

The Shaikh spread his hands. 'The waiting period is three months.'

Mariana searched his face. 'And Hassan will be here?'

'Of course he will. This is his house.' The Shaikh held Mariana's eyes with his own. 'If, Allah forbid, Hassan should die during that time, your waiting period will be another four months and ten days. But if he lives, and there is doubt about the need for divorce, the three months of waiting time may be used for reconciliation.'

'Three months? For reconciliation?'

Someone shouted an order in the courtyard above. At once, a booming volley of shots echoed down the stairs, but Mariana took no notice of it. Instead, she offered her father-in-law her beautiful, transforming smile.

They sat for what seemed like hours, while the firing went on upstairs. Crouched on the floor of the little room, Mariana prayed that the Afghan sharpshooters would protect them, that there would be no terrified screams as Sher Singh's men charged into the family courtyard.

She had also thought of Hassan, and of the three long months she had been given to woo him back.

When the gunfire at last ceased, the Shaikh rose to his feet. 'I must see what is happening outside,' he said.

Before he could stride away, someone clattered down the stone stairs, ran across the underground room and nearly collided with him in the doorway.

It was young Yahya. 'Good news, Lalaji!' he panted. 'Those on the roof are saying that Prince Sher Singh has prevailed at the Hazuri Bagh, and that at any moment he will ride into the city on his elephant and stop the violence of his soldiers!'

The Shaikh smiled and laid a hand on the boy's shoulder. 'Then go outside and tell the servants to return to their quarters.'

As he watched Yahya leave, the Shaikh seemed to age; he suddenly looked as old as he had when he had announced Hassan's death. He did not speak, but the single, hollow look he exchanged with his sister caused all Mariana's joy and hope to drain away.

In her happiness, she had forgotten the difficult truth: that Prince Sher Singh, now in full command of the city, believed that Hassan had tried to kill him. The Prince's guards had seen and shot Hassan in the Hazuri Bagh. His soldiers had stood under the windows of Qamar Haveli shouting threats at his 'enemies'.

Even now, nobles were whispering into the new Maharajah's ear, telling cruel lies about each other as they competed for his favour. Someone who coveted a place at court it would find it easy to embellish the already serious case against Hassan, to convince Sher Singh that the assistant Foreign Minister had been wooed into treachery and attempted murder by his calculating English wife and the British Political Agent. Assistant Foreign Minister would make an excellent appointment for a man with ambition.

Hassan might not have long to live. Once Sher Singh entered the city, he would not hesitate to act. A soldier accustomed to summary justice, he would end the matter in the crudest of ways. If the Shaikh refused to turn over his son, Sher Singh would bring one of his heavy guns into the little square in front of Wazir Khan's mosque. After he had blown open the doors of Qamar Haveli, he would send his men to storm the family courtyard and charge down the stone stairs, into these very underground rooms. The fact that women were present would not save Hassan.

'They will kill him,' Mariana cried thoughtlessly.

No one spoke. The Shaikh left the room and Safiya reached into her clothes and took out a string of amber prayer beads. She sat hunched silently over them, her lips moving as she counted. Then she said calmly, 'Allah Most Gracious is Protector of all. It is He, not Sher Singh, who will decide Hassan's fate, and ours.'

As Safiya uttered these words, Mariana's dream of the donkey caravan rushed back to her unbidden. Lady Macnaghten's elephants, she knew, were just ahead of her, round a bend in the path. Aunt Claire and Uncle Adrian were also there, riding between the rocks . . .

Understanding took a moment, but then Mariana sat straight. 'There is something I can do to help,' she announced. 'As soon as it is safe, I will leave here and go to Afghanistan with my uncle and aunt.'

She looked steadily into Safiya's stiffening face. 'I *must*, Bhaji. It is the best hope we have of saving Hassan's life.'

'Certainly not,' Safiya replied flatly. 'Wandering like a gypsy over the Punjab during your waiting period will do nothing to protect Hassan. It will only bring more shame upon you and us.'

'Please listen, Bhaji,' Mariana persisted. 'Everyone is saying that I am an English spy, even people in this house. Sher Singh knows it was the English Political Agent who plotted his death. He will never believe in Hassan's innocence as long as I remain here.'

Safiya Sultana did not reply. She looked at Mariana, her gaze suddenly as penetrating as the Shaikh's.

'I will leave for Shalimar as soon as it is safe,' Mariana repeated. 'If it appears that Hassan and I have fallen out, people may guess that I left him because he refused to join the murder plot and tried to stop it instead.' She dropped against the wall. 'I am sorry about my iddat,' she said, unable to keep the misery from her voice. 'I do not know how I shall live without Hassan, or Saboor, or you.'

Safiya turned to the door. 'Send one of the boys for Lalaji,' she called out.

The Shaikh reappeared, Saboor in his arms, followed by a crowd of women who stopped in the doorway behind him. Saboor had been crying. He flew across the little room and buried his head in Mariana's lap.

'What has happened?' the women asked, craning for a better view as the Shaikh joined his sister and Mariana on the floor. 'Why is Mariam so sad? What is wrong with Saboor?'

Mariana could not bring herself to look up. She bent over her luminous little stepson, her tears of farewell falling into his hair. He had known she would leave them, although Safiya had not guessed until she was told. So prescient already, Saboor would gain great wisdom as he matured. Perhaps in time he would be greater than even his grandfather and his great-aunt.

Would she ever see him again?

'Listen, all of you,' Safiya announced. 'Some of us have come to believe that Mariam is a British spy. This is wrong. She is no spy, and never has been. She had no hand in yesterday's violence at the Hazuri Bagh. She is returning to Shalimar today or tomorrow. After that, she will travel to Afghanistan with her relatives. I have consented to this plan because I believe her sacrifice in leaving us may persuade Sher Singh to spare Hassan's life.'

Saboor hiccupped in Mariana's lap.

The Shaikh cleared his throat. 'Daughter,' he said, 'you are a good woman, for all your boldness and indiscretion. You may have saved our lives yesterday, when you repelled those soldiers from

330

the upper windows. Do not think we have failed to recognize that service. And you have done more. We know very well what you did with the taweez that you no longer wear about your neck.'

'Only Allah knows whether Hassan will recover from his wound,' Safiya added, 'or whether Sher Singh will spare him. But you are right, Mariam. Go, then, to Shalimar, with our blessing. Our man who performs the cholera cure will go with you. We will also send a message to Firozpur suggesting that Shafi Sahib join you on your journey to Kabul.' She sighed. 'Perhaps it has been Allah's will all along that you should leave us again. Perhaps, in the end, your leaving will save Hassan's life.'

Mariana looked up and saw the Shaikh nod. 'Inshallah,' he intoned, 'when all this trouble is over, you will return safely to us. Between now and then, my daughter, may Allah protect you.'

'Hai, what a brave girl!' exclaimed Rehmana, the gap-toothed aunt.

Two months later, after waiting at Peshawar for warmer weather in the passes, Lady Macnaghten's party was travelling again. Mariana's donkey trotted rapidly, its dusty neck bobbing in front of her, as it climbed an upward-sloping path. The donkey was so small that Mariana's feet seemed nearly to touch the ground.

She shifted on its back to relieve the ache of riding without a sidesaddle.

It had taken some time for Aunt Claire's tears and recriminations to subside after Mariana reappeared from the stricken walled city, but Mariana had been too relieved to find her uncle still alive to pay much attention.

Everyone at Shalimar had expressed horror at the prospect of Safiya Sultana's cholera cure, but Uncle Adrian had ignored his wife's queasy disapproval and allowed the Shaikh's man to make an incision across his shoulder and sprinkle the German doctor's crystals into the wound.

His recovery had been slow. Even now he rode on one of Lady Macnaghten's baggage elephants, out of sight round a bend in the path, together with the rest of the English party. Ahead of them all trotted the cavalry escort that had joined them in Peshawar for the hazardous journey through the Khyber Pass.

Apart from Uncle Adrian, who had rasped questions from his pillows, the one person in camp who had shown any interest in the events at Lahore had been the reformed and now irritatingly subservient Charles Mott, to whom Mariana had recounted a censored version of her adventures over lunch in the dining tent the day after her arrival.

Only Mott and Uncle Adrian had been unsurprised at the Vulture's precipitous departure immediately after Mariana's return, two months earlier. As he rode off on 'a matter of some urgency that has just been brought to my attention,' followed by his train of servants, Lady Macnaghten was heard to say that she had never liked the gentleman at all.

'If anyone wants to know what *really* I thought of him,' she had announced at dinner that night, patting her beautifully arranged hair, 'I thought he looked exactly like a large, scavenging bird.'

Behind Mariana's donkey, Munshi Sahib's tall groom called out, his resonant voice echoing against the rocks on either side of the path. 'Bibi,' he said, 'someone is coming.'

Running feet approached, slapping on the dry ground. A moment later, a rough-looking man appeared, still running, beside Mariana, his pale beard grey with dust, his chest heaving.

'*As-salaam-o-alaikum.* Peace be upon you, Bibi,' he panted.

'And upon you, Ghulam Ali.'

Stiffening against sudden dread, she guided her donkey to one side of the path and waited, her fingers trembling a little on the reins, as loaded horses, camels, Aunt Claire's unoccupied palanquin, and more donkeys passed dustily by.

The albino reached into his shirt and took out a small cloth packet, sewn together with tiny, neat stitches, with Mariana's name written in Urdu on one side.

'I have been sent to give you this,' he said, pulling a knife from his belt. 'And,' he added, his tired face bright with what might have been joy, 'I am to remain with you, and serve you in Afghanistan.'

Two things lay inside the little packet: Hassan's neck chain and gold medallion inscribed with the verses from Sura Nur, and a short note written on a scrap of worn, dusty cloth. *Give this to my wife,* it read.

My wife. Mariana pulled Hassan Ali's beautiful old medallion carefully over her head, lifted her chin and breathed in the clear air.

An olive, read the delicately inscribed verse, *neither of the East nor of the West*.

You can buy any of these other **Review** titles from your bookshop or *direct from the publisher*.

FREE P&P AND UK DELIVERY
(Overseas and Ireland £3.50 per book)

The Seventh Son	Reay Tannahill	£6.99
The Blue Noon	Robert Ryan	£6.99
The Bounce	Betsy Tobin	£6.99
The Passion of Artemisia	Susan Vreeland	£6.99
A History of Insects	Yvonne Roberts	£6.99
The Long Afternoon	Giles Waterfield	£6.99
The Beekeeper's Pupil	Sara George	£6.99
Still She Haunts Me	Katie Roiphe	£6.99
Earth and Heaven	Sue Gee	£6.99
The Last Great Dance on Earth	Sandra Gulland	£6.99
The Lamplighter	Anthony O'Neill	£6.99
The King's Touch	Jude Morgan	£6.99
The Accomplice	Kathryn Heyman	£6.99

TO ORDER SIMPLY CALL THIS NUMBER

01235 400 414

or visit our website: www.madaboutbooks.com

Prices and availability subject to change without notice.